THE
SURROGATE

THE
SURROGATE

TANIA CARVER

PEGASUS CRIME
NEW YORK

THE SURROGATE

Pegasus Books LLC
80 Broad Street, 5th Floor
New York, NY 10004

Copyright © 2011 by Tania Carver

First Pegasus Books cloth edition 2011

Library of Congress Cataloging-in-Publication Data is available.

ISBN: 978-1-60598-256-4

10 9 8 7 6 5 4 3 2 1

Printed in the United States of America
Distributed by W. W. Norton & Company, Inc.
www.pegasusbooks.us

To David, thanks for everything

THE
SURROGATE

Part One

1

There was a knock at the door.

Claire Fielding and Julie Simpson looked at each other, surprised. Claire started to rise.

'You stay there,' said Julie. 'I'll get it.' She stood up from the sofa, crossed the living room. 'Probably Geraint, forgot something. Again.'

Claire smiled. 'Changed his mind about lending me his *Desperate Housewives* DVD.'

Julie laughed, left the room. Claire shifted a little to get comfortable, sat back and smiled. Looked around, taking in the presents on the coffee table. Babygros and clothes. Parenting books. Soft toys. And the cards. Claire had thought it would be bad luck to open them before the birth but the others had insisted so she had given in, her doubts soon forgotten.

She moved from side to side, tried to find a soft spot on the sofa, allow the springs to reach an accommodation with her huge, distended stomach. She patted the bulge. Smiled. Not much longer. She leaned forward, grunting with the effort, and picked up her glass of fizzy fruit drink. Took a mouthful, replaced the glass. Then a mini onion bhaji. She had heard such horror stories of women who couldn't eat anything during pregnancy and were constantly sick. Not Claire. She was lucky. Probably too lucky. She patted her stomach, hoping it was all baby, knowing it wasn't. She wished she could be like one of those celebs like Posh or Angelina Jolie who got their figure back in about four days after having kids. They claimed it was all diet and exercise but she knew it must be surgery. Real life wasn't like that for Claire and she knew she would have to work at it. Still. That was the future. She would get her body back, then start a new life. Just her and her child.

She was no longer anxious or depressed. Tearful or bereft. That was all in the past and finished with, like those things had happened to someone else. It had been painful, yes, but it was worth it. So, so worth it.

Claire smiled. She might have felt happier in her life but she couldn't remember when. She certainly had not felt as happy as this for a long, long time.

Then she heard sounds from the hallway.

'Julie?'

Thumping on the walls and floor, bangs and scuffles. It sounded like someone was playing football or wrestling. Or fighting.

A shiver ran through Claire. *Oh no. God no. Not him, not now . . .*

'Julie . . .'

Claire's voice was more frantic this time, unable to hide the alarm at what she was hearing, who she imagined was responsible for the noise.

A final thump, then silence.

'Julie?'

No reply.

With great difficulty Claire managed to pull herself upright from the sofa. The speed with which she got up left her feeling slightly light-headed. She picked up her mobile from the coffee table, left the room and stepped into the hallway. She had a good idea of who to expect there and was ready to call for help. Even the police if needs be. Anything to get rid of him.

She turned the corner. And stopped dead, her mouth open. Whatever she had been expecting, it wasn't the scene before her. No way could she have expected that. It was horrific. Too horrific for her mind to process. She couldn't take in what had happened.

Her eyes dropped to the floor and she saw Julie. Or what was left of her.

'Oh God . . .'

Then she saw the figure standing over her best friend and she began to understand. She knew that her own, ordinary life had stopped with the knock on the door. She was living through something else now. A horror film, perhaps. A nightmare.

The figure saw her. Smiled.

Claire saw the blade. Shining under the hallway light, blood dripping on to the carpet. She tried to run but her legs wouldn't work. She tried to scream but couldn't send the right signals from her brain to her mouth. She just dropped her mobile. Stood there, unable to move.

Then the figure was on her.

One punch and everything went black.

Claire opened her eyes, tried to sit up. But she couldn't move. Her arms, hands, back, nothing. Her eyes closed again. Even her eyelids felt heavy. Very heavy. She tried once more to force them apart, managed. But it was a struggle just to keep them open.

She could only look upwards. Not even from side to side. She recognised the ceiling of her bedroom. The overhead light was on, blinding her. She tried to blink the light away

5

but her heavy eyelids remained closed. She instinctively knew that wasn't good, so she forced them open, light or no light.

She tried to make out what was happening. A shadow was moving on the ceiling, large and looming, like something from an old black and white horror movie. Doing something out of her line of vision.

Claire remembered what had happened. The figure in the hall, the attack. And Julie. *Julie . . .*

She opened her mouth, tried to scream. No sound at all came out. A wave of panic passed through her. She had been paralysed in some way. Drugged. She felt her eyes close again. Forced them open once more. It was a struggle, the biggest of her life, but she couldn't allow them to close. She knew now that if she did, she would be dead.

She tried to move her lips, make sounds, call for help. Nothing. No matter how loudly she screamed in her head – and it felt like she was screaming all the time now – all that trickled out of her mouth was a puppy-like whimper.

She saw the shadow on the ceiling move closer to her.

No, don't . . . get off me, get away from me, don't touch me, don't touch me . . .

Useless. Just made her head hurt, her inner ear trill.

Claire felt her eyelids being pulled down again, fought to push them up. It was getting harder each time. As was breathing, her lungs slowing with each poisoned breath she took. Panic and fear only helped her heart to speed-pump the crippling drug round her body. She knew she didn't have long.

Somebody help . . . please . . . just break down the door, help . . .

The shadow of the figure now loomed above her, blocking out the overhead light. Claire felt confusion on top of fear and panic: who were they? Why were they doing this?

Then she saw the scalpel. And she knew.

6

Not my baby . . . please, not my baby . . .

The figure bent over her, light glinting along the scalpel's razor-edged blade.

No . . . help me, oh God, help me . . .

Began to cut.

Claire felt nothing. Saw only the intruder's grotesque shadow thrown across the ceiling, the light exaggerating the sawing motion of the arm.

God, no, please . . . please someone, help me, help me, no . . .

Eventually the figure straightened up. Stood over Claire. Smiled. Something in its hand, red and dripping.

No . . .

Another smile and the red, dripping thing was taken from her sight. Claire couldn't scream or move. She couldn't even cry.

The shadow moved towards the door and was gone. Claire was left alone, screaming and shouting in her head. She tried to pull her arms up, move her legs. No good. It was too much effort. Even breathing was too much effort.

She felt her lungs slow down. Her eyelids close. She could hear the pump of blood round her body slowing down, down . . .

She tried one last time to fight it but it was no use. Her body was closing down. And she was powerless to stop it.

Her lungs stopped inflating, her heart stopped beating.

Her eyes closed for the final time.

2

'**O**h my God . . .'

Detective Inspector Philip Brennan, Chief Investigating Officer with the Major Incident Squad, donned surgical gloves, pulled the hood of his pristine crinkling paper suit over his head and stood on the threshold of hell. He knew that when he pulled back the yellow crime-scene tape and entered, he would be crossing a line between order and chaos. Between life and death.

He lifted the tape, stepped inside. *So much blood . . .*

'Jesus . . .'

The tape fell back into place, the line crossed. No going back now. He took in the scene before him and knew he would never leave this apartment, mentally or emotionally, until he had found who had done this. And perhaps not even then.

The hallway looked like an abattoir. Covered in so much blood, as if several litres of red paint had been dropped from a great height, splashing up the walls and over the floor like a grisly action painting, fading to brown as it dried. But paint didn't smell like that. Like dirty copper and rancid meat. He tried breathing though his mouth. Felt it on his tongue. Tasting as bad as it smelled. Sweat prickled his body, adding to his discomfort.

'Can someone turn the heating off?' he shouted.

Other white-suited individuals moved about the apartment. Intense, focused. He noticed that a few of them were carrying paper bags, some full. They were issued in extreme cases to catch any vomit that might contaminate the crime scene. One of the officers acknowledged his request, went to find the thermostat.

The body still lay in the hallway, ready to be stretchered off to the mortuary for autopsy. The SOCOs had finished extracting every last piece of information from the scene but had left the body in place so Phil could examine it, find something to kick-start his investigation.

He looked down, swallowed hard. A woman was lying there, her torso twisted, her arms outstretched and grasping, as if she had been trying to hang on to the last breath as it left her body. She was dressed in jeans and a T-shirt. A vicious slash had taken out both jugular vein and artery on either side of her neck. He could see she had struggled by the patterns made by her arms in the blood on the wooden floor. Like bloodied angel's wings.

Phil looked to a SOCO officer standing beside him.

'Okay if I cross?'

The SOCO nodded. 'Think we're done with this one. Got everything we need.'

'Photos?'

The SOCO nodded again.

Phil stepped over the body, careful not to track blood into any other room. The bedroom door was open. He walked towards it, looked in. And felt his stomach pitch and roll.

'Oh God, this is a bad one . . .'

A white-suited silhouette heard Phil's voice, detached himself from a group of similarly dressed figures at the end of the hall, came to join him in the doorway. 'Like we ever get good ones?'

9

'Not as bad as this . . .' The smell was stronger here. He couldn't describe it; it was life, it was death, it was everything the human body was. It was something he had smelled before. It was something he knew he would never forget.

As he looked at the body on the bed, he felt his chest constrict, his arms shake. No. This was no time for a panic attack. He breathed deeply through his mouth, forced his emotions down, his breathing back to normal. React as a copper, he told himself; it's up to you to make order out of this chaos.

Detective Sergeant Clayton Thompson, one of Phil's team. Tall and in good shape, the white of his hood emphasising his tanned features, his usually self-confident, even cocky, smile replaced by a frown of concentration. 'Should have waited for you to turn up before going in, boss. Sorry.'

Phil always made a point of assembling his team at any crime scene. Entering together got them pooling their initial responses, sharing their theories, working towards a common conclusion. He was slightly annoyed that Clayton hadn't waited for him, but given the severity of the situation, it was understandable.

'Where's Anni?' he asked.

In response to his question a head poked round the frame of the bathroom door.

'Here, boss.' Detective Constable Anni Hepburn was small, trim, with variably coloured spiked hair that always contrasted with her dark skin. The strands poking out of her white hood were today mostly blonde. She gave a quick glance to Clayton. 'Sorry, we should have waited for you, but Forensics said—'

Phil held up a hand. 'We're all here now. Let's get going.'

A look passed between Clayton and Anni. Quick, then gone. Phil caught it, couldn't read it but hoped it wasn't what he thought it was. He always felt slightly jealous at the

10

amount of female attention Clayton attracted, and he knew the DS often did plenty about it. But not with members of his own team. Not with Anni. Still, now wasn't the time to think about that. They had work to do.

He turned back to the room, took in the scene before him. Forensics had set up their arc lamps, shining down on the bed, lending the central tableau an unreal air, as if it was a film or a stage set. They moved about in the light in hushed, almost reverential silence, kneeling, bending, peering closely at what was before them, scraping and bagging, sampling and storing. Like stage management or props making final adjustments.

Or supplicants before a sacrificial altar, thought Phil. A woman lay on the bed, spreadeagled and naked, wrists and ankles tied to the metal frame. Her stomach had been cut open and her eyes had rolled back in her head as if in witness to something only she could see.

Phil swallowed hard. The one in the hall had been bad enough. This one threatened to reacquaint him with the cup of coffee and two slices of wholemeal toast and Marmite he had had for breakfast. Just what he needed on a Tuesday morning.

'Jesus,' said Clayton.

'I mean, this is Colchester,' said Anni, shaking her head. The other two looked at her. She was visibly shaken. 'Things like this don't happen here. What the hell's going on?'

Clayton was ready with a retort. Phil sensed his two officers were starting to develop unprofessional responses. He had to keep them focused. 'Right,' he said. 'What do we know?'

Anni snapped back into work mode, pushed a hand down her paper suit, withdrew a notebook, flipped it open. Phil took a grim pride in the fact that she had recovered so quickly, that she was professional enough to work through it.

'The flat belongs to Claire Fielding,' she said. 'Primary school teacher, works out Lexden way.'

Phil nodded, eyes still on the bed. 'Boyfriend? Husband?'

'Boyfriend. We checked her phone and diary and we think we've got a name. Ryan Brotherton. Want me to look into it?'

'Let's get sorted here first. Any idea who's in the hall?'

'Julie Simpson,' said Clayton. 'Another teacher, works with Claire Fielding. It was her husband who contacted us.'

'Because she didn't go home last night?' asked Phil.

'Yeah,' said Clayton. 'He called us when she didn't come back. This was well after midnight. Apparently there was some kind of get-together here last night. He'd tried phoning and got no reply. Not the kind to be out on a bender, apparently.'

'Not on a school night, anyway,' said Anni.

'Has he given a statement?' said Phil.

Clayton nodded. 'Over the phone. Bit distraught.'

'Right. We'll talk to him again later.'

Anni looked at him, worry in her eyes. 'There's, erm . . . there's something else.'

She turned, gestured to the living room. Phil, glad of the excuse to not look at Claire Fielding's body any more, followed her, stopping at the entrance to the living room. He looked inside, instinctively trying to get some idea of her life, her personality. The person she used to be.

The room was tastefully furnished, clearly on a budget, but small flourishes and touches of individuality indicated that the budget had been used creatively. With books and CDs, foreign ornaments and framed photos, it spoke of a rich, full life. But something stood out.

On the coffee table were empty and half-empty bottles of wine, white and red, a sparkling soft drink and several glasses. In amongst the glasses and bottles was the detritus of opened presents. Boxes, bags, gift wrap, tissue paper. The presents were there too. Toys, both soft and primary-coloured plastic. All-in-one Babygros, shawls, hats, jumpers, socks, shoes.

'This get-together . . .' Anni said.

'Oh Christ . . .' said Phil. He was aware of Anni looking at him, gauging his reaction, but couldn't look at her or Clayton yet. His pulse began to quicken. He tried to ignore it.

'You'll see one of them wasn't drinking,' said a voice from the bedroom.

The three of them turned. Nick Lines, the pathologist, was straightening up from the bed, peering over the tops of his glasses at Phil. He was a tall, shaven-head, hook-nosed, slightly cadaverous man, with graveyard looks and a gallows humour to match. He always looked excited at a crime scene, Phil thought. As much as he ever looked excited at anything. Lines took his glasses off, looked at Phil. 'I'm guessing that's because, as far as I can make out from an initial examination, she was pregnant.'

Phil stared with renewed horror at the slit stomach. He didn't dare voice the question that all three of them were thinking. 'Shit,' was all he could say.

'Quite,' said Lines, his voice like Nick Cave's more miserable brother. 'She was pregnant. And before you ask, the answer's no. There's no sign of it. Anywhere in the flat. Once we realised what condition she had been in, that was the first thing we did.'

Phil felt his heart beating faster, his pulse racing; tried to calm it down. He would be no good to the investigation in that frame of mind. He turned to the pathologist, his voice urgent.

'What have you got, Nick?'

'Well, as I said, this is only preliminary; don't hold me to any of it. The obvious stuff first. Broken nose, bruising. She

13

was punched in the face. Hard. It looks like she's been injected with something at the back of her neck. Then again at the base of her spine. Obviously I don't know what it is yet but I'd hazard a guess that it was something to paralyse her.'

'And the . . . the cutting?'

Nick Lines shrugged. 'Carried out with a modicum of skill, it would seem. The one in the hall, they knew which arteries to go for. Likewise here. They had a fair idea of what they were doing.'

'Time of death?'

'Hard to say at present. Late last night. Eleven-ish? Sometime round then. Between ten and two, I'd say.'

'Any sign of sexual activity?'

A faint smile played on Lines' lips. Phil knew it was his way of displaying irritation at being asked so many initial questions. 'As Chairman Mao said when asked how effective he thought the French Revolution had been, it's just too early to tell.'

'Any clues as to who could have done this?' said Clayton.

Lines sighed. 'I just tell you how they died. It's up to you to find out why.'

'I meant what kind of person,' Clayton said, clearly hurt by the response. 'Build an' that.'

'Nothing yet.'

'How far gone was she?' asked Anni.

'Very well advanced, I'd say.'

'But how far?'

He gave her a professionally contemptuous look, clearly getting irritated. 'I'm a pathologist, not a clairvoyant.'

'And we've got jobs to do as well,' said Phil, matching Lines' irritation with his own. 'Would this baby be dead by now, or is there a chance it could still be alive?'

Nick Lines looked back at the body on the bed rather

than directly at Phil. 'Judging from the condition of her womb, I'd say almost full term. Only weeks away.'

'Meaning?'

'Meaning yes. There's every chance that this baby is still alive.'

3

Marina Esposito stepped slowly into the room, looked around. She was nervous. Not because of what she was about to do particularly, but because of the public admission. Because once she had taken that step, her life would be changed, redefined for ever.

The room was large, the walls painted in light pastels, the floor wood. It had that warm yet simultaneously cool feel that so many fitness centres had. She had tried to slip quietly into the changing room, not engage anyone with eye contact and certainly not in conversation, get changed as quickly as possible, hoping her body wouldn't mark her out as one of them. She had heard them and seen them, though, talking and laughing together, and knew instinctively she would never be part of that. Never be one of them. No matter what circumstances dictated. Now she saw the same women in here and her heart sank. Hair piled up or tied back, trainers or bare feet. All wearing brightly coloured, almost dayglo leotards and co-ordinated joggers. Full make-up. Marina was wearing grey jogging bottoms, a black T-shirt, old trainers. She felt dowdy and dull.

Someone stopped behind her. 'You lost?'

'Yes,' she said, turning. She tried to speak, but the words wouldn't emerge.

'Pre-natal yoga?' the woman said, seeing the mat under Marina's arm.

Marina nodded.

The woman smiled. 'That's us, then.' She patted her stomach. It was much bigger than Marina's. Taut and hard, the bright orange leotard stretched tight across it. It protruded proudly over the waistline of her rolled-down joggers. Marina could see the distended navel through the material, like the knot of a balloon. The woman smiled like being that size and shape was the most natural thing in the world. She looked at Marina's stomach.

Oh God, Marina thought. *Looking at stomachs. That's how I have to greet people from now on.*

'How far gone?'

'Just . . . three months. Four.'

The woman looked into the room. 'Starting early, that's good.'

Marina felt she had to reciprocate. 'What . . . what about you?'

The woman laughed. 'Any day now, from the size of it. Eight months. I'm Caroline, by the way.'

'Marina.'

'Nice to meet you. Well, come on in. We don't bite.'

Caroline walked into the room, Marina following. Marina sized the other woman up, looking at her face rather than her stomach for the first time. Mid-thirties, perky, cheerful. Probably a housewife from somewhere like Lexden. Kept herself in good shape, filled her days by lunching with friends, going to the gym, the hairdresser's and the nail salon, shopping. Not Marina's type of person at all. Caroline stopped to talk to other women, greeting them like old friends. All of them scooped from the same mould as her. Brightly coloured and round. Giggling and laughing. Marina felt she had walked into a Teletubbies convention.

She wanted to turn round, walk out.

But at that moment the instructor arrived and closed the door behind her, cutting off her escape route.

'See we have a new member . . .' The instructor beckoned Marina into the room.

Caroline waved her over and Marina, trying to disguise her reluctance, crossed the room, unfurled her mat and waited for the session to start.

There. She had done it. Admitted it in public.

She was pregnant.

4

P hil couldn't speak.

He looked at his two junior officers. They seemed similarly dumbstruck as the enormity of the statement sank in.

There's every chance that this baby is still alive . . .

'Shit . . .' Phil found his voice.

'Quite,' said Nick Lines. He looked back at the bed. 'Now if you'll excuse me?'

Phil nodded and ushered his team away from the bedroom, leaving the pathologist to carry on with his job. The three of them still didn't speak.

He felt his chest tightening, his pulse quickening. He could hear the blood pumping round his body, feel the throb of his heart like a huge metronome, marking off the seconds, a ticking clock telling him to get moving, get this baby found . . .

He called over one of the uniformed officers in the living room. 'Right, I want this whole—' He stopped. 'Liz, is it?'

She nodded.

'Right. Liz.' He spoke fast but clearly. Urgent but not panicking. 'I want this whole block of flats searched. Everyone questioned, don't take no for an answer, draft in

19

as many as you can on door-to-door work. You know what I mean: did anyone hear anything, see anyone suspicious. Someone must have done. Use your instincts, be guided by what they say. I noticed the flats have all got video entry-phones. If someone got in, they must have been buzzed in. And seen. And I want the area combed. Do it thoroughly but do it quickly.' He dropped his voice. 'You know what we're looking for.'

The officer nodded, went away to begin the search.

'Boss . . .'

Phil turned, looked at Anni. She was the highest-ranking woman on his team and he had requested for her to be there. She was trained to deal with rape cases, abused children, any situation where a male presence might be a barrier to uncovering the truth. But that wasn't why Phil wanted her. She had an intelligence and intuition that he had rarely encountered. And despite the ever-changing hair and the impish smile, she could be tougher than the best when needed to be. Even tougher than him. For all of that, he could forgive the affected way she spelled her first name.

'Yes, Anni?'

'What about Julie Simpson?'

Phil looked around, mentally trying to think through what must have happened. 'If it's all about . . .' he gestured towards the bedroom, 'then I'm afraid she was just wrong place, wrong time.'

Anni nodded, as if he had confirmed her thoughts. Then frowned. 'Shouldn't we keep an open mind?'

'Course.' He felt the blood pumping once more, his internal clock telling him time was running out. 'But . . .'

'So was this party a baby shower, then?' said Clayton.

Anni looked at him. 'You'd know about them, would you?'

Clayton reddened. 'My sister. She had one . . .'

Despite the situation, Anni smiled.

Phil cut their repartee short. 'Right. Let's think. So Claire Fielding was having a baby shower. If she, or her baby, was the one deliberately targeted, then whoever did this must have thought she was alone. Maybe they miscounted or something.' He sighed, trying to control his heart rate. 'But just in case it's anything to do with Julie Simpson, get the Birdies to follow up on her. Talk to the husband. See if he knows who else was here.'

The Birdies. DC Adrian Wren and DS Jane Gosling. Inevitable they got paired together. But no one was laughing about their names at the moment.

'You think it's about the baby, boss?' Anni again. 'He's taken it, hasn't he? Whoever did this.'

'Like I said, not jumping to conclusions, it seems the likeliest explanation.'

Anni looked into the bedroom once more. 'D'you think it's still alive?'

Phil sighed. 'Nick reckons it is, so we have to assume the same; bear that in mind.'

'Until we find out otherwise,' said Clayton.

'Yeah, thanks, Dr Doom.' Clayton had the potential to be an exceptional police detective, Phil knew. He had made no secret of his ambition, but despite what he thought and told people, he wasn't the finished article yet. And sometimes his comments, as well as irritating Phil, betrayed the fact. 'I'm aware of that.'

'Putting aside how fucked up this is,' said Anni, stepping between them, 'I think there's another possibility we should consider.'

'That it's *him*, you mean?' said Clayton.

Phil knew what they were both talking about, glanced round to see who was in earshot, bent in close to them. 'Not

21

here. You know what walls have got, and it's not ice cream.'
He sighed, ordering his thoughts, willing his training to kick
in, take over. He could still hear his heart beating, each beat
signalling inactivity that took him further away from catching the perpetrator.

'Right. A plan. Anni, chain of evidence. Accompany the
bodies through the post-mortems. See what you can find
there. Get Nick to prioritise. Don't let him fob you off. I'm
sure the budget for this one'll get upgraded.'

She nodded.

'Now. Claire Fielding's background. Who loved her, who
hated her. Friends, family, work colleagues, the lot. Her
boyfriend, Clayton, what was it? Brian . . .'

'Ryan. Ryan Brotherton.'

'Right. Let's see what we can get on him, then you and me
will pay him a visit. See what he has to say, where he was
when he should have been here.'

Clayton nodded.

'Now—'

Whatever Phil was about to say was cut short by the
sharp ringing of a phone. Everyone stopped what they were
doing, looked around at each other. An eerie stillness fell,
disturbed only by the insistent sound. Like someone had
just broken through at a seance. The living trying to contact
the dead.

Phil saw the phone in the living room and motioned to
Anni. Whoever it was would be expecting a female voice.
Anni crossed the room, picked it up. She hesitated, put it to
her ear.

'H-hello.'

The whole room waited, watching Anni. She felt their
stares, turned away from them.

'Can I help you?' She kept her voice calm and courteous.

They waited. Anni listened. 'Afraid not,' she said eventually.

22

'Who is this, please? . . . I see. Could I ask you to stay on the line, please?'

She held the receiver to her chest, cupping it with her hand. She called Phil over. 'All Saints Primary. Where Claire Fielding worked. They're wondering why she hasn't turned up for work.' She mouthed the next words. 'What should I tell them?'

Phil didn't like handing out death messages to work colleagues before close relatives had been informed.

'Have they spoken to Julie Simpson's husband yet?'

'Don't think so. He would have told them what was going on.'

'Good. Tell them we'll send someone round to talk to them this morning. But don't say anything more.'

'Why not?'

'I think next of kin should know first.'

Anni nodded, went back on the phone.

Phil turned to Clayton, his voice lowered so it wouldn't carry down the phone line. 'Okay. Like I said, the Birdies can follow up on Julie Simpson. Now, the media'll be here soon. Before we go, I'll call Ben Fenwick. Get him down here to deal with them.'

'King Cliché rides again,' said Clayton.

'Indeed,' agreed Phil, not irritated by this comment of Clayton's, 'but he's good at that kind of stuff and they seem to like him. Plays well on screen. They're going to be on our side with this one – at least for now – so we'll sort out our approach in the meantime. And find out if Claire Fielding's parents live in the area. Get someone over to talk to them.'

'Shouldn't we get the DCI to deliver the death message, boss? All PR to him.'

'Yeah, but he might want to take along a camera crew. See who's at the station. Get someone with a suitable rank to do it. Draw straws if you have to.'

23

'Yes, boss.' Clayton was writing everything down.

Anni came off the phone. 'We'd better get someone round there soon as. They're not going to keep a lid on this for long. And it *was* a baby shower.'

'How d'you know?'

'Lizzie, that's Lizzie Stone who just phoned, knew Claire was having a get-together with friends last night. Mostly other teachers, I think.'

'Right,' said Phil, thinking on the spot. 'Can't remember who said this, but it's true. My mind will change when the facts change. So. Anni, get the Birdies sorted. Adrian chain of evidence, Jane still sticks with what she was doing. You get yourself round to All Saints, take as many spare units as you can. Statements, the works. Separate them, don't give them a chance to collude. I want to know exactly what happened at that party last night. Get Millhouse up and running as gatekeeper for the investigation back at base. And get him to give the computer system a pounding. We're going to need extra bodies. DCI Fenwick'll sanction that, I'm sure, because I want the Susie Evans and Lisa King cases re-examined with a fine-toothed comb. Any similarities, no matter how small, they get flagged and logged. And get uniforms to check CCTV for the whole area, inside these flats and out, registration plates, the lot. Everything referenced and cross-referenced. Right?'

The other two nodded.

'Any questions?'

Neither had any. He looked at them both. They dealt in murder and violent crime and he had hand-picked them himself. There was mutual trust between them and he hoped that look he had caught earlier wasn't going to undermine that. He examined their faces, saw only determination in their eyes. The need to catch a double killer and a possibly living child. None of them would be going home any time soon. Or going out. He felt a pang of guilt, wondered how that would go down. Could guess.

He pushed the thought out of his mind. Deal with it later.

'Right,' he said. 'Let's go. We've got work to do.'

He strode out of the apartment as quickly as possible.

5

Phil stood outside the apartment block, ripping apart the Velcro fastenings of his paper suit, hunting for his phone. He thought of Anni's words once more: *I mean, this is Colchester . . .*

Colchester. Last outpost of Essex before it became Suffolk. If heaven, as David Byrne once sang, was a place where nothing ever happened, then heaven and Colchester had a lot in common. But as Phil knew only too well, something, like nothing, could happen anywhere.

He looked round. Claire Fielding's flat was in Parkside Quarter, sandwiched between the river, the Dutch Quarter and Castle Park. The Dutch Quarter: all winding streets and alleyways of sixteenth-century and Edwardian houses stuck between the high street and the river. An urban village, the town's self-appointed boho area, complete with cobblestones, corner pubs and even its own gay club. Parkside Quarter was a modern development of townhouses and apartment blocks, all faux wooden towers and shuttered windows, designed to fit sympathetically alongside the older buildings but just looking like a cheap toytown version of them.

He was on a footpath by the river, where weeping willows shaded out the sun, leaving dappled shadows all around. It took joggers and baby-carriage-pushing mothers to and from Castle Park. On the opposite bank was a row of quaint old terraced cottages. Up the steps and beyond was North Station Road, the main link for commuters from the rail station to the town centre. It seemed so mundane, so normal. Safe. Happy.

But today the Dutch Quarter would be silent. There would be no joggers or mothers along the footpath. Already white-suited officers were on their hands and knees beginning a search of the area. He looked down at the ground. He hoped their gloves were strong. Discarded Special Brew cans, plastic cider bottles were dotted around on the ground like abstract sculptures. The odd used condom. Fewer needles than there used to be but, he knew, no less drug-taking.

He looked up to the bridge, saw others peering from their safe, happy world into his. Commuters carrying cappuccinos, mobiles and newspapers on their way up the hill were stopping to stare down, the blue and white crime-scene tape attracting their attention like ghoulish magpies dazzled by silver.

He ignored them, concentrated on getting out of his paper suit. As he did so, he caught a glimpse of himself in the window of the downstairs flat. Tall, just over six foot, and his body didn't look too bad, no beer gut or man boobs, but then he kept himself in shape. Not because he was particularly narcissistic, but his job entailed long hours, takeaway food and, if he wasn't careful, too much alcohol. And it would be all too easy to succumb, as so many of his colleagues had done, so he forced himself to keep up the gym membership, go running, cycling. Someone had suggested five-a-side, get fit, make new friends, have a laugh and a few beers afterwards. He'd turned it down. It wasn't for him. Not that he was unsociable. He was just more used to his own company.

He tried not to conform to the stereotypical image of a

police detective, believing that suits, crewcuts and shiny black shoes were just another police uniform. He didn't even own a tie, and more often than not wore a T-shirt instead of a formal shirt. His dark brown hair was spiky and quiffed, and he wore anything on his feet rather than black shoes. Today he had teamed the jacket and waistcoat of a pin-striped suit with dark blue Levis, a striped shirt and brown boots.

But his eyes showed the strain he was under. A poet's eyes, an ex-girlfriend had once said. Soulful and melancholic. He just thought they made him look miserable. Now they had black rings under them.

He breathed deep, rubbing his chest as he did so. Luckily the panic attack he had felt in the flat hadn't progressed. That was something. Usually when they hit it felt like a series of metal bands wrapping themselves round his chest, constricting him, pulling in tighter, making it harder and harder for him to breathe. His arms and legs would shake and spasm.

It was something he had suffered since he was a child. He had put it down to his upbringing. Given up for adoption by a woman he never knew, he was bounced from pillar to post in various children's homes and foster homes as he grew up. Never fitting in, never settling. He didn't like to dwell on those times.

Eventually he was sent to the Brennan household and the panic attacks tailed off. Don and Eileen Brennan. He wasn't one for melodrama, but he really did believe that couple had saved his life. Given him a sense of purpose.

Given him a home.

And they loved him as much as he loved them. So much so that they eventually adopted him.

But the panic attacks were still there. Every time he thought he had them beat, had his past worked out, another one would hit and remind him how little progress he had made.

Don Brennan had been a policeman. He believed in fairness and justice. Qualities he tried to instil in the children he fostered. So Don couldn't have been more pleased than when his adopted son followed him into the force.

And Phil loved it. Because he believed that alongside justice and fairness should be order. Not rules and regulations, but order. Understanding. Life, he believed, was random enough and police work helped him define it, gave it shape, form and meaning. Solving crimes, ascribing reasons for behaviour, finding the 'why' behind the deed was the fuel that kept his professional engine running. He was fairly confident he could bring order to any kind of chaos.

He turned away from the window. Do it now, he told himself. *Put yourself in order.*

He would start with the two previous murders.

6

L isa King and Susie Evans. The two previous murder victims. Phil pulled those two names from his mental
Rolodex, focused on them. He had seen their faces so many
times. Staring out at him from the incident room whiteboard, imprinted on his memory.

Lisa King was a twenty-six-year-old married estate agent.
She had arranged a viewing of a vacant property on the edge
of the Greenstead area of town. She had never made it out of
that house. She was discovered later that day by one of her
colleagues. Laid out on the floor of the house, drugged, bru-
tally knifed. Her stomach ripped to pieces. Her unborn child
mutilated, killed along with her.

There had been a huge media circus and Phil and his
team had doggedly followed every line of inquiry, no matter
how tenuous or tedious. The appointment had been made
over the phone, from a cheap, unregistered pay-as-you-go
mobile bought from a branch of Asda with cash. Lisa had
taken all the details herself; the client was hers. A woman's
name had been given, according to the file in the office. No
such woman existed.

Phil and his team had tried their hardest but failed to make
any headway. No forensic evidence, no DNA, no eyewitnesses

coming forward, no CCTV pictures. Nothing. It was as if the killer had materialised, murdered, then vanished into thin air.

Appeals had been made to the woman who had called the estate agent to come forward. She was promised protection, confidentiality, anything. Lisa's husband had been brought in, questioned, and released. The usual informants, paid or otherwise, came up with nothing. Everyone was talking about it; no one was saying anything.

Then, two months later, Susie Evans was murdered.

A single parent living in a council flat in New Town. Pregnant with her third child and, as she had laughingly said to her friends in the pub, between boyfriends. A part-time prostitute and barmaid, she hadn't made such a sympathetic victim as Lisa King, but Phil and his team treated her exactly the same. He didn't hold with the view that one life was somehow worth more than another. They were all equal, he thought, when they were dead.

Her body was found in a friend's flat. She had asked the friend if she could borrow it as she had a client who was going to pay her handsomely. Her eviscerated, broken body had been dumped in the bath, the walls, floor and ceiling covered in arterial blood sprays, the baby cut out, left on the floor beside her dead mother.

A door-to-door had been mounted, but it was an area that was traditionally unsympathetic to the police. A mobile station had been set up on the estate but no one had volunteered any information. Again there was no DNA, no forensic evidence and certainly no CCTV. They had speculated on many things: that it might have been a particularly twisted punter with a pregnant woman fetish. Even that it had been an abortion gone horribly wrong. And, most worryingly, that it was the same person who had killed Lisa King and his crimes were escalating. But the investigation went nowhere. And they were left with just a dead mother and child.

31

Then nothing for another two months. Until now.

Phil took out his mobile. Eileen Brennan, worried that he was in his thirties and unmarried, had been trying to fix him up with Deanna, a friend's daughter, a divorcee the same age. They had never met, and weren't particularly keen to, but had agreed on a date to keep the two older women happy. This evening. He had to phone her and, with not too much reluctance, call it off.

He had the number dialled, was ready to put the call through, when his phone rang. Grateful for the diversion, he answered it.

'DI Brennan.'

DCI Ben Fenwick. His superior officer. 'Sir,' said Phil.

'On my way over now. Just wanted a quick chat beforehand.' The voice strong and authoritative, equally at home in front of the cameras at a news conference or telling a joke to an appreciative audience in an exclusive golf clubhouse.

'Good, sir. Let me tell you what we've found.' Phil gave him the details, aware all the time of the missing baby, the clock still ticking inside him. He was pleased the rubber-neckers on the bridge couldn't hear him. He hoped there were no lip-readers in the crowd. Hid his mouth just in case.

'Oh God,' said Ben Fenwick, then offered to deal with the media as Phil knew he would. It wasn't just that he never missed an opportunity to get his face on TV; he had so many media contacts he ensured the story would be presented in a way that would benefit the investigation.

'Sounds to me like we've got a serial. What do you think? Am I right?' Fenwick's voice was tight, grim.

'Well, we've still got the party aspect to pursue, the boyfriend to question . . .'

'Gut feeling?'

'Yeah. A serial and a baby kidnapper.'

'Wonderful. Bad to worse.' He sighed. It came down the

phone as a ragged electronic bark. 'I mean, a serial killer. In Colchester. These things just don't happen. Not here.'

'That has been mentioned, sir. A few times. I'm sure they said something similar up the road in Ipswich a couple of years ago.'

A serial killer had targeted prostitutes in the red-light area of the Suffolk town. He had been caught, but not before he had murdered five women.

Another sigh. 'True. But why? And why here?'

'I'm sure they said that too.'

'Quite. Look. This is a priority case. God knows how long we've got to catch this bastard and get that baby, but we've got to step up. You're going to need a bit of help.'

'How d'you mean, sir?'

'Different perspective, that kind of thing. Psychological input. Profile.'

'I thought you didn't go for that sort of thing.'

'I don't. Not personally. But the Detective Super's been on the phone from Chelmsford. Thinks it would be helpful. Sanctioned the money too. So there we are. Another weapon in the arsenal and all that.'

'Who did you have in mind?' A shiver ran through Phil, as if he had just plugged his fingers into a wall socket. He had an idea of what Fenwick was about to say next. Hoped he was wrong.

'Someone with a bit of specialist knowledge, Phil. And I know you've worked with her before.'

Her. Phil knew exactly who he was talking about. His chest tightened again, but this wasn't a panic attack. Not exactly.

'Marina Esposito,' said Fenwick. 'Remember her?'

Of course Phil remembered her.

'I know it all ended rather unfortunately last time—' Fenwick didn't get to finish his sentence.

33

Phil gave a bitter laugh. 'Bit of an understatement.'

'Yes,' said Fenwick, undaunted. 'But by all accounts a cracking forensic psychologist, don't you think? Or at least as far as they go. And, you know, what happened aside, she got us a result.'

'She did,' said Phil. 'She was good.' *And an even better lover*, he thought.

He felt his chest tightening again at his own words, tried to ignore it. He sighed. He remembered the case well. How could he not?

Gemma Hardy was in her mid-twenties, a dentist's receptionist who lived in a shared flat in the Dutch Quarter. She had friends and a regular boyfriend. Life was good for Gemma Hardy, she was happy. But that was all about to change. Because Gemma had also attracted a stalker.

At first it was just texts, then letters. Love letters, dark and twisted, the writer telling her that she was the only girl, his true love. That he would kill anyone who got in their way. That he would kill her rather than let her go with someone else.

Scared, she contacted the police. Phil was handed the case. He and his team went through Gemma's life intimately. They found no one, nothing that could possibly point to the perpetrator. They arranged for her flat to be watched. Saw no one apart from her friends and boyfriend. They were getting nowhere, she was still terrified. Then someone suggested bringing in a psychologist.

Marina Esposito, a lecturer in psychology at nearby Essex University, was called in to consult. She specialised in deviant sexuality. The case was tailor-made for her. Along with Phil she examined every aspect of Gemma's life, and they found their stalker: Martin Fletcher. Her flatmate's boyfriend. He was arrested and confessed.

And that should have been the end of it. But it wasn't. Not for Marina.

'I doubt she'd do it, to tell you the truth, sir.'

'I thought a bit of persuading, perhaps.' Fenwick sounded surprised.

Phil couldn't believe what he was hearing. 'Persuading? Last time she worked with us she nearly died. Severed all links. You sure you want her?'

'Super mentioned her personally. Good a place as any to start with. And if ever a case was right up her alley it's this one.' Fenwick's voice changed gear then, moved from politician to friend, counsellor. Phil didn't trust him when he did that. 'Leave it to me, Phil. I'll talk to her, see what I can do.'

Phil closed his eyes. Marina was there. He shook his head. Marina was always there. He sighed. Fenwick was right. Whatever else had happened, she was the best. And he needed the best on this case. 'Well, good luck with that.'

'Thank you.' Phil couldn't tell if Fenwick was being sarcastic or not.

There was a silence on the other end of the line. Then: 'Are you sure you can handle this, Phil?'

Phil was jolted back. 'Don't see why not. I've been CIO on high-profile cases before.'

'That's not what I meant.' Fenwick's voice was quiet. Solicitous.

Phil couldn't speak for a few seconds as he absorbed the impact of Fenwick's words. *He knows. The bastard knows.*

His heart started to beat faster again. It's the case, he told himself, the baby, the seconds ticking away. That's all it is, not . . . 'Yes, sir, I can handle it.'

'Good. Then I'll talk to her. Because we're going to need all the help we can get on this one. There's a budget for this; it's been upgraded as high priority so we don't need to worry about that aspect. Extra manpower too. Personpower I should say. Let us not speak the language of dinosaurs in this department.' He gave a snort.

Phil wasn't listening. He had butterflies in his stomach.

'Right. Well, we'd better get going. The clock's ticking and all that. '

'Right you are, sir.'

Phil broke the connection. Stood staring at the phone, stunned at Fenwick's words. But he didn't have time to think about them now. He had another call to make.

Somehow it didn't seem to matter too much.

Clayton emerged from the block of flats, joined him.

'Ready, boss?'

'Nearly,' said Phil. He looked at Clayton, looked at his handset. Do it now. Get it over with.

'Just got a call to make. Won't be a moment.'

He walked away for privacy, dialled the number. Hoped Clayton was out of earshot.

It wasn't good for morale to hear your boss get told off by his mum.

7

He had done it. Actually done it. Gone out and got her a baby, just like she had asked, just like he had promised to. Hester couldn't believe it.

But she looked down at the baby and frowned. It wasn't right. Not right at all.

She knew what babies looked like. Especially newborn ones. She'd seen them on TV. They were always happy and smiling, with hair. This one wasn't. Small, wrinkled, shrivelled and pinky blue. More like Yoda than a baby. And it didn't smile. Just twisted its face up and made a gurgling, wailing noise, like it was being tortured underwater.

But it was a baby, so Hester would have to make the best of it. A baby of her own. And when you had a baby, you had to clothe it and feed it and make it grow. She knew that.

It was wailing now. Hester brought her face into a smile.

'Do you want feeding, baby?' Her voice was an approximation of baby talk. Like she had heard on TV. 'Do you?' More wailing. 'Mummy's got something for you.'

Mummy. Just the word . . .

She went to the fridge, took out a bottle, placed it in the microwave. She had given him a list of what she wanted and he had got the lot. Powdered milk. Bottles. Nappies. Everything the books said.

She waited for the ping. Took it out.

'Just right,' she said, squirting some into her own mouth. She stuck the teat into the baby's mouth, waited while it sucked hard. 'That's it. That's better . . .'

Yes, it was tiny and pink and shrivelled. Yoda. But unlike Yoda its eyes wouldn't open all the way, no matter how much Hester pulled at them. That wasn't important, though. She looked down at the infant. She had wrapped it in blankets because that was the right thing to do, but it still looked cold. Like its skin wasn't the right colour. But it didn't matter. Hester had a baby. At last. That was the important thing. And she had to bond. That was important too.

She looked down at it again, feeding, managed a smile. 'I've been through a lot to get you,' she said, her usually broken voice sounding like a baby coo, 'a lot. I could have just walked in somewhere, taken you, but that wouldn't have been right, would it? No . . . Because you'd have been someone else's by then, wouldn't you? You'd have a different mummy and you'd have to forget her before you met me.' She sighed. 'Yes, I've been through a lot. But you were worth it . . .'

The baby spat the teat out, began to cough. Hester felt anger rising inside herself. It wasn't doing what it was supposed to. It should take all the bottle. The book said. TV said.

'Don't you fuckin' do that,' she said, no trace now of baby talk. 'Take it . . .'

She shoved the teat back in the baby's mouth again, forced it to drink. Pushed the rising anger back down.

The baby stopped coughing, took the teat. That was better.

It was shrivelled and the wrong colour. And it wailed and

shat all the time. She hated that. But it was a baby. And that was all she had wanted. So she would put up with it.

'But you'd better start to be like the TV babies,' she said to its bare head, 'the proper babies, or there'll be trouble . . .'

The baby kicked and wriggled, tried to get away from the bottle.

'No,' she said, 'you need to be big and strong. And you're not finished until I say you're finished . . .'

Milk ran down the baby's cheeks. It had finished feeding. Hester kept the teat in place.

She smiled, looked at her watch. Closed her eyes. It would be time for her husband to go out soon. Yes, she had a baby now but his work wasn't done. There was still the list to be attended to. Then, when he had finished, he would come back to her and they would all settle in. A real family. Complete. She opened her eyes. Smiled. Content with her life.

For now.

8

'Fancy a coffee?' The bright and perky voice was in Marina's ear once more.

Marina turned. Caroline was standing with some of the other women from the group, heading towards the door.

'A few of us usually head off into town,' Caroline said. 'Go to Life for a coffee. Well, those of us who can still drink it. And usually a little something else.'

'Doesn't that undo everything you've just done here?' asked Marina.

Caroline laughed, shrugged. 'What's life without a few little treats?'

Marina smiled. 'That's kind, thanks, but I have to get back to work.'

Caroline, Marina noticed, was now dressed in the latest in designer and high-end high-street maternity wear. She had also done her make-up in the time it had taken Marina to get showered and dressed. How had she managed that?

Caroline smiled again. 'You sure?'

And Marina saw something in her features she hadn't noticed earlier. Tiredness, lines around the eyes. Her smile too brittle. Caroline was older than Marina had first thought, older than her peers in the group. She dressed

younger, acted younger, but she couldn't quite hide the extra
years.

'It would be lovely to have you along.'

Marina returned the smile. 'Maybe next time.'

'Okay, then. Next time.' Caroline turned, went off with
her happy, chattering friends, all similarly dressed. They
smiled as they passed, and Marina reciprocated, letting it
fade once they had all exited.

She watched them go, talking and laughing. They were a
group Marina would have instantly categorised, even stereo-
typed. Middle class, husbands at work, the type of women
who would have pain-free births and, by hitting the gym and
the fad diets, get their pre-pregnancy figures back within a
week. The type of women other women would envy and even
secretly despise.

From a distance Caroline looked like she was one of the
group, but Marina sensed something different about her.
Something separate. Maybe that was why she had wanted
Marina to go with them. Or maybe she was just being
friendly. No matter. Not her problem. Marina waited until
they had all gone, walked through the foyer of Leisure World.

The piped muzak drowned out the shrieks, cries and
splashes of schoolchildren cramming in five minutes of play
after their prescribed swimming lessons, the multicoloured
flume and slide tubes sticking out of the side of the building
taking a pounding. She walked through the doors and on to
the forecourt. The noise was bad enough but the chlorinated
smell was seriously starting to assault her nostrils. She knew
things like that happened in pregnancy. The senses were
heightened; women became intolerant of scents that had
never previously bothered them. She knew one woman from
university who couldn't stand the smell of her own husband.
A shiver of dread ran through her body. She hoped nothing
like that happened to her.

41

Outside, she stood on the kerb of the car park on the Avenue of Remembrance, pulled her coat close to her to keep out the November cold, waited for the cab that would take her back to her new office and her afternoon clients. She had showered but her muscles were still aching, throbbing. She would suffer tomorrow.

A few minutes later, a 4x4 went past, tooted. Caroline and her friends. Marina gave a smile that disappeared as the car rounded the corner.

The changes in her life in such a short space of time had been huge. Leaving the comfort and safety of the university to go into private practice – although by the time she left it didn't feel safe or comfortable – and the fact that Tony, her long-term partner, had proposed to her. But the most important change had been the baby. Unplanned and, initially, unwanted, she was still coming to terms with it. She felt she always would be.

She looked at her watch, getting impatient for the cab, killing time by working out what she would be doing if she were still at the university. Probably preparing for her second-year class, gathering together papers, books and notes in her old office, readying herself for the seminar she would be about to give. Chimerical Masks and Dissociation in the Perception of the Self. Something like that.

The self. Her hands, as they so often did these days, went automatically underneath her coat to her stomach. Began stroking the bump. Slight to a disinterested onlooker's eyes, but to her enormous. And, she knew, it would only get bigger. This self – her self – was one she barely recognised any more. When she thought of her old life, her old self, she became choked, felt like crying. But she was beyond the tears stage now. Four months beyond.

She felt something flutter. Like butterflies in her stomach. Big butterflies. She jumped, startled and scared. Tried to breathe deeply, calm down. It was natural, it was expected. It was what the body did. But not her body. She didn't feel it was her body any more. She was just a carrier, a vessel for this child. Which was fine while she was carrying, but when it had left her, what would she be then?

The physical stuff was scary enough – the changes that would occur in her body as the baby grew and demanded life from her, the actual pain of childbirth itself and then how ravaged her body would be afterwards. And then there were the years as a mother to come.

Her first response to the pregnancy was to get rid of it. Get it out of her, don't let it grow, take her over, like some hideous invasion-of-the-bodysnatchers-type creature. And with her starting up in private practice it was the wrong time, if nothing else.

Tony said he would be fine with whatever she wanted to do. It was her body, after all. So she decided on a termination. But when the time came, she couldn't go through with it.

Marina had swallowed her fear, tried to live with it. Pre-natal yoga, relaxation and meditation, eating the right things, not drinking. Luckily she wasn't one of those women who were sick all the time and couldn't eat anything. Or at least not yet. Feeling the baby grow inside her was bad enough. That would have been intolerable. She also thought that being with other pregnant women would help. Take away the fear, the uncertainty. And it had, for a while. But now that she was alone again she felt the old doubts coming back.

She wondered how she had looked to the other women in the class. Long, dark hair, mercifully free of grey. Or rather chemically assisted to be free of grey. A pretty face for a thirty-six-year-old, she thought, just spoiled by worry. She had good bone structure due to her Italian parentage; the worry she had added herself. Her eyes looked sunken, hollow, like a ghost waiting to be brought back to life. Once she had resigned herself to the baby she had hoped it would do that. Four months in and it hadn't. She was beginning to doubt that it ever would. She needed something else.

She checked her watch, stamped her feet. The cab driver had said goodbye to his tip.

From within her bag, her mobile rang.

Sighing, she extracted her hand from her coat, went to answer it. 'Yes.'

'Marina? Marina Esposito?'

She knew that voice. It took her a few seconds to place, but she did it. And gave an involuntary gasp. DCI Ben Fenwick. She exhaled slowly.

'Ben Fenwick?'

'Yes, Marina, hi. Sorry to bother you. I need to talk to you.'

'Oh.' She looked round. And there in front of her was Martin Fletcher. Advancing on her, features twisted by hate.

She screwed her eyes up tight, opened them again. Nothing but the cold car park, the missing cab. The faint sounds of screaming children in the background. Martin Fletcher had gone. But Ben Fenwick's voice was still on the phone.

'Marina? You still there?'

'Yes . . . yes, Ben. I'm still here.'

'Look, I wouldn't ask if it wasn't important.'

That was all she needed to hear and immediately the barrier was back up. 'Look, I'm . . . I'm busy. Can we do this another time?'

'I'm afraid not. We've got a problem.'

'What kind?'

He sighed. 'The worst kind.'

She wanted to push the button, end the call. Get into her cab – if it ever arrived – and forget Ben Fenwick had phoned. Instead she said, 'What kind of problem?'

44

'A new case has come up and we need help. Your help.' He paused as if thinking over what to say next. 'Look, I realise this may be difficult for you . . .'

She saw Martin Fletcher advancing towards her out of the corner of her eye again, felt blind, trapped panic rise in her chest. She blinked him away, breathed deeply.

She kept her voice low, contained. 'What is it?'

'It's . . . it's not really the kind of thing we can discuss over the phone. Best if we talk in person.'

She felt a shiver run through her. *Say no. Say no. Say no.* 'Okay. Where . . .'

'I'll get a car sent to pick you up.'

'When?'

'No time like the present.'

'But I'm . . . busy. Clients . . .' The words sounded weak, even to her ears.

Fenwick sighed, evidently thinking again. 'Please don't take this the wrong way, but with all due respect, Marina, I think when you hear what I've got to say, you may find it takes precedence.'

She said nothing, thought. He took her silence as a need for more explanation, reassurance.

'Look, I'm sorry about what happened before. We all are. It was horrific, unacceptable. Totally. If there was . . . if we could have done things differently . . .'

'Not your fault,' she said, her voice small and unconvincing.

He sounded relieved. 'It won't be like that this time. I promise. I give you my word.'

Despite everything she felt a slight thrill at Fenwick's words. Perhaps enough time had passed to want to get away from the office. Like childbirth, she thought with a grim smile, the memory of the pain dissipates so you can go through it again.

'Okay, send the car. Give me a couple of hours.'

45

'Can you come quicker? It really is urgent.'

'Right away then. I'm standing outside Leisure World. Tell the driver to hurry. It's freezing here.'

'Thank you, Marina. He'll find you.'

She put the phone away while he was still thanking her. Smiled to herself. Didn't even attempt to suppress the thrill that ran through her. Whatever they wanted her for must be bad, she thought. Psychosexual deviance was what she specialised in.

Another shudder went through her. Phil. She would be working with Phil.

She had tried to put him out of her mind. Concentrate on her life with Tony, the impending baby. But there he was again, Fenwick's phone call summoning him up. He didn't dress like any of the other coppers, but his clothes always showed off his broad shoulders and slim waist. She had thought he played rugby when she first met him but she soon found out that wasn't him. He wore his childhood on his face; the nose that had been broken and reset, the small scars he still carried from fights that only showed up when he was angry. But it was the eyes she remembered most. The eyes that had drawn her in. His melancholic, poet's eyes. Because when she talked to him, he listened. Actually looked her in the eye and listened. He would remind her a few days later of something she had said, proving it. And it wasn't a trick, an affectation, it was the way he was. She imagined how this could make him a good policeman, but it had done something more to her. Made her feel wanted, special.

No wonder she fell for him. And now she would be working with him again. Well, things were going to be different this time. They would have to be. Because she might have told Fenwick that what happened with Martin Fletcher wasn't his fault. But with Phil it was a different story.

Her cab chose that moment to arrive. She waved him off,

told him he'd taken too long. The driver got out, started to argue, but the arrival of a police car behind him and the presence of a policeman seemed to shut him up.

Marina got in the passenger door of the police car.

Hoped this would be just the displacement activity she needed to take her mind off her own troubles.

9

He watched them go in and he watched them come out. They didn't see him, didn't even know he was there. Not a clue. So sure were they of their place in the world, their importance in it. Safely inside their own protective little bubble. They would soon find out how unsafe they were.

Or at least one of them would.

He knew they wouldn't see him. He was too good for that. Prided himself on it. Sitting in the car park of Colchester's Leisure World, a clear view of the front entrance, just far enough back not to attract any attention. But he could see them. Talking and laughing as they emerged from their yoga session, their full, distended bellies sticking out in front of them.

Surrogates. All of them. If he wanted them to be.

He had the list, knew which one would come next. Knew the order.

It wasn't for the babies. He didn't care about that. It was all about the hunt. Planning. Preparation. The chase. The thrill. The kill. He had always enjoyed hunting. The breed of animal was unimportant.

There she was, his next prey. She had stopped to talk to another one on the pavement. This one didn't have such a big belly; in fact she was barely showing at all. His prey wanted the new one to go with them. But she wouldn't. His prey didn't seem too bothered, just walked away with her pack.

Past his own vehicle. Didn't even stop to look at him. He grinned. An invisible god with the power of life and death.

She got into her own car, drove away.

He didn't need to follow her. He knew where she was going. He would catch up with her later. Instead he turned his attention back to the one left on the pavement. The new one who didn't want to go with them. He shouldn't have been interested in her but he was. There was something about her. She was alone, apart from the pack. But not because of weakness. The opposite, he sensed. A strength, an attitude.

He smiled. He liked that in his prey. A challenge. Something to work with. Something to break down.

He knew he should be driving away, but he couldn't take his eyes off her. She wasn't like the others. He sensed cunning, intelligence. Just from the way she stood, her body language as she talked on her phone. There was nothing he could do about her now, but she would be filed away. And one day, at a time of his own choosing, he would come back for her.

And then he would have fun.

He was about to start his engine when a taxi arrived. She bent down, spoke to the driver. The driver wasn't happy with what she said. There was going to be a fight. He sat back, watching. This would be interesting. But before anything could happen, another car pulled up and the driver got out. There was no mistaking who this person was. Even if he didn't know him, he knew the type. A policeman. He could see that from here.

The taxi driver drove away, clearly unhappy. The woman got into the unmarked police car and was driven away.

Interesting. Curious. He would look out for her, watch for her. She wouldn't be forgotten.

With nothing else to stay there for, he turned the ignition, drove away.

She had been marked.

49

10

It was nearly lunchtime when Phil Brennan turned the Audi off the main road. Aware of the constant ticking of the clock, he had made the drive to Braintree as fast as he could. He had pushed the Audi to the legal limit, done everything short of sticking the siren on the roof.

The satnav pinged, informing them that they had reached their destination. Clayton Thompson reached across the dashboard and turned it off.

'Hate those things,' he said.

'Thought you'd be all for them. Know how you love a gadget.'

Clayton shrugged. 'Yeah, but it's just their smug little voices. Like the top brass have put them here to spy on us. Like we have to stick to the journey. If we know a short cut or a better route they tell us we can't use it, that they know best.'

Phil gave a grim smile. 'Clayton, I think you've just discovered a metaphor for policing in the twenty-first century,' he said.

He looked out of the window. They were on an industrial estate in Braintree, a few miles south of Colchester, just off the A12. Low-level metal and brick buildings surrounded them, stretching all the way from the main road to the railway line running from London to East Anglia. Directly ahead of them was a double set of metal mesh gates bearing the name B & F METALS. Behind the gates was another low-level metal and brick building with a forecourt on which stood a pair of huge cranes and several trucks and lorries. Cars were parked at the side. Metal canisters were piled all around: old gas bottles, fire extinguishers. Further on were huge square bays made out of old railway sleepers in which sat various kinds of scrap metal, piping, wire and old electrical appliances. One of the cranes was moving, a grabbing claw on the end of it. As they watched, it lifted a massive handful of metal from a bay, swung it round and deposited it into the back of a waiting high-sided lorry.

Phil shared a look with Clayton, turned off the engine.

'Come on,' said Clayton, getting out of the car, 'let's do it.'

'Yeah,' said Phil. 'Clock's ticking.'

Clayton stopped to give him a look. 'Nothin' to do with the clock. Just a relief to get away from that awful music you keep playin'. Glasvegas? You listen to some shit.'

Phil stared at him, said nothing.

'With all due respect, boss,' mumbled Clayton, his eyes dropping.

Clayton had an attitude on him. Phil knew that. Most of the time he tolerated it because his junior was a damned good copper, but sometimes he overstepped the mark. Phil often wanted to hit him. But just as often wanted to praise him.

'Well at least it's better than that stuff you listen to,' said Phil. 'Just how many songs do we need by black ex-gang members boasting about their genitals and their bank accounts?'

Clayton didn't answer, just looked sullenly at the ground, a naughty schoolboy facing detention.

'Now get your head straight,' said Phil. 'We're going in.' He started off, Clayton trudging behind him.

They knew this wasn't going to be an ordinary death-message delivery. In running a routine check on Claire Fielding's boyfriend Ryan Brotherton before coming to his place of work, they had found something interesting. He had done time in HMP Chelmsford for assault. The reports were over five years old, but from what they could gather it had been a previous girlfriend he had assaulted. This had made them all the more interested in talking to him.

Phil and Clayton walked into the yard. Men, barrel-chested and shaven-headed for the most part, dressed in dirty work clothes, went about their business. Phil knew immediately that they had been clocked. He also guessed that most of the men who worked here had had run-ins with the police before so weren't inclined to help them or ask what they were doing here. They would assume it was bad news and hope it didn't concern them.

They found an office at the corner of the main building, the glass streaked with grease and dirt. They knocked on the door. It was answered by a woman; blonde and middle-aged, but fighting it hard. Petite but pneumatic, her breasts, lips and expressionless forehead screaming surgery, she was dressed like a secretary in an eighties porn film. As the smile she gave them faded once she worked out who they were, Phil reckoned she might have had a run-in with the law too. For something entirely different.

He held out his warrant card, Clayton doing likewise, and introduced themselves. 'DI Brennan and DS Thompson. Could we come in?'

'What's this about?' Her voice had a hardness that no amount of surgery could soften.

'Better we talk inside, I think.'

Looking round warily, she reluctantly led them into the

52

office. Inside was bare-walled and functional. Not a place for interior designers or feng shui consultants. Two desks, two computers, two phones. A charity calendar on the wall. Metal filing cabinets.

'What's this about?' she said, not offering them a seat.

'We're looking for Ryan Brotherton,' said Clayton, trying to move his eyeline away from her breasts and, Phil noticed, not entirely succeeding.

Knowing she had his DS, she turned to Phil, stuck them out further.

'What's it concerning?'

'It's a private matter.'

No one moved. The phone rang. She ignored it.

'Shouldn't you get that?' Phil said. 'Might be work.'

She still didn't move.

'Want me to?' said Phil, moving towards the desk.

She beat him to it, grabbing the receiver and saying, 'B and F Metals,' then listening. 'Right, Gary, can I call you back in a minute?' She put the phone down, turned back to them.

'Ryan Brotherton?' said Phil, reminding her.

'And I want to know why you need to see him.'

'Look,' said Phil, trying to keep a lid on his irritation, 'he's not in any trouble, he's not done anything wrong. We just need to have a few words with him.'

He looked at her, didn't break eye contact. She wavered, looked away. 'I'll go and get him.'

She left the office, walked across the yard. Clayton watched her go.

'You okay?' said Phil.

Clayton shook his head as if coming out of a trance. His face was unreadable. 'Yeah, uh . . . not your average scrap-metal dealer,' he said.

'This is Essex, remember,' said Phil, trying not to look, but unable to stop his eyes tracking her swinging hips like a spectator at Wimbledon. 'Wonder why she wants to work here? Surrounded by all those men?'

'Maybe that's your answer,' said Clayton, not bothering to disguise his leer. 'Might consider a change of career . . .'

'Focus, sonny. Think with your brain, remember. Look around. See anything that might help us?'

Clayton scanned the office, giving it close scrutiny. He shook his head.

'Me neither.' Phil returned his attention to outside the window.

As they watched, the pneumatic secretary walked to the bottom of the grabber and gestured to the man in the cockpit. He swung the arm over a bin and left it dangling there as he put the brakes on and opened the cab door, leaned out. Phil got a good look at him. He was big, and not unattractive, fine-featured. His hair was close-cropped, his upper torso very well muscled. He listened to what the woman said, his eyes going to the office, following her pointing arm. He didn't look pleased.

'Look at those guns,' said Clayton. 'Whoever he hit didn't stand a chance.'

Ryan Brotherton got out of the cab and made his way across the yard to the office. Not in a good mood. He reached the cabin, opened the door, stepped inside. The space was small enough; with his large frame as well as the two of them, he seemed to suck all the air from the room.

'Yeah?' he said.

Phil held out his warrant card again. 'DI Brennan and DS Thompson,' he said.

'So?'

'Can we have a word, please?'

Brotherton shrugged.

Phil noticed the pneumatic secretary trying to enter the office. 'In private.'

54

Brotherton noticed her entering too, didn't try to stop her. 'This is Sophie. Anything you have to say to me can be said in front of her.' His face twisted into an expression that on someone else could have been a smile. 'And I've found, Mr Brennan, that when your lot are around it's better to have a witness.'

Phil weighed his options. Reassure Brotherton that he had done nothing wrong, insist on privacy. Or just say what he had to say to this unpleasant man, no matter how painful, and get out. He decided on the latter.

'I'm afraid we've got some very bad news to tell you, Mr Brotherton.'

Brotherton said nothing, waited.

Phil and Clayton exchanged a glance. Phil continued. 'It's your girlfriend.'

Brotherton frowned. Sophie joined him. 'Girlfriend?'

'Claire Fielding. Your girlfriend.'

'You mean ex-girlfriend,' said Sophie quickly before Brotherton could speak.

Phil looked between the two of them. He knew what was happening. 'Ex-girlfriend. I'm sorry.'

'So? What about her? What's she done now?' He took a step forward, hands instinctively bunching into fists. 'What's she said about me now, eh? What lies has she come out with this time?'

Phil kept his face straight, his voice neutral. 'What lies has she told before, Mr Brotherton?'

Brotherton gave a harsh bark. It could have been a laugh. 'Don't pretend you don't know. You wouldn't be here otherwise.'

'Would this have something to do with your assault charges?' said Clayton.

'You know fuckin' well it does. Just because I've done time for assault over five years ago you think you can keep

55

dredgin' it up all the damned time. Every time some bird makes some allegation you automatically come to me. Well I'm sick of it. Any more of this and I'll get my solicitor on to you.'

'That won't be necessary, Mr Brotherton,' said Phil. 'There won't be any more allegations against you. At least not from Claire Fielding.'

Another snort. 'Why? She been given a restrainin' order? Stop pesterin' me?'

'No, Mr Brotherton,' said Phil, 'she's dead.'

He waited, scrutinising Brotherton and Sophie's faces for the slightest out-of-place expression, to file away for a later date. The two of them exchanged glances. Sophie looked to be about to say something but Brotherton shushed her. 'What happened?' he said, voice flat.

'She was murdered. In her flat, last night.'

His jaw sagged slightly open, his eyes went blank. Phil imagined that for him it was quite a display of emotion. Brotherton's usual range probably went all the way from anger to anger.

'What . . . what . . .' Then a thought struck him. 'She was pregnant, wasn't she?'

'She was, Mr Brotherton. With your baby?' said Clayton.

'So she said,' said Brotherton, the anger in his words indicating that whatever grieving process he had undergone for Claire Fielding was now officially over.

'What d'you mean by that?' said Phil.

'What I said. Oldest trick in the book, innit? You wanna catch a man, you tell him you're pregnant.' He made an expansive arm gesture, looked round the office. 'I mean, look at this place. I'm not bleedin' Alan Sugar, but this is all mine. I own it.'

'Your company?' said Phil.

Brotherton nodded. 'I do all right out of it. And women,

when they see that, they think, ooh, I'll have a bit of that for myself. Better than workin'. So what's the easiest way to do it?' He shrugged, gave a self-satisfied smile as if he had just explained a particularly thorny issue to the Oxford University debating society. 'Exactly.'

'Well she's dead now, Mr Brotherton, so your empire is safe.'

Brotherton nodded, failing to pick up the sarcasm in Phil's tone.

'So who's the F?' asked Clayton.

'What?' Brotherton was clearly irritated by the question.

'The F. In the sign out there. B & F Metals.'

Brotherton shrugged. 'Bought him out. Kept the name so people knew who they were dealing with.'

'And that's important, isn't it?' said Phil. 'Knowing who you're dealing with.'

Brotherton just stared at him.

'Why were you out on the crane if you're the boss of the company?' asked Phil, frowning. 'Don't you pay someone to do that?'

Brotherton's chest puffed out with pride. 'Good to keep your hand in. Keeps you fit, strong.'

'Never know when that's going to come in handy, do you?'

Brotherton turned to Phil, his muscles flexing, hands balling into fists. Clayton looked between the two, spoke.

'So you were no longer seeing her?' he asked. 'Claire Fielding?'

Another snort, attention diverted from Phil. 'Why would I?' He looked around, smiled triumphantly. 'I've got Sophie now, ain't I?'

Sophie returned the smile with all the warmth and animation her Botoxed features would allow.

'So why would you still be described in her diary as her boyfriend?' asked Phil.

'Bollocks.'

'It's true, Mr Brotherton. Her address book still has your name in it too, and she carried a photo of you in her wallet.'

'You know what birds are like,' he said, trying to remain cocky. 'Can't let go, can they?' But his features didn't mirror his words. And something unfamiliar entered his eyes. Fear?

'Mr Brotherton, where were you last night between the hours of ten p.m. and two a.m.?'

'What?' Brotherton looked between the two policemen.

'You heard the question,' said Clayton.

'I was . . .' He looked to Sophie for support.

'He was with me,' she said, picking up on his visual clue.

'Where?' said Phil.

'At my place,' she said quickly.

'Doing what?' said Clayton.

'What business is that of yours?' she said, her face finding animation at last.

'This is a murder inquiry; answer the question, please.'

'Watching a DVD. Bottle of wine, takeaway.'

'What film?'

'What?' she said.

'What film were you watching?' Phil said again.

'We . . . had a couple,' Brotherton said.

'What were they?' Clayton's voice was calm and emotionless.

'Something . . . something Sophie wanted and . . . and something I wanted.' Brotherton looked at her again, willing her to speak.

'Which was?' Phil's voice was also flat and emotionless. A question machine.

'*Atonement*,' said Sophie.

'*No Country for Old Men*,' said Brotherton.

'Is that out on DVD yet?' said Clayton.

'Got a pirate.'

Phil allowed himself a small smile. 'Want us to do you for that as well?'

'Look, just . . . fuck off. You've got what you wanted, we've told you what we were doin'. You've got your information, just . . . leave. Now. I've got a business to run.' Brotherton was talking himself into confidence again. 'And you're bad for it.'

Phil and Clayton exchanged another look, the purpose of which was to rattle Brotherton and Sophie even more than their questioning had. Leaving them with that, they made their way to the door.

Phil stepped through first, Clayton following. As he came abreast of Brotherton, he turned.

'What did you think of Romola Garai?'

'What?' he said, startled.

'Briony,' he said.

Brotherton's face was blank. He looked to Sophie for help, but she was as lost as he was.

'Romola Garai,' Clayton continued. 'She played the adult Briony. The lead character in *Atonement*.' He smiled. 'Thought you might have remembered that. I mean, you only saw it last night.'

He left, following Phil across the yard to the car.

'That's my boy,' said Phil when Clayton caught up with him.

'Thank you, boss. Everythin' I learned, I learned from you.'

'You like *Atonement*, did you?'

Clayton smiled. 'Never seen it. Saw some pictures of that Romola Garai in *Nuts*. Thought she looked hot. Remembered what film she was in.'

Phil's turn to smile. 'So there is some value in those magazines after all.'

They reached the Audi, got back in.

59

'So what d'you think, boss? Dirty?'

'Hard to say. Something's not right. He's big enough to do it and he's got previous. And from the way he responded, there seemed to be some unfinished business between him and Claire Fielding.'

'He didn't seemed too upset about her death,' said Clayton.

'He didn't.'

'And he was lyin' about where he was last night.'

'They all lie to us, Clayton. Haven't you worked that out yet?' He put the car into gear. 'Back to Colchester.' He thought of Marina. She would be at the station by now. He felt butterflies at the thought, tried to immediately tamp them down. He had work to do.

Clayton looked back at the office, then round again. He groaned. 'Not Glasvegas again . . .'

'No,' said Phil, thinking. 'About time you developed some taste, I think.'

Clayton's eyes brightened. 'Yeah?'

'How about some Neil Young?' Phil knew his DS would have never heard of him, but after the last admonishment he wouldn't dare to argue. 'A classic. Something to get the old brain cells working.'

Clayton shook his head. 'Kill me now,' he said under his breath.

Phil took a perverse and childish satisfaction in putting Clayton in his place.

They drove back to Colchester as fast as they could.

11

Marina bent over the washbasin and vomited again. One hand on the porcelain, one holding her hair away from her face.

'Oh God . . .' Her voice broken, riding out the waves of nausea, crying as she spoke. 'I can't . . . can't do this . . .'

She gasped, breathed hard, waiting to see if there was to be any more. A deep breath in. Held and let go. And again. She sighed, eyes closed, listening to her body. That was it, she felt. No more. There was nothing left inside her to come out.

Opening her eyes, she ran the cold tap, splashed her face, the water disguising the tears, and straightened up, running her fingers through her hair, looking at herself in the mirror. Her eyes more haunted than ever. More fearful.

And with good reason, she thought.

Her hands went automatically to her stomach as she tried to control her breathing, will herself to calm down.

So, she thought. She was one of those women who were sick. And she knew the cause: the photos. She had been shown into reception at Colchester's main police station on Southway. The duty sergeant had rung through; DCI Ben Fenwick had come down to greet her. He looked exactly the same. Smart suit, hair greying but neatly cut. His features were symmetrical and pleasing to look at, but somehow avoided being handsome. Marina assumed this was because he was too bland.

He came towards her, hand outstretched, smile in place, reminding her once again of the overeager head boy, welcoming newcomers to the sixth form. She felt sure he had done that.

'Marina,' he said, shaking her hand, moving her forward. 'Welcome back. Come through. Let's walk and talk.'

They went through the double doors, Fenwick striding urgently. 'You know,' he said without breaking stride, 'we could never have reached a successful conclusion in the Gemma Hardy case without you.'

'Thank you.' *And we know what happened with that*, she thought, almost running along behind him.

Fenwick must have picked up her thought telepathically. 'Of course, what happened afterwards, none of us could have predicted. And for that I am most deeply, deeply sorry. I am just so pleased that it was concluded successfully.'

And that I never sued the department, she mentally added.

'I'm fine now.' She was glad he wasn't level with her, couldn't see her eyes.

'I'm delighted to hear it. Delighted.' His voice changed, the pitch deepening. Through another set of double doors. 'Of course, there will be nothing like that this time. Nothing. You have my personal word on that.'

King Cliché, she thought. Of course. How could she forget?

'Thank you. Heard you on the radio on the way in, Ben,' she said. 'A double murder? Two women?'

Fenwick nodded, rounded a corner. 'A flat in that new development. Parkside Quarter. Neither showed up for work today. Both stabbed to death. Nasty. Very nasty.'

Marina nodded, already processing the information, making quick assumptions. Women, stabbing. The blade a surrogate sexual organ. Since her specialisation was psycho-sexual deviancy, that was obviously why she had been called in. 'Right,' she said. 'What else have you got?'

'Well . . .' Fenwick stopped walking, looked at her. She instinctively pulled her coat close around herself. A specially bought swing-cut coat to hide the baby bulge. And something told her she *should* disguise it. Despite numerous diversity training courses, she still believed that the police as an organisation remained not only institutionally racist but sexist too. And always would be: a brick house is always a brick house and no amount of beechwood cladding is ever going to change that, she thought. It was just something she had to accept if she wanted to work alongside the police. But she didn't want any of her findings being dismissed as the misguided thinking of a hormonally overcharged woman.

Fenwick sighed. And she saw beyond his politician's bon-homie a worried, weary man. 'We think it ties in with another two murders we've had,' he said. Marina could clearly see the stress lines etched on his face. 'It's a biggie. A real biggie. Under a lot of pressure on this. A hell of a lot. We've got to come up with a result, and soon.' Another sigh. He rubbed his eyes, then, aware that she was watching him, rallied. 'Come on. I've got the case files ready for you. And a desk too, come to that. This way.'

She was led through more corridors. She tried to remember the layout from the last time, but this time she was being taken somewhere different. Fenwick opened the door to the bar. She frowned, followed him in. The pool tables were covered over, turned into desks with computers and phones on them, likewise the tables, banquettes and booths. Filing cabinets next to fruit machines. And there were plenty of people working. More than she had seen last time.

63

'Bit unorthodox,' said Fenwick. 'Major Incident Squad is usually based up at Stanway, but they're having asbestos removed in the interview rooms. Plus we need a lot of space for this one. Lot of space.'

The shutters were down over the bar, whiteboards placed in front, dominating the room. They kept the team focused, reminding them all what they were working towards; the desks, tables and chairs in the bar were in satellite formation to them.

She looked at one of the whiteboards, saw photos of four women's faces. All smiling, anyone else cropped, leaving them the centre of attention, all unaware through their smiles that they would one day end up here. Names were attached: Lisa King, Susie Evans, Claire Fielding, Julie Simpson. Ordinary names, extraordinary deaths. Marker-pen lines linking them together like a grisly dot-to-dot. Other names, dates, locations beneath them. Nothing yet linking them. Marina knew there wouldn't be. She wouldn't be here if there were.

Fenwick gestured from a table at the side of the room. She crossed to him.

'Here we are,' he said. 'Not much, I'm afraid, but there's a computer and a phone. And these.' He tapped a set of files sitting by the keyboard. 'All yours. Photocopied this morning. If you could keep them on the premises we'd be grateful. But if you can't, you know, be discreet.'

'Thank you.'

'Can I get you anything?' said Fenwick, a smile playing on his lips as he gestured to the shuttered bar. 'Gin and tonic? Wine? Beer?'

Marina smiled. 'Coffee would be good, thanks.'

Fenwick arranged for a junior officer to fetch her a coffee. Marina sat down at the desk, took her notebook and pen from her bag, ready to read.

'There you go. I'll leave you to do your . . . whatever it is you do,' he said, looking at his watch. 'But I should warn you. The photos . . . they're pretty upsetting. And if I'm saying that, they must be. So be warned.'

She nodded and he left her to it. She opened the first file, marked Lisa King, and began to read. She hadn't reached the photos before she felt her stomach start to lurch. The uniform placed the coffee down on the desk and she took a mouthful. It tasted bitter. She felt it swirl around in her stomach. She kept reading.

Her head began to swim. She swallowed hard, blinked. Picked up the next file: Susie Evans. Read on. It became harder to breathe. Despite the room being large and open, it felt stuffy and hot. She needed air. Her stomach lurched and a heaving sensation began working its way up her chest. Her hand went to her throat, tried to hold down the rising acid and bile. She looked again at the photos.

And knew she was going to be sick.

12

Phil Brennan pulled the Audi into the car park, switched off the engine.

'Come on,' he said to Clayton, unfastening his seat belt and swinging open the door. 'Report to write. Let's see if Anni's back yet.'

Clayton didn't move. 'You go on without me, boss. Just got something I need to do.'

'What, put in a harassment claim because I made you listen to Neil Young? Again?'

Clayton managed a polite smile. It had sounded like the same three-note song all the way back. He had hated it. 'Just got an idea,' he said. As he spoke, his eyes darted round, looking anywhere but at Phil. 'Thought someone in that scrapyard looked familiar.'

'Who?'

Clayton began to get out of the car. 'Not sure. Give me a couple of hours.'

'Don't take too long,' said Phil.

'Yeah, I know,' said Clayton, turning and walking away. 'First twenty-four hours and all that.'

Phil bit back the retort, tamped down the irritation he felt at his junior officer. Let him go, he thought. Give him his head. He entered the building, pushing through the doors, swiping his pass. He felt tense, on edge.

Nothing to do with seeing Marina again. All to do with the clock ticking, he said to himself.

He made his way up to his office.

Marina stood outside the bar, trying to pluck up courage to enter once again. She knew what they must be thinking of her.

Civilian. Can't stand the heat. Can't take the pressure. Shouldn't do it, then. And a woman, what can you expect?

She knew. Was sure they were saying it out loud. Normally she would be in there, confronting them, facing down anyone who dared to question her fitness for the job. But not this time. This time she didn't blame them. This time she even agreed with them.

She put her hand beneath her coat, cradling the baby growing inside her. It might not have been planned, but she didn't want anything to happen to it. To her. Not like in those reports, those photos. Dead mothers. Dead babies.

Taking a deep breath, she opened the door to the bar, walked back in. A few heads turned in her direction, then went back to what they had been doing. She walked over to her desk, sat down again, picked up a report.

'You okay?'

She looked up. Fenwick was standing over her, concern in his eyes. She gave a quick look round the room. Saw only sympathetic looks in her direction, nothing judgemental.

She nodded. 'Yeah. It's just . . .'

'Don't worry. Nobody blames you for your reaction. I told you this was a bad one. I mean, I'm sure I've dealt with worse, but I really can't remember when.'

She nodded again.

'There's something else,' said Fenwick, leaning over her.

67

'Now that you've had a look at the files I should tell you. In the first murder the baby was cut up in the mother's stomach. In the second it was removed. The baby in this morning's murder is missing.'

'Oh God . . .'

'So work your magic, the quicker the better, please.'

He laid a hand on her shoulder that could have been either comforting or patronising and walked away, leaving her to it. She watched him go into his office, close the door.

She looked at the reports in front of her, then to her notebook. She opened the Susie Evans report again, began to read once more. She was here to do a job.

She became engrossed, didn't notice someone standing at her side until they spoke.

'Hey.'

Her breath caught in her throat. She stopped reading. She wanted to look up but didn't dare until she was ready.

'Hey yourself.'

He looked good. A bit thinner perhaps but that was no bad thing. She found a smile for him and sat upright in her chair. 'You still here, then?'

'They tried to get rid of me, kept coming back.'

'Bit like me,' she said.

Phil smiled, then looked round the room, as if aware that people might be staring. Marina was unsure how many people knew of their relationship or its ending and she felt herself blushing. She picked up the coffee mug to cover it, put it to her lips. Cold. She made a face, replaced it on the desk.

'I'll get you some fresh,' he said.

'Doesn't matter. I doubt it'll taste any better.'

Silence. She saw Phil's mouth move, as if rehearsing what he wanted to say. But knew he wouldn't say it.

'Ben Fenwick been looking after you?' he said eventually.

'My every whim catered for.'

Phil gave another smile. 'Is that right. You got everything you need?'

She nodded.

'Good.' Another look round, then back to her. 'How's . . .' He paused.

She knew he was only pretending to forget the name.

'Tony,' she said, prompting him.

'Tony. Right. He okay?'

'Fine.' She looked into the coffee mug. 'Everything. Fine and Jim Dandy.' She shifted uncomfortably in her chair, breathed in, her stomach suddenly feeling enormous.

'Whoever he is,' said Phil. 'Well, you look like you know what you're doing. I'll leave you to it, right?'

'Okay.'

'Right.'

'You said that already.'

He laughed. 'Right.' Laughed again. 'Well . . . I'm sure I'll see you later.'

'Later.'

He moved away, walking towards his desk. She kept her eyes on him the whole time, then shook her head. No, she thought, that's the last thing I need right now.

She put her head down, looked again at the paperwork in front of her but couldn't concentrate. There had been too many things left unsaid between her and Phil. Things they should talk about. If she decided she wanted to. But they would have to wait.

She went back to the reports. Concentrating this time.

Because lives depended on it.

13

Emma Nicholls sat down behind her desk and gave DC Anni Hepburn a smile intended to convey confidence and professionalism but which instead screamed tension and barely suppressed emotion.

She was dressed as if for a normal day at work as a head teacher: black two-piece trouser suit, light-coloured blouse, hair cut into a long bob. But the day was no longer normal. Two of her teachers had been murdered and now the school had been invaded by police.

DC Anni Hepburn had been a detective long enough to develop a detachment that enabled her to do her job effectively while still retaining sympathy for the victims of violent crime. She hoped she always would. Human debris, was how she often secretly referred to them. Broken remains needing – and hoping for – repair. But she had also been a detective long enough to know that that wouldn't always happen.

Emma Nicholls, she thought, would be all right eventually. She hadn't seen what Anni had seen earlier that day in Claire Fielding's flat, smelled what she had smelled. And, as the headmistress kept stressing, her relationship with Claire Fielding and Julie Simpson had been mainly professional.

'Please understand,' Emma Nicholls said, tipping her head back and appearing to audition words in her head before trusting them to leave her mouth, 'that my primary concern is for this school.'

'Of course.'

'By that I mean everyone. The welfare of the children and the staff I consider to be equally paramount.'

'Right.'

Words chosen, she continued. 'Having said that, I seldom interfere in the affairs of my staff unless they are personal friends or they ask for help.'

Anni nodded, knowing a disclaimer when she heard one. 'Okay.'

Emma Nicholls' office managed to be both professional and welcoming, with achievements and diplomas on the walls alongside schedules, year planners and pictures the children had made especially for her. She seemed to be popular and well thought of. It was how Anni thought a primary school head teacher's office – and a primary school head teacher – should be.

The school was old but had been modernised. Clean, bright and bursting with positive energy, and with children's work and achievements decorating the walls, it was clearly a place where the children were valued and well taught. But then, thought Anni, this was Lexden. An affluent suburb of Colchester. She would expect it to be like that.

The children, or at least most of them that Anni had come into contact with since she had arrived there, seemed so full of hope, of life, of potential and enthusiasm for the world. They had seemed thrilled by the arrival of the police. Something different, something exciting to break up the routine. But as Anni and her small team of junior officers and uniforms had gone about their business of interviewing staff and explaining what their procedures would be, the children, she knew, no matter how discreet her team or how careful the teaching staff in explaining things, would soon find out. There was no way the murder of two teachers – well loved, if the comments she had overheard were anything to go by – could not affect them. And then they would see what the police were really there for. And begin to understand that the world wasn't like they saw on TV; that it could be a horrible, cruel place. That was why Anni had never wanted kids herself. Because no matter how hard you tried to protect them from the world, the world would eventually claim them.

'So,' she continued, her notebook open, 'were Claire Fielding and Julie Simpson personal friends?'

Emma Nicholls seemed about to answer but instead sighed, her eyes drifting off, her forced pleasantness slipping away to be replaced by a dark, depressive air. Like a cancer victim who had momentarily forgotten their predicament.

'This is just terrible,' she said.

With nothing to add, Anni nodded.

'Oh my God . . .'

The dark, depressive air was increasing. Anni had to take control. 'Ms Nicholls,' she said. 'I'm most terribly sorry about what's happened. I realise this is an awful time, but I really do need to ask you some questions.'

Emma Nicholls pulled herself upright. 'I know, I know. You've . . .' Her mind drifted again, her features taking on the appearance of approaching tears. She managed to pull herself together. 'Sorry.'

'That's all right.'

The head teacher allowed a small smile to cross her face. 'At times like this I wish I still smoked.'

Anni gave a small smile. 'I'm sure you do. Right. Claire Fielding and Julie Simpson. Friends?'

Emma Nicholls nodded.

'Julie was Year Six, Claire Year Four, right?'

72

Emma Nicholls nodded again, her hands fidgeting as if an imaginary cigarette was there.

'And Claire was pregnant.'

Another nod.

'How long did she have to go until maternity leave?'

'A couple . . . a couple of weeks.'

'Was it planned, d'you know? Was she happy about it?'

Emma Nicholls frowned. 'Is that important? She's dead.'

'I know. But we have to ask these questions. Helps us find out who did it.'

'Right.' The frown slowly disappeared to be replaced by a sigh. 'She seemed happy about it, from what I could gather.'

'We believe she had friends round last night.'

'Yes. A baby shower.' Her lip trembled again.

'Ms Nicholls, we're trying to track down anyone one else who may have been there. Could you give me any names?'

Emma Nicholls didn't have to give the matter any thought. 'Chrissie Burrows. Geraint Cooper. They were talking about it this morning.'

'That's it? Just those two?'

'Just . . .' Tears threatened her eyes again.

Anni waited until the head teacher was once more under control.

'Ms Nicholls, I'll need to talk to them too.'

Emma Nicholls nodded. Anni looked at her notes. 'What about Claire's boyfriend? Did she ever mention him?'

The frown returned to Emma Nicholls' face, along with a guarded look in her eyes. 'Her boyfriend.'

'Ryan Brotherton,' said Anni, looking at her notes once more. 'At least that's what we're assuming. His name crops up a lot in her diary. Dates, that sort of thing. Did she ever mention him at all?'

'Well, Claire didn't have a very . . . easy relationship with him from what I could gather. As I said, it was none of my business. She was an excellent teacher, very professional, and the children adored her. Whatever else went on in her life, as long as it didn't impinge on work I couldn't get involved.'

Anni said nothing.

Emma Nicholls continued. 'Claire had recently split up with her partner.'

Anni frowned. She hadn't received that impression from the notebooks in Claire's flat.

'You look surprised.'

'I am. I was given to understand that the relationship was still ongoing.'

Emma Nicholls shook her head. 'Again, I must stress that I seldom interfere, but my staff know my door is always open for them. A few months ago Claire was looking very despondent. I asked her if she wanted to talk. She didn't. Julie . . .' Again the dark cloud descended as she spoke the name. 'Julie . . . told me that Claire and her partner had split up. And that Claire was taking it very badly.'

'When would this have been?'

Emma Nicholls thought. 'About . . . when she announced she was pregnant. Five months ago? Six months. Something like that.' Her fingers fidgeted again. 'Everyone rallied round, as I said. And she got over it eventually.'

'Do you think she wanted him back?'

Emma Nicholls looked surprised at the question. 'Of course. Wouldn't you?'

'Yes. I suppose I would,' Anni said, trying to smile.

'Yes. Even him.'

Anni leaned forward. 'Even him? What d'you mean?'

Emma Nicholls did her auditioning thing once more. 'He . . . I don't think he did her much good. Not just running out when she was pregnant, but . . .' She put her head back. Anni felt as if she was about to impart something important. Then she leaned forward, waved her hand.

Whatever it was she was going to say, the moment had passed. 'I don't know. I don't know. You wanted facts. Anything else I could say would be conjecture.'

Anni realised this would be as much as she was going to get on Claire Fielding. She checked her notes once more. 'What about Julie Simpson?'

'What about her?'

'Anything happened to her recently that strikes you as out of the ordinary?'

Emma Nicholls frowned in thought. Shook her head. 'Nothing . . . No. Nothing.'

'Any enemies?'

'Enemies?' Emma Nicholls looked round the room as if unable to believe what she had just heard. 'She was a primary school teacher, not a . . . an international terrorist.'

'No,' said Anni, 'but she's also just been murdered.'

Emma Nicholls' face fell. Her head nodded forward. 'No,' she said to the floor, 'no enemies. She was liked in this school. Well liked.'

'No . . .' Anni tried to be tactful, 'liaisons? Anything like that? Something that could go wrong?'

'No. Nothing at all. Nothing.'

Anni nodded. There were at least two people she thought would be able to help her more than the professionally guarded Emma Nicholls. 'Chrissie Burrows, Geraint Cooper,' she said. 'Where could I find them, please?'

Emma Nicholls made arrangements for Anni to see them. Anni put her notebook away, rose to go, thanked the head teacher for her time.

'Not at all. I just wish I could have been more help.'

'You've been fine.'

Emma Nicholls put her hand on Anni's arm, stopped her from leaving. 'There is one more thing. Perhaps you were right.'

Anni frowned. 'About what?'

'Ryan Brotherton. I know I said it was over between them. But I got the impression . . . and again this is just conjecture, not fact . . . I got the impression that it may have been over but it wasn't quite finished. Do you know what I mean?'

'I do. Some people are like that,' said Anni.

'Men in particular,' said Emma Nicholls.

14

Caroline Eades pointed the BMW 4x4 towards Stanway, drove out of the city centre. As she took it round the roundabout and down the Lexden Road, she felt once again that she wasn't just driving a car but manoeuvring a tank. She knew all her friends at the gym were jealous, told her how much they loved it, but she hated it. She wished she had never let Graeme buy it for her.

Her lunch had passed in a pleasant enough way, the same as it always did. Her friends were good company and it was always fun to catch up with the gossip. The Life café on Culver Street West wasn't Starbucks or Caffè Nero, and when it was her turn, she always insisted they went there. Everyone else went to the chains because they thought they were somewhere to be seen. And because they had the same menu all day every day in every branch and you knew what you were getting. But Caroline found that boring, depressing even. She preferred Life. And the others went along with her.

With original art for sale on the walls and iMac internet access, Life was individual, a one-off, and it made her feel like an individual going there. It was bright and airy and the coffee and cakes were good. Not that she allowed herself cakes all that often. She had compromised: a slice of rocky road with the marshmallows removed. Well, most of them.

She turned off the Lexden Road before it became London Road, feeling her arms ache as she spun the wheel – even with the power steering it was a beast to manage – and headed towards her estate. It was starting to feel like home now. She had moved there nearly two years ago from a small but very pleasant house in St Mary's, an area over the walkway from the Mercury Theatre, just outside the town's wall. Bordered to the west by Crouch Street, and on the east by the wall, it had the feel of a little village within the town, but the nearness to the centre meant it wasn't too cut off. Broad Street also had its delis, designer clothes shops, restaurants, pubs and furniture shops, all adding to the feel. However, like so much of the town, it had become choked by new apartment blocks and she took that as her sign to leave. By then it was just another suburban outpost of Colchester, the chi-chi shops of Crouch Street an affectation on what was really a main road off the Queensway roundabout.

The estate in Stanway was further away from the town centre. Secluded, the estate agent had said. Select. And it looked it. Large executive houses, tastefully designed, solidly built. No two the same, and each one with space for at least two cars on the driveway. It was what Graeme wanted. Caroline had loved the house in St Mary's but was trying to feel content here.

She pulled up in front of her house, the black 4x4 jerking to a halt with a slight squeal of brakes, the front tyre on the pavement. Hating the car once again. Maybe when she'd had the baby she might enjoy driving it more. Get hold of the wheel properly without her huge belly getting in the way.

She climbed out, took her gym bag from the boot, walked to the front door, humming a song she had been listening to on the radio. Let herself in. Put the keys on the table in the hall, went to the kitchen. It was symbolic of everything she had ever thought she wanted in life. A beautiful house. A great car. A childhood sweetheart who had turned into a handsome husband. Two gorgeous kids already and a third on the way. Life, she kept telling herself, couldn't get more perfect.

She crossed to the fridge, poured herself a glass of orange juice, took it to the breakfast bar. She sat down on one of the stools, took a mouthful, and a wave of tiredness over-whelmed her.

She sighed. Exhausted again. She told herself it was just the baby, that was all. The baby. She and Graeme already had two older children, nearly teenagers. Alfie, twelve, and Vanessa, ten. What was she doing having another baby? Now? At her age?

Thirty-nine wasn't old, she told herself. Not too old to be a mother again. Not too old to still be a desirable, attractive woman.

She took another mouthful of juice. Felt it travel all the way down her body. She shouldn't drink it too quickly, she would want to pee again. Especially if the baby decided to lie on her kidneys. Another deep breath as she tried to find a comfortable way to sit. Her mind flashed back to lunch. The girls. All younger than her, all expecting their first baby. They were a good bunch, friendly, fun to be with. But sometimes Caroline thought she saw them looking at her not in a friendly way. Like they were laughing at her. As if she was too old. Trying to look younger, pass as one of them when she should have been past all that. Like being out with their mum.

They had never said this, but it was a feeling she got. Only sometimes.

Caroline finished the juice, put the glass in the dishwasher.

As she stood up, stars danced before her eyes. She began to feel light-headed. She had moved too quickly. That started to happen now. More and more often as the baby got heavier and heavier. Natural, the doctor had said, but still bloody annoying.

She supported herself against the counter top, got her breath and her balance back. Checked her watch. Four hours until Graeme came home. She should have something prepared for dinner. She sighed again, too tired to stand upright let alone cook. Lucky she had remembered to call in at M&S. Roast shank of lamb plus prepared vegetables. Wouldn't take too long to heat up. And if Graeme complained, she would tell him to make dinner himself.

The kitchen gleamed, all beech and granite and matching appliances. Another sigh. At least she hoped it would be four hours until Graeme arrived home. Lately he had been coming back later and later. Working longer hours, he said. Getting in the overtime before the baby came along. Because they would need the money then. Babies were expensive, had she forgotten? And when he did arrive home he was tetchy and miserable. Jumping on the slightest thing she said or did. And he never wanted sex any more. Admittedly at the moment she was too tired for it, but even in the first stages, when she was feeling really horny, he hadn't wanted it. In fact, the last time they had made love was when she got pregnant. She would remember something like that.

And the kids were no help. Coming in straight from school, upstairs to their rooms, on the internet, watching TV. She may as well be by herself.

She sat down again on a bar stool. If this was her life and it was all so perfect, why did she feel so unhappy?

She wanted a bath. A long, lovely, luxurious soak to ease away all the aches and strains she carried round with her. But she couldn't do that while she was in the house alone.

What if she got stuck? What if someone came to the door and she couldn't get out? No. Too risky. She would have to settle for a shower instead. Again.

She went up the stairs, one step at a time, supporting herself heavily on the banister, into the bathroom, where she ran the water, began to slowly strip away the layers of her clothes.

At least all I have to do is stand there, she thought. I don't have to move.

She stepped into the shower. Closed her eyes.

Stood there until her legs ached. Then towelled off, went into the bedroom and changed into her pyjamas and dressing gown. She only meant to have a few minutes' rest. Just a quick lie-down on the bed. But as soon as she closed her eyes she was gone.

Her last thought before sleep claimed her was that it would all sort itself out. When the baby was born.

15

Chrissie Burrows had, Anni thought, been very eager to help but didn't have much to contribute. She had come across her type quite often. It was a common enough response in situations like this, to feel that you had to do everything possible to assist, even when you had exhausted your knowledge.

The woman was in her thirties, plain and round. But she had eyes that, under different circumstances, would have indicated a lively, fun companion. Not these circumstances, however.

The empty classroom they were talking in felt hot and cloying. Like the boiler was turned up too high to keep the children drowsy. Anni tried to ignore it, set to work establishing a timeline for the party.

Chrissie Burrows sat fidgeting with one paper tissue after another, dabbing her eyes, blowing her nose, reducing them to shreds with her fingers. 'Well, I . . . I left early.'

'What time would that have been?'

'Around nine. Nine thirty at the very latest. But nearer nine, I think.'

'Any particular reason?'

She thought, shook her head. 'We . . . we were all having

a good time. I'd given Claire her present, some Babygros . . .' The tears threatened again. She plucked another paper tissue from the box. Anni waited for her to ride the moment out.

'And you went home.'

She nodded. 'Still had some work to do for today. And I have a long drive, so I only had one glass . . .'

'And did you see anyone suspicious as you left? Anyone loitering outside or on the stairs?'

She shook her head. Her brow was furrowed, as if by concentrating hard enough she would be able to make the memory, or even the person, Anni wanted appear before them.

'So who else was there, apart from yourself?'

'Claire, Julie, Geraint . . . that's it.'

'No one from outside school?'

She shook her head.

'Not Claire's boyfriend? Ryan Brotherton?'

Chrissie Burrows sat up, something else in her eyes besides tears. 'No. Not him. Claire never wanted to see him again.'

Anni kept her expression professionally blank. 'Why not?'

'He was a . . . oh.' She shook her head. 'I can't say it. But he was bad for Claire. Very bad. Getting rid of him was the best thing she ever did.'

'What about Julie? Was there anyone in her background who might have wanted to harm her?'

Chrissie Burrows looked up. 'Julie? No. No one. No one wanted to harm her. She was, she was . . .' The tears started again.

Anni was beginning to see a pattern emerging.

She regarded the weeping woman intently, doubting there was anything more she could tell her. She was just a normal woman who couldn't believe that something horribly extraordinary had invaded her life and taken away two of her friends in the most brutal way imaginable.

Anni stood up, handed her a card. 'If you think of anything else, please call.'

Chrissie Burrows took the card without looking up.

With a uniform stepping in to take a statement from the distraught teacher, Anni went on to question Geraint Cooper. Relieved to be out of that hot room.

The police had requisitioned the nurse's room for questioning and he was waiting for her there. At least it was slightly cooler than the classroom. Geraint Cooper was black and, she surmised, in his mid to late twenties. Neatly dressed, he sat with his hands in his lap. Anni didn't believe in jumping to conclusions, and certainly not in stereotypes, but from his demeanour and attitude, she was sure Geraint Cooper was gay.

She sat down opposite him and introduced herself.

'Mr Cooper, I'm DS Hepburn.'

They shook hands. She felt from his loose grip that he was shaking slightly.

'I'll try and make this as painless as possible,' she said with a small smile. 'You were at Claire Fielding's last night along with Julie Simpson and Chrissie Burrows.' Not a question, a statement.

He nodded.

'What time did you leave?'

'Around ten. Something like that.'

'And where do you live?'

'Dutch Quarter. Just up the road from Claire.' His voice caught as he said her name.

'How did you get home?'

'Walked.'

'And what would you say the mood was like when you left?'

84

He shrugged. 'We were all having a good time. A good laugh.' He looked straight at her. 'Claire was enjoying herself. We all were.'

'No arguments, nothing like that?'

He looked as if the question offended him. 'No. Just having a laugh.'

'And it was a baby shower?'

He nodded. 'A baby shower. We brought our presents, opened some wine, had a laugh. God knows, she needed it.'

'Claire? Why d'you say that?'

He sat back, his body language defensive, arms wrapped over his chest. 'Because of *him*.'

'You mean Ryan Brotherton?'

He nodded.

'What did he do?'

'Oh, I'm sure you've heard all about it by now.'

'Tell me again.'

'He didn't want the baby. Wanted her to get rid of it. She wouldn't. She dumped him.'

Anni waited. He said no more. 'And that's it?'

He nodded, arms still wrapped tightly round his chest.

She changed her approach. 'When you left, at around ten-ish, did you see anyone suspicious hanging about?'

He said nothing, thinking.

'Either outside the flats, in the street, or even inside, on the stairs. Anyone. Anywhere.'

He sighed. His arms dropped, his posture relaxed. 'I've been thinking about this all day. Over and over in my head. Trying to think . . .'

'And was there? Anyone?'

He sighed. 'No. No one. Sorry. I wish there had been.'

'That's all right. And Julie Simpson was still there when you left?'

He nodded.

85

'Didn't she have to get back home?'

'Said she'd help Claire clear up.'

Knowing the answer, she asked the next question anyway, to check that the stories matched. 'And were you the first to leave?'

He shook his head. 'Chrissie went first. She had the furthest to travel. Wivenhoe way.' He looked at her pointedly. 'She didn't drink too much. Didn't want to get pulled over.'

Anni smiled again. 'I don't care about that. I'm just trying to find who killed Claire and Julie.'

He nodded, as if accepting that. 'Well I think we know who did that, don't we?'

'Do we?' Anni leaned forward slightly. 'Who would that be, Mr Cooper?'

Geraint Cooper looked her square in the eyes. Anni realised that he was shaking not from nerves but from anger. 'Well it's obvious, isn't it? Claire's ex. That bastard Ryan Brotherton. He killed her.'

16

DS Clayton Thompson glanced quickly round. No one about. No one following him.

He had left the station and walked down Headgate towards the town centre. The shops were thinking about closing, and with the night drawing in, the bars and restaurants in front of him along Head Street were becoming alluring. He felt their pull on him now, even on a weekday.

Clayton still liked nothing better than to hit a few bars on a night off with his mates, see what he could pull. He thought he would have had enough of it after years in uniform, clearing up on weekend nights when the town-centre pubs were swarming with squaddies from the garrison, hitting on town girls and students, hungry for anything they could get a hold of, ready to fight for it if necessary, but he hadn't. He looked back fondly on those times; it was good, uncomplicated fun. Bash a few heads together, a few free drinks or whatever else was going.

And it wasn't all one-way traffic with the squaddies: Clayton had seen plenty of predatory middle-aged women, their bodies squeezed into clothes designed for teenagers, desperately trying to remove the wedding rings from fattened fingers, as if that mattered, bar-hopping in the hope of attracting a young, fit squaddie for the night. In his uniform days he had been called on to break up plenty of fights as young men, having failed to get off with anyone their own age, fought over these women, the women themselves turned on at the sight, thrilled to be a trophy for the winner.

And if they failed to get off with a squaddie, he remembered, a smile crawling across his face, a copper would often do.

But alluring as that was, he had to ignore the memories, the pull of the bars. It would be so easy just to sit there, have a few beers, let it wash away. But he couldn't. Things had become serious. He had to take action. And he needed privacy for the call he was about to make.

He took out his mobile, dialled a number from his address book. It was a number he hadn't used for quite a while, but he hadn't deleted it. He had thought it might come in handy some time. One way or another.

He had lied to Phil when he told him he was following up a lead. Nothing personal, but he had no choice. This was damage limitation. This was his career at stake. He hadn't gone to look into anything. He had just been walking round the town centre trying to sort everything out, work out what to do next. Whatever he did, he had to tread carefully. Make sure any move he made left him protected.

He turned off the main road, ducked down Church Walk, all boarded-up shops and lock-ups, headed towards the church and the graveyard, ignoring the teen goths and the drinking school gathered by the rusted old gates. The trees and tombstones looked desolate against the darkening sky. It was like the backdrop for some clichéd old Hammer film.

The phone was answered.

'It's me,' he said.

There was a pause on the other end of the line. He waited.

'I knew you'd call,' a voice said eventually.

'Thanks for not grassin' me up,' he said.

'You're welcome,' the voice said, in a tone Clayton couldn't read.

'I need your help.'

The voice laughed. 'Course you do.'

Irritation ran through Clayton. He opened his mouth ready to spit out angry words, but stopped himself. That wouldn't help.

'I do.'

'Why?'

'To . . . square things. Make sure you're protected.'

The voice laughed. 'Make sure one of us is protected, you mean.'

Clayton felt the irritation turn to anger. Swallowed it down. 'Don't—'

'Play games?' said the voice. 'You used to like playing games, as I remember.'

Clayton kept a grip on his temper. 'This is important. We've got to talk. Tonight.'

The voice sighed. 'When and where?'

'You name the time and the place.'

'Nine o'clock. The Lamb and Flag, Procter Road, New Town. You know it?'

He did.

'And I'll need a lift home afterwards.'

'Right.'

He rang off. Looked round. The graveyard was fully dark by now. Ghosts and other horrors were free to lurk. He turned, walked back to the station. He didn't need those ghosts.

He had enough of his own.

17

Anni Hepburn was still questioning Geraint Cooper.
'So Ryan Brotherton killed Claire? Is that what you're saying?'

Geraint Cooper nodded. 'Not content with just Claire, he has to do Julie as well.'

'Why d'you say that, Mr Cooper?'

'Oh, come on. It's got to be him. That bastard.'

'Do you have any proof, Mr Cooper?'

He looked at her, anger abating slightly. 'Well, no. But it must be, mustn't it?'

'Why must it be?'

'Because of what he was like.'

'What *was* he like?'

'I told you.'

'You said he didn't want the baby and wanted Claire to get rid of it. She wouldn't and she dumped him. Hardly sounds like grounds for murder.'

'Well, he was a bastard. The worst kind of bloke. The kind kids leave home to avoid and spend all their lives hating.'

'Abusive?'

He rolled his eyes. 'Was he not.'

'To Claire?'

Geraint Cooper calmed down, nodded. His voice dropped. 'She always goes for the same type. Big blokes, look like they can handle themselves. Real macho. I've told her she shouldn't, they're trouble, won't do her any good, but she still does it.' He stopped, attempted to correct himself. 'Does . . . did . . .' He sighed again, fighting back tears, then used his anger to regained composure. 'Oh God . . . anyway. It's him.'

'Tell me more about him, Mr Cooper.'

He leaned forward. Anni didn't doubt the honesty or sincerity in his eyes. 'He was awful to her. Started out nice, but then they all do. Then a couple of months in, he changed. Little things. She was late home. Bang. She looked at someone in a pub a funny way. Bang. He didn't like the dinner she'd cooked him. Bang.'

'But she didn't leave him?'

He shook his head. 'She was unhappy, but she loved him. Kept going back to him. Every time. She would turn up at my house or Julie's in tears with a black eye or something, saying she was going to leave him. Then she'd get better and he'd call her, promise never to do it again, and that would be it. She'd have him back.'

'Right,' said Anni.

Geraint Cooper looked at her, his face hard. 'I suppose you're saying she deserved it, aren't you? That she brought it on herself for being so stupid? So soft? For letting him do that?'

'Not at all, Mr Cooper,' said Anni, her voice calm and even. 'I've seen this happen a lot. Too much, to be honest. And not to soft, stupid women. They're intelligent, sensible and mature. And often they don't know how they've ended up in that state either.'

Her words seemed to calm him down.

'So what happened next?'

91

'We had what you'd call an intervention. Julie, Chrissie and me. We were her best friends. And we hated what was happening to her. Hated it. Luckily we managed to make her see sense.'

'But the next thing, she was pregnant?'

Geraint Cooper nodded.

'By Ryan Brotherton?'

He nodded again. 'That's when she finally left him.'

Anni frowned. That contradicted what Emma Nicholls had said. 'Really?'

'Really. He said he didn't want a baby. At all. Under any circumstances. She did. Even his. So he decided she was going to get rid of it. And if she didn't do it, he would. Forcibly.'

Anni swallowed hard, kept her face as straight as possible. 'How?' Her voice was slightly less calm than she wanted it to be.

Geraint Cooper held up his hands, clenched them hard. 'With these.'

'Right.' She swallowed again. 'And that's when she left him.'

He nodded. 'And that's when he decided he wanted her back.'

'What about the baby?'

He shrugged. 'He wanted her more.'

'So how did he go about that?'

'Nice as anything. Charming, flowers, the lot. He'd changed, he was a new man, the usual.'

'And did it work?'

'No. Like I said, she had us with her now. We helped her be strong.'

Anni frowned again. 'So he didn't run out on her; she ran out on him?'

'Right.'

'And he didn't like that.'

Geraint Cooper rolled his eyes. 'He certainly didn't.'

'What did he do?'

'Got nasty. Phone calls, mainly. Threatening ones. Horrible ones. What he would do to her if he got hold of her. What he would do if she didn't come back to him. What he would do.'

'If she didn't come back to him. You keep saying that,' she said. 'I heard the story was that he left her. Is that not right?'

He shook his head, looked slightly uncomfortable. 'Some people may have been given that impression.'

'Why?'

'Because we wanted them to think that. It helped Claire. The three of us there last night, we weren't just her friends. We were her support group. We kept her going.'

Anni said nothing, knew there was more to come.

'Think about it. Isn't it easier to say that you're pregnant and single because your man's left you rather than because you've summoned up the courage to leave him after he threatened to kill your baby?'

'He actually said that? Those words? That's what the phones calls were about? He threatened to kill the baby?'

Geraint Cooper nodded. And kept nodding. And all those tears he had been holding back started to break out.

Anni closed her notebook. She had everything she needed for now.

18

'Thanks for doing this,' said Phil. 'Really appreciate it.'
Nick Lines shrugged; one case was much the same as another to him. 'Not my decision to make. Those on high deem it high priority; I just act accordingly.'

Phil had done a background check on Ryan Brotherton, and with Clayton still not back and everyone else out on jobs, he phoned Nick Lines. The cadaverous pathologist had been as good as his word, doing both post-mortems in record time. Phil had wasted no time coming straight to the mortuary at Colchester General, where he had released DC Adrian Wren to take care of other duties.

Nick Lines' office was, in contrast to the clean, sterile, stainless-steel efficiency of the cutting room, a mixture of professional clutter and personal effects. Newspaper articles pinned up on the wall, both serious and jokey, alongside schlocky film postcards, fifties sci-fi and horror. Superhero action figures struck ridiculous poses on shelves. Surprising things, Phil thought. But then it was that kind of profession. Nick Lines was clearly a surprising man.

As they spoke, a CD played in the background. Something gothic and baroque, Phil noted, yet tuneful. He couldn't place it.

'What's this we're listening to, by the way?' he asked.

'The Triffids,' said Nick, throwing a CD case across the desk, pleased that Phil had asked but hiding his pleasure. '*Calenture*. Brilliant album.'

'Right,' said Phil, as he listened to lyrics about sewing up eyelids and stitching up lips. He didn't ask any more. 'The results?'

Nick nodded, opened a yellow file, sat back in his chair, steepled his fingers before him. Like a Bond villain about to explain his plan for world domination. 'The same blade was used on both victims,' he said, the words drawling, as if his findings had thrilled him to the point of inactivity. 'About seven inches long, smooth, very sharp edge. Probably a hunting knife, something like that. Quite a heavy blade judging by the size and shape of the incisions.'

'Could this knife have been used in the previous two murders?' asked Phil.

'I think so,' said Nick, nodding. 'Of course I've only made a preliminary re-examination of the other two cases at this stage, but I think it's fair to assume.' He went back to his explanation. 'The knife was actually used in different ways. Julie Simpson, the first victim, was stabbed with a sharp slash to the throat. Death wouldn't have been long in coming.'

He paused for dramatic effect. The Triffids were singing about being blinder by the hour. That just reminded Phil that time was running out.

'The second victim was dispatched in a completely different way. Physically restrained while a drug was administered.'

'What drug?' asked Phil.

'Tests aren't back yet, but my guess is introcostrin. It's a neuro-muscular blocking drug. Controls spontaneous muscle movement during surgical procedures, usually given in very controlled doses.' He sounded almost regretful. 'However, this was administered in a much larger dose.'

Phil frowned. 'How big are we talking?'

'Very big,' said Nick. 'Paralysis would have been almost instantaneous.'

'So that was for . . . what? To stop her moving?'

'Larger than that,' the pathologist said. 'It would have stopped her breathing.'

'Shit,' said Phil. 'Can we trace the drug? How easy is it to get hold of?'

'It's worth a try. If it's local, you may be able to find it. But it won't be easy. If someone's taken it from a hospital, they'll have likely covered their tracks. And if they got it from the internet, a counterfeit . . .' He shrugged. 'Who knows?'

Phil made a note.

'Was it accidental, d'you think? Giving her that much? Or did he mean to?'

Nick smiled. Like he had set a secret test and Phil had passed it. 'That, in the rather overused and clichéd words of the Bard, is the question. My guess, and it's only that, is that he didn't mean to. He wanted her compliant. He then tied her to the bed. It was clear the drug had kicked in by then because there was very little abrasion on the skin against the restraints. She didn't – or rather couldn't – struggle. Then he got to work cutting the baby out of her. For that he used the same knife he dispatched Julie Simpson with.'

'Could he have drugged her to keep her silent? Block of flats, people home . . .'

'Very possible. Not easy to keep that kind of thing quiet.'

Phil thought for a moment. 'How fast d'you think he worked?' he asked.

Nick frowned.

'Would there have been time for the drug to have spread to the baby? Would it have been removed still breathing?'

96

'Speculation only, I'm afraid. There was very little finesse about the incisions. They were made quickly, which would suggest he was working towards a purpose. I'd say there's a chance that the drug hadn't reached the baby by then.'

'So we can assume it's still alive?'

Nick shrugged. 'That would be my assumption.'

'How skilled were they? I mean medically? Surgically trained?'

The pathologist mulled over the question. 'Trained . . . no. Skilled . . . perhaps. They might have had a rudimentary grasp of what they were doing. They knew where to cut. But not a professional. An enthusiastic amateur.'

'And Lord preserve us from them,' said Phil. 'What about DNA? Anything back yet?'

Nick shook his head. 'Too early. Could be anything up to a week, even more.'

'What about sex?'

Nick gave a thin-lipped smile. 'It's a kind offer but I'm afraid you're not my type.'

Phil shook his head. 'I'll bet you're a wow at the Christmas party.'

Nick raised an eyebrow, gave a small smile. Phil didn't want to think about it.

'No,' he said eventually. 'No evidence of sexual activity. Forced, consensual or otherwise. With either body.'

'Thanks.' Phil was digesting what he had heard. 'Right. Well, if that's it, I'll be off.' He moved to pick up the file.

'Couple of things,' said Nick. Phil stopped, waited. The pathologist slid another sheet of paper across the desk. 'Took the liberty of speaking to a colleague in Ob/Gyn. She factored in the variables: traumatic delivery, premature by four weeks – I checked Claire Fielding's records; she had a Caesarean booked for four weeks' time – drug administered to the mother . . .' He sighed. 'If the baby receives fortifiers along with plenty of milk and is kept warm, it might be all right.'

'Where would you find these fortifiers?'

'Anywhere. That's the good news. But if it doesn't receive constant quality care or it develops breathing difficulties, I think we're talking hours rather than days.'

Phil took the paper. Felt the familiar band tighten round his chest. 'Thanks. I think.' He ignored the pressure building inside him, made his way to the door.

'Something else. This was all done with some force. I think that that, along with the angle at which the blade entered Julie Simpson, would rule out the possibility of it being a woman. Unless that woman was a six-foot, sixteen-stone bodybuilder.'

Phil nodded. Thought of someone who fitted that description perfectly.

'Go get him, Phil,' said Nick.

Phil nodded. Left as fast as he could.

19

'Okay,' said Phil, striding into the bar. 'Gather and pool. What have we got?'

Everyone looked up.

'Just briefly,' he said, 'before we go home.'

It didn't look like anyone was about to go home. In fact the bar looked like his team had moved in for the duration and had no intention of leaving until the killer was caught and the baby found. Anni was writing up reports at her desk, Marina next to her. The Birdies, DC Adrian Wren and DS Jane Gosling, sat at their desks, Adrian tall and rake-thin, Jane round and squat. They looked to Phil like an old music-hall double act, but they were two dedicated coppers.

Ben Fenwick entered.

'Come and join us,' said Phil.

The overhead lighting compensated for the evening darkness outside, keeping the room unnaturally, even depressingly, bright. The whiteboard in front of the bar displayed grisly before-and-after shots of Claire Fielding, Julie Simpson, Lisa King and Susie Evans: one from life, one from death. Before: smiling, displaying contentment or the hope that being alive held. After: lifeless and soulless. Arrows pointing outwards from them, bloodied husks reduced to components and clues.

To the right, a map of Colchester, the scenes of death high-lighted. Below that, a photo of Ryan Brotherton. A marker invited anyone to fill the remaining white space with facts, sup-position, hypotheses. Make links, illuminate secret, occult connections, bring order to chaos, provide answers. Next to the board was a TV on a stand with a VCR/DVD combination underneath.

'Where's Clayton?' asked Anni.

'Following something up,' said Phil. 'He should be with us shortly.'

'Glory-hunter,' said Anni, just loud enough for Phil to catch. He knew Clayton had his eye on bigger places than Colchester, higher rank than DS. This was probably the per-fect case for him to move up on the back of. If they got a result.

Phil fixed her with his eyes, chastised her, but let her words go. This wasn't the time or the place.

'Right,' he said, 'it's roughly seven hours since the bodies of Claire Fielding and Julie Simpson were discovered, and that baby's still out there. Let's go. Anni?'

Anni checked her notes, told the team about her findings at All Saints Primary. Chrissie Burrows, Geraint Cooper and Julie Simpson, celebrating Claire's pregnancy. How they were more than friends, a support group for Claire Fielding. Because of Ryan Brotherton and what he had threatened. Phil stepped in.

'Ryan Brotherton,' he said, 'previous for ABH, assault. Done time in Chelmsford for it, too. Domestic-abuse-related, all directed against women.'

Marina put her head down, started writing.

'And he threatened to kill the baby if Claire didn't have an abortion?' asked Fenwick.

'With his own hands,' said Anni.

The sides of Ben Fenwick's mouth twitched as if they

100

wanted to smile but weren't yet allowed and his eyes lit up. 'Looks like we have an early front-runner,' he said.

'We'll see,' said Phil. 'We paid him a visit.' He told the team about the trip to the metal yard, Brotherton's response and his new girlfriend covering up for him. 'She was clearly lying.'

'Do you know why?' asked Fenwick.

Phil shook his head. 'Habit? First response? I don't know. I'd like to talk to them both again, separately. But I'm sure he'll be keeping her on a short leash at the moment. I've got the post-mortem from Nick Lines.'

He shared it with them. The blade used, the drug, the size and build of the attacker.

'I'm liking this Ryan Brotherton more and more,' said Fenwick.

Phil didn't answer him. 'But Lines did say we have only a limited window to find the baby alive. If it's not being looked after, it could be just hours. A day at the most.'

Silence as his team took in the words.

Phil turned. 'Adrian, Jane. CCTV? Door-to-door follow-ups?'

'Nothing as yet from CCTV,' said DS Jane Gosling, 'but we expect the tapes from the block of flats and the streets by tomorrow morning. We've looked into possible sex offenders in the area, anyone known to us with any kind of deviant behaviour that might overlap with this. Nothing. There was this, though. A couple of residents in the flats reported seeing a large figure dressed in a long overcoat and hat in the area last night. No sign of them after what we assume to be the time of death.'

'Brotherton?' said Anni.

'Could be,' said Fenwick. He had a hunter's gleam in his eye.

'Right,' said Phil. 'I think we can assume that this was

done to get Claire Fielding's baby. Julie Simpson's husband has been interviewed, and while we can't be entirely certain, I'm pretty sure she was just in the wrong place at the wrong time.'

'Like Claire,' said Anni.

'Absolutely. But if it's all about Claire, then that's one thing. However if this is the same person who murdered Lisa King and Susie Evans, it could be the baby they're after. Either way, that doesn't necessarily rule out Brotherton.'

'What d'you think, Phil?' said Fenwick. ' Gut feeling. Is it him?'

Phil frowned. 'If it had just been this one incident, these two murders, then I would have said yes. Case like this, it's almost always the husband or boyfriend. Well, nine times out of ten. But because of the other two . . .' He shrugged. 'I don't know. He's lying to us, but I think we need something more definite. We need to find a connection.'

'We need to find the baby,' said Anni.

'Let's pull him in, then,' said Fenwick, balling and unballing his fists. 'Get him in the box, sweat him. See what he has to say then.'

Nods all round the room.

'Good,' said Fenwick. He stood, impatient to be doing something. 'That's a plan, then. First thing in the morning, Phil, get him in. Get him talking. Get him singing.'

More nods, more assents. The team were buoyed, focused on their target. A voice cut through their thoughts.

'There is one thing you haven't fully considered.'

All heads turned to Marina. She was looking up from her notebook, waiting until she had all their attention.

'What?' said Fenwick, clearly irritated at the interruption.

'That it isn't him.'

20

'Stop it, stop it, stop it . . .'

Hester clamped her hands over her ears and stomped round the room, angrily shaking her head. No good. The baby's wailing still penetrated. She clamped her ears harder, opened her mouth.

'La, la, la, I'm not listening . . . no, no, no, I can't hear you . . .' Shouting at the top of her voice, stomping all the harder, her eyes screwed tight shut, flinging her body round, letting all the impotent rage out.

'La, la, la . . .' Screaming now.

But it was no good. She could still hear the wailing, no matter how hard she screamed.

Hester slammed to a halt, turned to look at the baby, the thing that had promised so much happiness and contentment but which was bringing nothing but trouble. It lay in an old rusted tin bath with a none-too-clean blanket underneath it and another one covering it. The cot that Hester herself, the whole family, had used as a baby. She should have been sentimentally attached to it – after all, it was a family heirloom – but she wasn't. Her mind didn't work that way. Perhaps as a baby she had felt safe and secure in her cot. But she didn't know. Couldn't remember that far back, she told herself, had blocked it out. Those memories belonged to a different person. And she never wanted to be that person again. She couldn't be.

She took her hands away from her ears. The baby was still making that noise. It wasn't the same crying as earlier, strong and loud; this was more like one unending cry of pain. If anything, it was worse than the shouting. She stomped back to it, picked it out of the cot, held it under its arms, looked right into its mewling, shrieking, stupid little face.

'Shut up!' she screamed. 'Shut up! I'll . . . I'll . . .' She shook it hard. The movement just made the sound vibrate. It sounded funny. She would have laughed if it wasn't so annoying. 'Shut up! Or I'll fling you against the wall! Yeah, that'll keep you quiet . . .'

But the baby didn't seem to understand her. It just kept on wailing. Hester looked between the wall and the cot, then, with an angry exhalation, flung the baby back down into the tin bath. It bounced on the blankets, looked startled for a few seconds, stopped wailing in surprise. She scrutinised it. Smelled that smell.

'You stink . . . urgh . . .'

The baby was thinking about wailing again. She could tell. She had to do something quickly. Maybe that was it. Maybe it needed its nappy changing. It was still wrapped in the blankets her husband had put it in when he brought it home. Wasn't even in a proper nappy. Not yet. That was okay; she had seen them get changed on TV. The babies always lay on their backs kicking their legs and laughing while the pretty young mums smiled and wiped their bottoms with a special cloth and put a new nappy on them. Well, that was easy. She could do that. And if she did, the baby would smile again and she could smile again. Easy.

She cleared space on the workbench by sweeping the tools out of the way with her thick, muscled arm and blew any

104

sawdust or iron filings off the surface before hefting the baby out of the cot and placing it down. It remained silent, startled at being moved. Hester smiled. This was what a mother would do. Good. It was working.

She unwrapped the blankets one at a time, pulling them off as quickly as she could, throwing them on the floor. The silence encouraged her to speak in baby talk again, like she was supposed to. She took a nappy out of the bag and picked up a cloth to wipe the baby with.

'Be prepared,' she gurgled in an approximation of baby talk. 'Mummy's got to be prepared . . .'

She looked at its body. All pink and blue blotches, like its face. But there was yellow in there too. Was that right? She didn't think so, but it was still moving so it must be. And it was cold as well. Were they supposed to be cold? She had thought they would be warm. Something else the TV and books had got wrong.

Hester smiled to herself. Maybe she should write a book on babies. Or go on TV to talk about them. Tell the truth about what they were really like. She grinned at the thought and began to undo the final blanket. What she found there wiped the smile off her face.

'Urgh . . . no . . .'

She didn't know what to do. She had the cloth ready but didn't want to touch it. She wished her husband was there to help, but knew he wouldn't do anything.

Lookin' after babies is women's work, he always said. *Don't mind gettin' you one, but you're lookin' after it yourself after that.*

And she had accepted that. So it was down to her.

She took the cloth and set to work, holding her breath all the time. She did it eventually, throwing the soiled cloth in the pile of blankets. She brought out the wipes that came alongside the nappies. When they were wiped with these, the babies smiled. She wiped it. It didn't smile. Or laugh. But it

105

didn't wail. That was something. She wiped it again. That was better. Getting it clean. She threw the wipe after the cloth and the blankets. Looked at the naked baby lying there.

It had a thing sticking out. Little and wrinkled, but with quite a big bump underneath. It was a boy baby.

'Oh.'

She reached out, got its little thing in her big fat hand. Tiny. Felt a sadness build within her. A tingling somewhere in her body to accompany it. The sadness increased.

No. That was in the past. She was what she was. She was Hester. She was a wife and a mother. She was happy. Happy.

She let go of its thing, started to put a nappy on it. It couldn't be that difficult. She looked at the picture on the packaging, tried to copy it. While she worked, she thought. About the baby's little thing. She hoped her husband wanted a boy. He should do. They did, didn't they? Fathers wanted boys. Another shudder of sadness rippled through her. Most fathers. Some wanted girls. Some made them girls.

She looked again at the baby as she covered its thing up. Smiled.

'Let's hope he wants a son,' she said, baby-talking again, 'or he'll have that thing off you quicker than you can say . . .' She thought. There was a phrase she should use but she couldn't think of it. 'Well, quick, anyway.'

She pulled a one-piece suit on to it.

'There. Don't you look handsome?'

It just lay there, kicking its legs slightly. Eyes still screwed tightly shut. But at least it wasn't screaming.

She checked her watch. Her husband had been back and gone out again. Should be back soon. She could usually feel when he was going to return. Time to feed the baby in the meantime.

She crossed to the fridge, took out a bottle of milk. She

knew she couldn't feed it from her body; that would be stupid. So she got milk from the shop. Full fat. She had read that it should be given powdered milk and something called fortifiers. But she didn't know what they were. And the powdered milk she didn't like the sound of. Better off with proper milk. From a cow. Full fat was good; that would have all the fortifiers and stuff in that it needed. That was being responsible, because she had read that children shouldn't be given diet things. Coke was all right when it was older, a few months maybe, but not yet. She knew that. She wasn't stupid.

She squirted the milk into her own mouth. Cold. Too cold. Pop it in the microwave. She did, waited for the ping, watching the baby all the while. It lay on the bench, kicking its legs again. She smiled. She liked it like that, when it was quiet. That's how she'd imagined it would be.

The microwave pinged. She took the bottle out, squirted milk into her mouth. Bit hot. But that might be good. It was cold in here, warm the baby up a bit. Put a bit of colour in its cheeks, make it smile.

She crossed to the bench, shaking the bottle in her hand to cool it a little. She scooped the baby up in one meaty, powerful arm, held the bottle to its mouth. Looked at it, just lying there, its face twisted into a permanent scowl, like a miniature gargoyle. Not what she'd imagined at all. It looked weak, too. Weak and yellow. Like a very old and wise Chinaman in a temple from a martial arts film. She smiled, looked again. No. It just looked tired, like it wanted to sleep. Well, it could. After it was fed.

She ran the bottle along its lips, moistening them. It moved slightly. She took advantage of that, put the bottle in. It jumped.

She laughed. 'Ooh, almost opened your eyes there.'

She jammed the bottle all the way in. Let it suck. It was good for it.

The sadness was still within her. She forced it away, along with the earlier rage. This was a time for mother and baby. A time for contentment. She had read that somewhere. She sat down in a chair. Sighed. It wasn't like she had expected it to be. But then she had also read that it never was.

This was her new life, she told herself. She was a complete woman now. Wife. Mother.

'This is me,' she said out loud to the baby. 'This is me. And look . . . I'm complete.'

The baby didn't reply. Just lay there, slowly taking in milk but too weak to swallow , letting it run down its sickly yellow face.

Hester didn't notice. Just smiled.

21

'It's all wrong,' said Marina. 'Nothing fits.'

Phil joined the others in looking at her. He knew what they would be thinking: the profiler should stick to her day job, leave the police work to the professionals. He suppressed a smile at her nerve.

She continued, 'I know I'm running to catch up at the moment. I haven't visited the crime scene yet or spoken to anyone concerned. All I've done is read the case notes this afternoon. And I still haven't delivered a profile.' She waited. No one interrupted. 'But based on what I've read about the previous deaths and what I've picked up about Ryan Brotherton, he's not the killer.'

'Why not?' said Fenwick, his irritation palpable.

'Because he's a spousal abuser, not a killer. They're two different things.'

'He could be both,' said Fenwick.

'I'll explain,' said Marina. 'For a spousal abuser, it's all about isolating their partner, keeping them locked away from the rest of the world in order to control them. He'd want to injure her, yes, but not kill her. What good would she be to him dead? He wants her alive to keep tormenting her.'

The silence in the room became very uncomfortable.

'Now, the baby . . .' Marina paused. 'And we're assuming here that Claire Fielding, or rather Claire Fielding's baby, was the subject of the attack . . . Well, most spousal abusers wouldn't be happy that their partner was pregnant in the first place. They're childish and needy and want attention. A baby will take that attention away from them.'

'Wouldn't that make them angry?' said Anni.

'Not that angry. Because the baby is still part of them. They'll be jealous that the woman is carrying it, but they won't try to harm it. And there are another couple of things. No links with the two previous murders—'

'That we know of,' said Fenwick. 'Yet.'

'That you know of,' Marina said. 'But there's the fact that he drugged her first.'

Phil understood what she meant. 'He would have wanted her to scream,' he said. 'Wanted her to suffer. The drug would have taken that away from her.'

Marina looked at him, smiled. Phil couldn't help but return it. Then straight back to business.

'Or he didn't want her to wake up the whole block,' said Anni.

'There is that,' said Marina. 'Now, putting aside the baby for a moment, let's look at what actually happened.' She pointed to the photo of Claire Fielding's body without actually looking at it. 'Here is Claire Fielding. Tied to the bed, spreadeagled. Why?'

'Ritual?' suggested Phil.

'That was my first conclusion,' she said, almost looking at him once more. 'But it seems to be more about control. She's been injected with a drug to induce paralysis. As the post-mortem report said, whoever did this is not a professional. Therefore they didn't know exactly how much of the drug was needed. If they got the dose wrong, the victim might scream or struggle. Kick. Hence the ropes.'

'So . . .' said Phil, 'it wasn't ritual, it was . . . what? Expedience?'

Marina nodded. 'It could well be. And her legs had to be open because . . .' She took a heavy breath.

'He enjoyed it?' said Phil.

'Perhaps,' said Marina. 'It could be as simple as that. But it's still an aspect of control, of subjugation.' She checked her notes again. 'Now what were the restraints made of?'

Phil consulted his own notes. 'Rope. Thick, heavy-duty. We're waiting on DNA.'

'So he came prepared,' said Marina. 'He brought the knife and the rope.'

'And the drugs,' said Phil.

'And the drugs.'

'Well, what about the sex aspect?' Fenwick's voice was rising in pitch, getting clearly agitated. He looked to Phil like someone who had been told their birthday party had been cancelled.

'Post-mortem states there's no evidence of sexual activity.'

'This still doesn't rule Brotherton out, though,' said Fenwick. 'If he wanted to, I don't know, show her who's boss, couldn't he do it by ripping the baby out of her? Wouldn't that show her who's in charge?'

The attention of the room turned back to Marina. 'Put like that, I suppose it sounds plausible, yes,' she said.

Fenwick held his arms up as if in triumph. 'Well then.'

'But it doesn't sound likely. And then there's the fact that it might not be a man at all.'

'What?' said Fenwick. 'A woman?'

'Why not?'

That was too much for Fenwick. 'Because a woman isn't physically capable of doing what this person did. And someone answering Brotherton's description was seen in the area.'

111

'Look at it logically,' said Marina. 'Who wants babies? Not men, women.' She paused, continued. 'I'm generalising. But you get what I mean.'

'So it could be a big, angry woman,' said Anni. Behind her, Fenwick shook his head.

'It's possible,' said Marina. 'There are a few documented cases of this kind of thing happening, but mainly in the States and always with some kind of personal connection. Partner leaves, takes up with a new woman, gets her pregnant. The spurned girlfriend takes revenge by cutting out the new baby.'

The room flinched en masse.

'Could be a man,' said Phil, almost thinking aloud, 'doing this *for* a woman. Getting a baby for her.'

'Brotherton,' said Fenwick. 'Doing it for his girlfriend.'

Marina sighed. Fenwick picked up on it. 'Something to say?'

Marina said nothing, just kept her head down.

Fenwick nodded. 'Good.'

Marina looked up. Phil saw the redness in her cheeks, the fire in her eyes. Knew she was about to unleash her Italian temperament. 'Yes,' she said, 'I do have something to say. You asked me here to give my professional opinion and you've done nothing but talk over me and attempt to belittle me.'

Fenwick shrugged. 'Yes, but a woman. I mean, please.'

'I was brought here to provide a profile—'

'Which you haven't done yet.'

'I've had less than a day here.'

Fenwick strode over to Marina. 'We have a suspect.'

'I was not brought in to rubber-stamp whatever you say.'

'Don't you want us to catch him?'

Marina looked him straight in the eye, didn't back down. 'I want you to catch the right person.'

112

Fenwick opened his mouth to say something else, but Phil was on his feet. 'Sir.'

Fenwick turned.

Phil looked round to the others in the room. He didn't want to do this but Fenwick's actions had left him with no choice. 'With all due respect, sir, I'm running this investigation and your comments aren't helpful.'

Fenwick stared at Phil as if he wanted to punch him, but managed to control himself. He put his hand on Phil's shoulder, steered him towards the door. 'Come with me.'

The two men walked out into the corridor, leaving the rest of the team staring after them.

Once outside, Fenwick turned to Phil. 'I brought her in to provide a profile, to help us catch a killer, which she hasn't done yet. Instead she comes out with all that, trying to undermine the investigation.'

'She's got a valid point. I'm listening to her.'

'We've got a suspect ready to bring in and she's trying to talk you out of it.'

'We should listen to what she's got to say.'

Fenwick gave an ugly snort, all vestiges of the training course designed to produce politically correct modern policemen gone. 'Oh yeah. She can say what she likes to you, get away with anything. Twist you round her little finger. And we all know why, don't we?'

Phil felt his hands ball into fists. His breathing came harsh and fast; his turn to struggle for control.

He managed it. 'Like I said. This is my investigation, sir. And I'll conduct it the way I see fit. Your comments aren't helpful. In fact, you're way out of order, superior or not.'

Fenwick said nothing.

'I'm going back inside,' said Phil, 'to continue the meeting. Will you be joining us?'

Fenwick held Phil's stare for a second or two before turning and walking away.

Phil watched him go, then, taking a deep breath and expelling it slowly, walked back into the bar.

22

'I'm afraid DCI Fenwick won't be rejoining us for the moment,' said Phil, his voice as light as possible. 'So let's finish up here and we can go home. Shall we continue?'

His team looked at him, eyes wide. He knew what they were thinking – had he punched out a senior officer? Had a senior officer had a go at him? Whatever, it would be round the station in minutes.

'Marina?' said Phil. 'You were saying?'

Marina looked at him, her face unreadable. Was that admiration he saw? Irritation? She looked down at her notes, began scanning.

'Erm . . . Yes. Here. What was I saying? Yes. Right. Escalation. Look at all these women. Lisa King, Susie Evans, Claire Fielding . . . with the unfortunate exception of Julie Simpson, you see a clear escalation.'

'Trial runs or unsuccessful attempts,' said Phil, getting back into the rhythm as quickly as possible. 'Technique refining.'

Marina nodded, picking up speed as she did so. 'This person wants a baby. A live one. And if that's the case, to the killer, these women are just breeders. Surrogates.'

'Why not just snatch one from somewhere? A maternity ward or outside Mothercare?' said Phil.

'Perhaps the risks are too great. I don't know, they think that a baby taken from the womb will be easier to bond with. Now,' Marina said, pointing to the map, 'the geographical aspect might be worth looking at. Usually you can put together a profile of the perpetrator from the area in which they've operated. Fix their position, their home, from where they've committed their crimes. But looking at the map, I can't find any kind of pattern.'

'Where does Brotherton live?' asked Anni.

Both Phil and Marina looked at her.

She blushed. 'I'm only asking.'

Phil checked his notes. 'Highwoods,' he said.

'Right in the middle of it,' said Anni, looking at the map. 'Well, almost.'

'Yes,' said Marina, 'that's true. But these women have different backgrounds, social classes, they come from different areas. There doesn't seem to be any kind of geographical overlap in terms of Brotherton meeting them.'

'Perhaps he bought a house,' said Phil. 'Used Lisa King's estate agency. Might be worth a look.' Jane Gosling made a note.

'Maybe he used prostitutes,' said Anni. 'Met Susie Evans in New Town.'

Jane made another note.

'I don't think we should rule Brotherton out,' said Phil. 'Let's investigate him further. See if we can find a connection between him and the earlier victims. And we'll get his phone records checked too. But he shouldn't be the only avenue we explore.'

'What if he's not living or working where he targets and kills?' said Anni. 'How's he picking his targets? Hospitals, antenatal clinics, that sort of thing. Could he have access to a database with pregnant women on it?'

116

'It's being looked into,' said Jane Gosling.

'And also,' said Phil, 'we still need full background checks on both Julie Simpson and Claire Fielding. They're both as important as the other. I want their last weeks traced, where they went, who with, who they spoke to, everything. Nothing is unimportant. If someone has asked them the time in the street, find out who. Find out when. Jane, can you do that?'

Jane Gosling, scribbling, nodded without looking up.

'D'you mind if I take a look at the murder scene?' said Marina. 'Might help.'

'I'll run you over there when we finish.'

He watched her nod; their eyes caught once more, then away.

'Right,' said Phil, 'that seems to be as much as we can do for now. Uniforms will continue to collate the door-to-door and CCTV stuff, Ben Fenwick can talk to the media again, give them an update. In the meantime, those who are going home get some rest. We'll need it.'

'Before we go, can I just ask,' said Adrian Wren, 'this serial killer—'

Marina cut him off. 'Please don't use that term. As soon as you say the words "serial killer", everyone goes all FBI and *CSI*. It's not helpful.'

'So, this person who kills more than one person sequentially,' Adrian Wren said, and got a few polite smiles as a response. 'Don't that sort usually try to communicate with us, or to leave clues to show off how clever they are? Taunt us? Or is that just in films and books?'

'No, in real life too, sometimes,' said Marina. 'Killers of that nature are often of low self-esteem and want to parade their intelligence. Sometimes it's a cry for help. They actually want, subconsciously, to be caught. That's one kind of serial killer, yes. But I don't believe we're dealing with that kind

117

here. This one seems to be fixated on a very specific goal.'

'The abduction of the baby?' said Phil.

She nodded. 'To the exclusion of everything else. And the end, in their mind, justifies the means.'

'Well, if they've got the baby now,' said Anni, 'and it's alive, that might be a good thing. They've got what they wanted.'

'Perhaps,' said Marina.

'Why perhaps?' said Anni.

'Because we're assuming this baby's alive,' said Phil. 'And being well cared for.'

'Precisely,' said Marina. 'What if, God forbid, this baby dies and they need a replacement? Or even worse, what if they get a taste for what they've done and want to continue?'

'Start a family,' said Phil.

Marina looked right at him and he at her. They held their look. Connection made. 'Exactly.'

'Jesus,' said Anni.

The whole room sat in silence for a few seconds, taking that information in.

The silence stretched on. Outside the window, people were making their way home from work, coming out for the evening. Life was going on in that other, separate world.

The door to the bar opened. Fenwick walked in, a look of triumph on his face.

'Right,' he said. 'Been on the phone to Chelmsford. They've sanctioned twenty-four-hour surveillance on Ryan Brotherton. Overtime in place. I'll leave you to draw up a rota for the uniforms, Phil.'

Phil stared at him.

'I said, and the Detective Super at Chelmsford agreed with me, that Brotherton should be brought in for question-ing tomorrow.' He turned to Marina. 'Of course, I think you should be there to take a look at him from the observation room. See what impression you get.' He looked round, gestured to Phil. 'All yours.' Then he strode out.

The silence his absence created was louder than a bomb. The door opened again. They all turned.

'So,' said Clayton, 'what have I missed?'

23

DS Clayton Thompson drove slowly down the narrow New Town road, cars parked on both sides allowing only one vehicle at a time. The rows of dark, dirty red-brick terraced houses just added to the closed-in, claustrophobic feeling. The only people around in New Town after dark either lived there, or were trying to get out of there. Or had business there. It wasn't somewhere most people went by choice.

Colchester might have been Britain's oldest recorded town, the capital of England during Roman times. It had the wall round the town centre and the grid-like road system to prove it. It also had an old castle, a theatre, open spaces and parks, lots of old buildings. The University of Essex was based there. It had boutique shops, good restaurants and bars. As big as a small city with the feel of a market town. No concrete tower blocks or sink estates to spoil the view.

But a town didn't need tower blocks to have their associated problems. It still had areas where poverty and deprivation gave way to rage and criminal activity. New Town was an area of warren-like Edwardian terraces running from North Hill at the fag end of the town centre down to the river's edge at the Hythe. Where Clayton was headed was bad enough, but there were parts of it that even he wouldn't visit after dark. At least not without back-up. And people here he never wanted to meet again, at least not without bars between them. Developers had recently tried to smarten the place up, building expensive gated apartment blocks in amongst the terraces. The locals had responded well, giving these new developments the highest rates of burglary, theft and criminal damage in the whole town.

Clayton parked the car in front of the street-corner pub, amazed that there was a parking space, but worried because he had to leave his ride unattended. He loved his 5-series BMW. Expensive to run and maintain, not to mention the monthly payments he made on it. But that was okay. He just compromised on other stuff. It was worth it.

He had been brought up in a house of women. A mother and two sisters, his father dying when he was six years old. His mother had wanted him to work in a bank, an office, do something with money, something steady. Much as he loved his mother and wanted her to be proud of him, he hadn't wanted that.

Whatever sense of masculinity he had came from films, TV, games. If the man had the car, he got the woman. The fact that he was well dressed and handsome didn't hurt either. So the police force had been natural for Clayton. And then the car.

He had planned it for years. Spent days fantasising about what he would do when he could eventually afford it. Lower the chassis; what rims and exhaust to fit, what sound system to give it, the whole nine-yards pimp job. All those teenage years spent devouring car magazines, especially *Max Power*. His favourite. That presented him with the lifestyle he wanted, showed him which cars to idolise and which girls too, come to that. And which girls would go for which car. Now, at twenty-nine, when he could actually afford the ride he wanted, he discovered that it didn't need any extra pimping. It was perfect as it was. That upset him slightly – he felt that a part of his childhood, and with it his adolescent fantasy, had died. But something stronger had been put in place. The mature, confident young man. The one who was actually able to live out that life, to make that fantasy a reality. A DS at twenty-nine; he was going places. And his mother was proud of him. Nothing would hold him back, no one. He would make sure of that.

He sat there a moment, engine idling, hip-hop on the stereo. The Game. Cool, hard stuff. Gave him the right kind of swagger. He pulled down the sun visor, checked his eyes in the mirror. This meeting was important. Thing had to be said. But more importantly, things had to be kept quiet. He had to be full-on for this; no doubt, no insecurity. Took a deep breath, then another. He wasn't going to lose his car, his lifestyle and most importantly his career over this. No way. So. Keep it firm, keep it strong. And if that failed, use any means necessary. Another deep breath. Another. Checked his eyes again. Flipped the visor back into place, took the key from the ignition, got out.

He opened the door to the pub, stepped inside, letting it swing closed behind him. The interior looked as bleak and depressing as the exterior. Tired red faux leather ran the length of one wall, old, scarred tables and battered wooden chairs before it. A carpet whose pattern had surrendered to age and various kinds of darkness covered the floor. A TV was mounted above the bar, the brightness and colour showing the few drinkers what they were missing elsewhere in the world. The bar was a semicircle curved round the centre of the pub. A lone barman stood at one end, chatting to an old man who might not have lived there but who certainly belonged there. Clayton saw a couple of men sitting at a corner table. He knew them. Brothers, supposedly builders, they were in fact behind most of the criminal activity in the area. Drugs, prostitution; they probably took a percentage of whatever was taken from the posh cars parked in front of the new flats. Clayton stared. They looked away. He did the same. A mutual thing: they wouldn't bother him if he didn't bother them.

He saw who he wanted, sitting at a table, alone. A glass of something clear, half drunk, before them, bag by the chair leg, workout gear sticking out. They saw him. Waited. He sat down opposite. Found a smile.

She flicked a smile in return. Sharp, practised. 'Hello, stranger.'

'Hello, Sophie,' he said.

Before he could answer, the smile was dropped. She looked quickly round, checking no one was listening or watching. 'You took your time,' she said.

'Briefing,' he said. 'And traffic.'

'Yeah. Well I haven't got time to sit around here all night, have I?'

Clayton smiled at her. 'Sorry.' She didn't respond. 'Anyone bothered you in here?'

She shook her head. 'Told them I was waiting for someone. Told them in a way that made them leave me alone.'

'Right.' He ran his eyes up and down her body. She had changed out of her working clothes. Jeans, trainers and a pale, tight, translucent blouse, her dark, lacy bra clearly visible through it, a generous amount of cleavage on display. Her hair was down, accenting her heart-shaped, make-up-caked face. 'You're looking good.'

'Not good enough, apparently. Haven't heard from you in ages. Years.' She leaned forward. He couldn't help but stare down her cleavage. 'But you only call when you want something. And I expected you to call after today.'

'Bit of a shocker, that,' he said. 'Didn't expect to find you there.'

123

She shrugged. 'And what was all that fuckin' DVD crap? What did you come out with that for?'

'Just doin' my job.'

'Yeah. Well I know what that involves, don't I?'

His smile disappeared. He felt edgy, uneasy. She was gaining the upper hand. He had to stop it. 'Yeah, well. That's in the past. And it's going to stay there. It's the present I want to talk about.'

She allowed herself a smile, adjusted her top. 'I'm sure.'

Clayton stared at her, his features hardening. He felt his control slipping. Wouldn't allow it to happen. 'And you do too, otherwise you wouldn't be here. Would you?'

Uncertainty flickered across her eyes. He tried not to smile. He had her. Yes, she could make things difficult for him, but he could do the same for her too.

'I must admit, I was surprised to see you when you came into the yard. You did a good job of not letting on you knew me. Really good. Should be an actor, you know.'

'You hid it well too,' he said.

She gave a sharp laugh. 'Nothing wrong with my acting skills.' Her turn to look him up and down now. 'You dress better than you used to. On more money?'

'More money, new job.' He swallowed hard. 'New me.'

Another laugh. 'Doubt it,' she said. 'Leopards and all that.'

He leaned forward. 'Listen, Sophie . . . do I have to call you that?'

'It's my name. Sophie Gale.'

'You used to have a different one.'

'Only for professional purposes. And anything that went on between us was always strictly professional.'

'Yeah, but that was after. I knew you before all that, remember? When you used your real name. Gail Johnson. When I busted you in that New Town brothel raid. You've grown up since then. Done all right.'

124

'And I suppose I've got you to thank for that, have I?'

'Amongst others.'

'Yeah. Well I think I've thanked you enough times.'

'Listen.' Clayton's voice dropped to a low, harsh hiss. 'I still remember when we dragged you in. Just a poor little teenage prossie runaway, terrified. Who would do anything not to go to prison.' His voice dropped further. 'Anything. So we made a deal, didn't we? You said you had intel on all the major drugs gangs operating in the area. You would provide us with that intel. As long as we looked the other way and kept you out of trouble. You were happy for our help then.'

'Yeah. And I gave you plenty of stuff. It put people away. But that wasn't enough, was it? You wanted something more.'

'So I took a few freebies.'

Her eyes hardened. 'You took more than that.'

He stared at her. Tried not to let her words scare him. Got himself under control. 'You want me to tell your new boyfriend all about it? About your old life?'

'Fuck off.' There was real anger behind Sophie's hissed words. Then she sat back. Smiled. 'Wonder if your new boss would be interested to hear about what you used to get up to? What you used to do to me instead of paying me the money you owed? What I had to do for you?'

Clayton's eyes hardened. Fear gave way to the promise of violence. 'Don't.'

'Then don't fuck me about, either. Just as long as we both know where we stand.'

They sat there in silence, staring at each other.

'What made you pick this place?' said Clayton eventually. 'Old times' sake? Didn't figure you for the sentimental type.'

Her eyes flashed with a dark fire. 'You don't know anything about me at all.'

Another silence. Sophie looked at her watch.

125

'Can't sit here all night,' she said. 'Got to go home soon.'

'Bet he doesn't like you being out on your own. Seems like the controlling type.'

Sophie said nothing. Clayton knew he had hit a nerve. He pressed on. 'Right. We've been doing some diggin'. Want to know what we found?'

Sophie shrugged.

He struggled to conceal his excitement at what he was about to say. Back in control again. 'I found out that when you used to be on the game, working for us, you knew someone we're interested in.'

'Who?'

'Susie Evans.'

Sophie shrugged again. 'So? Lots of working girls knew Susie Evans. I didn't know her very well. She was low rent. I always aimed higher.' She adjusted her top. 'Besides, I'm out of the life now.'

'So is she. She was murdered, remember? Course you do. It was in all the papers.'

Sophie looked away, not wanting to match her eyes with his.

'And there are similarities between her murder and Claire Fielding's. Your boyfriend's ex. Coincidence?'

'Yeah,' said Sophie. 'Ryan never knew her.'

Clayton sat back. 'How long have you been with Ryan?'

'Couple of months. Went for a job at his firm.'

'Really? Strange career progression. Why'd you do that?'

'Had this boyfriend who was a metal merchant. Told me there was a vacancy. Put me up for it. Got the job, met Ryan, the boyfriend got the push.'

Clayton said nothing. The boyfriend was probably a client. He doubted Sophie was totally out of the game. 'So you get the job and this boyfriend of yours gets an inside eye into another firm's dealings.'

126

'Except I started seeing Ryan and dumped him.'

'The old boyfriend mustn't have been very happy. What did he do? Go back to his wife?'

'He never left her.'

Clayton allowed himself a small smile of triumph.

'So now you're with Ryan. And his girlfriend—'

'Ex-girlfriend.'

'All right. Ex-girlfriend, then. She winds up murdered. Same way as an old mate of yours. Your new boyfriend has a history of violence towards women, and with you in the middle there's a connection between the two.'

Sophie said nothing.

'Not only that . . .' Clayton leaned forward, ready to play his ace. 'You lied for him. He was out when the murder happened, wasn't he? And you lied to us and told us you were with him.'

Sophie again said nothing.

Clayton sat back, pleased with himself, but slightly put out that she hadn't responded. 'So where was he?'

She shrugged. 'I don't know.'

Clayton studied her face. She wasn't just holding out on him; there was something else. 'You're scared of him, aren't you?'

He thought she would sit in silence again, but eventually she nodded.

'You know what he's done to other women and you're scared he'll do that to you.'

She nodded again. 'Yes.'

Clayton's voice carried a greater degree of warmth and concern than was perhaps professionally necessary. 'Then why are you with him?'

'He's . . . a good bloke. Looks after me. Never want for anything. You know.'

Clayton knew.

'And he's . . . he's not that bad. I know all that stuff with Claire, that got him down. But he's over it now.'

Her voice sounded thin, her words hollow. 'No he's not, Sophie. And you don't believe that either. You're worried. I'm guessin' he's still obsessed with her. He was out when she was being murdered. And he won't tell you where. Is that it?'

Another nod.

'And that's why you agreed to see me.'

'Yes.' She sighed.

'So what happened? Where do you think he was?'

Sophie leaned forward. Clayton got a great view of her cleavage, but he wasn't interested now. This was more important. This was work.

'I don't know,' she said. 'He went out saying he had to meet someone. That it was business. When he got back, I was in bed. I heard the shower, then he came and joined me.'

'Does he often go out on business?'

'Sometimes.'

'That late at night?'

She said nothing.

'And does he always need a shower when he comes back?'

Silence.

'And that's what he said when you asked him about it? That it was business?'

She nodded. 'I thought it was Claire at first. Because he's . . .' She sighed. 'He's not over her. The baby and everything.'

'He wanted her to get rid of it.'

'So he said. But . . . I think it just scared him. The whole thing.'

'He didn't say anything else? About the baby? Give you . . . give you anything to go on?'

She frowned. 'What d'you mean?'

He didn't know whether to tell her. The fact of the baby's disappearance had been kept out of the media. And she didn't seem to know what he was talking about. He decided to leave it at that.

'So you thought that's where he was?' he said, continuing with the questioning. 'With Claire?'

'I didn't want to think that.'

'Course not. What d'you think now?'

She didn't answer. Instead she looked at her watch. 'Shit, I've got to go. Take me home. We've got to go now.' She stood up, grabbed her bag. Clayton stood also, placed a restraining hand on her arm.

'Look, you don't have to go. We can help you. Keep you safe if anythin' happens.'

Sophie shook her head. 'Yeah, heard that one before. Thanks.'

'We can.'

'Just take me home. And keep my past out of this.'

'I'll try, but—'

She turned to him, eyes alight with angry fire. 'You'll fuckin' do it. If I'm keepin' you out of this, you can do the same for me.'

Clayton sighed. 'All right. I will.'

'Good. Come on.'

She led him to the door. The barman watched them leave, eyes on her buttocks, lewd imagination written all over his face. Outside, the air had turned cold. Clayton pointed out his BMW to her.

'Nice,' she said. 'Always thought you'd do well for yourself.'

Clayton smiled, got in, Sophie beside him. He drove off as fast as he could.

24

'**M**ind where you walk,' Phil said.

Marina didn't need to be told. The blood in Claire Fielding's apartment had dried to various shades of dark brown and black, but it was still unmistakably blood. And the carpet and walls of the hall were still covered in it. The earlier smell of dirty copper and spoiled meat had dissipated somewhat. But that didn't make the scene any less horrific.

'Oh God . . .'

Phil noticed Marina touch her stomach as she spoke.

There had been a tense silence in the car on the drive across town, the air thick with unspoken emotion. This was the first time they had been alone together since they had met again. They had nothing to say to each other, yet everything to say to each other. Not to mention the scene in the bar.

'So,' Phil had said to break the silence, 'Fenwick hasn't changed much, has he?'

Marina managed a small smile. 'Wanker.'

'Still, at least he made you feel welcome.'

Marina didn't reply. Another silence, then: 'Did you hit him? When you took him outside?'

Phil smiled. 'You like that, do you? The thought of two men beating each other to a pulp over you?'

'Defending my honour. And my professional integrity, of course.'

'Of course I didn't hit him. I took him away for his own protection. That famous Italian temper of yours was about to make its presence felt.'

She laughed. 'And he would have deserved it. I felt like walking out.'

Phil kept his eyes on the road. 'Glad you didn't.'

The rest of the journey had taken place in silence.

'You okay?' Phil asked, back in the flat.

Marina didn't turn round. 'I'm fine.'

'Your . . . stomach. Is it hurting?'

She still didn't turn, but he saw her shoulders tense. Her hand dropped from her stomach. 'No. Everything's fine.'

'This isn't upsetting you?'

'I'm hardcore.'

'Well, as I remember—'

'Shut it, Brennan. Concentrate.' She looked at the blood. 'So this was . . . Julie Simpson.'

'Yeah,' said Phil, glad to be able to focus on the case. 'She must have answered the door. Judging by the way we found her and the wounds inflicted, he killed her straight away.'

Marina nodded, looked at the wall. She pointed. 'Intercom,' she said. 'Videophone?'

Phil nodded.

'If she knew them, she would have buzzed them up.'

'Does that rule out or rule in Brotherton?'

Marina frowned. 'I don't know. Can't see her letting him up.'

'No,' said Phil. 'But perhaps the intercom didn't go. Perhaps he was already in.'

'Someone let him in and he was waiting? Planned, premeditated. It would fit.'

'So there's a knock at the door, say. Julie Simpson goes to answer it. Next thing . . .'

Marina nodded. She examined the walls in more detail, traced the arcs of dried blood with her finger. 'Very decisive. She opens the door . . .' She positioned herself in the doorway, taking the place of the attacker. 'He looks at her, knows she's not the one he wants – probably because she's not pregnant – then . . .' She scythed her arm in an arc, ending abruptly, sharply. 'Cuts her. Gets rid of her.' She looked at Phil. 'What does that tell you? What does that say?'

Phil didn't know if he was supposed to reply, or whether she was just using him as a sounding board. He ventured an answer. 'Well, he . . . Julie Simpson wasn't the primary target. So get her out of the way, move on.'

'Exactly what I think. Get her out of the way. He didn't knock her out, tie her up, anything like that. He didn't paralyse her with his needle. He killed her. Straight away. No hesitation.'

'So . . . she was just an obstacle,' Phil said.

'Just something between him and his goal.'

'Claire Fielding.'

'Claire Fielding's *baby*,' Marina corrected him. 'If I'm right.'

'If you're right.'

'So.' She again took the position of the intruder, mimed the actions. 'He slits her throat, drops her to the floor. Does he wait to see that she's dead? No. It doesn't matter. She can't move, can't call out. If she's not dead yet, she's as good as dead.' Marina moved down the hallway. 'Then he comes along here.'

'Just a minute,' said Phil. 'Slits her throat and drops her . . . doesn't see her as a person . . .' Something was coming to him. Connections were being made. 'Knife . . . Could this person work with animals?'

'How d'you mean?'

'Well, a farmer. Not a vet, obviously. Or someone used to slaughtering livestock? In an abattoir, maybe?'

Marina smiled in admiration. 'It's a possibility. Well done. We'll make a decent copper out of you yet.'

Phil couldn't help returning the smile. 'Right then. Off you go, and leave us professionals to get on with it.'

'My work here is done.'

They both stood there, smiling, not speaking. Unspoken emotions again humming between them like high-tension wires.

Marina broke the silence. 'Where was Claire Fielding?' She walked to the end of the hallway, her voice once again businesslike, focused.

'Here, we think,' said Phil, picking up the lead from her voice, following her. He stopped at the end of the hallway, pointed to scuff marks on the wall. 'Signs of a struggle here.' There was a potted plant lying on its side. 'Maybe he attacked her, knocked her into this.' He examined the wall. 'Not much damage, though.'

Marina joined him. 'There wouldn't be. If it's the baby he was after, he wouldn't want her harmed. Well, not too much.' She looked round. 'Then what?'

'We found her in the bedroom. Tied to the bed and . . . well, you know the rest.'

Marina stopped walking, looked round again. 'This is the living room, yes?' she said, pointing towards the room on her right.

'Yeah.'

'So . . .' She looked round again, examined every surface with her eyes, stretched out fingers.

'It's fine,' Phil said. 'Touch what you like. The lab boys have finished here.'

Marina nodded. 'Is this room how you found it?'

'More or less. Presents on the coffee table, not much disturbed.'

'So the living room wasn't touched. He either knows the layout of this flat, or he's supremely confident about what he wants and single-minded about how he's going to achieve it.'

'Which is it?'

She gave a small smile. 'I don't know, Phil. I'm not Derek Acorah.'

He laughed. 'You're better-looking, for a start.'

She closed her eyes, shook her head. 'Stop it,' she said. She looked irritated by his interruption, but a smile played round her lips. 'Now concentrate. He must have had some contact with her. She wasn't chosen at random. She was targeted, picked out for a purpose.' She rubbed her hand across her mouth. It was something she did unconsciously when she was thinking. Phil smiled inwardly at the memory. It was an endearing trait, he thought. 'But . . .' She took her hand away. 'That doesn't necessarily mean she was intimate with him.'

'Why not?'

'Well, most killings like this are sexual in nature. And I don't get a sexual feeling from this.'

Phil couldn't stop himself smiling. 'That's reassuring.'

Marina blushed. 'You know what I mean,' she said, trying to cover her reddening face. Eventually she smiled too.

'Right. So it's not Brotherton, then?'

'I don't think so.' She shook her head. 'He doesn't feel right. But . . . you never know. I may be wrong. It has been known.'

'Not in my experience.'

'Charmer.'

She looked at him once more and there was that connection again. She smiled, and as she did so, her features relaxed, tension leached from her body and her eyes became

134

lit not just by warmth but by an inner light. It was a light Phil hadn't seen for a long time. He moved towards her, smiling also.

'Marina, I've . . .'

Suddenly the light was extinguished. The tension returned, like an invisible barrier had once again been erected.

'Please, Phil,' she said, her voice strong but not harsh. 'Please. Don't.'

'But—'

'Just don't. Please.'

Phil felt exasperation build within him. He had to say something, whether she wanted to hear it or not. Whether she had given him permission to speak or not. 'Listen, Marina. It's been months now. You just—'

'Phil, don't. I can't talk about it now. Please.'

'But—'

'No. We can't – I can't have this discussion now.'

'Why not?'

'Because . . .' She pulled her coat around herself once more. Another barrier, thought Phil. Another shield. 'I just can't. Not at the moment.'

'When, then?'

'We will talk,' she said. 'But not yet. You'll have to wait.'

'For what?'

'Until I'm ready.'

He just looked at her. She was irritating, she was a control freak, she was mouthy, she was arrogant. He sighed. She was beautiful, she was warm, she was witty, she was brilliant. He knew how he felt about her. It had never changed. He said nothing. Just nodded. He couldn't blame her.

To take his mind off Marina, he looked once more round the flat. 'Murder scenes always make me feel lonely,' he said.

She looked at him, frowning, bemused.

The words surprised him. He didn't know he had been

135

thinking them and certainly wasn't aware he was going to articulate them. Unsure as to why he was talking, he continued. 'Yeah.' He nodded, looking round. 'Lonely. Depressing. I mean, beyond the obvious, you know.'

Marina seemed grateful for the change in subject and jumped on his words. 'In what way?'

'Well . . .' He felt suddenly shy talking about it. But if there was anyone he could share an intimacy with, even a verbal one, it was Marina. Wherever they were at with each other. 'It's like . . . office buildings at night when the workers have left for the day. Or . . . theatres when the play's finished and everyone's gone home.'

'When do you go to the theatre?'

He blushed. 'You don't know everything about me, you know.'

'Clearly.'

'But it is,' he said, warming to his theme now. 'You know in the theatre when they turn the stage lights off after a show and put the working ones on. To reset the stage and stuff. It's really bleak. Depressing. Like the thing that gave the place life, the play, the actors, the audience, whatever, has gone. And you're still there. And you shouldn't be, you should have gone with them. But you are there, on your own, and you've got to keep going.'

She looked at him, frowning. Gave a small nod of her head. 'I know what you mean,' she said.

He nodded also, wondering if she did know what he meant. Wondering also whether he had still been talking about crime scenes.

'I think I've seen everything for tonight,' she said. 'D'you mind giving me a lift home, or should I call a cab?'

'I'll take you home.'

He turned the lights off and they left the flat.

Dark and empty. A stage set with no actors.

25

*H*e was hunting again.

 He didn't really need to. Not yet. But it was good to plan ahead. In fact, it was essential. And he had to keep working at it. Hone his skills. Improve all the time. Never too old to learn something new. Plus he was good at it. And he enjoyed doing things he was good at.

 The animal had no idea he was watching her. And he liked that feeling. Just planning something that his prey had no idea about, sitting there watching her, that made him feel good. He drew power from that. Enormous power. He could feel his erection stirring at the thought. A feral lust.

 This one was tricky. But that didn't bother him too much. They all presented problems; all he had to do was work out the best way round them. They were obstacles in the path to his goal. And obstacles could be overcome.

 This one was about vantage point. The housing estate was open. If he sat watching from the side of the street he would be seen. He knew the type of people they were round here. Anything – anyone – that didn't look like it fitted in, and they called the police. So he had to be careful. Cunning.

 He had parked before the entrance to the estate and walked in. From there it had been easy to go to the house opposite and find *a shadow to crouch in. Simple. They all had huge plastic wheeled bins and large cars parked out front. Some of them even had skips and rubbish from home improvements. Plenty of places. Anyone looking at the street would see a normal housing estate. Nothing out of the ordinary. Nothing to be scared about. No one would ever notice him.*

He watched the house. She was moving from room to room like she couldn't settle. Like if she left a room for too long she would forget what was in it. And she had been alone all night. Her husband was coming back later and later. Like he didn't want to be with her. Didn't matter. Soon he wouldn't be with her at all.

She would be his. Or the part of her he wanted would be his.

Lights at the end of the street. Sweeping round. A car coming into the turning.

He stayed completely still. Head down, so the beams couldn't even catch his eyes, waiting until it had gone past. It slowed, stopped. Turned in to the house opposite.

The husband coming home.

The husband turned off the engine, the lights. Took his briefcase from the passenger seat, got out. Walked towards the house. Slowly, like he didn't want to go in. Closed the door behind him.

He stood up, slipped out of the shadows and down the road. He had seen enough for the night. Time to head back now. Things to do. Duties to perform.

But he would be back.

Very soon.

26

'Not here. Round the corner. He might see.'

Clayton put his foot automatically on the brake, then eased it off again. He drove the car past the house Sophie shared with Brotherton and parked around the corner. He turned the lights off. Highwoods was an area consisting entirely of housing estates with a huge Tesco at the centre of it. Most of the houses were large and fronted by laurel hedges but crammed so close together it made them seem smaller than they were.

Clayton looked at Sophie, her face lit by the overhead light in the car. 'How do you usually get home from the gym?' he said.

'Taxi. Sometimes I take the car. But sometimes I'll meet a girlfriend and have a drink.'

'Bet he doesn't like that.'

She gave a smile Clayton couldn't read. 'He would prefer it if I brought them back here for a drink.'

'Then he could keep an eye on you.'

Sophie nodded, gave a grim smile. 'Yeah. He does that all right. That's why most of my girlfriends want to meet me in town now.'

Clayton said nothing.

'I'm not saying I don't enjoy it; it's just . . . I like to pick and choose, you know?'

'You like to be in control.'

This smile wasn't grim but teasing. 'Sometimes . . .' She leaned across the seat towards him, whispered in his ear. 'But sometimes I do like to do what I'm told. If it's the right person telling me . . .'

Clayton could feel his erection springing up immediately. She moved in closer to him, licking the side of his neck. Goosebumps ran over his skin. He couldn't sit comfortably. Her hand was on his chest now, smoothing down the front of his shirt, heading down towards his belt buckle . . .

'No . . .' It sounded like someone else had borrowed his voice and was doing a bad, timid impression of him.

'That's not what your body's saying.'

He gasped as she found his erection. 'I can't . . .'

'Sshh . . . I won't tell anyone.' She eased his zip down. 'And neither will you, will you?'

'Wh-what?' He thought she had said something important but he didn't know what it was. There was also something else he should be thinking about, something important. but he couldn't remember. He could only concentrate on one thing at a time.

'I said,' said Sophie, working her hand into his trousers, 'you won't tell anyone, will you? About meeting me, about anything I've told you . . . You'll keep my name out of it, won't you?'

He felt her hand gripping him tight, working him up and down. She began to lower her head into his lap.

'Will you?' she said, looking up, eyes staring directly into his.

There was no love in those eyes. No warmth. Just calculated professionalism. His lust mirrored.

140

'No,' he said between gasps. 'No . . .'

She lowered her head. He closed his eyes.

Anni Hepburn was cold. She had taken over from the Birdies over half an hour ago, having asked for the job specifically. Sometimes she got so hyped about a case that Phil gave in to her, let her put her energy to use.

But despite remembering to wrap up warm, she was still cold. She couldn't put the car heater on in case it ran the battery down. The same with the radio. She knew they all did it, but if she needed to get away quickly and the battery was dead, the whole investigation could collapse and she would be in trouble. And she didn't want that. So she sat there, several layers of clothing wrapped tightly round her, staring at the house.

Scrap metal must pay, she thought. Nice house. Not her style, and bigger than she would be able to afford. Unless she married a scrap metal merchant, obviously. Though if they were all like Ryan Brotherton, she wouldn't bother.

She was just wondering how she was going to entertain herself for the next few hours to stop herself from falling asleep when a car approached. She sat up immediately, watching. The car came to an abrupt halt, then continued round the corner, away from the house. She sat back again. Probably nothing, she thought. But she would keep watching, just in case.

The lights on the car were turned off, but no one emerged. Strange, she thought. Maybe another car had been sent on surveillance. Not a BMW, though. Hardly a pool car.

She watched, waited. There were two people in there; she could make that out from the silhouettes. Then there was movement, the silhouettes rearranging themselves, one moving to the other side.

Oh God, she thought. Doggers.

She shook her head, tried not to watch as the woman's head disappeared under the dashboard and the man threw his back in ecstasy. If she had been feeling difficult she could have walked over, tapped on the window, flashed the warrant card and put the fear of God into them. But she was on surveillance. Still, it was tempting. Not because of the law-breaking aspect, but because it was so long since she had been in a relationship or had any real excitement along those lines and she was jealous.

She and Clayton had almost been an item. A work attraction, that kind of thing. They had gone for a drink a few nights ago. Just to see whether the fact that they got on so well was because they were friends who worked together, or if there was something more. Jesus, was it only a couple of nights ago? Felt like ages. And yes, she had gone back to his flat. And yes, they had had sex. Or something approaching sex. It wasn't very good. And afterwards they both knew it was something they had done more out of a sense of duty to each other than from anything approaching burning passion. The next day had been surprisingly easy and they had laughed it off as a bad idea. And that was that. The question had been answered. They were friends who worked together. Nothing more. She didn't want it to develop any further. Besides, she knew what he was like, knew his reputation. She didn't want to be just another conquest of his. Someone else to show off to the lads about down the pub. Just leave it at that.

As she watched, the silhouettes separated. The one in the passenger seat made some adjustments and rearrangements and got out. Anni reached for the binoculars. A thrill ran through her. The woman she was watching matched the description of Ryan Brotherton's girlfriend, Sophie.

'You two-timing bitch,' she said to herself, laughing.

She watched as Sophie walked to the front gates, let herself in, walked up the driveway and into the house.

She turned her attention to the car. The headlights came back on and it turned round, ready to come past her and drive away. She raised the binoculars to her eyes, tried to get a look at the driver as it went.

'Oh my God . . .'

Clayton. Unmistakably Clayton.

Her mind was racing. She reached quickly for her phone, ready to make a call. Who to, she didn't know. Phil? Clayton himself? And say what? Ask what was going on?

She sighed, put the phone down. No. She would wait until the morning, have a word with him.

She sat there, still watching the house, not expecting anything more to happen. Her mind was racing. She was no longer cold. She was hot.

And angry.

Clayton was with another woman so soon after her. The fact that there was nothing between the pair of them wasn't important. It showed a lack of respect. And it wasn't just that – the woman he was with was involved in a murder inquiry. And that was serious.

There would be no sleep now.

She sat there watching. Planning.

27

What you doin' standin' here in the dark?

    Hester jumped at the voice, opened her eyes.

'I'm . . .' She didn't know. What *was* she doing standing there in the dark? She looked down. The baby was in its cot where she had left it. She was standing over it. 'I'm lookin' at the baby.'

In the dark?

She blinked. Unaware of how long she had been standing there. She must have blacked out again. 'It . . . wasn't dark when I started lookin' at it.'

Her husband grunted. *You made my dinner?*

'It's . . .' She looked again at the baby. It wasn't moving, its breathing shallow. But it was peaceful.

Well?

She looked at the kitchen area. 'I'll get it for you.'

Disorientated from her blackout, she pulled the blanket up to the baby's chin, being careful not to wake it, and ignited the Calor Gas heater. Then she switched on the light over the baby's head. She had rigged up one of the electrician's work lamps at the side of the cot, clamping it to the bedhead so she could see the baby from wherever she was in the house. The lamp threw down hard light and heat. It illuminated the baby

144

all right, but she could also see the condensation on the bare brick and stone, glistening and running above the heater. The house would soon be warm enough, she thought. The baby was wrapped well enough.

She must have been staring at the still baby for a long time. She did that sometimes, stood still, not moving from the spot she was in. Losing all track of time. This time she hadn't noticed the day slip away, to be replaced by night. And she hadn't heard her husband enter. But that wasn't so strange. Usually she just heard him as a voice in her head, a presence, and she knew straight away that he was there.

She looked at the baby one more time and, satisfied that it was all right, crossed over to the kitchen area. Her husband had built it for her. He had put up plasterboard walls to divide it from the open space, built shelves and cupboards from what he had salvaged on his travels. He had even painted the bare stone and brick walls in the kitchen area white. She liked that. Thought it made the place look more homely. And that was important, now they were a proper family.

She stood in the kitchen area. She hadn't prepared anything. She looked round to see what she could make quickly. There were two skinned rabbits on the counter top, some root vegetables in a basket. That would do.

'How . . . how about rabbit stew?' she said, closing her eyes, hoping her husband wouldn't see her lack of preparation.

He grunted again. *I'm hungry. Now. Whatever you do, you'd better make it quick.*

She nodded and, as fast as she could, lit the stove, put on a pan of water to heat up. She looked round. The baby was lying still in the cot, making no sound. Good. Knowing no harm could come to it, she made their evening meal.

Later, after she and her husband had eaten and she had washed up and cleared away, she returned to the baby. She couldn't keep away. She had been getting up and checking on it all through dinner. She had heard her husband give a few exasperated growls, but he had said nothing. She had smiled inwardly at that. Perhaps he was an understanding man after all.

While she was staring at the baby, her husband slipped away again, leaving her alone with the infant once more.

It hadn't wailed for ages. Once she had changed and fed it, it had kept quiet, slipping into what she thought was sleep as she rocked it in her arms. She remembered, before she blacked out, studying it as it lay breathing shallowly but raggedly in her arms, its eyelids just about closed, leaving only a sliver of milky white showing through as its eyeballs rolled into the back of its sockets. It was so small, so helpless. She could have done anything to it. Cuddled it, kept it warm, squeezed it tight. Or put her fingers round its throat, choked the air out of its tiny, frail body. Anything. She felt a rush of adrenalin as that realisation sped through her. She had the power of life and death. She could play God.

Power. For the first time in her life. She had smiled at the thought. No wonder people went to such lengths to have babies.

Hester looked down at it now, deliberating what to do. She wanted to pick it up. After all, that was what mothers did. But it looked so peaceful lying there, hardly moving, hardly breathing.

That was when she thought something might be wrong.

She leaned in closer, angled the lamp over to see it better. The pink blotches on its face seemed to be lessening in number. Its skin now had a blue tinge all over and the yellow was increasing. Hester didn't think that was right. It most definitely wasn't what they looked like on TV. Something was wrong.

'Oh God, oh God . . .'

She looked round, panic welling inside her, willing her husband to turn up, but he was nowhere to be seen. She would have to cope on her own.

'Oh God . . . oh God . . .'

What to do, what to do . . . She looked down at the sleeping child. She couldn't take it to the doctor, she knew that. She hated doctors, had had a bad time with them all her life. So what, then? Did it need feeding? She checked her watch. No. Changing? She couldn't smell anything. Should she pick it up? Yes. That seemed like a good idea. Then what? Hold it. Why? Because that was what mothers did, she reminded herself. Because doing that would make it better.

She reached down, picked the still infant from the cot. She stroked its cheek. It felt cold to the touch, its skin clammy. Just like stroking the walls behind it.

She held it to her. Warmth. That was what it needed. She got into bed, holding the baby to her chest. Eventually her arms began to cramp up from keeping them in the same position for so long, so she put the baby back in its cot with an extra blanket on top of it. The tin cot was right beside her bed. She lay on her side, looking at the baby.

And that was how she lay well into the night. Staring at the baby, keeping vigil for signs of a worsening condition. Trying to keep awake but dropping off occasionally. At some point during the night, she woke to find her husband was back.

'The baby's not well,' she said.

He grunted. *So?*

She looked at the baby once again. For the first time she voiced the fear and doubt that had built within her. 'I don't . . . I don't think it's goin' to get better. Not on its own.'

It'll have to, her husband said.

147

'Can't we just . . .'

No. We can't. Don't be fuckin' stupid, woman.

She nodded. She knew that.

You'll just have to hope it gets better on its own.

'Right.'

If it lasts the night, it'll be all right.

'What if it doesn't?'

Then it doesn't. Go to sleep. You've still got jobs to do in the mornin'. Baby or no baby.

And he was gone again.

She took his advice, tried to get some sleep, but couldn't. Instead she lay there, watching the baby. At some point she plucked it from the cot, held it to her. She could feel something happening inside herself and she didn't know what it was. An unfamiliar feeling, like it was tearing a hole in her. She didn't like the feeling but she wouldn't have wanted to be without it somehow. Not now.

So she held the baby. Waited for morning.

28

Caroline Eades couldn't sleep. Her husband, lying on his back, mouth open and snoring like an angry lion growling, had no such problem.

She just couldn't get comfortable. Every time she did, moving her body around to a position that could accommodate her stomach and the rest of her, somewhere the baby wasn't lying on anything that would cause her discomfort, it would kick, or stretch, or shift about, and she was back to square one again.

But she didn't think it was the baby's fault. Not entirely. Graeme had come in after nine o'clock, put his briefcase down and announced he was going for a shower. He didn't want any dinner, which was a good thing, since the M&S lamb shank was ruined by then; said he had eaten on the way home. Then, following his shower, he had downed a can of lager and gone to bed. He didn't ask how she was, how her day had been, nothing. He barely acknowledged the children, who were putting themselves to bed. If she didn't know better, she would have thought he was having an affair.

He had been her childhood sweetheart. Proper Romeo and Juliet stuff. At least she'd thought so until she read the play and saw what happened to them. She vowed that would never happen to Graeme and her. She would make it work, whatever. Give them a happy ending.

And she had. In the early days, when he was building up his business, she had put her career plans aside, been there to help him. In fact, the majority of the work involved in drawing up the business plans was down to her. But falling pregnant had stopped all that. Then she'd become a stay-at-home mum, let Graeme go out to work. His business had prospered, selling his recruitment agency to a national company while still being allowed to run the local arm. This had led to the new house, the two big cars, the private schools.

And now the new baby.

Unplanned but welcomed, at least by Caroline. Because if she was honest – and lying in the dark awake when the rest of the world was asleep was the time for honesty – she had nothing else. No friends since the move, apart from the other young mothers. Her two kids treated her as their personal servant. Her husband ignored her. So yes, this baby was welcome.

She looked at Graeme again. The man she had given all her dreams and wishes to. Her heart and soul. Her one-time Romeo, now snoring and drooling from the side of his mouth.

He had better not be having an affair. That would mean the baby was all she had to look forward to. Please, let him not be . . .

The baby kicked again. She shifted, tried to get comfortable.

Sighed. It was going to be one of those nights.

29

Phil sat on the sofa in his living room, took a mouthful of beer. Held it in his mouth, rolled it round, swallowed. Head back, eyes closed. The remains of an Indian takeaway on the coffee table in front of him, Elbow playing on the stereo, 'The Loneliness of a Tower Crane Driver'. He sighed, listening to the song, Guy Garvey singing about there being a long way to fall.

He had come in from work thinking about the case, particularly Fenwick's behaviour. But a quick weights session on his home gym had worked that out of his mind. Now, when he should have been formulating approaches, strategies for tomorrow, he found himself thinking of Marina. Only Marina.

When she had walked out of his life she had broken his heart and he had been bereft. And the way she had done it, cutting him out completely, after all they had meant to each other. No phone call, text, email, nothing. Like he was dead to her.

His bursting emotions had gone through several recognisable stages. Firstly incomprehension at her actions. A creeping guilt that she blamed him for Martin Fletcher. Then anger when she wouldn't allow him to explain why he was innocent of her imagined charge. That anger upped to rage as he tried to hate her out of his system, telling himself she was no good for him and failing massively. Finally a numb emptiness as he realised he would be facing the rest of his life without her. All the while playing and replaying conversations with her, inventing and imagining new ones that they might possibly share, different scenarios and possible outcomes.

His reverie was cut short by the phone ringing.

He jumped to answer it, thinking at first that it might be Marina, but then in a more professional frame of mind realising it might be someone from the station with an update about the case. Or even another murder.

God, don't make it that. Please don't make it that . . .

It was neither.

'Hello, son.'

Phil relaxed. It was Eileen Brennan. The nearest thing he had to a mother.

'Hi, Eileen.' He flicked the remote, muted the sound. 'All right?'

'Very well, Phil. And Don sends his love too.'

Phil had forgotten. He always made a Wednesday-night call to Eileen. 'I'm sorry,' he said. 'I was going to call you.'

'It's all right. Doesn't matter.' She sighed. 'We saw the news. Those girls . . . terrible. I said to Don, that'll be our Phil working on that.'

Phil heard the pride in her voice. Smiled. 'Yeah, that's me.'

'And that's why you had to stand poor Lynn Lawrence's daughter up.'

'Oh, please . . .'

'Couldn't you even have met her later? Gone for something to eat?'

'I don't think I'd have been much company.'

152

'I know, Phil.' She sighed. 'Terrible. We live in a terrible world.'

'Not all of it,' said Phil.

'Don wants to know all about it. I said you couldn't tell him. He knows that but it doesn't stop him asking. So how's . . .'

And she was off. Phil relaxed, took another couple of mouthfuls of beer while he talked to her. Hearing Eileen's tales of friends he barely knew and Don's troubles with how to work their new DVD recorder was just what he needed to hear after the day he had had. It told him that, contrary to what Eileen might have said, the world wasn't the terrible place he saw all too frequently, but a place where people went about their normal, everyday lives. He heard some of his colleagues talk about parents and responsibilities as if it was something boring that they hated doing. Not Phil. He loved these phone calls with Eileen.

She was coming to the end now, building up to her familiar sign-off. 'I wish you could meet a nice girl, Phil. Settle down. You deserve someone nice. Someone to give you a bit of happiness.'

He responded in kind. 'I know, Eileen. But I never get the chance, do I? Never meet any women through work.' *Only dead ones*, he thought, but thankfully didn't add.

'Well, I did try. But you're a grown man, you can look after yourself. Anyway, Don wants to know if you're still coming over on Sunday. I think he just wants someone to go to the pub with and watch the football. Don't know why he wants to do that, either. We've got Sky here.'

Phil could imagine her sitting in the armchair of their big detached 1950s house in Mile End, just beside the mainline station. Mock Tudor, beamed inside and out. Tastefully decorated, torn apart by generations of foster children and lovingly repaired again. He loved that house. A noisy and

153

energetic environment but also a warm, comforting one. It seemed empty now since they had both retired from foster care and there was just the two of them. But Phil still loved visiting. It made his Sundays special.

'I'm still coming. And I'm looking forward to it.'

They said their goodbyes, Eileen rang off and Phil was alone once more.

He sighed. Her words had hit a nerve. He looked around the living room of his own home. It was well furnished, with books on shelves, CDs and DVDs. Prints on the walls. It told of an interesting life. A full one. He was happy with his own company. He had been on his own for most of his life. But sometimes, he thought, sometimes he would enjoy having someone to share it with. Someone to come home to.

He laughed out loud at how self-pitying he sounded.

'Maybe I'll get a dog,' he said, to no one in particular.

He took another mouthful of beer, pointed the remote at the stereo. Elbow started playing again and his mind was immediately cast back to Marina. He had been listening to the album when they first got together. Each track reminded him of some aspect of her, but one in particular stood out. He knew that was coming soon, looked forward to it with both longing and trepidation, knew it would bring back memories he found almost too powerful to cope with, but memories that he wanted to be reminded of nonetheless.

They had met through work. The Gemma Hardy case. And the attraction had been instantaneous. He had looked up from his desk that day as Fenwick had escorted her across the office and done a double-take that verged on the comedic. She was so beautiful. In an office full of hard-bitten, badly dressed, sweating, cynical police officers, even more so. It looked like she had arrived from another planet, a more cultured and enlightened place. He couldn't help but stare.

He vividly remembered their first meeting at the briefing, even down to what she was wearing. He recalled it now. A black velvet dress that accentuated her trim figure and flared out around her legs, plus high-heeled knee-length black leather boots that made her appear taller than she actually was. Thick black curly hair, pushed back at one side, held in place with a glittering hair slide that matched her necklace and earrings. Round, expressive hazel eyes. Full red lips. His first thought: he had never seen a woman that looked so perfect.

And his second: don't even think it – she's way out of your league.

But she'd soon proved him wrong.

They had been teamed up together in the case, her psychological expertise matching his experience as a detective. They had been left alone to work. At first he found it difficult to speak to her. When he tried to discuss the case he would catch her eye fleetingly, because he couldn't hold it too long, and find her smiling at him, those beautiful hazel eyes wide and shining. It was unnerving; he felt she was teasing him. The educated university lecturer laughing at the poor, plodding copper. He tried to ignore it, not let it get to him, just concentrate on finding the girl's stalker.

But she kept smiling at him. And he kept focusing on the case.

Then they touched. Accidentally, both standing over a desk, looking down at a spread of reports and photos. As she went to point at something, her hand came down on top of his. It was like an electric current passed through him. Like it jolted him awake, alive. Made him feel truly connected to another human being for the first time in his life. He looked at her as if shocked. And in that moment, that look, he knew: she felt the same way. She was still smiling at him, but he understood the smile now. She wasn't laughing at him, mocking him. There was affection there. And something more.

'Listen,' he had said, ignoring the reports and looking directly at her, her hand sliding slowly off his as if reluctant to move, 'I was just wondering, d'you fancy a drink or something some time?'

Phil had felt himself blush then, massively. What was he doing asking her out? What had possessed him to say that? He worked hard within the force to be seen as a man's man when he had to be and a thief-taker by trade. He had shrugged off death threats from criminals that other officers would be seriously concerned by. But with women, he was all but clueless.

His mouth was open, ready to attempt to take his words back, when she said yes, that would be lovely.

'Why did you say yes?' he had asked her on their first proper date, in the Olive Tree restaurant in Colchester's town centre. It was relaxed and comfortable with good, if slightly pricey, food. The kind of place professionals came to eat. But not usually police officers of his rank. He figured it for a safe place not to be seen.

They had made small talk on shared interests, discussed the case, whereabouts they both lived. Then Phil decided to move things on.

And her response was that smile again. Her wine glass at her lips, the deep reds matching, the candlelight dancing in her hazel eyes. 'Why not?' she said, taking a slow mouthful of wine. Phil watched as her lips lifted from the glass, glistening. 'You're handsome. You're intelligent. You look like you can handle yourself if you need to, but you're sensitive too.'

Phil laughed. 'Is that a professional opinion?'

She nodded. 'A personal one. But it's true. I can see it in your eyes.'

He didn't know what to say.

156

She laughed. 'Are you happy being a detective?'

Phil was surprised by the question. 'Yeah. Are you happy being a psychologist?'

Marina smiled. 'They say all psychologists are damaged and are just trying to find their way home.'

'They say all police are racist, violent thugs.'

'Not the ones with sensitive eyes.'

Phil was feeling uncomfortable but exhilarated by her honesty. 'So is that the case with you? Are you trying to find your way home?'

She shrugged. 'I'm on the right path.'

She asked what appealed to him about police work. He was going to give her something boring and mundane: the hours were good, the pension scheme, something like that. But seeing her eyes, feeling the way they bored into him, and after the answer she had given him, he couldn't just do that. She needed something more, something honest.

'Well, it's like this. You get a case. You get called out. Something's happened. A robbery, a murder. Whatever. It's a mess. There's usually someone in tears, a house torn up, lives in pieces. Something like that. And they don't know what to do next.' He shrugged. 'And it's up to me to find out what's going on. See what's gone wrong and help repair it. Make sense of it.' She was still looking at him. He felt suddenly self-conscious. This woman was unlike any he had ever met before. He picked up his wine glass to hide behind. 'That's it, really.'

She slowly nodded. 'Did you go to university?'

He shook his head.

'Did you want to?'

Another shrug. 'Maybe. Wasn't an option at the time.'

She toyed with the stem of her glass, frowning slightly. It left a lovely little crease in her forehead. 'You like reading, I bet.' A statement, not a question. 'But you don't tell anyone at work in case they have a go at you about it.'

He thought of the bookshelves in his flat. Filled with all sorts of stuff. Everything from philosophy and poetry to literature, biography and airport thrillers. He had a thirst for knowledge, for understanding, the roots of which he was sure lay in his childhood. He hadn't found what he was looking for, though. The only thing that gave him real satisfaction was police work.

He shrugged again, growing even more uncomfortable with her questions.

'You had a bad childhood, didn't you? Lot of hurt there. Damage.'

The exhilaration was gone. Phil felt only discomfort. 'Sorry. Off limits.'

'No, *I'm* sorry,' said Marina, looking down at her plate. 'I only mentioned it because I sensed it, that's all. Because . . .' She paused. 'I recognised it. ' She looked up, eye to eye. 'There's something in you that reminds me of me. I'm sorry if I've got that wrong.'

Phil looked at her, said nothing. She slid her hand across the table. They touched. Electricity sparked again. As if the touch confirmed that they understood each other instinctively.

'D'you want to know about me? I don't mind,' she said. She opened up then, told him of her home life, how her alcoholic, abusive father had walked out on her mother and two brothers when she was only seven years old, coming back occasionally into the lives only to cause anguish and upset.

'He was a bastard: a pathological liar, a bully, a cheat, a wife-beater,' she said, her eyes clouding over with unpleasant memories.

'And those were his good points,' Phil had said, trying to turn her from the dark emotional path her words were sending her down.

She smiled. Continued. Told him how she was encouraged

158

at school, how they praised her intelligence, cajoled her to push herself and her studies. She had willingly responded, eager to get away from her background.

'So you're not from round here? I didn't think you had an accent.'

'I'm from Birmingham originally,' she said. 'And that's an accent you don't want to carry round with you.' She continued, telling him how she had been awarded a scholarship to Cambridge and chosen psychology.

'I suppose I chose it because of my dad. I wanted to understand what made him the way he was. Why he did what he did.'

'And did you?'

'Yeah. But I didn't need a degree in psychology to work out that he's just a vicious, lazy bastard.'

Her mother had died soon afterwards of cancer, robbing her of the chance to see her only daughter graduate. 'And I feel bad about that. I wanted her to be proud of me.'

'I'm sure she is.'

Marina nodded, her eyes averted.

'And what about your brothers?'

A shadow passed across her eyes as she spoke. 'Let's just say they grew up to resemble their father. I'm sure your colleagues in the Midlands have more to do with them than I do.'

Phil raised an eyebrow, didn't push it.

'So, you're from Colchester?' she said. 'Lived here all your life?'

'Not yet,' he said, hoping she would laugh. She did. Politely. 'And you're not married,' he said, changing the subject. 'Is there . . . anyone?'

A curious look crossed her face. 'I'm living with someone.'

Phil's heart sank. 'Oh.'

159

Marina shrugged. 'It's . . . we've been together a long time.'

'I see.'

'He's . . . I was his student. He was my lecturer.' She shrugged. 'At least we waited until I'd finished the course. Well, more or less. He was . . .'

'A father figure?'

'I suppose so.' Before Phil could say anything more, she went on. 'Maybe it's time I . . . Sometimes I feel more like his . . .' She looked at her drink, swirling it round in the glass. 'I don't know. So that's me. What about you?'

Because Marina had been honest with him, Phil felt that honesty should now be reciprocated. He spoke. And Marina listened attentively.

He told her of the pain of being abandoned, of growing up in various children's homes and foster homes until Don and Eileen Brennan took him in.

'They gave me everything I'd been lacking. A home. A sense of belonging, I don't know . . . a purpose.' He smiled, took a drink of wine. 'Sorry. I'm not very good at talking about all this. It's . . . I can't express myself well.'

Her hand was on his again. She smiled. 'You've told me everything.'

Their eyes locked once more. Different colours but the same in every sense that mattered. They went straight back to his flat.

He hadn't had time to fully take in her body before they began making love. The connection continued. Nerves evaporated as they quickly fell into rhythm with each other, complementing and second-guessing what the other enjoyed, linked almost by a carnal telepathy. It was hot, physical, intense. Connected by more than just bodily sensations.

At one point, her legs wrapped round him, pulling him

into her as deeply as he could go, he had opened his eyes to see her staring up at him. She had smiled. He had returned it. And in that moment he knew there was something between them stronger than lust or physical attraction. It was stronger than any bond he had ever experienced. It thrilled him beyond description.

It scared him beyond imagining.

He came.

Later, lying spent and exhausted, their bodies intertwined, Phil tried to work out what had just happened. It was more than just a physical release. He glanced across at Marina. Knew without asking that she was experiencing the same thing. It was the biggest thing that had ever happened to him. Again he was thrilled. Again he was terrified.

Early-morning sunlight eased round the curtains. They had barely slept. Phil pointed the remote at the CD; Elbow played gently in the background: 'One Day Like This'. The euphoric love song establishing and nourishing the mood.

'Aren't you going to be in trouble when you get home?'

Her face was half in shadow. 'Leave that to me.'

'Okay.'

'I don't do this normally, you know,' said Marina.

'What, you do it abnormally?'

She gave him a shove. 'You're hysterical. I meant that. Jumping into bed with people.'

'People? You want a threesome now? Foursome?'

Another shove. 'You know what I mean.'

Phil laughed. 'I know. Then why did you do it?'

Their eyes connected. 'Why did you ask me out?'

Phil couldn't bear to look at her; the intimacy was too naked, too knowing. 'Felt right.'

'More than right,' she said.

Phil couldn't reply. He just held her tighter. Felt the

161

damage and uncertainty slip away, to be replaced by the beautiful, terrible peace of a love that reached down to his soul.

Held Marina like she was about to stop being real, turn into smoke. Knew she was experiencing similar emotions.

Knew that, whatever happened, his life would never be the same again.

Phil pointed the remote at the stereo, silencing Elbow before the album reached the track that reminded him of Marina. It wasn't healthy: like picking a wound, stopping it from healing.

He drained his bottle, put it down. Looked at the half-eaten takeaway before him. He couldn't eat. There was another bottle in the fridge if he needed it. He felt the start of a headache. Forced it away. He couldn't indulge himself. He had to work.

Trying to push Marina out of his mind, he made himself re-examine the day he had just gone through. Close up his heart to her, compartmentalise his life and concentrate on finding a killer. And a baby.

He played back the events of the day, starting with the discovery of Claire Fielding's body. Went over everything once again, looking for something they might have missed, attempting to make hidden connections.

Ignored the loneliness in his flat, his life.

Focused on his job.

Unaware that the song was still on his lips.

30

Marina stood at the window, glass of sparkling apple juice in hand, wishing it was something stronger. In front of her was a path, and beyond that the River Colne moved slowly past. Her house, a painted brick cottage with clematis climbing round the porch, was on the front at Wivenhoe, a quaint old fishing village now colonised primarily by academics working at the nearby university. The whole village had a relaxed, cultured ambience. A homely, safe place. But, putting the glass to her lips, Marina was feeling neither of those things.

Tony was cooking a late dinner. Nothing special, pasta arrabiata. It should have been Marina's turn but he had taken one look at her as she entered and, handing her a glass of juice and kissing her forehead, declared he would do it. She had made a half-hearted attempt to refuse.

'No,' he had said, fussing around her, his reading glasses still perched on the end of his nose, 'my last seminar finished at five, and since then I've done nothing but read and drink wine, so . . .' He sat her down in an armchair as if she was an invalid and handed her a newspaper, then, pleased with himself for being so solicitous, retreated into the kitchen. She had smiled at him, accepted it. He was good to her, she told herself.

She had looked round the living room of their cottage, filled as it was with books, interesting one-off pieces of furniture, subdued lighting, unexpected pictures, plants and wall hangings. They had done that to show visitors and themselves that they were interesting people leading a full, rich life. The opposite of the house she had grown up in. But crossing to the window and looking out at the slow-moving, sluggish, dark river, Marina felt as if it all belonged to someone else and not her.

Music wafted from the kitchen – some chilled Brazilian beats Tony had picked up somewhere – along with delicious cooking odours that any other night would have had her stomach rumbling in anticipation. But not tonight. She took a sip of her drink, grimaced, disappointed in herself that she had expected something that wasn't there.

She saw Claire Fielding's dead body. Julie Simpson's too. The other two women. Phil had been right about the murder scene. It felt like they shouldn't have been there. Like life had passed on.

Phil. She had planned what she was going to say to him the next time she saw him. Several times. But as the weeks had passed and life had ground on without him, she had resigned herself to never seeing him again. And perhaps, she had thought, that was for the best. She was back with Tony, pregnant, with a fledgling private practice. Her life had moved on. Or at least back. Back into her safety zone.

But here they were, together again. And she hadn't been able to say anything to him. Because every time she thought of him, she saw Martin Fletcher's face. The locked door. She felt the cold fear bubble and boil inside her once more, and then she thought of Phil. And it all rendered her speechless.

She hadn't realised how much of a rut she had fallen into before the police called her in on the Gemma Hardy case.

164

Routine had turned to drudgery without her noticing. Her safe job, her pension. And Tony, her safe man.

But then she hadn't wanted an exciting man. Before she met Tony she had been attracted to the kinds of men who reminded her of her father. She knew it was wrong, not to mention unhealthy, but nevertheless she kept going back, kept seeking them out. Until one day she had looked in the mirror and seriously questioned what she was doing. And found that she couldn't do it any more.

Tony had been there. A good man, solid, dependable. Thoughtful, pleasant, companionable. Old enough to be her father, but his diametric opposite in every other respect. He didn't thrill her or excite her, but he made her feel comfortable. Safe. He was kind to her. And those, she told herself, were admirable qualities. He asked her out, she accepted. And that was that. He wanted her to move in with him, out of her town-centre flat, into his cottage in Wivenhoe. She had done so. And felt comfortable. Content. Or so she thought.

By the time of the Gemma Hardy case she was ready for a new challenge. And she got one. It taxed her, stretched her. Being forced to turn something she only dealt with theoretically into a practical application, with a young woman's life potentially at stake, terrified her. But it also pushed her, confronted her. And when she helped provide the team with a positive result, it gave her a thrill teaching never had. Never could.

Not only that, but she met Phil.

She knew as soon as she saw him. There was something about him, an immediate connection. At first she tried to deny it, claim it was a symptom of the case she was working on, confusing adrenalin and lust for something stronger and more profound, but the more time she spent with him, talked to him, the more she became convinced she was right and they connected on a much deeper level. A soul deep level. She recognised something in him. Something she had never encountered in anyone else in quite the same way. Something she had only ever seen in herself. She knew that if there was a man who could understand her – totally – it was him.

So when he asked her out, she couldn't say no. Despite having Tony. She slept with Phil. Repeatedly. And surprised herself: rather than feeling guilty about betraying Tony, she began to feel increasingly that her future lay with Phil.

And then came Martin Fletcher.

The Gemma Hardy case was finished. Martin Fletcher had been caught, the team had celebrated. Marina included. Her first foray into police work had been a resounding success. She had put her name forward for more. Everything was looking good for her.

She had gone back to university after the case had concluded, and was in her office one evening, straightening out some of the paperwork that had accrued in her absence. She was meeting Phil later, happy to work until that time. He had arranged to pick her up from her office, said he wanted to see where she worked. She was pleased about that, looking forward to showing the place off to him. No qualms about being seen on campus with another man, because she had decided to tell Tony it was all over. Consequently, her mobile was switched off in case he phoned her.

There was a knock on the door. Hesitant at first, then more self-assured. She shouted for the person to come in. He did. As she looked up, her heart seemed to stop. Her pen fell from her grasp. Martin Fletcher was standing in her office.

'What . . . what d'you want?'

He gazed around, as if searching for the answer to the question on the shelves of her office. Then looked directly at her.

'You,' he said. 'You.'

Marina was terrified. She glanced to the door, calculated the distance, the obstacles in her way. Fletcher must have had the same idea. He turned, and before she could even rise from her chair, he had locked it and put his back against it.

'Don't scream,' he said, menace in his voice. 'Don't.'

She swallowed. It felt like there was a stone in her throat. 'There's someone . . . someone coming here in a minute. Very soon.'

'No there's not. They've all gone home.'

'Yes, yes there is.' She was breathing so hard, her heart felt like it was going to burst. 'Phil . . . Phil Brennan. Detective Inspector. He's meeting me here.'

A wave of fear passed across Fletcher's features at the mention of the police. Despite being terrified, Marina was thinking like a psychologist. *He's scared of the police but not of me. He's angry but can't take it out on them, so I'm the target.* The thought was less than comforting.

'What are you doing out?' she asked. 'I thought you were on remand.'

He smiled then. It was eerie, like he was listening to a joke told by a ghost on a distant radio. 'They let me go. On bail. Technicality.' Then the anger returned. 'You. You ruined my life.'

'No, I didn't.'

'Yes you did.' He was starting to get angry now. He moved away from the door, started coming towards her. 'You took away my life. Turned Gemma against me. You did that.'

Marina looked round for a weapon, something she could use. Could see nothing. *Phil,* she thought, *hurry up . . .*

She had to keep him talking, try to reason with him. 'No, Martin, you're wrong. I didn't ruin your life.'

'Yes you did!'

She flinched at his anger. Forced herself to keep calm.

167

Breathed deeply. 'No. No I didn't. And Gemma was never your girlfriend. That was Louisa, Gemma's flatmate.'

'No . . .' He put his hands to his head, started hitting his temples. 'No, no . . .'

'Yes she was, Martin. Louisa was your girlfriend. Not Gemma.'

'No, no . . .'

'Gemma was her friend. But not your girlfriend. Let it go, Martin, you've got to let it go . . .'

His next words were inaudible, just a shriek of pain as he kept hitting himself, eyes tight shut, seemingly trying to knock her words out of his head.

Marina looked round once again for a weapon, anything. There was no time to turn her mobile on. She saw the phone on the table. If she could get to that, quickly make a call . . .

She looked at Martin Fletcher, eyes closed, still hitting himself, then back to the phone. She could do it. Just reach out, grab it . . .

As her hand wrapped round the receiver, he opened his eyes and, with a scream, lunged forward. She tried to punch in the numbers but he was on her, his hand over hers, pulling the receiver from her, wrenching the phone from the wall, flinging it on the floor.

'Bitch! You're going to pay . . .'

She made a lunge for the door, knowing that she probably wouldn't reach it. She was right. He was on her straight away, pulling her back by her hair. She put her hands up to her head, tried to prise his fingers away, but to no avail. He flung her to the floor. She felt hair being pulled out by the roots, thought parts of her scalp could have gone too.

She landed hard and curled up into a ball, instinctively trying to protect herself while she got her breath back. She knew blows were coming and closed her eyes, placed her hands over her head and face.

'Please, don't hurt me . . . don't hurt me . . .'

He knelt on her, his weight pushing her down, making it hard for her to catch her breath, clamped a hand roughly over her mouth. 'Shut up. Don't say anything. Don't scream, don't . . . just don't . . .'

She kept her eyes screwed tightly shut. Said the same words over and over again like a prayer, a mantra: *Phil will be here soon, Phil will be here soon* . . .

Then the slapping started. More startling than painful. She felt him attacking her around her face. She quickly moved her hands to ward off the stinging blows.

'Bitch . . . bitch . . .'

He was using the words to build himself up. The slaps were getting harder, more forceful. Then she felt a punch to her chest. She grunted. That hurt. Then another one. Then another.

She had to do something, try to stop him before he lost control completely.

She opened her eyes, squinting at the expected blow. She looked up, saw Fletcher, his face twisted ugly with anger and hatred, his eyes almost closed. She glanced to the side. Saw the phone lying there. That would have to do.

She could move her left arm; he didn't have any weight on that. Good. She snaked it out, groped for the phone. Found it. Flinching from the slaps and punches, she gripped it, hefted it in her hand and brought her arm round as fast and as hard as she could.

The phone connected with the side of Martin Fletcher's head.

Not trusting to luck, she did it again.

He opened his eyes, looked at her. The anger had gone, replaced by shock. She didn't have time to think about his

169

reaction now; she just had to capitalise on it. So for a third time, roaring as she did so, she hefted the phone, putting all her strength behind it, feeling it crunch once more against the side of his head.

Martin Fletcher sat back, stunned. Marina used his confusion to wriggle her body free of his. She dashed to the door, tried to undo the lock, but her hands were shaking so much she couldn't get a grip on it. Instead she started banging.

'Help! Help me! Somebody help me! Help!'

'No . . . don't . . . don't do that . . . please . . .' Martin Fletcher's voice was small and fragile. He stayed where he was on the floor, rubbing his head where the phone had connected, from where blood was beginning to trickle.

Marina ignored him, kept shouting.

'No, please don't . . .'

His anger was completely gone now; just that tremulous, fearful voice in its place. She turned to him, the psychologist in her ascendant once more.

'Your power's gone, Martin. I'm not scared of you any more . . .'

He shuffled away from her, squashed himself into the corner of the room. Covered his head with his hands.

Then came the sound of banging on the door.

'Phil!' Marina shouted. 'I'm in here!'

There was more than one voice, muffled by the heavy wood. Marina took strength from the voices, managed to turn the lock. The door opened. There were two overseas students standing there, along with a maintenance worker. But no Phil.

She turned back to Martin Fletcher. He had stood up and was trying to get out of the window.

She rushed forward but he shouted, stopping her.

'Stay back or I'll jump!'

170

She stayed where she was. 'Come on, Martin, don't be stupid. You'll break your neck if you jump from here. Kill yourself.'

'I shouldn't have come here . . .' Martin Fletcher was crying. 'It's my fault. All my fault. I shouldn't have come here . . .'

'It's not that bad, Martin, come on. Let's talk about it . . .' She tried to edge closer to him.

He moved further out on to the ledge. 'I said stay back!'

Marina stayed where she was.

'There's nothing for me. Not now. Just prison, with the nonces and the paedos . . .'

'Martin . . .'

'Tell Gemma, tell Gemma . . . I loved her . . .'

'Martin, no!'

But her words fell on empty air. He had jumped.

'Be about another five minutes.'

Tony's words called Marina back to the present. She gave a grunted reply, took another drink.

And that had been that. Martin Fletcher had jumped, killing himself in the process. And Phil hadn't been there to help her. To save her. He had tried to contact her afterwards, when he had heard what happened. But she wouldn't take his calls. She also discovered that he had tried to contact her when her phone was switched off. He'd wanted to tell her that at best he would be late, and at worst he wouldn't be able to make it. There had been a murder and he had been called out to attend.

That didn't make it better. None of it made it better. She had needed him to be there for her and he had failed. That was all there was to it.

She couldn't help feeling like that. It was the Italian in her, and she couldn't escape her ancestry. If a man said he

171

would be there, he would be there. No question, no argument. And if he didn't, if he let her down, then she had every right to be mad at him.

For over a week she awoke screaming during the night, Martin Fletcher's face the final thing she would see before waking. Tony had been there for her every time. Safe, dependable Tony. A good man who looked after her when she needed it.

But she couldn't face the university again. Not after what had happened. So she had left and set up on her own.

Then she discovered she was pregnant. Tony was fine about it. Happy, even. She might have thought that the pram in the hall meant the death of romance, but Tony had never been the most romantic of people to begin with. It didn't even mean the death of his personal freedom, because he never went anywhere.

He was the one who insisted she drank only soft drinks. He had even talked about redecorating the upstairs study for the baby, suggested colour schemes, murals. He had gone so far as to pick up a Mothercare catalogue and ask her opinion of baby buggies. He was enjoying her new pregnancy and she wished she could join him. As it was it just scared her, sometimes even depressed her.

She did see Phil once more. He was waiting for her when she came out of work on one of her final days at the university. She saw him loitering behind a pillar and immediately turned the other way. He chased after her.

'Please, Marina, please . . .'

She hurried away from him.

'Please . . .'

She just kept walking, didn't even acknowledge him. Eventually he realised that his words were having no impact and that she wasn't going to slow down. He stopped, let her walk away. Out of his life.

She turned another corner, found herself in part of the campus that was almost deserted. She flattened herself against the rough concrete wall and cried her heart out.

Eventually she returned home. Tony had been watching *Question Time* on TV. She had walked past him, straight up the stairs, and gone to bed. And that was the end of Phil.

Until Ben Fenwick's call.

She looked out of the window once more.

'I'm dishing up,' Tony called from the kitchen.

Marina called back that that would be fine. She looked again at the slow-moving river. She thought of the dead women, the missing baby. And Phil. She tried to keep him out of her mind, but there he was. His eyes staring into hers.

'Have I got time for a shower?' she said.

'Well it's ready now . . .' Tony came into the living room, glanced at her. Saw how tired and careworn she looked. Smiled. 'Go on. Get your shower. I'll keep it warm.'

She managed to return the smile, then made her way up the stairs.

Trying to ignore the conflicting emotions running through her.

Her arm across her stomach all the time.

31

*H*e held the hen down forcibly on the square block of wood. Its eyes were wide and staring. Its beak was open but it was too terrified to make any sound. It couldn't call for help or raise an alarm. It just lay there, a heavy hand, callused, rough and dirty, not allowing it to move.

Cross-hatched with blade indentations, the wood was ingrained and stained from dried blood and matter that had seeped into it through years of use.

The hen looked up, made one last attempt to escape and then gave up, mutely accepting its fate. The blade of the axe arced through the cold morning air. Landed with a thud in the wood, slicing through bone, feathers, flesh and skin. Blood spurted upwards and outwards, a gory ejaculation. The hen's head lay there, staring sightlessly upwards. Its body twitched and jerked like a carnival sideshow geek, held firmly in place by the hand until its gyrations and spasms came to a halt.

He wiped his hands down the sides of his long overcoat. Left long streaks of blood and gore, dark against the dark material. Glistening. Soon the marks would sink into the fabric. Join the other old stains that made up the texture of the coat.

He straightened up, looked round. The house was on the edge of the river, just up from the muddy sands. The river moved slowly

174

towards the sea, flat and oily in the weak early-morning light. The
surrounding area was flat and bleak, the marshland stretching to
the sands, away to the river, the sea. The trees bare and spindly,
late autumn naked, like bone sculptures painted with dried, dark
blood.

He put the axe down, closed his eyes. Things were different this
morning. Because Hester was no longer a mother.

She had lain awake most of the night, staring at the baby.
She found it fascinating. Its little chest moving up and down.
Its fingers clasping and unclasping, grasping at invisible
creatures. Angels or demons, Hester thought. Its face con-
torting, mouth twisting and chewing. It was like a little
creature from a Disney cartoon. Not a real, dying baby, just
a pretend special effect.

Gradually it weakened until it could move no more. Its
breathing became so shallow it eventually stopped. Its face
and hands stopped twisting. Still fascinated, Hester put her
head on one side, leaned in close, tried to hear the last trail
of air leave its body. Its final sigh. She missed it. But it
changed nothing. The baby was dead.

It lay in the cot, still and lifeless. Like it needed its batteries replacing. Hester poked it, prodded it. It didn't move.
She prodded again, harder this time. It still didn't move. She
leaned in closer, used both hands this time. It rocked slightly
but returned to its original position when she took her hands
away.

So that was that. The baby was gone. Hester was no
longer a mother.

She felt something then, an ache inside, like something
had been taken from her and could never be replaced.
That feeling sparked another one. An older but similar
feeling of something being taken from her body. Cut from
her. She had tried not to remember it, fought against it

175

returning to mind. Failed. She had tried to keep it from her head for years because when it arrived it was so painful she couldn't cope and it spun her into a deep depression that could last for days, weeks even. She would just mope around the house, get no work done, make no food, just cry for what she had lost. And there was no cure. She had to ride it out.

She fought against it again. Pushed her hands between her legs, clamped down hard with her thighs.

'No . . . no . . . Don't come back, it's fine. It's going to be fine . . .'

Rocking backwards and forwards in the bed while she did it.

It was no good. The memory, long suppressed, was already there. Once again she could feel the guilt lance through her, the hurt and humiliation. Crawling naked along the floor, blood and other bodily secretions oozing from her, those cruel, hateful words still ringing in her ears. And all that pain, working through her body, pounding in her head. More than one person could stand. Certainly more than the person she used to be could stand.

Once again she remembered how that hurt and humiliation had driven her to the kitchen. Told her to open the drawer. In her mind's eye she could barely see what she was doing, tears had been streaming so hard down her face.

'Stop it . . . stop it . . .' Rocking in the bed, curled up in a foetal ball, hands still pushed firmly between her thighs. But sparked by the dead child lying next to her, those long-suppressed memories just kept coming. They wouldn't stop.

'Oh God . . . no . . .'

She was seeing her own hand once again open the drawer, reach for the knife . . .

'No . . .'

She clamped down harder, screwed her eyes tight shut.

176

'Make it stop . . . no . . . I don't want to . . .'

Take the knife, place it against her skin . . . Feel how cold and sharp the blade was against the soft flesh of her lower stomach. Push – tentatively at first – to see what it felt like, to see if it was a pain she could stand . . .

No words now, just muffled, inarticulate sobs.

But what was one more kind of pain against the rest that were swirling around inside her? She pushed, harder again. Felt blood trickle down her skin from underneath the path of the blade. It tickled, felt like it was nothing at all. She couldn't call it pain. Not really. Not compared to the rest of her.

She felt once again her hand grasping herself between the legs, pulling out the skin and gristle, stretching it out . . .

More sobs, more rocking, more shaking.

Pulling, stretching as far as it would go . . . willing this to be an end, hoping and praying that the pain would stop when she had done it . . .

Just get it over with . . .

And then, with the realisation that whatever she did couldn't be worse than what she was at present, she took the knife in her other hand and brought the blade swiftly down.

It didn't go as planned. It was harder than she had imagined, tougher to cut through. But she managed, sawing backwards and forwards. The pain was so much more intense than she had thought it would be. And the blood, so much blood . . .

She felt she might black out. But she didn't, she couldn't. Looking down, she saw the job half finished, that hateful piece of gristle hanging off her body, bloodied and mangled. With a surge of rage she plunged the blade in once again and, in a fresh bout of arterial spray, resumed cutting.

And then, eventually, it was off.

She held it in her hand, that offending piece of flesh now looking so small and harmless. Shrivelled and lifeless.

Hester had smiled then, out of relief or respite from the pain she couldn't remember. But she knew she had smiled.

Before she collapsed.

32

When Hester opened her eyes, she was standing in front of the cot, looking at the baby. Her memories receding, waiting for her husband to arrive.

What the fuck's the matter with you now, woman? What you standin' there like that for?

He was there. She quickly wiped her eyes, willed the last smoky trails of her memory to be gone. She didn't want him to know she was thinking of *that* again. Anything but that.

'The . . . the baby . . .'

What about it?

'It . . .' She knew she had to deflect her attention away from her memories. She took her hands from between her legs and pointed at the cot. 'It died . . .'

'It's dead,' she said again when he didn't respond.

I can see that.

'What . . . what should we do?'

Bury it.

So she did. As soon as it was time to get up, she climbed out of bed and took the now cold and stiffening body from the cot. She carried it outside and picked up a shovel. It was difficult. The cold, hard earth proved unyielding to anything less than her pickaxe. So she swung it down, over and over, until she had loosened enough ground to dig a shallow grave.

And there she stood, looking down at the empty patch of earth, the weak early-morning light casting a deep, spidery shadow into it. Hester and her husband were the only people around along the bleak, deserted coastline. She put the pick-axe down and picked up the tiny body in one hand. The sky was grey and oppressive, like it was pressing down on her, trying to squash her into the ground too. She took the blanket from the baby, knelt down and placed the body in the hole.

She stood up, looked down at it. And felt something. Again there was that emptiness, that strange aching feeling inside her. It seemed to well up inside her, building in her chest. She opened her mouth, put her head back. And out came a wail, as surprising to her as it was plaintive and heartfelt. It sounded like a wounded, cornered animal that could fight no more and knew it was about to die. The sound had a pained inevitability to it. She kept howling and screaming, her head back, her eyes closed. Just howling and screaming.

She didn't know how long she stood there. Time for Hester became elastic and stretched, then fluid and flowed away. Then finally solid once more as she opened her eyes. Her voice was silent, her throat raw. She felt empty, spent. She looked round. The baby's body was still lying in the grave. She picked up the shovel, began to heap earth on to it. Each spadeful fell with a flat, spattering crash until eventually the body was covered. She tamped and smoothed down the earth, stood upright once more.

The emptiness she had thought she felt wasn't there. The pain inside her that had caused her to wail was. It had returned when the baby had become obscured by dirt. In fact, it was growing stronger. Her earlier memories of shame and rage were now totally forgotten, or at least suppressed once more. This was a more immediate pain. This called for a direct resolution.

She was holding the dead, headless chicken.

Here, said her husband. *You'll know what to do with that.*

She couldn't take her eyes off the patch of smooth earth. 'The baby's gone . . .' she said once more. The words, she knew, were unnecessary, but she felt she had to say something. Fill in the gap between the earth and the sky.

'We were goin' to be a family,' she said.

Her husband was silent. She continued.

'The baby was goin' to make us a family.'

We'll get another one.

Hester smiled, eyes shining. 'Can we? Because that's what couples do when things like this happen. It's what makes them families.'

There's more on the list.

Another smile played across Hester's features. 'Have you got one in mind? Have you been out hunting again?'

I've got one in mind.

Hester could have kissed him, she was so happy.

'When can we get it?'

Soon. Now take that hen inside and get to work. I'm gettin' hungry.

Hester went inside. She gave barely a backward glance to the flattened mound of earth. She didn't need to now. That was in the past. Water under the bridge and all that. This was the present.

She had something to look forward to. She was going to have a baby. She was going to be a mother again.

She was going to be complete.

Part Two

33

'Morning.'

Clayton locked his car, strode across the car park, smiling at Anni. She tried to return the smile, found her facial muscles wouldn't allow her to be wholly successful. Instead she nodded. He reached her, stopped, his own smile evaporating. Scrutinised her face, caught her mood. Frowned.

'What's up?'

She dug deeper, crinkled the corners of her lips upwards. 'Nothing. Everything's fine.'

Clayton's smile returned, reassured. 'Good. Glad to hear it.'

It didn't take much, she thought, to make Clayton's world right again. But then he wasn't the deepest of thinkers. He was charming, though. And handsome. And she was sure she wasn't the first woman who had been taken in by him.

'So,' she said, still deciding what she was going to say, 'what did you do last night?'

He shrugged. 'This an' that. Went to the gym.' He smiled, as if at a private joke.

She nodded.

'What about you?'

'Surveillance. Brotherton.'

A shadow passed over his face. 'When?'

She shrugged, tried to keep her voice non-committal. 'Late on. Not been long off it. Should still be in bed.'

'Why aren't you?' he said, very quickly.

Anni smiled inwardly. Feeling guilty? she thought. Think I've come in to have a little chat with Phil? 'Suppose I should be. Still, got to make the most of the overtime, haven't you?'

He smiled again, clearly relieved to see she was thinking the way he was. 'Too right.'

She had come straight to work from the surveillance, telling herself she would get cleaned up at the station. She had sat in her car in the car park, waiting for Clayton to turn up. She didn't have anything specific planned to say to him, but she wanted to confront him before they went in, see what he said about escorting Brotherton's girlfriend back to the house last night. About what happened in the car.

'You have a good workout, then?'

Clayton looked puzzled. 'What?'

'The gym.'

'Oh yeah.' Another relieved smile. 'Yeah. Should join me sometime.' The smile took on another, unmistakable meaning. 'Work up a sweat together. Might be fun.'

Her turn to smile then. But not in the way he necessarily imagined. She opened her mouth to speak, the thought transferred directly to her lips, bypassing her brain. *Why don't you take Sophie?* she thought. *Give more than her facial muscles a workout.* But she stopped herself in time. She had nothing to gain from doing that. And everything to gain from keeping silent.

'I'll think about it,' she said.

'Good. I'm lookin' forward to it.' Clayton gave her another smile, as if he could imagine exactly what would

186

happen. This was the moment, she thought, when she was expected to squirm and look grateful. He should know her better than that.

He began walking towards the doors.

Anni held back. 'I'll join you in a bit. Just got something I want to check out first.'

He shrugged. 'Suit yourself.'

He turned, walked away. Smiling at another woman he passed.

Anni shook her head. He just couldn't help himself, she thought.

She paused, looked at the entrance, watched Clayton disappear inside. She tried to analyse her feelings, her reactions to Clayton's responses. She felt spurned, for sure. He had used her for sex, and while she had tried to pretend to herself that she was using him too, she had found herself hurt all the same. But if that was all it was, she would have confronted him about it, told him exactly what she thought of him.

No, it was something more. It wasn't just the fact that she had seen him with another woman. That woman was at the very least a witness in a multiple murder case. Possibly an accessory even. He was keeping things from the team. Things that could potentially harm the investigation. And she wasn't going to allow that to happen.

She had thought about the best way to deal with it, and had given him the chance to say something. He hadn't taken it; in fact he had lied to her, looked scared that she might have found him out.

Anni turned, walked towards the double doors, her mind made up. She would say something, but not yet. First she was going to find out everything she could about possible links between Clayton and Sophie Gale.

★

187

Phil looked round the room. The Birdies were there, Clayton; even uber-geek Millhouse had torn himself away from his computer screen, his eyes red-rimmed behind his black-framed glasses. Anni sat at her desk, Marina at hers. His gaze lingered on her a beat too long.

No sign of Fenwick.

The room was exactly as it had been the previous day. The board still dominated in front of the bar, the TV/VCR/DVD set up next to it. Phil scanned the room once more. Already the strain was beginning to show on his colleagues' faces. It wasn't so much that they were tired but that they were all feeling the collective responsibility of having to come up with a positive result, and quickly. And in the intense spotlight glare of the media and the public. Not to mention the police themselves. Catch the killer, find the baby alive. No pressure there, then.

'Okay,' he said with energy, trying to inject some adrenalin and focus into his group, 'let's make this quick and get out there. What have we got?'

'CCTV,' said DC Adrian Wren. He crossed to the TV, turned it on. Slipped a disc in, took the remote, sat down in the nearest seat. 'Came through first thing. Watch.'

The TV screen showed a grainy image of Claire Fielding's block of flats. It was night-time.

'Night before last,' said Adrian. 'Here's the time we want.' He froze the frame. It showed a figure moving up by the side of the apartment block. A tall, stocky figure wearing a buttoned-up overcoat and a hat pulled down, disguising its face. Adrian let the footage move again. The figure walked purposefully towards the entrance of the block, looked round, waited. Adrian froze the frame once more.

No one in the room spoke or moved. Their attention was focused solely on the TV. Phil was no different. He was thinking exactly what everyone else in the room was thinking: *This is him. This is our first glimpse of the murderer.*

'Big bloke,' said Clayton, the first to speak. He was voicing what everyone in the room was thinking: it could be Brotherton. A few nods, grunts of assent in return. They waited for the footage to resume once more.

'Time here?' asked Phil.

'Just after seven thirty,' said Adrian. 'Now look. He wants to get in but can't find a way. No key. So he waits.'

He clicked and pointed with the remote once more. The figure tried the double doors, then moved away and disappeared round the corner. A slight fast-forward, then he returned carrying three bags of shopping.

Phil frowned. 'We didn't find any shopping anywhere . . .'

The figure stayed around the side of the building. Eventually a woman approached the double doors, took out a key to enter. The figure detached himself and struggled towards her, making the bags look as heavy as possible. The woman turned, her hand keeping the door pushed open.

'It looks like he's calling to her,' said Adrian, 'asking her to hold the door.' He looked at the screen again. 'And she is, look. There. She's smiling.'

The woman held the door open for him. He seemed to be bobbing his head in thanks. The door swung shut behind the pair of them.

'And he's in,' said Adrian.

'Who's that woman?' said Phil. 'Have we spoken to her? Has she given us a description?'

Adrian gave him a look that managed to be both elated and exasperated. 'We've seen her. But we haven't spoken to her.' He paused the recording, rewound until she reappeared on the screen. 'Look again.' He pressed play. They all moved forward, staring intently.

'Fuck,' said Clayton.

'Exactly,' said Phil. 'Julie Simpson.'

It was like a collective sigh of exasperation had been heaved in the room. Phil shook his head. 'She let her own murderer in . . .'

'If it was Brotherton, she'd have recognised him,' said Clayton.

'Not if he was disguised,' said Anni. 'His face hidden.'

The room fell silent as they watched the screen.

Phil held up a hand. 'Shopping bags? We didn't find any in Claire Fielding's apartment . . . Have we checked the stairs, everywhere else in the flats?'

'He's going to reuse them,' said DS Jane Gosling.

'Very eco-friendly,' said Clayton.

'Right,' said Adrian, bringing the focus of the room back to him and the TV. He restarted it. 'So he's in. At seven thirty-eight.'

He fast-forwarded again. Stopped it when the double doors were opened.

'Nine ten,' he said. 'Chrissie Burrows going home. Fast-forward again . . .' He stopped the footage. Geraint Cooper was seen walking out. 'Nearly twenty-five to ten.'

'So we don't know what he does or where he goes,' said DS Jane Gosling, 'but we know he's in the building all the time. Biding his time. If he gets stopped, he's got his carrier bags as cover. He can look like he's making his way up the stairs.' She looked at the screen again. 'Probably on his way to the flat by this time. Probably inside. Doing what he set out to do. Let's see what happens when he comes out.' She ran the images through until she found the one she wanted. The double doors opened, the figure emerged. He was dressed exactly the same, still carrying the shopping bags from earlier.

'He must have had his equipment in the bags, his tools, disguised by groceries,' said Jane. 'And something to wrap

190

the baby in.' Her voice dropped. 'There'd be an awful lot of blood.'

'But he must have put the set dressing somewhere,' said Phil. He noticed Marina look up, smile slightly at his choice of phrase. He felt his cheeks reddening, looked round. No one else had noticed. He continued. 'I still want Claire Fielding's flat checked for groceries. And see if we can find which supermarket he was in beforehand. Check their CCTV.'

They returned their attention to the screen. The figure was moving briskly but unhurriedly round the side of the building and away down the street. They watched as he faded from view.

'We got any more footage?' asked Phil.

Jane pointed the remote at the screen once more. 'This. Taken from the camera on Middleborough, just past the roundabout.'

They all looked at the screen as the same figure hurried past on the pavement.

'Now watch.' She pointed the remote again, slowing the picture down. 'He turns round. Here.' She stopped the image.

They all leaned in closer to the screen. Phil, like the rest of them, stared hard at the image. Willed it to take shape as Brotherton, assume Brotherton's features, close their case for them. But it was grainy, indistinct. He sat back. Tried not to sigh aloud in frustration.

'Can we get this sharpened up?' he asked.

'We can try,' said Millhouse. 'Might take some time to do it properly. And money.'

Adrian turned the TV off.

'Thanks for your hard work,' said Phil. 'Appreciate it. What about phone records? Claire Fielding's? Brotherton's?'

'We're still waiting,' said Jane Gosling.

'Right.' Phil rubbed his chin, noticed where he had missed an area shaving this morning. 'Well it's not conclusive,' he said, 'but—'

The doors opened. Fenwick entered.

34

Phil stopped talking, stared at his superior officer.

'You've seen the CCTV, then?' Fenwick said, not moving forward.

'Just now,' said Phil.

'Then you should be in no doubt. You know what to do next. So get a move on.'

Marina stood up, turned to him. 'It's not Brotherton,' she said. All eyes were focused on her. The room held a collective breath.

Fenwick gave a bitter smile. 'Well it bloody well looks like him. Maybe he's got a twin brother. Has that shown up in the profile?'

Marina's face burned. 'I'm sure a few interesting things would show up in your profile.'

Fenwick took a step towards her. Phil moved between them.

'Sir, I'm the CIO here. Not you. Please leave.'

Fenwick didn't hide the anger in his eyes. 'Don't order me around. The Super wants Brotherton brought in. And so do I.'

'Brotherton is a liar and a manipulator,' said Marina, anger in the ascendant now. 'He's a bully who preys on women weaker than himself. But he is not a killer. He wants his victim alive so he can keep hurting her. And he would never kill his own child.'

'Really?' said Fenwick, shaking his head.

'Really,' said Marina. 'You want reasons? Here they are.' She spoke quickly, getting as much information out as she could in as short a time as possible. 'As I said before, and clearly you didn't listen, this type of abuser is essentially narcissistic. And childish. On the one hand he would resent the fact that his woman, or object or property or however he likes to think of her, is carrying something that will take the focus and attention away from him. But on the other hand, he wouldn't harm it because it's a part of him. And by extension, he wouldn't hurt the woman while she is carrying it.' She looked round at the faces staring back at her. 'Check with Claire Fielding's friends. I'm sure you'll find that the abuse stopped once she was pregnant.'

'Well perhaps he killed her accidentally,' said Fenwick.

'And what about the other three murders?' said Marina. 'Did he accidentally commit them too?'

Fenwick stared at her. Phil stepped forward, ready to physically remove the senior officer if necessary. Or to get in his way if he made a move on Marina.

Instead Fenwick managed another smile. 'We'll ask him when we bring him in.'

'He's speeding up. The time in between murders is getting shorter.'

'All the more reason to get a move on, then.'

Marina moved over to Fenwick, stared him right in the eyes. Fenwick flinched but remained where he was. 'So if there's another murder while you've got Brotherton in here, that's all right is it? You'll take responsibility for that?'

'Psychology's one thing, Marina,' Fenwick said, his voice as patronising as possible, 'physical evidence is another. Get him.'

He turned and left.

The silence that followed was louder than their arguing.

'And while that's happening,' said Marina, her voice thrown into the silence like a rock down an abyss, 'the killer's still out there.'

Her voice died away but it was clear her anger remained. All eyes turned from her to Phil. He was aware of their stares, knew he had to do something. Regain charge.

'Let's bring Brotherton in,' he said.

Marina turned to him. 'But Phil . . .'

'We've no choice. We've got reservations, but we've got nothing else at the moment. We bring him in.'

Marina turned away from him.

'But I want you working on him with me, Marina. If it's not him, I want him eliminated as soon as possible.'

Her back still to him, she nodded.

Phil sighed. Ignored the band round his chest. 'Right,' he said. 'Let's go get him.'

35

Hester looked round the house, pleased with what she saw.

She had tidied away the tools, hung the scythes on their wall hooks by the double doors, polishing and oiling their blades before doing so to keep them keen. She had then swept the living area and put the old tin bath central to the room so it was the first thing the baby saw when it entered its new home. She had done the dishes and tidied the kitchen area too. She had even got up on the ladders and restapled the black plastic sheeting over the rotten wood around the front corner of the house, to stop the wind and rain from getting in. Everything was in readiness.

She sat down on one of the old armchairs.

'A woman's work is never done,' she said, smiling to herself.

Everything was going to be fine. Her husband would be out soon, finding the next surrogate. Then he would bring her new baby back home. She giggled. Wasn't that a song? Sounded like a song. If it wasn't, it should be.

She put her hands in her lap. She didn't think about the baby that had died. Didn't allow herself to. It was buried now, out in the garden beside the pigs. She hadn't marked the grave. Didn't want anything to remind her. That was the past. And it didn't pay to dwell on the past. She knew that from bitter experience. Every time she started to think of the past, she started to feel sad. If she thought about the dead baby she might feel sad for it too. And once she started to feel sad for that, who knows what she would start thinking about next? Herself before the . . . before she became who she was; her sister . . .

Her sister. She tried not to think about her sister. Ever. She still missed her. They used to be close. But she was gone now. Long gone.

Hester stood up, knocked her fists against her temples to clear her mind, to stop her thoughts from wandering down that path again. Grunted with each punch. She needed to do something to take her mind off . . . off . . . off that.

She opened the side door, went outside into the yard. It was as she had left it. The axe lay next to the chopping block. Wood was piled by the side of the house, a tarpaulin stretched over it. Rusting engine and body parts from several old cars sat on the hard red earth, flaking away. Two old fridges, a magazine rack, a waterlogged sofa, some plastic crates, a pile of bricks. Scavenged items to be cannibalised and put to use. In their wired enclosure at the side by the fields, the chickens pecked. Further along, fenced off from the yard, were the pigs. She breathed deep, the scents mingling in her lungs. That was what home smelled like.

The day was cold and sharp, the wind like a shower of ice needles against her face. She stood at the back of the house, looked across the river. She saw the familiar sights of the port where the ships came from Europe and disgorged their cargo. Huge they were, the containers. She didn't know what was in them, had never given it a thought. Just watched them pull in, unload, pull out again. Back home to another country. Hester had never been to another country. She had never even been across to the port. Anywhere that wasn't her home was like a foreign land. But then a woman's place was in the home. It was her husband who went out and about.

She looked across the beach. The tide had gone out, leaving stones, mud and moss along the waterline. Small boats were left anchored and landlocked in the silt, their chains dripping seaweed and debris, their hulls mildewed and algaed.

Hester knew the beach. Knew where it was safe to walk, knew the spots where you could be pulled under. She had seen it happen. Someone walking a dog, throwing a stick. The dog, too fat, too slow, had run too far out, wouldn't listen. The mud and sand and water got hold of it, wouldn't let it go. By the time its owner turned up, there was nothing left of it. Hardly a mark to show it had ever been there. Just a muddy stick lying on the ground.

The beach had secrets. And it held them. Hester liked that. Because she had secrets too. And she knew how to hold on to them.

The houses that edged the marsh grass and sand looked sad and lonely. Made of wood and built on stilts, they looked like they had been left stranded when the tide went out. Like it had promised to come back for them but never had. So they stayed there, gently rotting.

Along from the beach houses, reached by a muddy dirt track, was the small caravan park. The vans were stationary, unchanged for at least the last thirty years. There had been houses there before, big old ones, but they had been knocked down, their foundations and outlines still visible where the grass had grown over them. Hester hadn't seen many people come to the park, whatever time of year it was.

The beach was bleak. And depressing. In weather like this it was windswept and cold. But to Hester it was home. The only home she had ever known. Ever would know.

She started to feel the cold then, creeping into her bones. She didn't mind it that much, was used to it really. But she still went back inside.

Because there was something she had to do. Before her husband appeared, before the baby arrived. Something she had to do alone.

She closed the door behind her and crossed to the stairs. Unbuttoning her clothes as she went.

36

The rain had started while they were on the A120 on the way to Braintree. Freezing and pounding. Phil was pleased to be in the car and not doing door-to-door legwork like the uniforms were still engaged in. That was something. Next to him, Clayton was unusually quiet. Phil didn't think anything of it. He had enough to worry about. He didn't even play any music.

'D'you think,' said Clayton as they approached the Braintree roundabout, 'that what Marina said was right?'

'What about?'

'What Brotherton did to Claire Fielding, he's been doin' that to Sophie?'

'Perhaps,' said Phil. 'Might not have started yet. But she works for him and lives with him, so it sounds like he's well on the way.' He turned, looked at Clayton. 'Why are you so bothered?'

Clayton shrugged. 'M'not. Just wondered.'

Phil smiled. 'Got a little thing for her, have you?'

'Shut up,' said Clayton, not laughing. He looked out of the window, said nothing more.

The rest of the journey passed in silence.

The scrap metal yard looked just the same but the

pounding rain lent it the air of a black and white photo. Something grim and depressing from a sixties documentary, thought Phil as he drove the Audi through the gates. He was expecting the place to be deserted because of the weather, but men were still working out in the yard, unloading trucks and lorries, filling containers with metal.

Phil looked up at the cab of the grab. Brotherton was again inside it, swinging the huge arm from one of the bays, taking handfuls of twisted metal and transferring them to the open container on the back of an articulated lorry. Phil pulled the car up at the side of the office, facing the grab. He knew Brotherton had seen him; now he wanted to see if he would make eye contact. Brotherton ignored him, continued with his work.

'Come on,' said Phil, 'let's go and give the happy couple the good news.'

He got out of the car, Clayton following silently, and made his way to the office. He knocked on the door and, without waiting for a reply, went straight in. Sophie Gale was sitting at her desk, talking to a middle-aged man who was standing next to her wearing a pair of filthy overalls. She was laughing at something the man had said while he was watching her prominently displayed breasts for any sign of a reaction. They both looked up as Phil and Clayton entered, the man reluctantly dragging his attention upwards.

'I'll be with you in a—' Sophie stopped mid-sentence. 'Oh. It's you. I'm busy, you'll have to wait.'

'Sorry to barge in,' said Phil with a smile. 'Hope you don't mind, but it's pouring out there.' He gestured to her with his hand. 'Please, don't mind us. Pretend we're not here.'

The man in the overalls looked between the two new arrivals and Sophie and picked up the undercurrent of tension in the room. Phil reckoned he had clocked them both for police straight away. He was used to that kind of reaction. He just stood waiting patiently.

Clayton on the other hand seemed decidedly fidgety. Nervous, even, Phil might have said.

Sophie paid out several twenty-pound notes to the man, gave him a receipt. All thoughts of her breasts gone, he couldn't get out of the door quick enough. Once he had closed it behind him, she turned to the two of them, keeping her eyes on Phil as she did so.

'So what is it this time?' Her expression as hard as her cleavage was soft.

'We need to talk to your boyfriend,' said Phil, keeping his eyes on her face. He glanced to the window as a figure made its way towards the door of the office. 'And here he comes now.'

The door slammed open. 'What the fuck is it now?' Brotherton's voice was more irritated than angry, although there was enough in it to demonstrate that it could reach anger levels very quickly.

Phil looked at the big man, wearing just a T-shirt despite the cold and rain, and wondered how best to proceed. Take it easy, he thought. Come in fast and hard and the results might not be pretty.

'We just need a word, Mr Brotherton.'

Brotherton opened his arms expansively. 'Then have one. And make it fuckin' quick.'

'Not here,' said Phil, his voice quiet but authoritative. 'Down at the station, if you don't mind.'

The anger that Brotherton had barely concealed suddenly surfaced. 'Don't mind? Don't fuckin' mind? Well I do fuckin' mind. So say what you want now and get out, or I'm callin' my brief.'

'We want to talk to you down at the station, please.' Phil kept his eyes on Brotherton. Made them calm and cold, the opposite of the big man's. 'The sooner we do this, the sooner you can get back to work.'

'I'm callin' my brief. I ain't sayin' another word till he gets here.'

'Fine,' said Phil, sighing inwardly. As soon as a suspect got lawyered up, there was nothing he could say or do. 'Get him to meet us at the station. I'm sure he knows the way.' He gestured to the door. 'Please?'

Brotherton turned to Sophie. 'Get Warnock on the phone. Now.'

'We'd like Sophie to come along too,' said Phil.

Brotherton turned back to him. His rage had just reached a new plateau, Phil could see. He was waiting to take it a step higher and then it would be released.

'We'd like a word with her too. So if you could both just come this way?'

Sophie looked between Phil and Clayton. She seemed to be about to say something to Clayton, but – and here Phil couldn't be sure – appeared to change her mind on seeing Clayton shake his head. Just a small, surreptitious movement, and Phil couldn't swear that he had seen it, but she fell silent after that. With a burning anger that seemed to match Brotherton's.

'I've got a fuckin' business to run! Who's goin' to look after that?'

'That's not our problem, Mr Brotherton. We need to talk to you both. Right now.'

Brotherton looked at the two men, then at Sophie. 'We'll see about that,' he said, and stormed out of the office, slamming the door as he went.

Sophie came out of her angry trance. 'Ryan, no . . .' She ran into the yard after him, but not without giving Clayton a hard, venomous look.

Phil looked at Clayton. 'Don't think she likes you,' he said.

'No,' said Clayton, shaking his head. Was that fear on his junior officer's face? Phil wasn't sure.

'What's brought that on, then?' he asked.

'No idea,' said Clayton. He took his eyes away from the yard, turned to Phil. 'You didn't say anything about her coming in for questioning too. Why?'

Phil shrugged. 'Why not? She lied for him the other night, remember? If we're going to break him down, she might be our best chance.'

Phil waited for a reply, but Clayton said nothing. From out in the yard they heard the angry screech of gears.

'I think we'd better get out there, don't you?'

They hurried into the yard. Suspecting that Brotherton might make a dash for his car and try to escape, Phil had blocked him in with the Audi. But Brotherton wasn't going to give in easily. Sophie was standing in the middle of the yard, screaming at the cab of the grab.

'Ryan, don't . . .'

The other workers had stopped what they were doing and were watching what was going on. Phil could do nothing as the grab, with Brotherton at the controls, dug into the bin of metal it was in the process of transferring to the lorry container, coming up with a huge handful of scrap. But instead of placing it in its intended target, with another angry squeal of gears it swung round towards the centre of the yard. To right where Phil and Clayton were standing.

Sophie screamed and ran out of the way. Phil looked up and saw the huge claw wavering overhead; Brotherton had swung it so quickly it was shedding smaller pieces of metal, joining the rain in falling. Phil was no expert, but he was sure the arm of the grab was swaying dangerously.

He tried to catch Brotherton's eye in the cockpit, call to him, make him stop, but the man's features were twisted with rage, his powerful arms working the levers furiously. Phil realised there would be no reasoning with him.

'Boss, run . . .'

Phil didn't need to be told twice. He grabbed hold of Sophie and pulled her back with him into the office. The other workers had scattered, most of them into the large storage area at the side of the office. He looked out of the window. Clayton had tried to follow him back inside but had been unable to. Phil stood watching helplessly as his DS was left standing underneath the grab, frozen, looking round for somewhere to run.

Phil heard the claws of the grab opening and the metal start to rain down in earnest. Clayton suddenly seemed to decide that the office was his best bet, and ran towards it. Fast. There was another squeal of gears: Brotherton was trying to swing the grab round, chase Clayton with the arm. The DS ran even harder.

Phil turned to Sophie, grabbed her by the shoulders. 'What's he doing?'

Sophie just stared, slack-jawed.

'Can't you get out there? Stop him?'

No response. Phil turned back to the window. Clayton was nearly at the office. He made it to the door, tried to open it. It was locked. It must have slammed shut behind Phil and Sophie.

Phil ran over to it, ready to open it. But he didn't reach it.

'No! Get away!'

Sophie was on his back, clawing at him, trying to pull him away from the door. She was surprisingly strong. Through the office window, Clayton saw what was happening, knew he wouldn't be able to get inside in time. Instead he turned and started running in the opposite direction.

Once he had gone, Sophie relaxed her grip. Phil turned to her. 'You're in trouble now, missy.'

Sophie just responded with a brief, vicious smile.

Phil turned back to the window. Clayton was running towards the storage area. It had huge doors on the front, big

205

enough to admit several articulated lorries at one time. Luckily all the doors were open. Clayton ran inside, diving the last few metres. Phil was sure he must have hit the concrete hard.

He looked at a door at the back of the office. 'Does this lead to the storage area?'

Sophie nodded.

Phil ran towards it, pulled it open, ran through. The storage area was a massive corrugated metal and poured concrete shed. Clayton was lying on the floor, nursing his shoulder.

As Phil appeared, the scrap crashed to the ground outside. Amplified by the corrugated metal walls of the storage area, it sounded like a Stockhausen symphony played by a band of drunken maniacs. Phil screwed his eyes tight, as if that would somehow stop the sound clashing inside his skull. Clayton took a deep breath, let it go. Sat up.

'You okay?' Phil shouted to compensate for the ringing in his ears.

Clayton nodded, then winced. 'My shoulder . . .' He flexed his arm, clenched his fingers into fist. Nodded. 'Least it's not broken.'

Phil crossed to him, helped him to his feet. They stepped out into the yard again, crunching twisted metal underfoot. Phil looked up at the cab of the grab. Brotherton was slumped forward, his head in his hands, the reality of his angry actions having sunk in. Phil couldn't be sure, but it looked like the big man was crying. At least he'd be no trouble for a while.

'What d'you reckon, boss?' said Clayton, still rubbing his shoulder. 'Attempted murder?'

'Reckon so,' said Phil.

Going to be one of those days, he thought.

37

Hester stood before the mirror. Naked. She hated looking at herself, couldn't bear the sight of her body, but sometimes she just had to. It was a compulsion, a need, and she had no choice but to obey it.

Her body was her diary. It catalogued who she had been, who she was, who she would be. Every scar, every cut, every modification. Every change just one more signpost on the road map of her life. It told her story, and although there were parts she hated to face, she still felt the urge to view them over again. She had to remind herself who she had been to fully appreciate who she was.

The mirror was upstairs, in front of the newly repaired plastic sheeting wall. It was cold, the heat from the Calor Gas heater and the wood-burning stove not reaching this far. She tried not to shiver as she ran her hands over her head and body.

Her hair had started to thin shortly after she first became a woman. When she was recovering from her night with the knife. She tried to grow it long at first, brush over the places where it was thinning, but eventually that got too much. So she shaved the lot off and wore a wig. Long and black, thick and matted. Sometimes, if she was at home by herself, she didn't bother with it, just kept her bald head uncovered. But she didn't do that for too long because it began to confuse her and make her depressed. If she was a woman, she should have hair. That was all there was to it. So she wore the wig. It was old and tatty, but she restyled it regularly, brushing the knots out and trying to cover the bare patches. Usually she managed, but sometimes she couldn't and had to wear her outdoor scarf indoors just to keep it in place.

Her hands left her head, came down the sides of her face. She kept it shaved, as smooth as possible. That was the way her husband liked it. And there was no excuse. There was no shortage of blades in the house.

Then over her shoulders and down her chest to her breasts. She knew she was touching her nipples because she could see herself doing it in the mirror, but she couldn't feel it. She pushed harder, stuck her nails into the flesh until it went white. But she still felt nothing. That dark feeling came over her again. She knew it would once her hands were on her tits. It always did.

It reminded her of the night with the knife and what happened afterwards. She had taken the blade to herself when she could no longer bear his words. His voice. That taunting, raging voice. Their father's voice. Telling Hester what he was, what he wasn't. Hitting him. Hurting him. And then turning to Hester's sister. Smiling. Because she was the special one. He made no secret of that. He did special things with her, from when she was tiny. Hester hated him for it. He hated what the man did to his sister. But even worse, he hated the fact that he didn't do it to him. Because Hester wasn't special the way she was. And never would be.

His sister hated her father so much she tried to leave and didn't care how she did it. She got away. But Hester stayed. Then it all changed. She couldn't remember exactly what happened. Every time she thought back, it got hazier and hazier. Like she had wiped it out of her mind. But she knew some things. Her father disappeared. And then her husband appeared. And they became so close that she began to hear him in her head. His voice in her head all the time. Like he wasn't just next to her, he was inside her, part of her. She liked that. That was what love was supposed to be.

She remembered something else too. Something he had said when he first appeared and saw her naked: *If you want to be a woman I'll make you a fuckin' woman.* And he did.

Hester was taken to see people who knew what to do with bodies, how to make them different. They had done things to themselves and proudly displayed their work to her. Bodies shaved, tattooed, branded. Pieces, sometimes important ones, missing and parts stuck on. Metal lizard spikes implanted in their arms or steel balls under their skin. Tongues cut and forked like snakes.

They took her out, introduced her to others. Took her to clubs where she watched people on stage having their mouths and eyelids sewn up, getting cut and stitched, being whipped, suspended over the audience by hooks through their skin and bleeding on the watchers below. People hurting themselves for other people's amusement. For the first time in Hester's life, surrounded by freaks and outsiders, the mutilated and the modified, she felt like she belonged.

But it wasn't to last. What she needed doing was relatively easy. Her own handiwork was cleaned up and she was given breasts. It wasn't a very good operation, happening as it did in the back room of a specialist club in east London, but it worked. She was asked if she wanted a vagina instead of the scarred gash she had created, but her husband decided that wasn't necessary. One hole was enough for him, he said.

And then it was back to the house, and life with her husband.

And here she was. She ran her hands over the stubby,

scarred area at the tops of her thighs, between her legs. Where Hester should have had a womb, there was just an aching, painful void. She put her hand once more over where her heart should be, felt only insensitive scar tissue. Barren. Just a cruel joke of a woman.

The darkness was beginning to fall inside her once more. She closed her eyes. She couldn't allow it. Not now, not today. Because today was special. Today was the day that her new baby arrived.

She managed a smile at the thought. The new baby.

Hester closed her eyes, the earlier blackness disappearing. It would soon be time for her husband to go to work. Then she would get things ready for when he came back. She would dress up in her good frock, make a nice dinner. Might even have a bath. Get herself all nice and prepared for the baby. Ready to be a proper mother. Because that was what it had all been for. The journey she had taken, the pain she had endured. All for this. To be a proper woman. A proper mother.

A proper family.

38

'Right,' said Phil, 'earpiece and throat mic.' He tucked the wire behind his ear, pointed to the desk Marina was sitting at. There was a receiver and a microphone built into a console in front of her. 'Comes through here. You want to talk to me, flick that switch. I'll hear you, Brotherton won't.'

Marina managed a small smile. 'I do remember, you know.'

He paused, looked at her. She could see from his smile that her response had jolted him out of his professional mode for a few seconds, broken through that thin veneer that separated their feelings from their ability to function as work colleagues. She didn't want that to happen. Certainly not now.

'Just get it over with,' she said. 'And we can move on.'

'Words to live by,' said Phil.

Marina didn't answer him.

'So,' he said, changing the subject, 'same neurolinguistic interview techniques we used last time?'

'Why not?' said Marina. 'Stick with what works.'

She nodded, looked down once more at the folder before her, trying to familiarise herself with what was in there even

though she had gone over it countless times and was as prepared as she could ever be. To an extent it didn't matter what
was in the file or what notes she had made. She had to follow
the interview, be in the moment, ready to interject only if she
thought Phil had missed something or felt a line of enquiry
could be pursued further.

'Look,' said Phil, 'before, with Fenwick . . .'

'Let's not think about it,' she said, looking up.

Phil nodded. 'Right. He's a tit at the best of times. Even
worse under pressure.'

She smiled. 'I agree.'

The observation room was functional. The desk was
anonymous, blond wood and metal that could have come
from any office in any enterprise park in the country. It was
a clone of the one Marina had had in her university office.
The walls were two tones of beige, the carpet industrial grey,
matching the filing cabinet. There were two office chairs,
black, adjustable and with arm rests, both well used.
Overhead strip lights provided illumination; a desk lamp
added more directed lighting. The room was cramped and
airless but not oppressive; for one thing, the two-way mirror
into the adjacent interview room acted like a window. But
the main reason for the lack of stuffiness was the function of
the room itself. There was a crackle of energy round the
walls that came not just from the nylon carpet, but because
whoever used the room did so for the sole purpose of controlling the lives of others. And with that control came
power, which in its turn bestowed superiority. It could
become a rush, a thrill, if allowed to. Marina could imagine
why so many police came across as arrogant.

But not Phil, thankfully. Beside her, he busied himself
with his wires and battery pack. He wasn't having much success. Every time he pushed the pack down into his
waistband, his earpiece pulled loose.

'Bugger . . .'

'Oh, give it here.'

Marina stood up, took the earpiece from his fingers. She stood directly in front of him and fitted it into his ear, holding it there with two fingers. 'Plug it in now,' she said.

Phil reached round to the small of his back, pushed the battery pack into the waistband of his trousers. Marina adjusted the wire behind his ear, smoothing it down the side of his neck. She was aware of his breathing, of the warmth of his skin. She wasn't aware that she had stopped breathing.

Phil was saying nothing, his eyes on her. She knew that without looking at him. She couldn't look at him. Not now. Not yet. Her fingers were trembling. She smoothed the collar of his shirt, his jacket. Stood back.

'There. That's better.'

Phil didn't move. Marina didn't either. The two of them stood before each other, Marina still avoiding eye contact. She should pull away, sit back down. Look at her notes. She knew that. She stayed where she was.

'Marina . . .'

Phil put a hand out towards her. She wanted so much to let him touch her. So much. And to reciprocate that touch. Despite everything that had happened between them. But she couldn't. From somewhere deep within she found a reserve of willpower, pulled away. Phil withdrew his hand.

'Not now, Phil. Concentrate. Get in there and do what you're best at.'

He nodded. 'How do I look?'

'Like a policeman who's just had a fight in a scrap metal yard.'

'Did I win?'

She smiled. It was tense, tight. 'On points, perhaps.'

'Well.' He smiled. It was equally tense and tight. 'That's all right then.'

Phil closed his eyes, took a deep breath, another. Anchoring himself, she knew. Zoning in for what he had to do.

'Right.' He opened his eyes. There was no trace of the earlier Phil, Marina's ex-lover still conflicted over the end of their relationship. There was only Phil the copper. A dedicated professional with a job to do. And whatever needed to be said between them could wait.

'Right,' he said. 'Let's go.'

39

Brotherton was slumped in his chair, legs spread out underneath the table. He looked broken, defeated even before Phil had started in on him.

The room was small, barely big enough for the chairs and the table, and despite the efforts of the cleaners, it still smelled of unclean bodies and filthy minds, of stale sweat and desperate actions, of human waste in all its forms. Air, like hope, seemed to have been sucked out of the room.

Three of the windowless walls were covered with acoustic tiles and painted a depressingly institutional shade of grey-green; the fourth wall held a mirror. If Brotherton had looked up, he would have seen his own reflection. The door was heavy and grey. One overhead strip, quietly fizzing like a dying fly, threw out shallow, flat light. The kind of light that depressed Phil, reminded him of what he had said to Marina about the aftermath of murder scenes and empty theatres, places from which the life had departed. This, he knew, was deliberate. Just as the observation room was all about power, this was the opposite. It was all about powerlessness, help-lessness.

He sat down opposite Brotherton, trying not to be aware of Marina watching him. He looked down at the table. It was scarred and marked, layer added upon layer like recidivist geological striations: names both written and carved into the surface, protestations of innocence and sometimes love, anonymous attempts to grass up members of the criminal community, experiences of the police in general and certain individuals in particular. Phil always checked for his own name and the context in which it appeared. It was a little slice of immortality – at least until it was scribbled over – and he took a perverse pride in the fact that he had affected someone to such a degree that they wanted to tell the world about it. Even if they did just want to tell the world that he was a cunt.

He looked at Brotherton, who kept on ignoring him. He took a deep breath. Looked at Brotherton once more.

'Okay, Ryan,' he said, looking straight at him, hoping to establish eye contact, 'this is not a formal interview under caution. We won't be recording it or anything like that. Not just yet. This is just a chat between you and me.'

Brotherton shrugged. 'I've got nothin' to say to you.'

Phil smiled. 'No. You let your actions do the talking.'

Brotherton looked up. 'What's that supposed to mean?'

Phil leaned forward. 'Oh come on, Ryan. Chasing my DS round the yard with the grab? Dropping a whole load of metal on him? I mean, that's imaginative, if nothing else.'

Brotherton shrugged, but with the compliment, Phil felt the man's attitude was thawing slightly. He pressed on. 'You didn't need to do that, you know.'

'No?'

'No. No need at all. Why didn't you just talk to us? Talk to me.'

Brotherton's eyes narrowed. 'What d'you mean?'

'What do I mean? You know what I mean.' Phil smiled conspiratorially, leaned forward over the table. 'Man to man.'

Brotherton eyed him quizzically. Phil pressed on.

216

'Ryan, I kept saying to you about Claire, you know, it's a difficult situation, I appreciate that, but let's have a chat. And if you've got something to tell me, tell me. But you insisted Sophie was there all the time.'

'What would I have to tell you?'

Phil smiled. 'Come on. You're not the first person to have woman problems. And I doubt you'll be the last. Happens to all of us.'

Brotherton snorted a laugh. 'Even coppers?'

Phil shook his head, sighed. 'Like you wouldn't believe. And not so different from your troubles, either.'

Brotherton seemed interested now. Phil looked at him, the expression on his face showing uncertainty as to whether to tell him any more, share any more intimacies with someone on the other side of the table. He leaned in even closer to Brotherton. Before he spoke he looked round, as if checking for eavesdroppers, and lowered his voice.

'All I'm saying, Ryan, is I know what it's like. Sometimes you have to . . .' He balled his hands into fists. 'You know what I mean?'

Brotherton's face was a battlefield of warring emotions. Phil knew he wanted to believe him, hear him talk further, find a kindred spirit, someone who might be able to understand him, help him in this hell of a mess. But he was naturally wary. Phil pressed on.

'I had a girlfriend,' he said. 'My last girlfriend, actually. And you know what it's like. Everything's great in the beginning, you can do no wrong, always there for you, wanting to please you . . . and then they start, don't they? Wanting to change you. You don't dress well. Don't look right. They don't like your friends. You know what I mean?'

Brotherton nodded. 'Yeah. Know exactly what you mean.'

'And then they stop wanting to please you. And before you know it, you can't do anything right, can you?' Phil

217

shook his head in despair. 'I mean, why do they go out with you in the first place if everything you say or do is so wrong and they want to change it?'

'Claire was like that,' said Brotherton. 'Just like that. So fuckin' . . . exasperatin'.'

Phil smiled knowingly. 'Yeah. Exactly. And what can you do? Sometimes you just get so . . .' He flexed and unflexed his fists, grimaced as if in anger. 'You have to, don't you? It gets to you.'

Brotherton sat back slightly, wary again. 'You've never done that. Hit a woman.'

'Really?' Phil gave another look round, another check for eavesdroppers, lowered his voice even further. 'Like I said. You're not the first or the last. You're not the only one.'

A kind of hope sprang up in Brotherton's eyes. Cautious, but wanting to believe what Phil was saying. 'Yeah?'

'Yeah,' said Phil, as if imparting a particularly deep truth. 'Not the only one in here, either. Tell you the truth, loads of blokes in here hate prosecuting cases like yours. Waste of resources when we could be doing proper police work. Like catching paedophiles or real villains.'

Brotherton nodded. 'Absolutely right.'

'Way it should be, isn't it? Only natural. Course, you can't say that now. Political correctness and all that. They'd have you for it.'

Brotherton shook his head. 'Don't I know it. You can't do anythin' these days. Don't know what the fuckin' world's comin' to.'

Phil sat back, swallowed the smile. 'Tell me about it.'

He had him.

40

*I*t was nearly time.

He had parked in just the right place – not too near to the entry of the estate, not far enough in to attract suspicion from residents. Not that they bothered him too much. He could have walked into every house on this estate if he had wanted to and stolen something from each of them without them realising. The kind of people that lived in these types of houses were so intent on looking out for leering tabloid monsters that they missed the ones already in their midst.

Broad daylight. Or as broad as the grey November sky would allow. The time when most home invasions occurred.

He switched the engine off, waited. He made a mental plan of what he would do, based on his surveillance and research, what obstacles to look out for, random factors to try and account for. He checked he had everything he needed in his bag on the passenger seat. Satisfied, he sat back. Thought himself into the right frame of mind.

This was being done hurriedly. Normally he would spend weeks – months, even – planning something like this. But he didn't have months or weeks. Or even days. He needed another baby now to replace the other one. That wasn't important to him, though. It was all about the hunt. The chase. The kill. That was all that mattered. Everything else was justification. Excuse. This was everything.

He made one more inventory, one more mental check, and was ready.

He tucked the hammer up the sleeve of his overcoat, got out of his vehicle.

Walked up the road.

He could smell his prey on the wind.

41

Graeme Eades could barely keep his hands steady on the steering wheel he was so excited.

A whole afternoon with Erin. Not just a snatched lunch break in an empty storeroom or a quick fumble in the front seat of his Seat parked up in a shadowed corner at the back of an out-of-town supermarket car park. No. Actually the whole afternoon. Together.

He pulled up in front of the Holiday Inn, switched off the engine. The hotel was outside Colchester at Eight Ash Green, laid out in what Graeme supposed was a low-level American ranch style, holding the usual business-traveller facilities. He knew this from arranging stays there for associates. But that didn't bother him now. He wouldn't be using the gym or the pool or going for a spa treatment. For one thing he wouldn't be there long enough, and for another, his time was all accounted for. And it was sufficiently out of the way of the town centre so he wouldn't run the risk of bumping into anyone.

He got out of the car, grabbing the carrier bag from the passenger seat, locking the door behind him. He had paid a visit to Ann Summers before leaving the town centre, stocking up on clothing and accessories to make his afternoon as memorable as he had imagined it would be. Stockings, a basque, crotchless panties, all in Erin's size. He had checked when she hadn't been looking. Then there were the accessories. Creams, lotions, oils, toys . . . he had gone to town. Once inside he hadn't been able to stop himself. Just had to have everything. The girl behind the counter had looked taken aback and he'd replied with a wide grin. She wasn't bad either, he had thought. A bit short, perhaps, and could do with losing a few pounds, but he wouldn't have said no. Could just imagine using some of the stuff he was buying on her. Imagine her face as she came . . . He knew what she was thinking when she was ringing up the prices for his items and bagging them up. *Someone's going to be lucky.* That's what. The thought of that made him grin all the more. He had winked at her as he took the carrier bag. She hadn't returned it but that didn't matter. He didn't need her and had forgotten about her as soon as he left the shop. He had Erin to think about. And Erin was all he needed.

Erin. He crossed the car park to the front of the hotel. Erin. He couldn't believe his luck. When she'd started in his company he hadn't been able to take his eyes off her. None of the men had. And probably a few of the ladies if they were honest, thought Graeme with a lascivious smile. She was young, brunette and well curved. And she liked everyone to know it. He didn't know what she actually did, something in accounts, perhaps, but he knew the effect she had on him. He had watched her move around the office, her hips rolling, her breasts held high, a smile for everyone. That was it, he thought. She just looked so happy to be there, so happy to be herself. Her smile saying she would be up for anything as long as it was fun.

Not like Caroline at home. She had changed, and really quickly. Big and fat and complaining all the time of aches and pains. And her hand constantly out. Money for the hairdressers. For new clothes. A new fucking car, for Christ's sake. He had bought them all, just to keep her quiet. He thought the arrival of a new child was supposed to be a joyous affair, but this was nothing like that. He was glad to get away from her. And what a relief to be with someone who was totally the opposite of that.

He couldn't believe how easy the whole thing had been. How it had come together. Erin had been in his office one day, bringing in something for him to sign, bending over the desk so he got a good shot right down her cleavage, and before he could stop himself he had blurted out: 'God, I bet you're good in bed.'

Before he even had time to turn red she had replied: 'I am. Want to find out how good?'

And that had been that. Not an office romance, because romance had very little to do with it. Just lust. Sex. Pounding, thrusting, hard sex. Anywhere and everywhere they could. At any opportunity. It was brilliant. And so much cheaper than paying for it. But Graeme wasn't stupid. He knew that there was a chance she might not be doing this if he wasn't her boss. She had already mentioned promotion a few times. Graeme didn't mind. Anything he could do to help. Anything that would keep her there longer.

He entered the foyer, went up to reception. 'Room booked for Mr and Mrs Eades,' he said to the young girl behind the counter. She checked her screen.

As she did so, Graeme caught sight of himself in the mirrored surface in front of him. He had lost a little weight since Erin. Started dressing better too, even getting his hair cut more fashionably. He looked again at the image. But he still couldn't hide the fact that he was, essentially, a man tottering on the brink of middle age, doing what he could to turn back time. Oh well, he thought, chasing the image away and getting ready for some fun, at least he hadn't bought a red sports car.

The receptionist came back from the screen with the details, asked him to fill in a card. Told him what time breakfast was, ran through the list of amenities the hotel provided. Graeme wanted to scream: *I don't care about your fucking breakfast! I'll only be here this afternoon to fuck the brains out of one of my employees! After that I'm gone!* But he didn't. Instead he listened patiently and smiled when she had finished. Took his key card and went to the room, where he laid all his purchases out on the bed and let his fevered imagination start to run riot.

As he took objects from their packaging and inserted batteries, checked they were working, a thought crossed his mind. He was supposed to have gone home this afternoon. Caroline knew he was leaving early. He had promised to do the supermarket run, as she was too heavy to move. Or too fucking lazy. Still had time to meet her friends for lunch. That he paid for.

Ah well, he thought. She'll just have to wait.

He turned the pink jellied vibrator on, felt it buzzing in his hand and smiled. Perfect, he thought, checking his watch, and adjusting his trousers to accommodate the pleasantly uncomfortable bulge that was growing there.

Come on, Erin, he thought, *I'm waiting for you . . .*

42

C aroline Eades was beyond tired.
    She couldn't even be bothered to get dressed today;
just sat on the sofa, staring at the TV. She usually had something planned for the day: yoga or lunch with her young
friends, or shopping for the family. Today it was a hairdress-
ing appointment. But she had phoned up and cancelled. Just
couldn't face making the effort to get dressed.

It had hit her when she woke up. Like a huge mattress had
smashed into her and knocked her back on to the bed. She
had forced herself to get up, help her children off to school,
but flopped back down afterwards. And from then on she
couldn't move. It was even worse than she had felt in the
first three months of pregnancy. Not surprising, lugging all
that extra weight around. And the heartburn . . . like she had
been eating curries for a week.

So that was it for today. On the sofa with a cup of tea and
daytime TV for company. *Loose Women*, or *Hormonal Harpies*,
as she called it, was on. All of them shouting over one
another, vying for attention. Making risqué remarks to John
Barrowman while he responded in kind. It wore her out just
watching it. She turned over. *Diagnosis Murder*. That was
more like it. She started to watch it but found even that

simple plot was too much for her to follow. She couldn't be bothered to try any more channels so she flicked the TV off with the remote.

She took a mouthful of tea. It tasted awful. She had been able to manage coffee, but her taste for tea came and went. She hadn't realised just how much sharper her sense of smell had become. Everything heightened, accentuated. Things she used to like, or at least not notice, now repulsed her. Like the smell inside the fridge or Graeme's aftershave. Even the smell of the tea made her gag.

She leaned back, closed her eyes. Tried to relax. But she couldn't. No matter how she positioned herself, which way she shifted, she just couldn't get comfortable. She looked around. Her usually spotless house was becoming messy. Graeme wouldn't pay for a cleaner, said it was a waste of money when she was doing nothing all day. But she didn't even have the energy to get up, never mind clean up.

Dinner needed making, she knew that too, and she had no one to help her with it. And no food in the house again. At least Graeme had said he would go to Sainsburys on the way home. He hadn't seemed happy about it but then he didn't seem happy about anything these days.

She checked her watch. He should have been back by now. He'd said he was taking the afternoon off. He had been getting increasingly distant lately. Spending more time at work, snapping at her when he was at home. And he had started dressing better, too. Got a decent haircut. Lost a bit of weight. Those thoughts about an affair went through her mind again, but she didn't have the energy, or the courage, to face them fully.

She took another sip of tea, grimaced. Awful.

She replaced the mug on the coffee table, sat back, checked her watch again. He was late. But just at that moment, when she was allowing all sorts of ridiculous fantasies about his whereabouts to run through her mind, she heard the front doorbell. She sighed. He must have forgotten his house key. Or had too much shopping and wanted her to carry it in. Idiot. In her state. But it was the kind of thing he would do.

Prising herself up from the sofa, she managed to waddle slowly from the living room into the hall. The bell rang again.

'Yeah, all right, I'm coming . . .'

She reached the door, turned the knob to open it. And thought: Graeme wouldn't have forgotten his house keys; they're with his car keys.

She opened the door fully, looked up. It wasn't Graeme.

And then the hammer came down.

Her last thought: she wished she had gone to that hairdresser's appointment.

43

'I shouldn't be here, Clayton. You know that. You promised me.'

Sophie Gale's voice was low, hissing. She leaned across the table, kept hard, unblinking eye contact with Clayton. She was angry, he could see that. But he knew that underneath the anger there was something more. He just didn't know what.

'Yeah, I know. But what can I do? You've got to come in if the boss says so. You know the score. Look,' he said, leaning across the table also and keeping his voice low, though where hers had been hissing, his was controlled, 'don't worry. And don't panic. That's the main thing. Main two things.'

Sophie Gale said nothing in reply. Just stared at him, her eyes no less hostile, her arms wrapped tightly around her body. She stayed like that, staring, for what seemed to Clayton like several hours but was probably only seconds.

Clayton and Sophie were in the twin of the room Phil was talking to Ryan Brotherton in. The same drab colour, depressing light, scarred table, absence of hope. There was no mirror, though. That, thought Clayton, was something.

He had asked to conduct the interview on his own, wanted to press on with the inquiry. But he knew the rules.

He had been attacked while working on a case. There was a charge of attempted murder against his attacker. It was now deemed personal and there was no place for him on the investigation. Standard procedure. But still, he had hoped.

So he had sneaked in, tried to have a quick word before Anni arrived to take over. Out of all of the team it would have to be her, he thought. He knew that time was tight and he and Sophie would have to come up with something plausible very quickly.

'I am so fucked,' said Sophie.

'No you're not,' said Clayton. But the phrase sounded weak even to him.

'Don't be an idiot,' she said. 'If I say Ryan was at home with me the night his ex got killed and you find out he wasn't, I'll get done by you lot. But if I tell you he was out that night, then he'll have me. Either way, it's not pretty.' She sat back. 'Thanks a lot.'

Clayton felt himself begin to get angry with her. And he knew that his anger had its roots in the same place as hers: fear. 'Look,' he said, his arms out wide, imploring, 'it's not just you, is it? It's me as well. Whatever comes out about you comes out about me. And then we're both fucked. And now thanks to your shithead boyfriend I'm off the case. So I shouldn't be here and we haven't got long. We've got to make this work for us. Think. We've got to sort this together.'

Silence descended once more.

'This is what I think,' said Clayton, speaking quickly. 'This is what we should do. I go to my boss with what you said about Brotherton going out the night Claire Fielding was killed.'

She began to interrupt but he silenced her with a hand.

'Just listen. I tell him all that. But I also say that you're terrified of him. You didn't want to tell me and only want it used on the condition that Brotherton be charged and kept inside. No bail. Because . . . because your life's in danger.' Clayton sat back, pleased with himself. 'That'll work. Yeah. What d'you think?'

Sophie kept staring at him. 'And where's the risk to you, then?'

Clayton frowned. 'What?'

'You said this is a risk to both of us. I don't see no risk to you there. Just me.'

Clayton sighed. 'It's the best I can think of.'

'Well you'll have to think better. Because if I say that and they don't keep Ryan in, I'm fucked. No job, nowhere to live. Not to mention what he might do to me.'

'If he does anythin' he'll be back in custody.'

She rolled her eyes, threw her arms up. 'Oh great. And I'll be in the bleedin' hospital.'

'Sophie, it's the only way out.'

'For you, maybe.'

'Well have you got any better ideas?'

'Yeah.'

Clayton didn't like the nasty light that had started to glow in Sophie's eyes. 'What?'

'I tell them everything. Not you, your boss. About the informin' I used to do. All the intel I supplied. The convictions that led to. Remind them what a good source I was.' The light got nastier. 'Then I tell them you remembered me from those days, came to see me. Wanted me to keep quiet about the freebies you used to get. But it wasn't just freebies, was it?'

Clayton said nothing.

'No,' Sophie continued. 'You weren't content with that. You wanted to run the show as well, didn't you? Keep your friends supplied. Strangers, too. That was you, wasn't it? PC Pimp.'

'Shut up . . .'

230

'Yeah. That's what you came to see me about. Because freebies, that's nothing. But running your own little business empire . . . I don't think that'll go down too well. And I'll tell them. That you said you'd keep my name out of it if I kept my mouth shut. That you even asked for a blow job for old times' sake.'

'That's not—'

Sophie smiled. It wasn't pleasant. 'It's the only way out,' she echoed, mirroring his words back at him.

Clayton sighed, sat back. 'This is so fucked.'

'Ain't it though.'

'We have to think of something. Fast.'

The room, small already, began to feel overpoweringly claustrophobic.

They stared at each other.

Neither of them could think of anything to say.

44

'You know,' said Phil, as if imparting an intimate secret to an old friend, 'you didn't have to do all that. With the grab and the metal.'

'No?' Brotherton looked genuinely interested.

Phil was working Brotherton hard, but not letting the other man know what he was doing. The technique was working well. He had seen hardened criminals respond to it. Even coppers who had strayed over the line and ended up on the other side of the table responded to it. And they had been trained not to.

But Phil didn't want to get cocky. He stayed focused, concentrated. He still had a long way to go.

'No,' he said. 'If you'd wanted to do Clayton or me some damage, why didn't you just hit one of us?'

'That would have been assault, wouldn't it?'

'Yeah, but it could have bought you time; you could have got away. And then a good lawyer could have argued it out later. Said I was harassing you or something.'

'Yeah?'

'Yeah.' Phil thought it best not to mention the attempted murder charge now hanging over Brotherton's head. He didn't want to break the flow. 'You could have done that. I mean,' he said, 'you've got the muscles for it.' He waited a few seconds, let his words sink in, then continued. 'I like to think I keep myself in pretty good shape, but to get the kind of body you've got, you must be very dedicated. That's not just from working in the yard, is it?'

'Nah,' said Brotherton, unconsciously flexing his biceps. 'I work out.'

'Thought so. How long have you been doing that, then?'

Brotherton's eyes looked to the right. 'Since my early twenties. About fifteen years?'

'That is dedication. Whereabouts?'

Again a look to the right. 'Used to work out in the leisure centre on the Avenue of Remembrance. But now it's the gym up in High Woods.'

'Good place. I like a good workout but I'm between gyms at the moment. Just moved house.' He laughed. 'But I'm nowhere near your league. What's High Woods like? Would I like it?'

Brotherton frowned, his eyes falling down to the left. 'Yeah. It's a gym, you know? Leisure facilities, they've got a pool, sauna.' He nodded. 'Not as bad as some places, not as cliquey. But you know. Gym's a gym when it comes down to it. You get out what you put in.'

Phil nodded, apparently giving the matter some thought. 'Good.' He put his hand behind his back, moved it up and down. There was a knocking on the mirror.

Brotherton jumped. Phil affected to.

'Sorry,' he said. 'They must want me. I'll be right back.'

He got up and left the room.

Marina was waiting for him when he entered the room.

'Did you get all that?' he said.

'Yep. Eyes to the right, he's remembering. Eyes to the left, he's thinking.'

233

Phil gave a grim smile. 'Let's hope he doesn't have a squint or a nervous tic. Then we're completely buggered.'

Marina returned the smile.

'Right,' he said. 'We good to go?'

'I think so.'

Neurolinguistic interviewing technique involved two different kinds of questions: remembering and cognitive. The innocuous questions, as well as lulling the subject into a false sense of security, established a yardstick to judge all subsequent answers by. A subject's body language would be different for each kind of answer. When asked a remembering question, Brotherton looked down to the right. But when asked a thinking question, he looked away to the left. Phil and Marina now knew that if he was asked a remembering question and answered as he would for a thinking question, he was buying himself time, working on an answer. In short, probably lying.

'Sorry about all that . . . stuff. In there,' said Phil.

'Doesn't matter,' said Marina, her head down in her notes. 'You were working. No apologies necessary.'

'Right,' he said, and picked up a file folder from the desk. It had Brotherton's name written on the front. 'Off I go. Wish me luck.'

She smiled. 'You don't need it.'

He returned the smile. 'Do it anyway.'

'Good luck.'

'Thank you.'

He left her alone once more. She looked at the mirror. Waited for it to start again.

45

Clayton looked around the room. He was beginning to know how it felt to be on the other side of the table. Like he was the one trapped, about to give himself away, be caught out by his own lies. He looked at Sophie. She caught his eye, glanced away in disgust. He didn't blame her.

He checked his watch, sighed. It seemed to be showing the same time as when he had last looked. Another sigh. Like waiting in a doctor's surgery, he thought. For test results to come back and confirm the worst. Something bad. Something terminal.

Another sigh. He resisted the temptation to check his watch again.

'Your boyfriend's probably given it up by now.'

Sophie stared at him. 'I doubt it.' Her words seemed strong but he sensed nervousness behind them. 'He's not the type.'

Clayton shook his head. 'They're all the type.' He drew his sleeve back, fought not to bring his eyes to his wrist. Let his sleeve fall back into place. 'He's no different.'

Sophie sat forward, about to argue, but decided against it. Slumped back into the seat. Defeated.

Clayton could empathise with her. He had never felt so—

His thought went uncompleted. The door to the interview room opened and Anni Hepburn entered. She was carrying a document wallet under her arm and had a look of triumph in her eyes. She gave a start when she saw him but controlled it well, crossing to the table, pulling up a chair placed against the wall and sitting down next to Clayton.

She gave him a brittle, yet unreadable smile and looked at Sophie. 'Sorry to keep you waiting,' she said. 'I'm DC Hepburn. I believe you already know my colleague DS Thompson.'

She looked towards Clayton as she spoke. There was no mistaking the message in her eyes. The doctor had arrived with the test results.

'Right.' Anni opened the folder, read down. Clayton knew there was often nothing in these files they brought out in front of suspects; they were just props. There was nothing someone who had a problem with authority found more terrifying, a training officer had once explained, than someone in authority holding a file on them.

Anni looked up, seemingly startled to find Clayton still there. 'I thought you were off this case now?'

Clayton felt his cheeks warming up. 'Yeah. I'll just . . .' He rose, scraped his chair back along the floor. Made his way reluctantly to the door and out. He glanced at Sophie before he left, but she wasn't looking at him. She was staring straight ahead, her face unreadable.

Once outside the room, Clayton looked quickly round, then made his way as fast as he could to Ben Fenwick's office. There was a CCTV relay in there and he could watch the interview on it. He ran up the stairs, stood outside, getting his breath back, knocked. No reply. He tried the handle. Open. He went inside, set the TV monitor up. Started watching.

'Sophie Gale,' Anni was saying as he turned it on.

'Yes.' Sophie's voice was dry and cracked.

Anni looked up from the file, directly at her. 'But that's not your real name, is it?'

'It's . . .' Sophie looked towards where Clayton had been sitting. She seemed to have guessed which way this was going to go and, now that he was no longer there, suddenly needed an ally.

'It's not your real name,' said Anni; not a question, a statement.

Sophie nodded.

'Gail Johnson. That's the name under which you first came to our attention. When you were a prostitute.'

'Yes.'

A tight smile from Anni. 'Good.' She looked down at the file again, pretended to be reading. 'Charges were never brought against you, were they?'

Something hardened in Sophie. 'You know they weren't. And you know why.'

'Yes. I know why. Just found out today.' Anni's gaze went to the screen.

Clayton jumped back. Was she looking at him? Did she know he was watching?

She continued. 'You were an informant. You were protected.'

Sophie nodded.

Anni's voice changed. Became less accusatory. 'Very good. Can't have been easy to do that. Downright dangerous at times, I would have thought.'

Sophie shrugged. Clayton could tell she was thawing. He knew Anni was playing her.

'Having to go with men you didn't want to was bad enough. But then having to come and tell us about it . . . bad men, dangerous men . . . that's real bravery. I mean it.' And she sounded like she did. She smiled.

237

'Thank you.' Sophie returned the smile.

'How long did you do that for?'

Sophie thought. 'Oh . . . feels like for ever. But it also feels like it happened years ago. To someone else.'

'So how long?'

'About five years.'

Anni looked impressed. 'Long time.'

'Felt like it.'

Anni nodded, smiled. 'But that's all in the past now.'

'Absolutely. New life, new everything.' Sophie gave a tentative smile. Even on CCTV, Clayton could see that her guard was starting to drop. He knew exactly what Anni was doing. And what the end result would be. And he was powerless to stop her.

'So.' Anni looked back at the file. Pretended to be reading. 'Wednesday the seventeenth. You were at home. With Ryan Brotherton. Your boyfriend. In the house you share together.' She looked up. 'That right?'

'Yes.'

Back to the file. 'And you were there all night. Watching DVDs. Eating takeaway food.'

Sophie nodded.

Anni looked directly at her, the earlier friendliness now completely absent. 'No you weren't. You're lying.'

Sophie was taken aback by the words.

The test results were back, thought Clayton. And they were positive.

46

'**B**ut let's put that to one side,' said Anni. 'We'll get to that. Let's talk about Ryan first. How did you meet him?'

Sophie, shaken from Anni's previous words, trotted out the same story Clayton had heard the previous night. She was seeing one of Ryan's competitors, she heard there was a job going, she applied, was taken on, then dumped her boyfriend and took up with Brotherton. Anni listened, nodded, said nothing.

There was silence while she consulted the file once more. Clayton watched the monitor helplessly. There was nothing he could do. Anni was controlling things now.

'Did you know Susie Evans, Sophie?'

Sophie seemed to be deciding on what her answer should be. 'Yes,' she said. 'But not very well.'

'You got pulled in with her. On a raid.' Anni read down. 'Couple of raids.'

Sophie nodded, but said nothing.

'Did Ryan, your boyfriend, know Susie Evans?'

Clayton saw the fear and desperation in Sophie's eyes as she stared at Anni. 'No. I don't know. Not that I know of.'

'Which one is it?'

'I don't know.'

'You don't know.'

'If he did, he never mentioned it.'

'Right.' Anni flipped over a few pages, brought out another sheet of paper. 'Funny, that, because his name has come up a couple of times where hers is concerned. Quite a few times, actually. And yours is there too.'

Sophie again looked round, trying to find help and support from some corner of the room, fear now rampant in her eyes. Clayton, in the office, looked at Anni, knew that look on her face. She was trying not to smile. She had something.

'Yes. When you and she were picked up a few times, he was picked up too. Never charged, which was why it took me so long to find the information, but his name was taken. Don't you think that's a strange coincidence?'

Sophie looked at the table. 'Yes. It's a coincidence.'

'A coincidence. Right. So it's a coincidence that you knew Susie Evans. Worked with her. And that Ryan Brotherton knew Susie Evans. And that Ryan is now your boyfriend. And Susie Evans is dead. Murdered. And Ryan's ex-girlfriend, Claire Fielding, is also dead. And Ryan, your boyfriend, the one you were eating takeaway food with and watching DVDs with the other night, has a history of violence towards women. A problem with women, in fact. A very serious problem.' She sat back, her eyes locked on to Sophie like laser beams. 'Quite a coincidence.'

Sophie looked frantically at Anni.

Anni leaned forward. 'You want to tell me the truth now?'

Sophie's head dropped into her hands. 'No . . . He'll kill me . . .'

'Yes,' said Anni, her tone conciliatory yet steely. 'He very well might. So I'm your only chance, Sophie. You'd better talk to me. Right?'

She nodded.

'Truth this time.'

'Yeah,' she said. 'The truth.'

Phil walked back into the interview room holding a document file. On the file was Ryan Brotherton's name. He set it on the table, resumed his seat. Brotherton looked expectantly at him. Phil opened the file, glanced at the contents. Raised his eyebrows.

'Oh, Ryan . . .'

'What?' Brotherton craned his neck forward, trying to see what was written there. Phil moved it further away from him.

'Jesus, you have been a naughty boy . . .' He held his gaze on the pages for a few more seconds, just long enough for Brotherton's anxiety levels to increase, then flipped the cover of the file closed and looked levelly at him. This was a different Phil from the one who had left the room. He had appeared to be Brotherton's friend, someone on his side. This new Phil was something different. A professional. A heat-seeking missile zeroing in on his target. And he wasn't going to miss.

'Where were you on the night of Wednesday the seventeenth of November?' he asked.

Brotherton looked startled at Phil's abrupt tone.

'Where were you?'

'I was . . .' His eyes slipped away to the left. 'At home. With Sophie. We watched a DVD, I told you this.'

'Liar. Where were you?'

'I told you where I was . . .' Eyes straight ahead, imploring, trying to hold Phil's gaze, saying: *Would I lie to you?* 'That's the truth.'

'You're lying, Ryan. Where were you? Between eight p.m. and two a.m.? When Claire Fielding, your ex-girlfriend, the mother of your child, was being murdered, where were you?'

'I've told you.' Eyes left. 'At home. Watching a DVD. With Sophie. Ask her.'

Phil gave a small, tight smile. 'We will. Don't worry about that. Can you trust her?'

'What?'

'Can you trust her? To lie for you?'

Eyes away to the left. Thinking. 'I can trust her. Yeah.' Defiance in his voice.

Phil sat back, not taking his eyes off the other man. Time for something else. 'When did Claire first tell you she was pregnant?'

Brotherton thought, looking down to the right. 'About . . . five, six months ago.'

'And what was your reaction?'

'I've told you. I didn't believe her.'

'But you soon did.'

Brotherton shrugged.

'She soon convinced you. Because you told her you wanted her to get rid of it, didn't you?'

Brotherton stared at him, said nothing.

'In fact you said that if she didn't, then you would. With your own hands. Isn't that right?'

Fear appeared on Brotherton's face. 'I . . . I want my solicitor . . . I'm not sayin' another word without my solicitor bein' present.'

'We've called her, she's on her way.'

Rage and fear clouded Brotherton's face. '*She?* What the fuck d'you mean, she? Where's Warnock?'

Phil could barely keep the smile off his face. 'We phoned your solicitor, Mr Warnock. He's . . . unavailable, apparently. But they're sending someone from the practice. Bit young, but very good, they say.' The smile appeared. 'She's just fin-ished working with victims of domestic abuse in a women's refuge, I think they said. I'm sure she'll be very interested in all this.' Phil didn't know anything of the sort, but he knew what kind of effect his words would have.

Brotherton said nothing. Phil knew he had hit the bullseye. Brotherton would talk to him now.

'So you offered to give Claire Fielding, your girlfriend, an abortion. With your own bare hands, is that right?'

'It wasn't like that . . .'

Phil leaned across the table. 'What was it like then, Ryan? Tell me. Make me understand.'

'She . . . I didn't believe her at first. But then I had to.'

'And you got angry.'

He nodded.

'You didn't want a kid around the place. It would stifle you, tie you down, that right?'

Another nod.

'Too much responsibility. So you made that very generous offer.'

Brotherton said nothing.

'And what was Claire's response?'

Brotherton still said nothing.

'No? I'll tell you then, shall I? She left you. Summoned up the courage to walk out on you.'

'No she didn't. I threw her out.' His eyes away to the left as he spoke.

'No you didn't. That's a lie. She left you. But you couldn't take it, could you? Couldn't take some piece of skirt walking out on you. Especially not a pregnant one. How hurt was your pride? Your ego?'

Brotherton shrugged. 'Same as anyone else's.'

'Same as anyone else's. So what did you do next?'

'Nothin'.'

'Liar. You phoned her. Texted her. Threatened her.'

'No I didn't . . .'

'Yes you did, Ryan. We've got her phone records.' Not

243

strictly true, thought Phil, but they were on the way. He was confident they would show that he was telling the truth.

Brotherton's head went down. Phil had been right. He didn't have time to gloat; he had an advantage. He had to press it.

'You stalked her?'

'No.' Eyes away to the left. A lie.

Phil hid his smile. Another bullseye. 'Yes you did, Ryan. You stalked her. Why? Because she'd dared to escape, to run away? Because you couldn't have her where you wanted her to torment? Yeah?'

Silence.

'So what did you think you would achieve by stalking her? Would that get her back?'

Brotherton said nothing.

Phil regarded him coolly. He was well in the zone now, thinking and acting intuitively. On fire but controlling it.

'Did you like the feeling of power it gave you, is that it? Do you think it scared her?'

'Fuck off.'

'Because you like scaring women, don't you?'

'Fuck off!'

'Like hurting them . . .'

Brotherton stood up, swinging his arms. 'Fuck off!'

The uniformed officer waiting at the door stepped forward, ready to grab him if he made a move. Phil got to his feet too. Brotherton moved forward. He was going to go for him.

47

*H*e stood up, opened his eyes. Allowed himself a few seconds of indulgence. Smiled.

His prey was gone. Dead. The birthing room trashed. Order had become chaos. He could feel the blood of his prey soaking into his clothes. He loved that feeling. Luxuriated in it.

It had started when he used to hunt rabbits and deer in the woods. There was the planning, the preparation. Then the chase, the thrill of the kill. Then that moment of power, looking down on something that had recently been alive, knowing he had had the power of life and death over it. And had chosen death. He used to get his knife out and quickly slit the animal open. Steam would rush out as the hot innards and blood collided with the cooler air. Blood would spurt and fountain and he would catch it. Spray it on to himself, feel the hot, glistening liquid warm his skin, smell the dark, coppery scent of his prey. Spraying it down his throat, swallowing it down. It felt like he was taking the spirit of the slain beast, ingesting it, letting it feed him.

He looked down at his prey, lying there on the floor of her living room. He had wanted to do just that. Catch her blood in his hands as it had spurted out, strip naked, rub it all over himself, feel her on his skin.

But he hadn't. He had to be disciplined about this hunt. Focused on his objective. He had no time to ingest the spirit.

Or did he . . . He looked down at the small, kicking baby he had cut out of her. Birthed in blood, its midwife a blade and a dying host. He smiled. There was the spirit, the life force from within her. He was taking that instead.

He took out the blanket he had prepared, wrapped the baby up, put it in his rucksack.

Left the house, closing the door behind him.

He walked down the street feeling like a god amongst mortals. No one saw him go.

48

The door of the observation room opened and Anni Hepburn rushed in. Marina reluctantly took her attention away from the mirror.

'I think Phil needs help,' she said.

'Never mind that,' said Anni. 'He can handle himself. We've got something. Ryan Brotherton used prostitutes. He knew Susie Evans. And Sophie Gale. That's how they met. He's known her for years. She's also told us that Brotherton was out on Wednesday night. The night Claire and Julie were murdered.' She looked at the screen, took in the standoff that was taking place. 'Tell Phil. Now.'

'Ask him about prostitutes.' Marina's voice was loud and sharp in Phil's ear.

'What?'

'It'll calm him down, wrong-foot him. Anything. Just ask him. Now!'

'What about the prostitutes, Ryan?'

The big man was close to hyperventilating. The uniformed officer ready to intercede.

Phil raised his voice. 'Prostitutes, Ryan. You ever used them?'

Brotherton's head jerked suddenly upwards. He stopped in his tracks. 'What? What's that got to do with anything?'

'Come on, Ryan. You hate women that much, sometimes it's easier to pay to vent your frustrations, isn't it?'

'No.' He sounded disgusted. His eyes went away to the left. Lying.

'He knew Susie Evans,' said Marina in his ear. 'Was a customer of hers. That's how he met Sophie Gale. They worked together. And she's also told us he was out on Wednesday night.'

Phil tried not to let his emotions show. He kept his face as blank as possible. 'Sit down, Ryan. Let's talk.'

Phil sat down. Brotherton, getting his breath back, did likewise.

'Now,' said Phil. 'You sure? You've never used prostitutes?'

'No. Never.' Eyes again to the left. Another lie. 'I don't have to pay for sex. I don't need to.'

'Might not just be for sex, though, might it?'

'What d'you mean?'

'You know what I mean, Ryan. You like beating up women. Sometimes the women in your life don't like it and walk out. Or testify against you and get you banged up. So you need an outlet. A bit of release. Would have thought prostitutes would fill the bill nicely.'

'You'd have thought wrong.' His voice sounded weak.

Phil sat back, regarding him again. 'I don't believe you, Ryan. You see, I'm good at my job. I sit here and I listen to people sitting where you are. They want me to believe what they're telling me. And most of them are liars. Some of them are very good. Some of them I nearly believe.' He folded his arms. 'But not you, Ryan. I know you're lying.'

'Prove it.' Brotherton aimed for defiance in his voice, missed.

'Okay,' said Phil.

★

Anni Hepburn had just left the observation room to return to questioning Sophie Gale when the door opened again and an out-of-breath Ben Fenwick entered. Marina took her attention from Phil, looked at him. She had never seen him so dishevelled yet so elated. He looked wired.

'Let me in,' he said, making for the desk.

Marina moved aside, let him take over the microphone. Fenwick took a few seconds to regain his breath before he spoke. While waiting, he turned to Marina.

'How's he doing?'

'Good,' she said. She didn't want to commit herself to anything else. Especially after the way Fenwick had spoken to her earlier. She didn't want to tell him that it looked like Phil was about to crack Brotherton, that he was homing in for the kill. That Fenwick had been right and she had been wrong.

Fenwick smiled. It was the kind of glassy-eyed leer a coked-up City trader would give. 'Well he's going to be even better after I tell him this.' He opened the channel, spoke into the mic. 'Phil? Ben Fenwick.'

Marina watched Phil's expression through the mirror. His head jerked upwards and he stopped talking immediately. He didn't reply but they knew he was listening.

'The Birdies have been singing.' Fenwick laughed at his own joke.

Technically, thought Marina, now irritated with the man, the Birdies had been making other people sing.

'They've gone through the records of the estate agency Lisa King worked for. Guess what? Brotherton was registered with them. He looked at houses through them. Lisa King's name comes up a couple of times as showing him round some properties. Phil, we've got the bastard!'

Fenwick turned to Marina, a leering smile on his face. 'Police work,' he said.

★

In the interview room, Phil once again did his best not to respond. Instead he leaned back, regarding Brotherton quizzically. Brotherton looked down at the table, clearly scared.

'You asked me to prove it,' said Phil. 'Prove you killed Claire and Julie. Okay. I will. There's a few ways I could do that. Let me ask you something. How long have you been in your house?'

Brotherton frowned. It wasn't the question he had been expecting.

'How long?'

He shrugged. 'Couple of months.'

And you were on the books of Haskell Robins estate agents?'

'Yeah, but I didn't buy from them.'

'But one of their estate agents turned up dead, didn't she?'

Brotherton frowned again.

'Lisa King. Twenty-six years old. Married. Found in an empty property with her stomach ripped open. Pregnant.'

'Wait a minute . . .'

Phil pressed on. 'Right. Just circumstantial. Tenuous. I know. Try this, then. I could tell you that your name's come up as someone who's been questioned in brothel raids. A few of them. What would you say to that?'

Brotherton, visibly shaken, said nothing.

'Okay. So you've got a hatred of women. You beat up girlfriends, you beat up prostitutes. Now, one of these prostitutes you say you didn't know was Susie Evans. And you know what happened to her. She was murdered too. While she was pregnant. Her stomach ripped open, the baby taken out. Was that yours too?'

Brotherton looked frantically round the room, realised there was no escape.

250

'You stalk women who dump you, threaten them. Your own girlfriend is pregnant and you offer to rip the baby out of her.' Phil leaned forward. 'And then what happens? She turns up dead. With the baby ripped out of her. Just like the other two who you claim you don't know. And you lie to me about where you were on the night it happened. So, how am I doing so far, Ryan? How much more proof do you need?'

Brotherton put his head in his hands. His shoulders began to shake. He was crying. Phil saw his advantage, pressed on.

'We've got you on CCTV outside Claire's flat. We've got her phone records.'

He shook his head. 'No . . . no . . .'

'You killed her, Ryan, didn't you? Just admit it, then we can start sorting it out.'

No reply, just crying.

'You were out that night, weren't you? The night Claire was killed.'

Brotherton said nothing.

'I know you were. Sophie told us.'

'Sophie . . .' His voice was small and fragile, like a child who had been told there was no Father Christmas.

'Yes, Sophie. She's not going to lie for you any more, Ryan. So tell me the truth. You were out that night, weren't you?'

Brotherton nodded. Breakthrough. Phil could barely sit in his seat, he was so excited. He swallowed down his rising excitement, controlled it, kept his voice steady, his breathing even, pressed on.

'You went to her flat, didn't you? You crept in and killed her.'

Phil waited. Here it comes, he thought. The confession. The climax he had been working for, building towards. Brotherton looked up, eyes shining, face wet.

'Didn't you, Ryan?' Phil's voice was gentle, coaxing. 'You killed her.'

Brotherton shook his head. 'No. I didn't. I swear I didn't . . .'

Phil studied him. Watched his eyes for deviation.

'You killed Claire, Ryan. And Julie. Didn't you?'

Brotherton shook his head once more.

'Yes you did. Claire. And Julie. And Lisa. And Susie. You did. Didn't you?'

'No . . . no . . .' Brotherton's eyes slid down to the right.

'*Didn't you . . .*'

'*No . . .*'

Phil sat back, exhausted. He had seen it. Marina's voice in his ear just confirmed it.

'Oh my God. He's telling the truth, Phil. He didn't do it.'

Then, just to emphasise the point, Brotherton started talking. 'Yes, I was out. There's this . . . this girl that I've been seeing . . . a young girl. I . . . I didn't want Sophie to know . . .'

Phil stared at Brotherton until he could look at him no longer.

Marina was right. Brotherton was telling the truth.

49

Graeme Eades felt like Superman.

He parked in front of his own house in Stanway, switched off the engine, sat back, closed his eyes and sighed contentedly. The afternoon with Erin had been beyond fantastic. She had joined him in the hotel room not long after he arrived, seemingly delighted at what he had bought for her. Cooing and squealing, she had gone straight into the bathroom and changed into the first outfit, telling him to just lie himself down on the bed and get comfortable, and she would give him a treat.

And what a treat. She came out, filling the basque beautifully, walking slowly and predatorily in her heels, a lascivious smile on her face. Once in the bedroom she moved the armchair to the end of the bed and proceeded to put on a show for him involving at least half of the toys he had just bought. He was pleased he had remembered the batteries.

He was so excited he almost came there and then but she wouldn't let him. A quick change of costume and she joined him on the bed, making use of the lotions and oils. She smiled all the while at his reaction to her perfect and surprisingly gymnastic body as she joined it with his rather less than lithe one.

As he was about to come, Erin controlling and restraining the juddering, electric orgasm that was ready to burst from within him, she asked once again about promotion. Yes, he had gasped. Whatever. She went on to tell him how good she was at her job and whose job she thought she should have. Naturally, he agreed. That person needed sacking. Would he do it? He would. And give her the job instead? Yes. Yes. Yes. She smiled. Good. And allowed him to come.

He pulled the key out of the ignition, grabbed his briefcase, got out. His senses had been left reeling from his encounter, with more than his mind blown. As he walked up the drive he thought back over the promise he had made. He had known it wasn't in his power to hire and fire. But Erin didn't know that. Okay, perhaps he had exaggerated his importance and position in the company. So what? All men did that. Especially to impress women. He had promised her the job, yes, and she had reminded him of that promise as he had left, but again, so what? What could she do about it? He would tell her that, boss or not, these things took time, there were procedures to be gone through, but not to worry. She would get the job. No hurry. Yeah. String her along. And in the meantime . . .

He smiled. Best of all, he had put the whole afternoon, including his purchases, on expenses. Whatever, it was definitely better than paying for it.

As he approached the house, it felt like a black cloud was descending over him. With every step that took him nearer to his front door, the cloud darkened until it was almost pitch black as he put his key in the lock. He reluctantly tried to force Erin out of his mind as he prepared to confront Caroline. He had an excuse ready for being late – a meeting went on longer than expected, a client turned up he had to see, something like that, the usual – but to be honest, he didn't care. He'd had enough of seeing her pained, pale face

254

haunting the house as she dragged her lumpen body around, never happy. Put her next to Erin and there was no comparison. Before the pregnancy, maybe. The first one. But not now. Perhaps he should do something about that. Something to seriously think about.

He opened the door. He sighed, shook his head and entered. Should he shout? Tell her he was home? No. She might be sleeping. Hopefully.

He put his keys on the table as he always did. The hallway was in darkness. He tried the switch. It didn't work. Puzzled, he walked down the hall. Opened the living room door. Ready for arguments, ready for misery. Ready for any of the normal responses he was greeted with when he arrived home.

But he wasn't ready for this.

The lights were on in here.

He screamed.

And screamed and screamed and screamed.

50

C layton pulled deep on his Marlboro Light, held it and exhaled slowly, feeling his body relax against the side of his BMW as he did so. He was in the car park behind the police station. It was freezing. He was trying not to let the cold get to him. But his chattering teeth betrayed him.

What a balls-up. The whole thing. What a balls-up.

Sophie in the interview room, and then Brotherton. Phil hadn't been able to break him. Even with all the circumstantial evidence, CCTV footage, everything, he still couldn't do it. They were all coming to the conclusion that maybe Brotherton actually was innocent. And Clayton was off the case. Unable to influence it. His future in everyone else's hands. He hated that most of all.

Another drag, and another exhale. Movement at the back of the police station caught his eye. Anni was striding out of the building, wearing her usual T-shirt and jeans but with no jacket, arms tightly wrapped around her body in a vain attempt to keep out the cold. She approached him, slowed. Stood opposite him as he smoked. Said nothing.

Clayton swallowed. Again. Took another drag. She was making him nervous. He was letting her. He had no choice. He looked at her. She was waiting for him to speak. He noticed that his stomach flipped and his breathing had quickened. His teeth were still chattering. He tried to stop them.

'Thanks,' he said.

Anni's face remained impassive. 'What for?'

'You know.' The wall to the left of her shoulder was fascinating; he kept his eyes on it.

'Yes,' she said, a trace of angry emotion seeping into her voice, 'I know. But I want to hear you say it.'

He took another drag of the cigarette, tried again to keep his teeth still in his mouth. Exhaled. 'Thank you,' he said. 'For not grassin' me up to Phil.'

She said nothing. Waiting once more.

Clayton felt that since it had now been acknowledged between them, he was expected to say something further. 'I recognised her straight away,' he said. 'At the metal yard. And I thought . . .' He sighed. 'Maybe I could get something from her, something important that I could use for the investigation. Now, I know I was bein' selfish, not thinkin' of the team—'

'Don't insult my intelligence, Clayton, I saw what happened.'

Another sigh. 'It was just the once,' he said. 'Last night in the car.'

'I don't want to know. I don't need to know.' She still wouldn't look at him.

'Yeah . . . just the once. That's all it was.' He fell silent. Risked a glance at her. He was sure she had been looking at him when he had been looking elsewhere, sure her eyes had just darted away from his. 'It was . . . I've never done anything like that before.'

'I don't care.'

'Whatever, but look—'

This time she looked at him. Directly at him. And her eyes were so fierce and strong, he wished she hadn't.

257

'Clayton, when I say I don't care, I don't care. It's none of my business what you get up to in your own time.'

Clayton frowned. Wasn't she angry because she had seen him with another woman? Wasn't that it? 'I just thought because of, you know, the other night, that you were—'

She gave a laugh, harsh and abrasive. 'What? You think because we had a fumble that somehow we're . . . what? Lovers? That I've caught you cheating on me? Is that it?'

'Well, yeah . . .'

Another laugh, just as harsh but more disbelieving. She shook her head. 'That's what you think this is all about? Really? You arrogant bastard.'

'So . . . why then?'

She gave him the pitying kind of look she would reserve for a backward child. 'Think about it. Because, Clayton, you were spotted in a car with a witness who was, as the tabloids say, performing a sex act on you. While under surveillance. Doesn't that scream unprofessional conduct to you? Conflict of interests, at the very least? Don't you think it's the kind of thing that could put a conviction in jeopardy? Not to mention this shining career you think you're going to have.'

'Well, yeah. When you put it like that, yeah.'

'So?'

'I know that. I just thought, you know. You were mad at me because of, you know. Us.'

Anni looked him directly in the eye. There were things she was about to say but she stopped herself. Instead she shook her head and walked off. 'I'm going back inside.'

Clayton flicked his cigarette away, turned to follow her. 'Me too.'

She turned to him as she kept walking, her arms still wrapped tightly round her body. 'Piss off, Clayton. Leave me alone.'

She reached the door before he did. He ran towards her,

258

stopped her from opening it with his palm against it. She turned and faced him, angry.

'Let me go. Now.'

'What you goin' to do? About what you saw?'

'Let me go.' She struggled to open the door. He still wouldn't let her.

'Please, Anni, I need to know.' Clayton's voice had dropped to a begging, wheedling tone. 'Look, it was just a one-off. I've never done it before, I'll never do it again. Please.'

'I don't know . . . I don't know what happened . . .'

She pulled the door again.

'Please, Anni. You have to tell me. Are you goin' to tell Phil?'

'I should do.'

'Yeah, I know. You goin' to?'

She stopped struggling, looked at him. Sighed. She was still angry, he could tell. But her features had softened slightly. 'I don't know. I should do. But I don't know.'

He took his hand off the door. She walked through it and strode away from him. Clayton looked back into the car park, saw his BMW sitting there, gleaming. He sighed, shook his head.

What a balls-up.

He followed her back in, letting the door swing shut behind him.

51

Marina sat in the canteen in the police station, note-book open before her, a cup of something at her lips. Someone had made a vague attempt to cheer the place up, make it appear welcoming by providing primary-coloured chairs and tables and non-institutional colours on the walls. But it still looked like what it was. A fuelling station for time-poor public employees.

She took a sip of her drink, not knowing whether it was coffee or tea, suspecting it was veering towards coffee because that was what she had ordered. But not really caring. She sighed, pen poised above her notebook, ready to write something. Process what had just happened, what she had just witnessed, find a way to move forward. She looked at the blank page. Willed the words to appear. Couldn't do it. Couldn't think of anything to write. With a sigh she placed the pen back on the table, took another sip of coffee.

She had been right all along. Brotherton was not the killer. Phil had tried to break him down, kept going even after she had spoken to him, told him he wasn't the killer. He'd repeated the evidence back to Brotherton, over and over again, like a mantra of guilt, asked him to confess, shouted at him to confess, even tried to cajole him into confessing. But he'd got nowhere. Nothing. Not because Brotherton couldn't be broken down, but because, as Marina knew, he wasn't guilty.

Eventually Phil had given up, terminated the interview. She hadn't seen him since. Nor, for that matter, had she seen Fenwick, Anni, any of them. They had all gone straight down the hall once Phil had emerged from the interview room. She didn't know whether she was supposed to follow them, but none of them had looked back, made any attempt to include her. So, with nowhere to go and nothing to do, she had come to the canteen, planned what to do next.

Go home, she thought. Get back to her day job, back to her life. Just have her baby, build up her private practice, live happily ever after with Tony and never work with the police again. Fenwick had made it quite clear that her expertise wasn't appreciated and her points weren't going to be listened to. So why didn't she just go home? She already had a career. She didn't need to do this. Leave them to get on with it, sort it out themselves. Forget them. All of them, even Phil.

As soon as the thought was formed, she felt a deep stab of discomfort and instinctively put her hand over her swelling belly. The baby seemed to be registering displeasure at something. Probably the coffee, she thought. Or maybe something more. Like it was reminding her that there was more at stake than the careers and reputations of a few police officers. Dead babies and their mothers. Giving them a voice. *Jesus Christ*, she said to herself, *I must be getting superstitious. Not to mention simple-minded.* She moved around in her seat, tried to find a comfortable position to sit in. Couldn't. She took another mouthful of warm brown liquid, began to pack her notebook away.

So engrossed was she in doing so that she wasn't aware of another person at her side until he spoke.

'May I join you?'

She looked up. Ben Fenwick was standing there. She wouldn't have recognised him from the contrite voice. But it matched the general state of him. He seemed to be disintegrating before her eyes. She hadn't paid his appearance that much attention in the dark of the observation room, but she looked at him now. The smug political air that he usually affected had now unravelled and dissolved as the pressure of the case increased. He needed a shave, his hair was messed up, and so was his suit. His tie was askew and there were dark half-circles beneath his eyes. She hadn't noticed it at his press conferences; maybe he saved his grooming for then. Perhaps, she thought, this was what actors looked like when the camera wasn't on them. She thought again of the seminar she would have been delivering had she still been teaching: Chimerical Masks and Dissociation in the Perception of the Self. How true, she thought.

'Feel free,' she said, still packing her bag. 'I was just leaving.'

'Where to?'

'Off.'

'Where?'

'Back to work.'

He nodded. 'You mean leaving us? For good?'

She stopped what she was doing, looked at him. 'Why not? I don't get paid enough to put up with the abuse you give me. To say you haven't valued my professional opinion or input barely covers it. You've belittled and derided anything I've said. And in front of the whole team as well.' She felt her voice rising again, knew that people were starting to stare. She didn't care.

'Well, I . . .'

She didn't want to let up. Time for some home truths, she thought. 'You ask me what I think, and when I tell you you ignore it because it doesn't fit in with what you want to believe. And now you've got an innocent man sitting in an interview room—'

'He's hardly innocent.'

She felt her face reddening, her anger deepening. She kept her voice down but focused. 'Innocent of the crime you want him to be guilty of. Well, good luck.' She stood up, swung her bag on to her shoulder. 'I'll invoice you.'

'Wait.' He placed a hand on her arm. She stopped, looked down at him. There was more than contrition in his eyes. There was also a desperate hope. The kind a shipwrecked man has when clinging to a piece of wreckage. 'Please. Sit down again. Don't go yet. Let's talk first. Please.'

Marina knew what she should have done. Just shaken off his grip, walked out of there. But she didn't. Instead she took the bag from her shoulder and, anger barely abating, resumed her seat. She said nothing, sitting upright, waiting for him.

'I'm sorry,' he said.

She waited, still said nothing. Made him work. Knew there would be more.

There was. 'I was . . . I was wrong.' He sighed. 'Yes. I was wrong. And I admit it. I was wrong to ignore your findings. And I was certainly wrong to speak to you like that in front of everyone at the briefing. That was unforgivable. I was . . . out of order.'

'You were.'

He nodded. 'And I'm sorry.' Another sigh. His shoulders drooped as the air left his body, like he was deflating. 'I'm very sorry.' He rubbed his eyes, his face. 'But we just . . . We need a result on this one. A quick result. It feels like . . . the eyes of the world are upon us.'

Despite the situation, Marina stifled a smile. *King Cliché rides again*, she thought.

'So that excuses it. Your behaviour towards me, your grasping at straws . . .'

'It wasn't grasping. It was good, solid police work.'

'It just wasn't the right man.'

Fenwick sighed. 'We need to find him. It's as simple as that. We need to find him. And I thought we had him.' He balled his hands into fists as he spoke. 'I wanted, really *wanted* to believe we had him . . .' He let the fists go. 'But we didn't. And I think that maybe, deep down, I knew it.' Another sigh. 'So I'm sorry. I'm afraid you were just a casualty of . . . that.'

Marina nodded, her anger ebbing slightly. Not that she would let him see that, though. 'They say that when you're under stress your true character is revealed,' she said.

He offered a weak smile. 'Then I'm a twat. And an obnoxious one at that.'

She couldn't return the smile. 'You'll hear no argument from me.'

'True.' He put his hands on the table, reaching out to her. 'I suppose what I'm trying to say is that we need you. This investigation needs you. Your input is invaluable. If we are to catch whoever has done this, then I think we need to drastically alter our approach.'

'In what way?'

'My approach hasn't worked. So I want you and your expertise central to the investigation from now on. I want us to be guided by your experience.'

Marina raised an eyebrow.

'Yes, I know, I know. You should have been central from the start. I said you would be and didn't carry it through. I got anxious. What with everything going on . . . I'm sorry.'

'So you said.'

'So.' He rubbed his hands together, gave her another smile. 'Are you still on board? We need you. Please.'

She looked at him. His smile was thinly stretched, papering over the doubt, anxiety and guilt on his face. Marina's first response was to tell him where to get off, and walk; her second to make him suffer a while longer for her answer. But her third was the direct one, the honest one. The one that reminded her of the photos of the murdered women on the board in the incident room. The before and after shots. She felt for the child inside her once more, her arm going instinctively, protectively round her stomach.

'Yes, Ben. I'm still on board. But not for you.'

His smile was genuine this time. Relieved. 'Thank you. Thank you so much. I'm—'

'But you keep your word. I am not here as an optional extra. Got it?'

He held up his hands. 'Got it.'

He was about to say something further, but the sudden appearance of Phil at the table stopped him. Phil was breathless, wired. His brow furrowed, his body tense. Marina sensed what he was going to say before he said it. She just knew it. She was standing up, grabbing her bag, her coat.

'He's done it again,' Phil said. 'Another murder.'

Fenwick stood up too.

'Marina,' said Phil, looking at Fenwick. 'Not you. Sir.'

He didn't wait for a reply; just turned and hurried away.

Fenwick sat down again. Stayed where he was.

52

Hester held the baby in her arms and smiled. She was a proud mother again.

She had wiped most of the blood off it with an old rag that she had washed out and dried specially for use with the baby. It was smothered in blankets and she was sitting by the heater so it would keep warm. She wasn't going to make the same mistakes again. That was what life was, she had read somewhere or seen on TV or something, a learning process. So that was what she was doing. Learning how to take care of the baby.

Her husband had been buzzing when he brought the baby to her. She had never felt him so alive. The hunt, he had said. The hunt had done it. She didn't care. All she wanted was the baby. He had stayed around afterwards, like he was so full of energy he couldn't go anywhere else. But he had, eventually.

Somehow she didn't think this baby was going to be as weak as the last one. It was bigger for a start, moving its arms and legs round more. It even had its eyes open a bit. And it was a girl. She had checked. She had smiled when she saw, giggled.

'My husband's going to like you,' she said, still smiling and giggling.

Then felt something wrench inside her at the thought. Something dark and sad. She hoped he wouldn't. That might mean he went off her. Then she might be abandoned. For the baby. She would have to watch it grow, knowing that it was going to replace her. That couldn't happen. She wouldn't allow it. Better to not be a mother at all than be a mother betrayed.

The darkness and sadness inside her crystallised, hardened at the direction her thoughts were taking. Her face twisted with sudden anger. She stared at the baby, breathing hard.

'You'd better not,' she said. 'You'd better fuckin' not . . .'

The baby just lay there, trying to look round, its arms and legs doing their jerky, spasming movements. She tried not to be angry with it. Because that was all in the future. That was to come. First there was the here and now. There was motherhood. There was bringing up baby.

She sat there looking at it. She didn't know how long for. Eventually all the anger drained out of her, leaving just a placid, calm look on her face. Her body was still again, her breathing even and shallow. She wasn't angry. She was a mother again. Just a mother. And this was the time she should spend with her baby. Bonding time. Special time.

After all, that was why she had gone to the trouble of getting the babies the way she did. So they came straight out of their surrogate and into her arms. No time to bond with anyone else. Hers from the start.

The baby's face began to twist. Hester knew what would be next. Crying. Then wailing. She knew what to do this time.

'You hungry, eh? Want feedin'? Want some milk? I'll get it for you.'

She stood up, put the baby down on the armchair she had been sitting in. It writhed and screamed. She crossed to the kitchen, the screaming seeming to follow her.

267

'It's all right, Mummy's warmin' your milk now . . .'

She put the bottle in the microwave. It was old, rusting at the edges, the enamel chipped, the buttons worn and it made no sound any more, but it seemed to still work okay. Still heated things up.

The baby kept wailing. Hester tried to placate it while she waited for the microwave to do its work, but the baby wouldn't stop. She sighed. She had forgotten about that. In so short a space of time, she had forgotten. How it was at that certain pitch to cut right through you. Down to the bone, in your head. That loud, insistent wail. Even when it stopped you could still hear it. Hester felt anger rise inside her once more.

'It's coming . . .'

But the baby didn't understand. Or if it did understand, that didn't make it stop. Just kept on wailing. Hester watched the microwave, waiting for it to ping. That wailing . . .

'Shut up! Just shut up!' If it was going to do that all the time . . . She remembered how the last one had been, crying, shouting, screaming . . . she hated that. Had wanted to kill it. If this one kept doing the same . . .

The microwave pinged. She flung open the door, grabbed the milk. The bottle felt a bit hot to the touch. Hester didn't care. She crossed the room, picked up the baby, put it on her lap, stuck the end of the bottle in its mouth. The baby's eyes widened in surprise, then it started sucking. It took one mouthful, two, then spat it out, milk running down the sides of its face.

Hester felt anger clouding in again, her face twisting in rage once more. 'What's this about? Eh? You said you were hungry. You wanted feedin'. Here it is.'

She tried again, pushing the teat in once more. The hot liquid ran down the baby's cheeks again. Hester's anger increased.

268

'Have it . . . have it . . .'

The baby wouldn't take it.

Hester looked at the baby, at the bottle, didn't know what to do. Emotions were tumbling through her, so fast she couldn't recognise them, catch them. Anger, fear, impotence. She looked once more at the baby, the bottle . . .

She stood up. Put the baby on the seat once more, the bottle beside it. The baby's flailing arm knocked the bottle over. Milk began to ooze out, soaking the blanket the baby was wrapped in.

Hester didn't care. Couldn't think about that. She had to get out. Get away from the baby and its incessant wailing.

She opened the side door, stepped out into the yard. It was dark now and still bitterly cold. The air carried the threat of rain or worse, snow. But Hester didn't care. She would take all that just to get away from the baby. From that noise, that need . . .

She took a deep breath, let it out as one long sigh. She looked across the river to the lights from the port. Ships would be coming in, going out once more. No screaming babies there. Just the vast, open water. The sea. The ocean. Calm. How Hester wanted to be there, to be miles away from here.

She sighed. It wasn't the first time she had thought that in her life. It wasn't the first time she had thought that this week. But she knew that even though all that was just over the river, it may as well have been a million miles away. On another planet, even. She would never go there, not even to the port, let alone over the sea. Here was where she was from. And here she would stay.

Her sister had escaped. Or tried to. She closed her eyes. Didn't want to think of her sister again. Of the night she got away. Of the night she became Hester. No. All that horror, that screaming, wailing . . . No. Don't think of it. Too upsetting.

Yeah, her father had said. Her sister had got away all right. Got away for ever. Hester knew what that meant. And what she had to do. So she had stayed.

Hester sighed. From inside, she could hear the baby still screaming. She closed her eyes, willed it away, but it was no good. She opened her eyes again. Her husband was there.

Fuck's the matter with you? he said. *What you doin' out here?*

'The baby,' she said, 'it's the baby. I can't . . .' She was about to say 'cope', but she knew her husband wouldn't like that. Would think her weak, maybe even try to get rid of her, replace her. She thought again of the baby. Her possible replacement. She definitely wouldn't tell him those thoughts. Didn't want to give him ideas.

It's makin' a hell of a fuckin' racket. You'd better get in there, sort it out.

She couldn't answer, just shook her head.

Hey, he said. *You wanted it. You can look after it.*

'Can't . . . can't you do it?'

I can do it all right. I can go in there an' make it stop. But if I do, it'll never start again. That what you want?

Hester thought for a moment. Was that what she wanted? It would make everything so much easier. So much quieter. Just go in and . . .

You can always get another one. There's still the list . . .

She knew what he meant. He was so high on the blood lust that he wanted to go again. And if it meant getting rid of this one and finding a replacement, then fine. But no. She couldn't do that. Not after everything they had been through to get it. She couldn't just let it go like that.

She shook her head. 'I'll deal with it.'

Then sort it. Shut it up.

Hester nodded. It was what she was, what she had wanted, what she did. She was a mother. She had to cope.

And she could. As long as her husband was with her, as long as they were a family, she could cope.

She opened the door. Immediately the noise was amplified. She walked inside.

53

S tanway had once been a village with its own identity. It wasn't that long ago, Phil thought, twenty years at the most. But first came the zoo, then the retail park. Now it was rapidly becoming just another part of Colchester's suburban sprawl.

He stood in a modern estate comprised of boxy houses of varying sizes in red and yellow brick, designed to hark back to some unspecified architecture of the past, something that would endow the flimsy new houses with a sense of tradition and solidity. They were billed as executive dwellings, but from looking at the cars parked there, Vauxhalls, Fords, Renaults, a few Volvos and Audis, he would have said they were more for middle management with either ambitions or delusions.

Phil knew it would be the kind of place that the residents would have moved to from inner cities and town centres, associating them with violence and fear. Thinking money would protect them. And now they found themselves reluctantly embracing those things in the form of a brutal murder. He knew what they would be thinking: the people they had tried to escape from had followed them here. But Phil knew different. From sickening experience, he knew there were no boundaries. Money wouldn't protect them. Nothing would. Murder could happen anywhere.

The house he was standing in front of was one of the yellow brick ones. It had small, square windows and a pillared porch and was, he supposed, designed to project a vaguely Regency air. It looked, outwardly, as ordinary as could be. But once that threshold was crossed, Phil knew that once again he would be stepping into a different and much darker world.

The circus had been called out. The street had been closed off, the white tents had gone up, arc lights erected and pointing at the house. Rubbernecking residents had gathered at the corner, some evicted from their own homes, some being questioned by uniforms. Phil spotted Anni. He crossed the street. She saw him coming, nodded.

He looked round, took in the scene once more. 'What's the damage?'

Anni, bundled up in her parka and scarf, put her hands in her pockets, exhaled steam in the darkness. 'Nasty, boss,' she said. 'Stating the obvious, but there you go. It's him, though. She was pregnant. No baby. No sign.'

Phil nodded, his eyes on the threshold of the house. 'Where's the husband?'

Anni pointed along the street. 'Ambulance,' she said. 'He found her.'

'Poor bastard,' said Phil. 'Any children?'

'Two. Twelve and ten. They've been bundled off to Grandma's.'

'Right.' He made to cross to the ambulance. Anni stopped him.

'Boss,' she said. 'The husband. He's holding something back.'

'Any idea what?'

'Just being a bit secretive, that's all. Bit vague on his whereabouts this afternoon.'

273

Phil gave a grim smile. 'I think we know what that usually means.'

Anni returned the smile. 'Maybe thought I would pre-judge him. Probably happier sharing with another bloke.'

Phil walked over to the ambulance. The night was properly dark now, autumn changing to winter. He had once read somewhere that a writer had suggested six seasons instead of four, with the extra two either side of winter. Locking and unlocking, he had proposed they be called. A time when the world closed itself up, clutched itself in something more like death than hibernation. Looking around at the stunted, denuded trees at the fringes of the estate and feeling the icy wind blowing towards him, he had to agree. The world was locked, holding itself in. Itself and its secrets.

He reached the ambulance. A man, mid-forties, Phil guessed, overweight, balding but disguising it and wearing a suit that looked expensive but still didn't seem to fit very well, was sitting on the gurney, a foil blanket draped over his shoulders. He held a mug of something warm in his hands, absently, as if unaware that it was there. As if unaware that he had hands.

Phil remembered his name, spoke to him. 'Mr Eades?'

The man looked up. It was as if his eyes were at the back of a long, dark cave and he was having trouble seeing out.

'I'm Detective Inspector Brennan.' Phil offered his hand. The man detached his from the mug he was holding, absently shook it. 'I'm sorry about what's happened.'

Graeme Eades nodded.

'I'm going to have to ask you a few questions, I'm afraid.'

Another slack, absent nod.

Phil started in on his questions. He knew this was often the worst time to be asking them, but he pressed on because he didn't have time to wait. Sometimes he got lucky: a witness in shock would remember something with startling

274

clarity, and like a thread that could unravel a jumper, it was something that could be worked on, teased out.

Graeme Eades was clearly in shock, struggling to give answers, to be consistent. The more Phil went on, the less he thought there would be some kind of revelation, but he still kept plugging away. He also bore in mind what Anni had said while he asked the same things over and over: where were you this afternoon, what time did you get home, did you speak to your wife during the day, if so what time . . . and each time he received the same vague answers. He was about to give up, leave the questioning for later, when Graeme Eades looked up, grabbed his arm.

Phil, surprised by the action, looked down at the fingers. The grip was strong; not, Phil thought, because Graeme Eades' strength was returning, but more likely because the shock was bubbling up inside him, building him up to some kind of mania.

'I'm sorry,' he said.

'You're sorry?' said Phil, his heart skipping a beat. A confession would be too much to dare to hope for. 'What for?'

'It's my fault. I'm sorry . . .'

Phil sat down next to him once more. 'What are you sorry for?'

'I was . . . I was . . . with Erin. I should have been home and I was with Erin . . .' And then the tears started in earnest.

Phil could work out the rest from that. Graeme Eades was a liar. But he clearly wasn't a murderer. Just an adulterer. A very remorseful – and guilty – adulterer.

Phil stood up. He doubted there would be anything more Eades could tell him. Not in that state. Not at the moment. He left the ambulance, spoke to a uniform waiting by the back door chatting to a paramedic.

'See if you can get a statement when he calms down,' he

said, then walked over towards the house. He couldn't put it off any longer.

Marina was standing by his car. She was already suited, the hood pulled tight round her face, paper overshoes Velcroed round her legs. She was taking several deep breaths, her arm once again round her stomach, he noticed, her other arm on the bonnet of his car for support.

'You sure you want to do this?' Phil said, getting his own suit out of the back of his car and taking it out of the plastic bag.

She nodded, without making eye contact, keeping her focus on the front door. She didn't say anything.

'You don't have to,' he said, slipping into the suit. 'No one expects you to. No one would blame you if you waited until the body had been cleared out.'

'No.' She still didn't look at him, kept her eyes on something he couldn't see, something he wasn't even sure was there. 'I want to do it.'

'I should warn you. Once you step over that threshold, you're in hell. You might step out again, but it'll never leave you.'

'I know.'

'Well if you're sure. I don't want it messing you up, though. So much so that you can't function when we need you.'

She looked at him, right in the eyes. 'I won't mess up.'

He kept eye contact with her for perhaps longer than he should have done. His voice softened slightly when he spoke. 'I know you won't.'

He saw the ghost of a smile on her face. They both looked away at the same time.

Anni came to join them, similarly attired.

'Right.' Phil pulled his hood up, fastened his boots. He was ready. 'Let's go.'

276

54

P hil had been right, thought Marina. It was hell.

She had hoped that seeing Claire Fielding's apartment would have prepared her for this, but it hadn't. Nothing could have done. She had seen the flat after it had been cleared, the bodies removed. She had looked at the crime-scene photos, tried to imagine the two together. It still wasn't enough.

She had a flashback to when she was little and her mother used to wash her hair over the sink, rinsing it through with jug after jug of warm water. The school announced they were taking her year to the local swimming pool for lessons. Marina had never been swimming in a swimming pool before. She imagined it would feel like jug after jug of warm water over her head. But that gentle feeling was nowhere near the experience of plunging head first into the pool: the sheer weight and pressure of the cold, chlorinated water bearing down on her, pushing her under. She had felt like she was going to freeze and drown simultaneously.

Walking into the house had felt exactly the same. Viewing the photos, going round Claire Fielding's had just been a dry run. Now she saw first-hand the way an ordered, regular life had been torn apart and destroyed in the most horrific manner imaginable. She could feel the violence, the hatred and – there was no other word for it – the insanity in the atmosphere of the house. It was like an indoor fog had descended and refused to move. Her legs weakened and she stumbled. Phil looked at her, concern on his face.

'You okay?'

She nodded, kept her eyes away from his. The hall was carnage. The wallpaper, beige with gold designs, had bloodied handprints smeared down the length of it, showing signs of a desperate struggle, one she had no trouble imagining. The crunch of broken glass underfoot, a smashed light fitting helped her see it. But it was the bloodied spray over the walls, floor and ceiling that brought it to vivid life. The slaughterhouse decoration caused her to see the knife enter, break skin, slice muscle and tendon, watch as the bright arterial blood fountained and geysered out . . .

'You sure?'

'Yes.' Her throat was hot and dry, her voice cracked.

He didn't move for a few seconds, so she went on ahead of him. 'Let's . . . let's see the rest.'

He looked at her once more, decided he had to take her at her word and moved on. 'Must have been a struggle here,' he said aloud. 'She answered the door, he . . . what? Takes a swing at her? Cuts her?' He looked down at the carpet. The bloodstains had been flagged, samples taken for analysis.

'Looks like it,' Anni said. 'Why, though? That's changing what he did last time.'

'Serial killers . . .' Marina took a deep breath. 'Serial killers will do that sometimes.'

'We're saying that?' said Phil. 'Calling this the work of a serial killer?'

'You think there's any doubt now?' said Marina.

'And there's no chance Brotherton could have done this before we brought him in?' said Anni.

'Highly unlikely,' said Phil.

'So why's he done it like this?' said Anni, getting them focused once more. 'This serial killer? To throw us off? Make us think it's someone else?'

'Perhaps,' said Marina. 'They do that. Or they might find a . . . a different way of working. Something that . . . that . . . suits them better.'

'Let's find out where he cut her,' said Phil. 'Might give us more of a clue.'

Phil leading, they followed the bloodied trail into the living room. And stopped dead.

'Oh God . . .' said Marina. 'Oh Jesus . . .' She screwed her eyes tight shut, but not before the image had seared itself on to her retinas.

What was left of Caroline Eades' body lay in the centre of the room, on the floor. Her stomach had been slit in a crude circle from her groin to beneath her breasts. The baby had been removed. That was horrific enough, but whoever had done it hadn't stopped there.

'Throat cut,' said Phil.

'Not just cut,' said Anni. 'He's nearly taken her head off.'

The cut went right through her neck. Marina could see the glistening white bone of the woman's spine in amongst the gore.

'Maybe she started to scream,' said Anni. 'Had to keep her quiet. That accounts for the amount of blood in the hall.' She looked again at the body. 'What's . . . what's he done with her arms and legs?'

'Broken them,' said Phil, trying to sound as neutral as possible, failing to keep the revulsion out of his voice. 'Then . . . held them down . . .'

Caroline Eades' arms and legs were splayed out at impossible angles to her body. Heavy objects from around the room held them in place. Hardback reference books. A vase. The DVD recorder. The coffee table.

'Oh God . . .' said Marina again. 'Oh God . . .'

Phil turned to her, grabbed her by the shoulders. Eye-to-eye contact. 'Marina, look at me.'

'But, but I . . . I know her . . .'

Anni joined Phil in staring at Marina. 'How?' asked Phil.

'Oh God . . .'

'How?' Phil asked again, his voice managing to be both soft and firm.

'Yoga . . . she was at yoga . . . She . . . she asked me to go for a coffee . . .'

Phil needed Marina to concentrate. He couldn't allow her to slip into emotional memories. 'Marina, that's awful. Horrible. But I need you to focus now. To put that to one side and focus. I want to know what you see.' His voice was calm, solicitous. 'Tell me what you see.'

She glanced at the body again, then quickly back to Phil, her lip trembling.

'What Marina Esposito the trained psychologist sees. What this means to our investigation. What you see on that floor that's going to help us catch whoever did this.' His voice dropped even lower. 'Look again. Tell me what you see.'

She took a deep breath, steeled herself. Looked again. Tried to take in the scene dispassionately, clinically. Put aside her feelings, her emotions, work analytically. Put those years of theory into practice.

'He's . . . I say he, I don't . . .' She shook her head. 'I'll leave that one for now. The perpetrator came in through the front door; she . . . she answered it; he wanted to silence her. Maybe she started to scream . . . maybe he didn't want to take that chance. So he did it fast. He's . . . he's in a hurry. On a schedule? Wants it over quickly?' She shook her head. 'No.'

Another look at the body on the floor, the bloodstained

walls. 'He's here to do a job. He wants that baby. No time to mess about. He's escalating again. More ferocious this time, less focused.'

She then did something that she wouldn't have believed herself capable of doing. She knelt down before the body, peered at the stomach wound. 'He knew what he was doing. This is controlled. The cutting isn't frenzied or hurried. The rest of the attack is.'

She let her eyes rove over the other injuries. 'He didn't have time to tie her down, to control her as he did Claire Fielding. The restraints, the spreadeagling. I bet there's no drugs, either. Maybe he couldn't get them in time. Maybe he'd run out.' She looked again. 'Or maybe he doesn't want to use them any more. Maybe he's really getting a taste for this. He's doing a job, but he's starting to enjoy it. Really, really enjoy it . . .'

She checked the position of the body. 'Right. So he pushes her down . . .' She saw the action on her mind's eye. 'Not content with that, he smashes her arms, her legs. She's not going anywhere. Then he . . . he wants her to stay still, be controlled. No drugs, so he improvises. Finds what's at hand to do the job of keeping her in place. Then he gets to work.'

'What does that tell us?' asked Phil. 'What's your impression?'

She kept staring at the body, thinking. Phil and Anni waited. 'I don't think it's an escalation in the sense of him getting out of control,' she said eventually. 'But this is a fierce attack and it's come right after the last one. Usually in cases of this nature there's some time between them. The perpetrator likes to rest up, let his lusts die down, play with his trophies until the urge builds again. There's nothing like that here.'

'Why not?' asked Phil.

'Because . . .' An idea struck Marina. She felt cold and

281

empty as it took hold of her. 'The baby's dead. The last baby he took. Claire Fielding's. That's it. That's why he's back again so quickly. He wants a replacement.'

'And this baby could still be alive?' said Anni.

'Not my department. But I hope so. I'd guess so.'

'And the position he's left the body in?' said Phil.

'Doesn't matter,' said Marina, staring at the body. 'I don't think there's any significance. He's got what he wanted and he's off.'

'So this confirms things,' said Phil. 'That it's not the woman who's the target; it's the baby.'

'Right,' said Marina. 'She's just a . . . a husk, a carrier. He doesn't care what happens to her. Like you don't care what happens to an eggshell when you crack it and take out the egg.'

Phil and Anni stared at the body, taking in what Marina had said.

Eventually Marina turned to Phil. 'Can we step outside now, please?'

'Certainly.'

They did so. Marina was surprised at what she saw. Teams of white-suited police were going about their jobs in what was once a peaceful suburban street. Now it looked like it was the centre of a chemical attack. Nothing had been spared. Fingertip searches were taking place. The house and surrounding area were being examined in forensic detail. She saw door-to-door inquiries being carried out. A mobile police station had been set up by the end of the turning for anyone to give information anonymously. Nick Lines and his pathology team had arrived.

The press were behind the barriers at the end of the road, erected to stop them actually seeing anything, their cameras and lights adding to the police lights, creating an unreal film-set atmosphere. They were getting restless, hovering, hoping for that one glimpse, that overheard remark, the mistake that would provide them with their story.

Phil stopped walking. Spoke to the other two. Started to take charge once more. 'Anni, chain of evidence. Follow the body to the mortuary. Get Nick Lines over here now. I want timelines established for Graeme Eades, for Caroline Eades and for this Erin woman. I want her found and questioned. See if she wanted a baby and he wouldn't give it to her. I want Forensics working overnight, I want everything double-checked. He must have left some trace here, he must have done . . .'

'Who's going to do all this?' asked Anni.

Phil sighed. 'I wish we still had Clayton. The Birdies should be here soon. I'll make a couple of calls. Get all available ranks here and working on it.'

Marina looked over at the press once more. Flashbulbs popped in her direction as she did so. 'Should have brought Ben Fenwick after all,' she said to Phil. 'He could have kept them quiet.'

'I suppose he does have his uses,' said Phil.

'We're going to need to tell them something,' said Anni.

Phil nodded. Looked up. 'Would you two do it?'

Anni and Marina exchanged surprised glances.

'Aw, boss,' said Anni, 'that's not my thing. Come on . . .'

'You've had media training, you can do it,' said Phil, warming to his theme. 'Both of you. Together. Say what's happened – don't give details – then if you, Marina, could look at the camera and make some kind of plea to . . .' He shrugged. 'Whoever's got the baby. Ask them to give it back, ask them to come forward and we'll help them, that kind of thing.'

'You think that'll help?' asked Marina.

'It won't hurt.' Phil sighed, and Marina saw just how

much stress he was under. 'I know it's not what you signed up for, but if anyone knows the words that'll hit this person's buttons, it's you.'

She just looked at him.

'Please.' He glanced over at the news crews, then back to Marina and Anni. 'It's national now, not local. We need as much help as we can get.'

Marina shook her head, looked at Anni. 'Well?' she asked.

'I will if you will,' said Anni.

'Thank you,' said Phil.

The two women walked over to where the press were waiting, Anni complaining that if she'd known she was going to be on TV, she would have remembered her make-up. Phil watched them go. He couldn't hear what they said, but the audience seemed to lap it up. Anni was sur-prisingly poised, he thought. And Marina sincere. He noticed that she kept touching her stomach as she spoke, in that new nervous habit of hers. Then they were finished and walking back towards him. Flashbulbs popping once again.

'Well done,' he said.

Marina smiled. 'Thank you. I can now add media star to my CV,' she said with a grim smile.

'Yeah,' said Anni. 'Judge on *X Factor* next.'

Marina smiled once more. It covered the weariness and the tension.

Phil looked away, but she kept scrutinising him. His hand went to his chest, clutching it as if in sudden pain. She knew he was hiding it from Anni and his team, but she caught it. She knew what it was too. A panic attack.

She felt suddenly protective of Phil as he stopped rub-bing, took a few deep breaths.

'Come on then,' he said, turning back to them. 'Let's get started. Time's running out for that baby.'

He turned, walked away towards the mobile incident room. Marina caught up with him.

'Thanks,' he said, keeping his eyes straight ahead, his jaw set. 'I owe you one.'

Marina didn't reply. Just smiled.

55

The baby was quiet. Finally. Hester had picked it up, held it, shushed it. Rocked it from side to side. The motion must have made it sleepy. It closed its eyes. Eventually it had woken up and wanted feeding. She had given it milk. It had taken it. Hester felt good. Proud. Like she could cope.

Now the baby was sleeping in its cot. Hester had the TV on. Hester loved the TV. Especially the adverts. The stuff in between them she often didn't understand. She saw people doing things and heard laughter at the result but didn't know what was supposed to be funny. She watched people being serious with each other but couldn't work out what they were so worried about. She heard singers and dancers getting whooping applause and failed to see what the audience was getting excited about. You had to phone in and vote for the best one. She couldn't work out who that was. But sometimes it was the other way round: things that were supposed to be serious she laughed at. Things that were supposed to be funny she found serious. But the singers and dancers she still didn't get, still didn't know what was supposed to be good or bad.

She was watching the news. She had started watching it

when her first baby arrived. And got hooked. Photos of happy women on the screen would cut to a reporter standing in front of a crime scene. She knew it was a crime scene because the police were always there. And the reporter said so, in a voice that didn't smile.

Hester knew better. They weren't crime scenes. Birthing rooms, her husband called them. Where the surrogates – *her* surrogates – had given up their babies for her. So she could be a mother. She felt a tingle inside herself when she watched. She picked a word that the reporter used – random. She frowned. It wasn't random, it was her list. Pinned to the kitchen wall, the ones already used crossed out, the ones still to go unmarked. And there were lots more to go. She shook her head, frowned again. Some people . . .

She expected to see the same policeman again. The tall, smooth-looking one, with his good suit and his neat hair. Handsome, she thought, in a way. Then felt guilty at the thought: there should be no other man for her but her husband. She never listened to his words, just watched the shape of his mouth as he spoke. It had lines at the sides, tense little lines that seemed to be increasing every time she saw him. She smiled. It was becoming a familiar little ritual. Comforting, in its way.

But this time was different. He wasn't there. Hester stopped smiling. She didn't want that. Instead there was this black girl with a harsh voice that Hester instinctively didn't like, and someone with her. Another woman. Young, attractive. The black girl stood back and let her speak. Hester felt anger build within her. Who was this woman? What did she want? Where was the smooth policeman with the nice voice? She was talking, leaning forward and saying something serious. Hester was too angry to listen to the words.

But the woman kept going, talking and looking. And Hester felt she was looking right at her.

'What are you lookin' at?' she shouted.

At the other end of the room, the baby made a noise.

Hester didn't care. She felt uncomfortable with the woman staring right at her. 'Why are you lookin' at me?' Her voice was louder. The baby moaned, thrashed.

Hester wasn't stupid. She knew the woman wasn't really looking through the TV at her. She knew they couldn't do that. Or thought they couldn't. But it still didn't feel good. She tried to calm down, listen to what the woman was saying. Maybe when she did that, when she heard the words, she could get the woman out of her head.

'. . . implore you. Please. If you have this baby or if you think you know the person who does, then get in touch with us. We urgently need to talk to you. We have professional care waiting. Please. We just need to talk to you.'

The woman's face got even more serious. Like she was saying something and she desperately wanted to be believed. Like when Hester told a lie and knew it was a lie but knew it would be worse to admit it.

'Please.' The woman hardly blinked. 'For the baby's sake. For your sake. You must be hurting. Please. Come forward. And let us help you.'

Then it went back to the reporter.

Hester thought she would be feeling anger at the woman's words. But she didn't know what she felt. It was like the anger she had expected to feel was in there but was getting churned around with some other stuff that she didn't know the name of so that it wouldn't come out properly. In fact, the other stuff felt like it was going to come out more. She didn't know what it was but she didn't like it. It made her feel sad. And that wasn't good.

So not knowing what to do and wanting to get rid of the feeling, she screamed at the TV. And kept on screaming.

The baby woke up. Hester felt it all in her head, couldn't

tell who was screaming the most. Eventually she stopped, leaving just the sound of the baby. Hester was breathing hard, like she had just been for a long run or worked outside in the yard. And the baby was still screaming.

He was watching the TV alongside Hester when the woman came on. Speaking to the camera, looking serious. Begging whoever had the baby to give it up. At first he was surprised. He recognised her but couldn't think from where . . . then he got it. Leisure World. The yoga class. Same as the last one. He smiled. She was pregnant too.

That gave him something to think about. Something to consider . . .

The baby kept crying.

Shut that fuckin' noise up, or I will . . .

The woman had gone from the TV and the news was on to something else. Hester got up, went to the baby, picked it up, looked at it. Feeling not anger or love but other things. Like when the woman had been talking. Things she didn't know the name of. Things she hated the feel of.

She sighed, knew what her job was. What her job would be.

To find ways to stop the baby crying.

56

Phil sat on the sofa, Marina next to him. In front of them sat Erin O'Connor.

Phil could see why a man like Graeme Eades would fall for her. She sat curled in an armchair, her legs tucked underneath her, long-stemmed glass of white wine in her hand. Her body was as warm-looking and inviting as her eyes were not. Like twin adding machines. But Phil doubted Graeme Eades had looked at her eyes much. Mid-twenties, he guessed, her long dark hair pulled back, wearing pink velour jogging bottoms and matching hoodie with a tight white T-shirt underneath. The tracksuit said she had been working out. Taking care of her greatest asset, he thought.

She sipped at her white wine. Phil and Marina hadn't been offered any. The house was small, a two-up two-down terrace in New Town. It was pleasantly furnished but didn't feel lived in. Phil got the impression that Erin O'Connor didn't intend to be living here, or anywhere like it, much longer.

Phil had got her phone number from Graeme Eades. It had been a simple matter of calling, explaining who he was, getting her address, then going round. He didn't tell her what it was about, only that it was an important matter.

Marina sat next to him. He had intended driving her home, but Erin O'Connor's was on the way. He didn't mind her listening in, since she was part of the investigation. Marina, however, didn't seem all that comfortable. She sat on the edge of the sofa, looking round the room. No doubt, thought Phil, sizing its owner up, making assumptions. Hopefully ones that would be able to help them.

'So what's this about, then?' Erin O'Connor was trying to look composed and nonplussed, but failing. An unexpected night-time visit from the police would do that, thought Phil. There was tension in the set of her jaw. Her voice was well modulated, as if she had taken elocution lessons to obliterate any trace of an Essex accent.

Phil leaned forward, confidential but professional. He felt weary as he did so, his muscles complaining. The stress of the day and the aftershock of the panic attack was making itself felt. He needed a bath. A long, hot bath. And a large glass of whisky. Something expensive and peaty. Or a good bourbon. He blinked. Concentrate.

'Well,' he said, pulling all his focus together on Erin O'Connor, 'I couldn't say much on the phone, but I believe you're familiar with Graeme Eades.'

Erin O'Connor stiffened, the wine glass halting on the way to her lips. 'Yes,' she said, her face as blank a mask as she could make it, 'I am. He's my boss at work.'

Phil nodded. 'More than your boss, I believe.'

She held her wine glass so tight that Phil thought she might be wearing her drink before too long. She must have reached the same conclusion, as she put it down, clasped her arms tightly round her body. 'What's this about?'

Cut to the chase, thought Phil. She can take it, she's a big girl. Very big girl, he mentally added. 'We believe you spent the afternoon with him at the Holiday Inn.'

'So? What if I did? It's not illegal.' Then, before Phil could say anything more, 'Do I need to get a lawyer?'

Phil shrugged. 'You tell me. But while you were with Mr Eades this afternoon, someone broke into his house and attacked his wife.'

Her jaw dropped. Phil was treated to the sight of some expensive dental work and wondered whether Graeme Eades had paid for that too. 'Are you . . . but I was with Graeme . . . do you think I did it?'

Her Essex accent had started to creep back, Phil noticed.

'No.'

'You think I know who did it?'

'Do you?'

'No!' Her accent had returned completely. 'Course not. Oh my God . . . Did they . . . what happened? Did they get away with much?'

Phil knew Marina would have noticed that remark. Not asking whether Mrs Eades was all right, but was there anything taken. From that, he knew that Erin didn't have anything to tell them. It would just be a matter of sorting out timelines. Ruling out rather than ruling in.

'Robbery wasn't the motive, we don't think,' he said. 'She was murdered.'

Her hand flew to her mouth. Stayed there. Her eyes widened. 'Oh my God . . .'

'I just need to know what time you were with Mr Eades from and what time you left.'

'Oh my God . . .'

'Please.'

'Oh . . .' Erin O'Connor became thoughtful. Before she spoke, her eyes narrowed. 'Am I going to lose my job for this?'

'That's not for me to say,' said Phil. He had had enough of this woman. 'You'll have to talk to Graeme Eades about that.'

292

'Oh . . .'

'What time were you there from, please?'

She thought. 'About half one, two-ish, I think. I left, we left, about five. Something like that.'

'Can anyone verify that? Did you check out?'

She shrugged. 'Graeme paid for the room. It was all done upfront. When we were finished we just walked out.'

Phil blinked again, stifled a yawn. He shouldn't be doing this. He was too tired. A voice came from his side.

'Would you describe Graeme as your boyfriend, Erin?'

Marina. Her voice soft and gentle. No longer uncomfortable. Phil didn't look at her, kept his eyes on Erin. Waited to see what her response would be.

She frowned again, took a sip of wine. She seemed more at ease with Marina. 'I suppose . . . we're . . .'

'Lovers?' suggested Marina.

She nodded. 'Yeah. That's it. Lovers.'

Marina smiled. 'Seems an odd match. I mean, you're young and very attractive . . .'

Did Phil notice Erin O'Connor blush?

'And Graeme's . . . well. I met him.' Marina smiled. 'I would have thought you could have done better.'

'He's my boss,' she said, as if that explained it. And in a way, thought Phil, it did.

'Does he have lots of girlfriends?' said Marina. 'Lovers who he's the boss of?'

'I don't know. He said he doesn't.'

'Did he promise to . . .' Marina shrugged, as if the question had just come to her. 'I don't know . . . advance your career?'

'That's exactly it!' Erin O'Connor almost shouted as she jumped enthusiastically on the suggestion. 'He said I would get promotion if I slept with him.'

'And did you?'

293

'He promised I would. He was going to do it. Start the ball rolling tomorrow, he said.'

Marina shrugged. 'I think all that's changed now, don't you?'

Erin nodded. Then she became reflective. Phil looked at Marina, impressed. Marina stifled a small smile. Phil knew they would get no more from Erin O'Connor. He knew she would just move on to the next man who fell for her charms. He made to stand up. Then Erin O'Connor spoke.

'You know what he said?' There was a bitterness in her tone, as if she was realising not only that she wouldn't be getting her promotion through Graeme Eades, but that she had wasted all that time with him when she could have targeted someone else.

Phil stopped moving, stayed where he was. 'What? What did he say?'

'Today. This afternoon. He was . . . when we were . . . doing stuff. And I . . . I asked him if it was okay. If he liked what I was doing. And d'you know what he said?'

Marina and Phil waited, knew it was a rhetorical question.

'He said, at least I don't have to pay for it any more.'

'Charming,' said Marina.

'At least I don't have to pay for it . . .'

There was nothing more to say. They said goodbye and left Erin O'Connor to her thoughts, her wine, her small house and her plans for the future.

Outside in the street, Marina pulled her coat tightly around her. Phil looked at her.

'Waste of time,' he said. 'Just another gold-digger.'

Marina shrugged. 'See a lot of them, do you?'

He smiled. 'Only professionally. Not personally. Come on. I'll get you home.' He started walking towards the Audi. Marina hesitated, then stayed where she was.

'No,' she said.

He stopped, waited for her to catch him up. She didn't move. He had no choice but to turn round, walk back up the street towards her. 'What's up?'

She didn't answer immediately. Phil waited, saw an expression on her face that he couldn't read. She looked like she was at war with herself. Eventually she spoke.

'I . . . I . . . don't want to go home.' She kept her eyes away from his.

Phil didn't know how to respond. 'Why? What's . . . what's wrong at home?'

'Nothing,' she said quickly. 'Well . . .'

Phil felt a flutter in his chest. Not a panic attack, he knew that. But something just as dangerous. Hope?

He stood directly in front of her. When he spoke, his voice was soft, gentle.

'Is something wrong? Tell me.'

'It's . . .' Her hand went up to her face. She dabbed quickly and sharply at the corners of her eyes, as if angry with herself for crying. Certainly in front of Phil.

'What? Tell me.'

Marina sighed, looked round, looked anywhere but at Phil. The street was narrow, tight. Terraced houses on both sides, cars parked either side of the street, allowing only single-file traffic through. The night was cold. When they exhaled, their breath left their bodies as clouds of steam.

'I . . .' She shook her head. 'I wasn't going to do this. I said I wasn't going to do this . . .'

Phil waited. Watched the clouds leave his mouth, dissipate in the dark.

'I saw things today . . . I can't, can't just go home after that. Take them with me.' Then, in a quieter voice, almost to herself, 'Again.'

'There's nowhere else to go, Marina.' Phil wasn't sure he meant those words. But he had to say them.

She shook her head. 'There is.' She looked up. Eye to eye.

Phil didn't know what to say. It was the moment he had been waiting for for months. It was the moment he had been dreading for months.

She turned away, looked up and down the street once more. They were the only people there. 'I . . . I missed you. I missed you . . .'

'I missed you too,' he said, not daring to believe his luck.

'But I couldn't. We couldn't. Not after . . .' She sighed. 'And then today. Everything that's happened today . . .' She looked back to him. 'I saw the kind of things today that I only ever deal with in books. How can I go home after that?' Her voice fell away, as small and fragile as a child's whispers. 'What if I have nightmares?'

'I'll be there for you.' He smiled. 'I might be having them as well.'

She smiled, the tears starting again. Phil gently put his arms round her. She fell into his embrace. She turned her face upwards to his, eye to eye once more. The tears in her eyes making them glitter like diamonds in the streetlights.

On that cold, narrow street, they kissed.

And Phil, tired beyond endurance only a few minutes ago, had never felt more alive.

57

The Hole in the Wall pub was, as it claimed, in a hole in the wall. The old Roman wall that ringed the town loudly proclaimed its heritage, having been preserved and patched up over the centuries. Built into the Balkerne Gate, an old Roman entry point, the pub had its own kind of heritage. It was near the town centre but didn't attract squaddie or townie drinkers, which meant less violence, which in turn meant, for Clayton, less chance of bumping into colleagues.

He walked inside, unused to the surroundings, trying quickly to get his bearings. Not a coppers' pub, he thought, then amended that: he could imagine Phil in here. But certainly no one else.

Walls bare except for flyers advertising gigs at the Arts Centre and plays at the nearby Mercury Theatre; stripped floorboards; deliberately mismatched old wooden furniture. At a table sat a bunch of people in paint-splattered overalls, scenery painters and designers on a break from the theatre. Some goth types sat at the bar, and despite their spiked piercings and fierce tribal make-up, Clayton presumed they were harming no one but themselves.

The layout of the pub was haphazard. It looked as if sections had been added over the years. Consequently the floors were uneven, with steps up and down to various levels. There were open spaces and hidden spaces, high ceilings and lower, sloping ones. Clayton scoped the place, frowning at the noise coming from the jukebox, something thrashing and insistent, something he would never appreciate if he lived for ever, looking for the person who had texted him. He found her sitting on a leather sofa in a secluded section at the back of the pub, underneath slanted wooden roof beams.

Sophie.

She was sitting with a drink in front of her – vodka and Coke, he imagined – wearing jeans, boots and a shiny black padded jacket. He noticed there was a very large handbag at the side of the sofa. He crossed over to her, looked round once again to make sure there was no one he knew in the pub.

'They let you go then?' he said.

'Had to. Had nothing to keep me on,' she said, taking a mouthful of her drink.

He sat down next to her. 'I'm takin' a big risk meetin' you here. This better be worth it.'

She put the glass back on the low table, moving her shoulders back, thrusting out her breasts in the process. A faint, fleeting smile played across her lips. 'I'm worth it.'

Clayton said nothing.

Sophie's mood changed. The smile disappeared, to be replaced by something darker. 'I've left him,' she said.

'Brotherton?'

'Who else?' Her voice matched her features.

Clayton wished he had bought a drink at the bar now. 'What did he say?'

Her face dropped, her eyes on the table. 'Haven't told him yet. Just went home, grabbed my stuff and left. He'll find out when he comes home.'

'He'll be well pissed off.'

'That's his problem.' She took another mouthful of her drink, a large one.

Clayton sneaked a look at his watch. Wondered what Phil and the team were doing. He felt bad about being dropped from the team. Like a striker who was having a goal drought. He knew that wasn't the case, but that was how it felt. He was embarrassed about it. His first thought: what do I tell my mum? She was always so proud of his achievements. And he gets dropped from the highest profile case he's ever worked. Not his fault, but how would she feel when she found out? He should have been out there, working, investigating. Not sitting here worrying about his future. But he knew he had no choice. So when Sophie called, he didn't know what it was about, but if it was something that could save his career he had to go. And now he knew.

'Well, good luck.' He stood up, made to go.

'What you doing?' She looked up at him.

He turned, stood over her. Looked right down her cleavage. Well, he thought, it was there, rude not to. 'Leavin'. Nothin' more to say, is there? You're leavin' him. Good luck.'

Anger flashed in Sophie's eyes. A kind of anger Clayton hadn't encountered before. 'That's it, is it? Good luck? Good fuckin' luck? Oh no you don't. You owe me, Clayton.'

Clayton felt anger of his own begin to build. 'Really? I owe you? Yeah? You're a big girl, Sophie. You make your own decisions.'

He started to walk away. She stood up, came round the table, grabbed hold of his arm. There was a surprising strength to her grip. Her fingers dug in. He turned.

'You walk out of here, Clayton, you walk out on me, and you'll be sorry. Really fucking sorry.'

'Yeah?'

'Yeah. Because there's still things about you I can tell your boss. Or your mate. DC Hepburn, isn't it?' A smile crept

299

back on to her face. No warmth, just a sick, calculating cold-
ness. 'She doesn't like you, does she? Or maybe she does.
Maybe that's her problem. Perhaps she's the one I should
talk to. Tell her about your past. What d'you think?'

And once again, Clayton felt scared of Sophie. Not just
because of what she could reveal – he had experienced that
before – but because of the way she was behaving. This was
a side of her he hadn't seen before. One he didn't want to see
again. Not just scary, unnerving. He opened his mouth to
speak. She stopped him.

'And don't tell me I wouldn't. 'Cause you know I would.'

Clayton sighed, too angry, too scared to speak. She smiled
again, and this time there was warmth in it. Or an approximation of warmth.

'Why don't we sit down again?' she said. 'Talk this
through.'

The grip on his arm relaxed, becoming a gentle guiding
hand. Another smile. This was more like the old Sophie. The
one he knew. Or thought he did. He allowed himself to be
led, sat down next to her.

'Right,' she said, as if they were two old friends together.
'Let's discuss this properly.' She took another mouthful of
her drink, prepared herself. 'I've left Ryan. I've got nowhere
to go, nowhere to live, Clayton.'

A shudder passed through him as he realised what she
was saying. 'You're jokin'.'

'No I'm not, Clayton.'

Saying his name again, building up repetition, like a sales-
person trying to sell him something. That was what she was,
he thought. That was what she had been as long as he had
known her.

'No. You can't . . .'

She leaned in close to him, the warmth in her voice now
spreading to the hand she placed on his thigh. Another

smile. If anyone glanced over from the bar they would just assume that they were a courting couple sitting in a private part of the pub, having a close, intense conversation that would end up in bed.

'I'm staying with you, Clayton. You live alone, you started this. You've got no choice.'

He sighed, said nothing.

'Besides, when Ryan finds out what I've done, he won't be happy, will he? He'll come after me.' She moved in closer, her hand snaking round his arm, her thigh against his, slowly moving backwards and forwards. 'I'll want protecting. And who better to do that than a big, hunky policeman . . .'

Clayton felt his head spin, his hands shake, as if his whole body was in a whirlpool and he was being sucked down into some dark vortex. But he felt something else, too. Something that he shouldn't have been feeling. Because despite her words, her threats, he was getting an erection.

Sophie guessed what was happening, shifted her eyes to his groin. She smiled, snaked her hand gently over it. He gasped.

'Ooh,' she said, 'is that for me?'

He couldn't reply. She laughed.

'Well,' she said, pulling away from him and throwing back the remainder of her drink in one go, 'now we know where we stand, I think we'd better get going.'

'What d'you mean?'

'Back to your place,' she said, as if explaining the obvious to a slow child. She patted the bag at the side of the sofa. 'I brought my stuff.' Her eyes darted to his groin once more. 'And I thought you'd want to get there quickly so I can show you my gratitude.'

He stood up, adjusting his overcoat around his erection. He felt terrible, as if he had a virus or food poisoning, shaking like he was going to throw up.

301

Sophie grabbed her bag, stood up too. She put her arm through his, guided him to the door of the pub. Once outside, she stopped, looked at him.

'You hungry? I haven't eaten all day.' She hugged him again. 'And I'll need my strength. Let's get a bite to eat.'

Food was the last thing on Clayton's mind. But he knew he had no choice. From the moment he had laid eyes on Sophie in Brotherton's metal yard and recognised her, he'd known he had no choice. He wondered again what his mother would say.

'Come on, then,' she said, and almost skipped along the street.

Clayton allowed himself to be dragged along with her, as eager as a death-row inmate with an imminent appointment in the mercy seat.

58

Marina walked into the living room, looked round.

'Look familiar?' Phil was closing the door behind him, coming down the hall. He joined her in the middle of the room.

She kept looking, taking in everything about the man that he had put on show. His books she remembered from before. His CDs likewise. His small collection of DVDs. Mainly old films, Hitchcock, film noir. Despite the lack of feminine touches, it didn't seem overly masculine, just comfortable; two sofas, and table lamps offering subdued lighting rather than one harsh overhead light. Prints on the wall showed surprising taste, she thought, for a police officer: Rothko, Hopper. But then he was a surprising man. She turned to him, smiled. 'Just like I last saw it,' she said.

'Good job I tidied up this morning.'

Her smile became teasing. 'You were expecting to bring someone back tonight?'

He opened his mouth to reply and for a second he seemed about to give a serious answer, but then a smile split his face, equally teasing as hers. 'I'm always expecting to bring someone back.'

She laughed. 'Oh, you're pathetic.' She made to sit down

but her attention was drawn to a CD case on the sound system. She crossed, picked it up. Smiled. Elbow.

Phil tried to shrug. 'Good album.'

'Course it is, Mojo man.' She nodded, put it down again. Sat down on the sofa, her mood suddenly changing. She sighed; her smile disappeared.

Phil looked at her, concerned. 'You okay?'

'Yeah,' said automatically. Then another sigh. 'No. Sometimes when you see what we've seen today ... I just ... Why do they do it, Phil?'

'You're the psychologist, you tell me.'

Her hands clasped and unclasped. 'I said something to you once. You probably don't remember.'

'Try me.'

'When we were out. That first time. You asked why I became a psychologist. I said it was to understand my father. I lied. It was to understand me. I also said that all psychologists are just looking for a way home. That's not strictly true either. It's not just psychologists, it's all of us. Everyone. We're all looking for a way home.' She lifted her head, fixed him directly. 'Even you.'

He didn't contradict her. He said nothing.

She continued. 'We all want to be safe, to find some place in the world, in our heads, our hearts, where we can be understood and that we can understand. Where we can belong.'

Phil nodded, saying nothing.

'Then I think of what we saw today. And what we have to do to catch them. What's their idea of home? Where's their head and their heart at? I've got to understand them. That's my job. I have to look into my head and my heart and find parallels. That's what I have to do.'

'And the abyss looks into you and all that; that's the job.'

'I know.'

He turned to her. 'Look, Marina. You're the best I've worked with. You know you are. You'll manage.' He looked at his hands. They were shaking. Then back to her eyes.

She smiled. 'This isn't doubt, Phil. It's just . . . I can ascribe reasons for aberrant behaviour. I can examine chains of cause and effect. But we'll never understand, will we? We'll never truly know what makes a monster. Or what makes someone do monstrous things.'

'You always said we create our own monsters.'

'And we do. But . . .' She sighed. 'Oh, I don't know. I suppose what I mean is, that's all for tomorrow. Tonight I just want to be somewhere . . . safe.'

They looked at each other, eyes locking once more. Phil moved towards her. Marina seemed to be moving to him but she stopped herself.

'You let me down, Phil. That's why I couldn't see you again.'

Phil stopped moving, sat back.

'You let me down and I could have been killed.'

'I . . .' This was it, he thought. The chance to tell her everything he had wanted to say, to speak aloud all those speeches and conversations he had rehearsed in his head over the months. To explain where he was and why he was needed. *Because Lisa King's body had just been discovered. Because I had to track down a killer. And I couldn't let you know because you had your phone switched off.* And everything else. On and on. But he didn't. Instead all he said was, 'I'm sorry.'

'It wasn't just that. It was . . . I knew. I had a choice to make. And if I chose you, then that was what it was going to be like. I might never feel safe again. And I wasn't sure I could handle that.'

He said nothing.

'I said I wanted to be somewhere safe tonight,' she said. 'So I can put myself in the mind of a monster tomorrow.

305

And safe . . . didn't mean home for me. It meant you. Even though you let me down. Even though . . . I was scared. What d'you think of that?'

'It was Lisa King,' he said. 'The start of this case. Her body had just been discovered. I phoned you.'

'I know.'

'Lots of times.'

'I know.'

He sighed. 'I didn't know what would happen . . . no one could know . . .'

She said nothing, looked at his face, scrutinised his eyes, reading them as if looking for any trace of a lie, an untruth, a hesitation. Found nothing but pain in his voice, his features. Sincerity and honesty.

'I'll never let you down again. Ever.'

She smiled. 'You'd better not.'

They kissed.

They were hungry for each other, wanted to consume each other.

They had started on the sofa, kissing. Breathing hot, warm, wet breath into each other's mouths. Tongues twining. Phil ran his hands over Marina's face, neck, down over her shoulders, the tops of her breasts. Marina put her hands round Phil's neck. Stroking, touching, experiencing the sensation of the other's skin beneath their fingertips, reacquainting themselves, confirming that they were both real, that this was actually happening once more.

Pressure increased, bodies pressed closer together. Fingers became more confident, more probing. Passion, need became urgent. Breathing came in harder, shorter gasps. Hands roved, explored, found buttons and zips, began undoing.

'Let's go to bed,' Marina said, her words gasped, whispered.

They pulled apart reluctantly, not wanting to separate but wanting to take it to the next level. Phil stood, Marina came with him. Hands, mouths still locked. They stumble-walked up the stairs.

Into the bedroom. Phil turned on the bedside light.

'No,' Marina said. 'Keep it dark.'

'I want to see you . . . look at you . . .' His hands were on her again, finding clasps, zips. Uncovering her shoulders, his mouth tracing down her neck, kissing her bared skin. Marina gasped. His hands moved further, pushing her top from her body. She helped him, responded. Pulled out his shirt, began unbuttoning. He shrugged it off, was naked to the waist. She did likewise with her top.

Phil smiled, lifted one bra strap, then the other, easing them down her arms, unclasping it from behind. He looked at her, drank in her nakedness in the half-shadowed room.

He smiled. 'You're beautiful.'

She smiled in response, then began unbuckling his belt. Remaining clothes and footwear were stripped in a blur. Naked, they held each other, feeling the sensation of each other's body through their own skin. Kissed once more, then pulled apart. Phil took Marina in once more: the shape of her breasts, the colour of her nipples, the way she had trimmed her pubic hair, her soft thighs. Her belly perhaps curved more than he remembered it. It didn't matter. She did the same for him: his broad shoulders, lightly haired chest, strong thighs, his penis, hard for her. She smiled.

'You're beautiful,' he said once more.

'So are you.'

Time froze. It was a moment both had fervently wanted but neither had believed would ever happen again. It felt so right, so comfortable. But beyond the passion, they were both terrified. It was more than just sex. They both knew that. It was a line. Once it was crossed, neither could retreat back over it.

'I love you.' The words were out of Phil's mouth before he could stop them.

'I know. Don't let me down.'

'I won't.'

The line had been crossed.

They moved to the bed.

Together.

59

Marina heard voices. Strong, opinionated voices. Her eyes jolted open and for a few seconds she didn't know where she was. Then, as a lost piece of jigsaw completes a whole picture, she remembered. Phil's bed. The radio alarm clock had just gone off, Radio Four's *Today* waking her up. Her eyes closed again. She smiled.

They had made love another three times, eventually drifting off to sleep some time in the early hours. It had been beyond what she remembered, beyond what she had imagined: intense and sacred at times, hot and filthy at others. But always physically and emotionally satisfying. She had drifted off to sleep with Phil's arms encircling her. She had felt safe. Coming back to Phil's house had been the right decision.

Now she lay there, letting the voices from the radio wash over her. It was familiar, the same show she woke up to at home.

Home.

She thought about Tony. She had phoned him as they left the crime scene, telling him she wouldn't be back, giving him an excuse about pulling an all-nighter to work on the latest murder. He had been his usual understanding, reasonable self, asked her if there was anything she wanted, anything he could do to help. She had felt guilt at those words. But not because she wanted to be with him. Just because he was so good to her. Like a father should have been. She thought of the cottage in Wivenhoe. Not warm and comforting, just hot and enclosing. Maybe it was time to leave home.

She turned over, stretched out her arm, expecting to feel Phil. Nothing. His side of the bed empty. Opening her eyes once more, she sat up, looked around. Just in time to see the door open and Phil enter carrying two mugs of coffee – freshly brewed, from the smell. He crossed to the bed, placed one on the table at her side, one on his own, took off his dressing gown and slid, naked, back under the sheets with her.

'Thought you'd gone to work without me,' she said, smiling.

'As if I'd do that,' he said. He took a mouthful of coffee.

She took a sip. Lovely. Milk, no sugar. Just as she liked it. She replaced it. 'You remembered how I take it.'

He frowned. 'Why should I forget?'

Warmth spread inside her at his words. He had always been a good listener. 'Why should you?'

The smile lingered on his face as he turned and looked at her. His eyes began to travel down her body.

'We haven't got time,' she said.

He gave a mock sigh. 'I know.'

A thought struck her. 'Should we go in to work together or separately?'

'Nobody else's business.' He placed the mug on the bed-side table, lay back. 'Does it bother you, what people might say?'

'Does it bother you?'

'Did last time. The gossip. What people were thinking, what assumptions they were making.'

'And now?'

He looked thoughtful. 'Perhaps for the investigation. If anyone tries to use this as an excuse for us not getting results, it would bother me. But other than that, no, I don't care.'

She snuggled in to him. 'Good.'

They lay there in silence for a while, both sleep-and-sex-hungover, comfortable in each other's silence.

'So,' he said eventually, 'what happens next?'

'I'm going to leave him,' Marina said. The words, said aloud, surprised her. Like an idea made real by speaking it. She hadn't known that that was what she was planning until she said it.

'For . . . for me?'

Silence once more. Then, from Marina, 'Let's see.'

Phil nodded. Said nothing. Eventually looked at his watch. 'We'd better get going.' He threw back the duvet, got out of bed. Found his dressing gown once more. 'You want the shower first?'

'No, I'm okay. You go.'

He started to walk to the door, turned before he reached it. 'I . . . look. I meant what I said. Last night. I won't let you down.'

'Good.'

'Right.'

And he left the bedroom.

Marina reached for her coffee, took another mouthful. Replaced it. Sighed. She heard the sound of the shower. She stroked her stomach, felt the baby moving inside her. Thought of other conversations she had to have with Phil.

She finished her coffee, then got out of bed. It would all have to wait until later.

She had a monster to catch.

311

60

'Phil? Call for you.'

Phil looked up from his desk, where he was gathering notes and photos together, preparing for the morning briefing. Adrian was holding up the handset on his desk, motioning to him. Phil mouthed the words, 'Who is it?' Adrian mouthed back, 'Solicitor.'

Phil picked up the receiver, transferred the call. 'Detective Inspector Phil Brennan,' he said.

'Good morning, Detective Inspector,' a female voice said. 'You're CIO on the dead babies inquiry?'

Phil said he was.

'Linda Curran of Hanson, Warnock and Gallagher.' She paused as if he should know them. He certainly did. He had dealt with them, and Linda Curran, before. Many times.

'Hello, Linda, how can I help you?'

'I'm representing Ryan Brotherton, Detective Inspector, and I'm informing you that my client has instructed me to sue Essex Police, and in particular your department.'

Phil's features hardened. His grasp on the receiver tightened. 'Is that right?' he said.

'Indeed it is,' Linda Curran said. From the tone of her

voice, she took no particular joy in the message; she was merely doing her job.

'Oh come on, Linda,' he said. 'That's ridiculous. What is it? Harassment? How does he work that one out? We're charging him with attempted murder.'

There was the rustle of paper down the phone. 'Harassment, wrongful arrest, deprived of basic human rights whilst in custody, loss of earnings and emotional distress.'

'Okay,' said Phil, 'let's go through these. Can I do that? Or will it prejudice the case?'

'Feel free.'

'Okay. Harassment. Brotherton's name came up several times in a murder inquiry. We went to see him at work, and when he attacked my DS, we brought him in for questioning. He was never arrested.'

'He attacked your . . .? You allege he attacked your DS?'

'Dropped a ton of metal on him. Or would have done if he hadn't got out of the way in time. No "allege" about it. Didn't he mention it?'

Silence. Linda Curran clearly hadn't been informed of the circumstances. 'And that's the attempted murder?'

'It is in my book. What about this basic human rights thing? When did that happen?'

'In custody. You denied him access to a solicitor.'

'News to me. Warnock'd been called but was unavailable. You were on your way; we were just . . . chatting till you arrived. What was the next one?'

'Loss of earnings.'

'Blaming me for the credit crunch now, is he? And emotional distress.'

'Apparently his girlfriend has left him.'

'Good for her. Let's hope she finds someone who doesn't want to use her for target practice. Is that it?'

Another rustle of paper. 'Yep. That's everything.'

'Right,' said Phil, a weary smile on his face. It was all just part of the game. He sighed. 'Well, thanks again, Linda. Always nice to talk to you.'

'You too, Phil.'

'I wouldn't want to do your job.'

She gave a small laugh. 'And I wouldn't want to do yours. Let's catch up sometime.' She hung up.

'Or let's not,' he said to the dead line, putting the phone down. They had once gone out on a date. One of his least successful ones. And that was saying something. She must just be saying that out of politeness, he thought.

He leaned back in his chair, stretched. That was all he needed. Brotherton making trouble. He wasn't worried, though. He could make it go away. It was just extra hassle he didn't need, something to divert his time and energy.

He drained the last of his coffee, threw the paper cup in the bin. He had driven Marina in to work, then gone off to get takeaway coffee from a nearby sandwich shop. That way, he thought, it wouldn't look like they were arriving together. Phil imagined, once again, all eyes on them as they entered the building. Questioning, knowing. That was one of the reasons he had gone out again. In reality, no one paid them the slightest bit of attention. Still, he couldn't think about that now. Not with a briefing for the whole team in less than five minutes.

He gathered up his papers, made his way to the door.

'Ben Fenwick sends his apologies,' said Phil, sitting down
    Marina fought the urge to smile smugly.

'Over to you.' He gestured to Marina. She nodded, looked round. Phil, Anni, the Birdies, herself. The core members of the team. Phil was trying his best to pretend he wasn't watching her with more than professional interest. She tried not to look at him too much.

'Thanks,' she said. 'Right. We know it's not Brotherton. If the profile didn't help, the last murder did. I've had a look at Caroline Eades' murder and tried to fit it in with the others. And there are some interesting developments. Not to say worrying ones.'

She looked down at her notes, back to the room.

'Serial killers usually work to a routine. And yes, we're using the phrase serial killer now. I don't think there's any doubt. They usually follow a pattern. Same type of victim, some method of death, same type of location. But with this killer, there have been some striking deviations. I don't know if they're significant; I think they may be.'

She felt a twinge of pain in her stomach, automatically pressed her hand on it. She noticed Phil watching her.

'Right,' she said, 'the first time a serial killer kills – or at least the first time we hear about it; there will have been other incidents before this – they usually kill in an area of geographical significance. It could be where they live, work, where they lost their virginity, whatever. So far, we haven't found anything significant about the first murder.'

'But we're still working on it,' said Phil. 'Every new case that comes in, we match against it.'

'Good. But I don't think the location is significant in this killer's case. There's something more important to him than that. Each murder has presented an escalation. With Lisa King, the baby was killed too. Susie Evans, the baby was beside the body. Claire Fielding, the baby was missing. Same with Caroline Eades. But the timing is also significant with the latest one.'

'Why?' said Anni.

'Because serial killers don't just enjoy killing, they enjoy having killed. They usually take a trophy or two from the scene, take it back to their lair and . . .' She shrugged. 'Well, I'll leave that to your imagination.'

Everyone's face registered disgust.

'But that doesn't seem to be the case here. Which would suggest that he's differently motivated.'

'Bit of an understatement,' said Adrian.

'Indeed. But even amongst the noble brethren of serial killers, he's different. For most serial killers, the primary motivation is usually sexual. I don't think that's the case here. He wants the babies. He doesn't care how he gets them. The women are nothing.'

She turned to the whiteboard behind her, took out a marker pen. Started making notes. 'So this is what we've got. Different locations, different victims. The only thing they have in common is pregnancy.'

'And some kind of link to Brotherton,' said Phil.

'All except Caroline Eades,' said Marina.

'At the moment,' said Anni.

'Too many links, though,' said Phil, 'and I don't believe in that many coincidences. Maybe someone's trying to set Brotherton up? Shift the blame? Draw our attention, misdirect us, make us look at him to avoid looking at the real killer . . .' He put his hands behind his head, frowned. 'But that would have taken a huge amount of planning.'

'True. Next thing, escalation. Caroline Eades' death looked improvised. He didn't have time to restrain her properly, so he used whatever was at hand. And used it very crudely. Which leads me to believe that the baby he took from Claire Fielding is dead. He wanted this one as a replacement.'

'You sure about that?' asked Anni.

'As sure as I can be, given what I saw last night.'

'What about this baby?' said Phil. 'Is it alive?'

'I've spoken to Nick Lines,' said Jane Gosling. 'And he says that judging by the health of the mother and how far gone she was, plus looking at the way the baby was cut out –

316

and he's getting better at that, apparently – there's every possibility that it is.'

'Let's hope so,' said Marina. 'So let's assume that it is. But there's something else, as well. A question of gender. Normally, serial killers are male.'

'This big woman thing again,' said Adrian. 'But we've got a picture, CCTV. Millhouse has got the techies working overtime on it, but it's still not sharp enough. And we don't want to rush it. Might get the wrong person.'

'It could be a woman,' said Marina. 'Or it could be a man and a woman working together.'

'Or a man providing for a woman,' said Phil.

'Exactly,' said Marina. 'Now, there are usually two kinds of serial killers. Psychopathic and sociopathic. The psychopaths are wild. They prey on victims, don't care if they get caught. Sociopaths are harder to find. They can blend into society, hold down jobs, lead normal lives. Then one day something goes. And they have to feed their desires.'

'Will they have a job?' asked Anni.

'They might do,' Marina said, 'but it won't be anything prestigious. They won't be head of Microsoft or anything like that. They can use a knife. Maybe slaughter animals? Farm worker? Abattoir? Something along those lines. Also the disregard for the victim. Just another piece of meat.'

She looked round at the assembled faces. She had their total attention.

'At first I thought our killer was the first kind, a psychopath. Which, on reflection, might be better. This person lives on the edge. Single-minded. Not interested in taunting us or leaving messages. They're doing this for a reason. They want something. The baby. They don't see themselves getting caught because they don't think about getting caught. They're clever, cunning. Like an animal. This, theoretically, should make them slightly easier to catch. However . . .'

317

They waited.

'If there's two of them, one may be the psychopath, one the sociopath . . .' She could feel an idea coming to her. 'If . . . if there are two of them, then one, the contained one, the sociopath, could be finding the victims . . .'

'And the other one ripping them up?' said Anni.

'It's a theory.'

'If that's the case, then there's another idea,' said Phil.

They all looked at him.

'Split personality. Is that viable?'

'Could be,' said Marina. 'Two in one. I think that's even scarier, actually. But the same principles apply.'

'So how do we catch them?' asked Phil.

'Well, I don't think they're based in Colchester. I think they're coming in to do this. The geographical profiling supports that. And because they're all over the town, I think that means he's targeting them another way.'

'How?' said Phil.

'I don't know,' said Marina. 'But I think that's the key. Find out how he's choosing them and we've got him.' She nodded at Phil. His turn.

'Thanks, Marina. Right. I want all the individual cases re-examined today.' He scanned the room, making sure his words registered. 'Similarities flagged, everything. Old reports gone over, the lot. Marina, would you help with that, please? I'd like you teamed with Anni.'

'Sure.'

'Good. Anything that sticks out, flag it up. We can cross-reference it against Brotherton and Caroline and Graeme Eades. Look for another match. Forensics are still going through the data from the last two crime scenes. No conclusive DNA yet, but they'll keep looking. And there's something else. I don't know how significant it is.'

They waited.

318

'Sophie Gale has done a runner. Brotherton's solicitor was on the phone this morning.' He told them about the call.

'Good luck to her,' said Anni.

'Let's keep an eye out for her, though. We should still talk to her again.' He scanned the room once more. Despite the tiredness, he could see that they were all ready to go. 'Get pounding those files, those streets. Good old-fashioned police work. We might have lost one baby but there's another one out there and the clock's ticking. Let's get going.'

They all filed out.

As Marina got up, Phil moved in to talk to her.

'Marina,' said Anni, 'come on. You're with me.'

She looked at Phil, gave an apologetic little shrug and turned away. Phil walked out alone.

61

Clayton couldn't concentrate. He looked round the bar, at the walls, through the windows. Anywhere but where he was supposed to be looking. Down at the report in front of him.

He was deskbound, tasked with paperwork. Unable to work the case, unable to function like the copper he wanted to be, believed himself to be. He hated it. He saw faces, clocked movements. He knew what they were doing, what they were thinking. About him. They knew. *They knew.*

His heart was hammering in his chest, his hands shaking. But how much did they know? If it was everything, then that was it, finito. But if wasn't . . . he might have a chance. A slim one. He shouldn't have done it. Let Sophie stay at his place. He shouldn't have taken that blow job from her in the car the other night. Hell, if he traced it all the way back, he shouldn't have got involved with her in the first place.

All he wanted to be was a good copper. Well respected by his peers, well liked by his colleagues. And the ladies. But he couldn't see that happening now. Because he was weak. And being weak made him do stupid, cowardly things. Like getting involved with Sophie.

He looked round again. Phil was at his desk, attacking a

pile of paperwork he had allowed to accrue. He kept his head, down, focused on his task. Didn't catch Clayton's eye. Millhouse was geeking away at his computer, in his own virtual world as usual. But it was Marina and Anni that he felt most scared about. Anni had pulled her chair up to Marina's desk and was sitting alongside her, poring over reports and statements, scrutinising photos. Every once in a while Clayton would look across, find Anni staring back at him. He would look quickly away, his eyes nervous, shifty. Guilty.

She hadn't told. He knew that. Otherwise Phil would have said something. But it was only a matter of time. She wouldn't keep that to herself. She was as ambitious as he was, and hard-working. She wouldn't want to be seen to collude in mistakes he had made.

They would find out where Sophie was. Because they might still need to talk to her. And when they did . . .

He had to get a grip, think about what to do next. Get a damage-limitation plan in operation. Clayton sighed, went back to his paperwork.

Still unable to concentrate.

Anni read the statement over once again. Geraint Cooper, Claire Fielding's friend at school. She reached the end. Read it once more. Put it down, rubbed her eyes.

'Nothing?' said Marina, looking up.

'I think it's just . . . I want to see something there, find a connection so much that I'm imagining things . . .'

'Take a break,' said Marina.

Anni shook her head. 'Not yet.' She took a mouthful of bottled water. 'Right. Let's go again. Connections.' She looked down at the list she had made in front of her. 'Lisa King. Killed in an empty house. Had shown properties to Ryan Brotherton. Susie Evans. Prostitute. Ryan Brotherton one of her customers.'

'And Sophie Gale,' said Marina. 'Where he met her.'

Anni nodded. 'And she informed for the police. In return for certain leniencies. Right. Claire Fielding. Julie Simpson. Girlfriend of Brotherton and her best friend. Then Caroline Eades.' She looked through the piles of paper on her desk. 'No connection. None.'

'Caroline Eades. Never worked?'

'Her husband's an area manager for a recruitment agency. She was a stay-at-home mum. No connection with any of the others.'

Marina sat back, thoughtful. Sucked one of the arms of her reading glasses. 'What do we know about Sophie Gale?'

Anni rifled through her pile of papers, brought one out. 'Born Gail Johnson. First known address is in New Town. Pulled in on a raid, let go, works for us. Changes her name to Sophie Gale.'

'Reinvents herself.'

'Up to a point. Then appears with Ryan Brotherton.'

'So we have to assume they've known each other for a number of years. And in a number of capacities.'

Anni nodded. 'We'll never know now. She's gone.'

'Won't she turn up again?'

Anni gave a small smile. 'Probably. One way or another. They usually do. And usually attached to a man.'

Marina got a quick mental image of Erin O'Connor then. Sitting in her little New Town house, looking like she wouldn't be there too much longer. Erin O'Connor. Sophie Gale. Both sounded like made-up names. Manufactured girlie names. Names a man might enjoy saying, especially at certain times and in certain situations . . .

'Marina? You all right?'

Marina blinked. Anni was looking at her, concerned. 'Sorry?'

'You'd gone for a few seconds.'

322

She shook her head. 'Yes . . . miles away . . .' She was still thinking, grasping for something . . .

Something Erin O'Connor had said: *At least I don't have to pay for it any more . . .*

'Phil and I went to talk to Graeme Eades' girlfriend. Erin O'Connor.'

'His alibi.'

'Have you checked to see if she's got a record?'

Anni sat upright. It looked like electricity had been run through her already spiky hair. 'What kind of a record?'

'Prostitution.'

'I'll check.'

'I may be wrong,' said Marina, thinking how disgusted the woman had looked when she had said the phrase, but wondering if that could have been an act put on for their benefit. 'I may be doing her a great disservice, but I just get the feeling there might be a connection.'

'Go with your gut instincts. That's how it works.' Anni stood up. 'I'll go and check.'

She walked across the office. Marina watched her go.

So did Clayton.

Anni asked Millhouse to run a check on Erin O'Connor. While she waited, she looked round the office. Clayton was sweating like it was midsummer. And shaking like he had Parkinson's. She hadn't told anyone about his involvement with Sophie. Not yet. And if he didn't give her cause to, she wouldn't. But he didn't know that. She bit back a smile. Good. Let him suffer.

'Urm . . . yeah . . .' Millhouse was staring at his screen. 'Here . . . No, er . . . nothing . . .'

Eloquent as ever, thought Anni.

'Okay,' she said, 'what about Graeme Eades?'

'The victim's husband?'

'The very same.'

'Right . . .' He started pressing buttons, scrolling through information.

Anni waited. As patiently as she could.

'Uh . . .' said Millhouse eventually, 'here. Yeah, here. God . . . wow . . .'

Anni bent down to see what he was looking at. And there it was.

'Graeme Eades, picked up, cautioned,' she said. 'Four years ago. Was anyone picked up with him? Either buying or selling?'

'Uh, yeah, I'll see . . .'

Millhouse worked away on the screen. Anni felt excitement rising within her. She tried not to let it show. So many times in similar situations she had allowed herself to hope, only to have those hopes dashed by reality. So when Millhouse asked her to look at the screen, she tried not to harbour too much hope.

'Here . . .'

She smiled. Felt her toes curling. For once, her hope hadn't been misplaced.

'Fantastic, Millhouse. I could kiss you.'

'Erm . . .'

She smiled. She could almost see the phrase 'does not compute' running through his mind. She all but ran back to Marina.

Clayton watched her go. He didn't know what it was she had discovered, but he doubted it was good news. Anni didn't even sit back down next to Marina, just leaned over the desk and spoke hurriedly to her. Marina then got up, and in a similar hurry to Anni, rushed over to Phil's desk.

Oh God, oh fuck . . . She's found something. There must have been a record left of his connection with Sophie. She had discovered it. That must be it. He was breathing so hard he thought his heart would develop an arrhythmic problem. Like having too much coke.

He tried to calm down. Think straight. Maybe it wasn't him. Maybe they had discovered something that would further the investigation. A breakthrough. That was it. It might not be about him after all.

He forced his heart rate down, his breathing to steady. There was only one way to find out. He stood up from his desk, crossed the office to where Millhouse was sitting.

'Hi,' he said, aiming for nonchalance, but missing by several miles.

Millhouse barely grunted in response.

'What was, er . . . what was Anni looking for just now?'

'Graeme Eades,' said Millhouse, clearly upset at being disturbed from whatever he had been doing. Obviously Clayton didn't hold the same appeal that Anni did for him.

'Can I have a quick look?'

'You're off the case.'

Clayton gave a smile that he hoped said they were all mates together but somehow just died on his face. 'Come on, Millhouse. You know what it's like. Please. Just for me.'

Millhouse sighed, went into the system. 'There,' he said. 'That's what she wanted to see first.'

Clayton swallowed hard. 'Right. First? What did she look at next?'

Another grunt and a sigh, as if Millhouse was being asked to move a mountain with only a teaspoon. 'This.'

He put the screen up, sat back. Clayton looked. And felt the shakes returning. Big time.

He stood up. Walked slowly back to his desk, as if in a trance.

'Don't mention it,' said Millhouse after him.

But Clayton didn't hear. He sat down before the screen. *Oh God, oh fuck . . .*

The door to Phil's office opened. Phil came out, shrugging into his jacket, Anni following. They both made their way to the front door.

Clayton sat there, watching them go. He had to do something, but he was too stunned to move. He had to be careful. Whatever he did next was important. Very important. His future career depended on it. He had to think. Find a way to make this work, come out of it clean.

Yes.

But first he had to make a phone call.

62

Graeme Eades opened the door. He looked to Phil like a different man. Like he had aged enough to become his own father in the space of a day. But worse than that, he looked like a ghost that hadn't realised it was dead yet. Guilt will do that to you, thought Phil.

He was staying in a Travelodge on the outskirts of Colchester. His own house was being treated as a crime scene, examined for potential forensic clues, and would be for some time.

'Would have thought he'd had enough of cheap hotels by now,' Anni had said as they had walked up to the front desk and shown their warrant cards.

Phil hadn't answered, just asked for directions to Graeme Eades' room.

'Mr Eades?' he said. 'Just a few more questions, please. Won't take long.'

Eades opened the door fully, walked back into the room. He was dressed in a pair of chinos and a sweatshirt. It looked as if he had slept in them too. He needed a shave and his remaining hair had been sculpted into interesting swirls and whorls. He sat on the bed and waited, head down. Like a death-row inmate awaiting execution. But from the look in his eyes, he was already dead.

Phil stood before him, leaning against the built-in set of drawers. Anni sat in the chair.

'We've been looking into your background, Mr Eades, and there are a couple of things we'd like you to clear up.'

No response.

'Four years ago you were picked up and cautioned for kerb-crawling, is that correct?'

Eades looked up. He frowned. 'What?'

Phil started the sentence again. Eades cut him off. 'What's that got to do with . . . with . . .'

'So that's correct? You were kerb-crawling? Looking to buy sex?'

He put his head down, sighed. Humiliation piling on top of guilt. 'Yes,' he said, his voice a broken thing, 'yes, I was.'

'Just the once, or more often?' said Anni. 'Was this a regular thing?'

Eades looked up, eyes away from Anni. 'Does it matter?' He tried to hide his embarrassment, worked it up as anger instead. 'How does this have any bearing on . . . on my wife? Is this relevant? Is this part of the inquiry?'

'Yes it is, Mr Eades,' said Phil, keeping his voice steady but authoritative. 'We wouldn't ask if it wasn't.' He said nothing more, waiting for an answer.

Eventually, Eades, seeing that they weren't going away until they got an answer, sighed. 'I used prostitutes . . . a bit.'

'A bit?' said Anni.

'A fair bit. All right, quite a lot. Yes, I paid for sex. Happy now?'

Phil took a photo out of his jacket pocket, handed it to Eades. 'Do you recognise this woman?'

Eades looked at the photo. Susie Evans' face was smiling up at him. He frowned. 'She looks . . . familiar. A bit.'

'Have you had sex with her?' asked Anni. 'Was she one of the women you picked up?'

He kept looking at the photo. Eventually shook his head. 'No. I don't think so. Not really my type. But she does look familiar.' He handed the photo back.

'She was murdered a couple of months ago,' said Phil, repocketing the photo.

Eades' head jerked up, eyes wide. 'And . . . and you think . . . the same person did it?'

'It's a possibility we're looking into,' Anni said.

'We're exploring all avenues,' said Phil.

Anni took a photo out of her jacket, handed it to Eades. 'What about her?'

Eades looked at it, and there was no disguising the fact that he knew her. He sighed as he looked at her face.

Phil picked up on it straight away. 'You know her?'

'Has she been killed too?' It sounded like genuine concern in his voice.

Phil ignored the question. 'Do you know her?'

Eades looked again at the photo. 'Yes. Yes, I remember her very well.'

'You met more than once?' said Phil.

'Yes. Regularly. We met . . . she had a flat we went back to. I didn't pick her up on the street. Sometimes in a hotel. Yes . . .' He drifted off at the memory.

'And would you say you developed a relationship with her?' said Anni.

'Well, I think so. We were together for . . . we used to see each other for quite a while.'

'And you talked about . . . what, exactly?' said Phil.

'Oh, all sorts. Life, my family. Everything.'

'So why did it end?' asked Anni.

'I met Erin,' he said.

Anni folded her arms. 'And you didn't have to pay for it any more.'

'That's right.' Eades looked up, realised what he had just said. 'I didn't mean it like that . . .'

'That's all right, Mr Eades,' said Phil. He held his hand out for the photo.

Eades seemed reluctant to hand it over. He sighed, looked at it once more. 'Oh, Sophie,' he said.

Phil and Anni exchanged glances. They made to leave.

Graeme Eades stood up.

'Please,' he said, looking unsteady on his feet. 'Please. Find my baby. My girl.' He looked up. 'It was a girl, you know . . .' Then away again. 'And she's the last part of . . .' He couldn't bring himself to say his wife's name.

He crumpled to the bed, curled up and sobbed.

They left him to his grief.

Outside, Phil shook his head, as if to dislodge Graeme Eades' voice, the image of him lying there.

'We have to find her,' said Phil. 'And fast.'

They drove back to the station.

Clayton stood outside in the car park. It was freezing, wind whipping his jacket back, promising ice and snow. He didn't notice. He had his phone to his ear.

'Come on,' he said, 'pick up . . .'

It switched over to answerphone. 'Hi, this is Sophie. Leave a message and I'll get back to you really, really soon.' Her voice dropped, low and teasing, on the last three words, holding the promise of fun and sex. It worked. Clayton knew that.

'Listen, Sophie, it's me, Clayton. I need to see you. Now. It's important. I don't know where you are, but go back to the flat, I'll meet you there.' He ended the call. Sighed.

Fuck . . .

He put his phone away. Thought. Took it out again. He would try his flat. Maybe she was there already. In the shower or something. He dialled, waited. Heard his own voice on the answerphone.

He started to leave a message.

'Sophie? It's Clayton. If you're there, pick up.' A long pause. Then a sigh. 'Okay. Look, I'm coming back to the flat now. I really need to talk to you. Now. I've left a message on your mobile. If you're there, wait.' Another sigh. 'This is so fucked. I've . . . we've got to . . .' Another sigh. 'No. I can't say on the phone. We have to talk it through. We have to sort it.' The message ended.

Across the room, sitting on one of Clayton's dark leather armchairs, Sophie Gale took another drag on her cigarette, held it, let out a long plume of smoke.

The red light on the answerphone flashed. She didn't move. Just put the cigarette to her lips once more, took down another mouthful of smoke, slowly exhaled.

Waited.

63

Phil was pushing the Audi as fast as he could without breaking the speed limit down the Avenue of Remembrance on the way back to the centre of Colchester. Beside him, Anni was feeling troubled.

'Boss,' she said, with evident trepidation.

'Yeah?' he said, not taking his eyes off the road.

'I think there's something I should have told you.'

He risked a glance at her. Her head was angled away from him but he could clearly see the tension in her neck. 'Go on.'

The engine seemed to roar in the silence between them. Eventually Anni spoke. 'It's about Clayton.'

Phil waited.

'He's . . .' She sighed. 'I saw him. The other night. When I was staking out Brotherton's house.'

Phil looked at her, frowning. He said nothing, waiting for her to continue.

'He was . . . he brought Sophie Gale back home. In his car.'

Phil took his eyes fully off the road. 'He did what?'

'And . . .' She had to keep going. There was no turning back now. 'And she gave him a blow job. In the car.'

Anni turned her face away to the window once more. She

could feel Phil's eyes on her, burning into her intensely. The road taking care of itself.

'Why didn't you tell me?' His voice quiet, controlled.

Anni knew that wasn't a good sign. 'I . . . I didn't know if it was my place, boss. I just thought he was being a dick. I confronted him with it.'

'And what did he say?'

'He said he would tell you. Sit down and tell you everything.'

'Everything? What's everything?'

Anni sighed, shook her head. 'About . . . Clayton used to work vice. He knew Sophie from back then. Was one of the team she used to be an informant for.'

'Why the fuck didn't he tell me?' His voice seemed all the louder in contrast to its previous quiet and control. His hand left the steering wheel, began massaging his chest. Anni noticed he seemed to be having problems with his breathing.

'You okay, boss?'

He ignored her question. 'Why didn't he tell me?'

'I don't know. He said he was going to. But he didn't. But it made me look into her background. That's when I came up with the whole prostitute thing.'

'Which he wasn't going to say anything about.'

'I . . . I don't know. Boss.'

Phil sighed and kept sighing, his breath coming in short, ragged gasps.

'Boss . . .'

'Christ . . .' His hand clenched harder at his chest. Anni began to worry that he might be having a heart attack.

'Shouldn't . . . shouldn't you pull over?'

Phil gave an angry shake of his head. 'Call him. Phone him now. I want to know what the hell he's playing at.'

Anni took out her mobile, speed-dialled Clayton. She waited. Looked at Phil. 'Answerphone.'

333

'Bastard . . . leave a message. Tell him I want to see him back at the station. Now.'

Anni did so, hung up.

'He was in the office when we left,' said Phil in between gasps. 'Call them. See if he's there. No, call Marina. Ask her.'

Anni did what she was told, spoke to Marina, listened to the reply. Rang off.

'He's gone. Left just after we did.'

Phil seemed to be breathing through clenched teeth. 'Did . . . did she say why?'

'She said he went to talk to Millhouse just after I did. Then left in a hurry.'

'And you were asking Millhouse about Sophie Gale.'

'Yeah.' Realisation hit her. 'Oh God . . .'

'You know the way to his place?' said Phil.

Anni nodded.

'Direct me. Now.'

Phil put the siren on.

64

'Oh God, oh God . . .'

Marina stood in the toilet cubicle, the door locked. She didn't care if anyone heard her or not.

After Anni's phone call she had started to feel unwell. She couldn't describe what it was exactly, just a pain in her lower stomach. Sharp, stabbing. She knew that wasn't right. She hurried off to the toilets, locked herself in. And had her worst fears confirmed.

Blood. She was bleeding.

'Oh God . . . the baby . . .'

The baby. All the conflict she had been undergoing disappeared in an instant. There was something wrong with the baby. She had to get it sorted. She clutched her stomach as another wave of pain rippled through her. She gasped, rode it out. Then reached for her phone. Speed-dialled her GP. Hoped he could see her straight away.

Her call was answered, an emergency appointment booked. She made a note of the time, closed her phone. Case or no case, this was important. She hadn't realised just how important until this moment.

She flushed the toilet, just in case anyone was listening outside, rearranged herself, went off to the doctor's.

★

'Sophie?'

Clayton rushed into his flat, left his keys on the side table in the hallway, ran into the living room, looked round. He saw her over by the window. She was sitting in an armchair, unmoving. The blinds were drawn behind her. He let out a sigh of relief.

'Thank Christ, I thought somethin' had happened to you.'

'I'm fine,' she said, without moving.

Her voice sounded strange, remote. Not at all like he was used to. But he didn't have time to think about that. He had too much to tell her.

'Listen,' he said, crossing the room, sitting on the arm of the chair, 'they've found a connection. Between you and Graeme Eades, the husband of the last victim. From when you used to . . . when you were workin'.'

She said nothing. Clayton frowned. He had expected a bigger reaction than that. He pressed on.

'They want to talk to you, yeah? So we've got to think of the best way to do this. How it looks like I'm gettin' in contact with you and you're comin' in, yeah? To chat. How we goin' to do that, then?'

Sophie said nothing. Just continued to stare straight ahead.

Clayton began to get exasperated. 'Sophie . . .' He stood up quickly as if the arm of the chair was too hot to sit on any longer, paced the floor until he stopped in front of her. 'Have you been listenin'? Sophie, we're in trouble.'

She moved her head to the side, inclined her eyes upwards to him. '*You're* in trouble, Clayton.'

'What? We both are! We've got to, got to . . .' He put his hands to his head, screwed his eyes up tight, beat his fists against his temples. Opened his eyes again, looked at her. 'We've got to sort this. Now.'

Sophie said nothing for a while. Just as Clayton was

beginning to think she hadn't heard, she sighed. There was no sense of resignation in the sigh, just a weary acceptance of a tedious situation. She kept her eyes on him.

'I suppose it had to happen sometime. Sooner or later.'

'Yeah, it did.' He stopped. Was she talking about the same thing? 'What had to happen?'

She stood up, moved towards him. Pressed her body right against his as she spoke. 'There's no point in pretending any more. I should say it's been fun. But I'd be lying.' She put her hand on his chest, started moving it slowly in circles. 'And we've had too many lies, haven't we?'

'What . . . what you talkin' about?' He stared at her, seemingly hypnotised by her touch.

'A chain is only as strong as its weakest link. I learned that working in a scrap metal yard. Same with a police investigation. And that's you, Clayton.'

He was totally confused now. 'Wh-what?'

'Finding you were on the team was a bonus. Something I could work with. And when it all went wrong with Ryan, moving in with you seemed the perfect thing to do. Keep an eye on you, keep them away from me. But now it seems like that won't work out. You're off the team. And they've found out about Graeme Eades and me.'

'So? We can sort it. We just need to get our story straight . . .'

She gave him a sad smile. 'No, Clayton. I think it's got beyond that. We've all got to make sacrifices now.'

'What you talkin' about?'

'Family, Clayton. Family. Family ties. Stronger than anything.' There was sadness behind her words.

She was still stroking him, pressing her body against him. He didn't understand her words but he enjoyed the feeling. Despite everything, he found himself getting an erection.

'So I've got to go now.'

337

'No, listen—'

'Sorry, Clayton. You are the weakest link. Goodbye.'

He didn't feel the blade at first. Not the first blow. Or the second. But by the third he was feeling it. The pain had caught up with the shock by then. Sophie moved away. He looked down.

She had stabbed him in the stomach. Hard, fast. His shirt front was covered in blood. No longer required to make its way to his heart, it was pumping out of him in gushing torrents.

'No, no . . .'

He put his hands on his stomach, tried in desperation to catch the blood in his fingers. Couldn't. It just ran straight through.

'Oh God, oh God . . .'

He stumbled round, not knowing what to do, his panic increasing the rate his blood pumped out at. He looked to Sophie for help. But she had put on her coat, grabbed her holdall, which had been at the side of the armchair. She wasn't even looking at him.

'Help . . . help me . . .'

His voice, like the rest of him, was becoming weaker.

She ignored him, walked towards the door.

Something clicked inside him. He mustn't let her get away. He had to stop her. Call an ambulance, call for assistance. He fumbled inside his jacket for his mobile, his fingers slippery with blood. Eventually he got it out, punched in 999. No use. He had turned it off on the way to the flat.

'Oh God . . .'

He tried to thumb it on. Waited for it to power up, to find his network.

'Come on, please . . . come on . . .'

Dancing black stars were moving into the edges of his vision. He tried to blink them away. But every time he blinked, they just seemed to increase in number. He looked round the room, tried to focus. He was aware of Sophie reaching the door.

'No . . .'

The phone had eventually found a signal. He managed to dial 999, held it to his ear. It was ringing. His legs were weak. He felt like he wanted to sit down. He fought it, remained on his feet. Waited for the phone to be answered.

It was. He was asked which emergency service he wanted.

'Ambulance. I've been . . . stabbed . . .'

Sophie heard his words, turned. She crossed the room, took the phone from his hand, threw it as far away from him as she could. It hit the wall. Broke. She nodded, pleased with her action, turned, walked back to the door.

'No . . .'

His legs were ready to give way. With one last surge he managed to lurch across the room, blood following him, keeping pace as he went. He reached her by the door, put his hands on her. She turned, ready to swat him away.

Clayton knew he was fighting for his life. He knew his last breath wasn't far off and he had to do something. He grabbed her, tried to remember his training. Hung on to her as hard as he could.

They were fighting by the door when the entryphone buzzer went.

65

'This the place?' said Phil.

Anni nodded. 'Yeah.'

They shared a grim look. She pressed the button, waited.

Clayton and Sophie stopped struggling, looked at the buzzer in surprise. They both had an idea of who it would be.

Clayton reached for the receiver, ready to press the release button. But Sophie got there before him. Stopped him from pressing it.

The black stars were increasing. He knew he didn't have long left. With all his remaining strength he knocked her hand away, pressed the release button. Shouted down the receiver.

'Help . . . help me . . . somebody fuckin' help me . . .'

Phil and Anni looked at each other. They didn't need to hear any more.

'Which floor?' asked Phil.

'Second.'

They ran inside and up the stairs.

Clayton's strength was gone. His legs would no longer support him. The black stars were almost obscuring everything else before him. He crumpled in a heap in front of the door. Before his eyes closed, he felt a pang of guilt in amongst the pain. His mother. How he had failed in the dreams she had for him.

Then his eyes closed. For the final time.

He didn't feel Sophie drag him by the legs, try to move him out of the way.

'This one,' said Anni, outside Clayton's flat.

Phil pushed the door. It was locked. 'Fuck.'

Then, to his surprise, it began to open.

He gave a quick glance at Anni. She was prepared too.

The door opened. There stood Sophie Gale. She stopped moving, surprise on her face. She was hurrying, clearly expecting someone to arrive, but not expecting them to be there waiting for her.

Phil began to read her her rights.

'Sophie Gale, I—'

He didn't get any further. She dropped her holdall, gave him a swift kick between the legs with her booted foot. He crumpled over as pain flooded through him. He thought he was going to throw up; he thought he would never feel the same again.

Sophie Gale tried to step round him.

But Anni was waiting for her.

Although small, Anni was a fierce fighter. She had studied martial arts, picked up a few moves to give her the advantage against someone bigger or stronger than her. Before Sophie could try anything, she curled the fingers of her right hand inwards and flattened the palm of her hand. Then, with as much speed and strength behind the movement as she could manage, she hit Sophie just between her nostrils and her upper lip.

It was, as Anni knew, a part of the body with plenty of

nerve endings. It didn't take much to have an effect. And Anni had hit hard.

Sophie Gale's hands flew up to her face. She screamed in pain. Anni pressed forward.

'Sophie.'

The other woman's hands dropped. There was real anger in her eyes. She was readying herself to fly at Anni.

Anni did the same again, even faster and stronger this time.

Sophie went over backwards. Anni moved over her, knelt beside her. Punched her in the nose this time. Hard. Blood flowed even faster.

Then she took a pair of PlastiCuffs from the back pocket of her jeans, grabbed Sophie's wrists, pulled them behind her back and secured them as tightly as she could.

She looked at Phil. 'You okay, boss?'

He was getting to his knees. 'Yeah . . .' He pointed at the open doorway. 'Get Clayton . . .'

Anni jumped over Sophie's prone body, saw what was waiting for them in the flat.

'Oh my God . . .'

'I'll . . . I'll call an ambulance,' said Phil, getting out his phone.

Anni moved sadly to the door, stood there, head down.

'Too late for that, boss. He's dead.'

Part Three

66

Hester looked down at the baby as it lay sleeping in its cot. It was pinker, bigger, healthier than the last one. It was just like she'd seen on TV and in the books. It was everything a baby was supposed to be. And as she looked at it, she expected to feel an overwhelming outpouring of love for it, like the books said. But she didn't. In fact, she didn't know what she was feeling.

No, it wasn't love. Or at least she didn't think it was. Because love didn't make comparisons. Love didn't judge one against the other. She kept thinking of the last baby. She knew this was a different baby from the last one, with different needs and everything, but even though that one had been sick all the time, she still thought it was better than this one. There didn't seem to be anything wrong with this one. It was big and strong, like a baby was supposed to be. But Hester felt nothing for it. Why was that?

She had read somewhere that this happened sometimes, mothers not bonding, rejecting their babies. They got depressed and wouldn't do anything for them. Maybe that was it. Maybe she was rejecting it. Maybe she was wrong about not looking back and it was too soon after the last one.

Maybe. Or maybe she just wasn't interested any more. Bored with babies, time to do something else.

She was thinking all this while she was staring at the TV. The news was on. Hester was watching again to see if they said anything. Something seemed to be happening, because the reporter looked even more serious and the smooth policeman, the one she liked, was talking to the camera again. She couldn't understand the words, though.

The phone was ringing in the background. Hester didn't like answering the phone, so she closed her eyes, called for her husband. Asked him to answer it. He didn't reply and it was still ringing. She would have to do it herself.

Reluctantly she crossed the room, picked up the receiver. Listened.

It was for her. And it wasn't good news.

Call finished, she replaced the receiver and stood there. It was like she had been physically hit. Punched in the face. And that punch had more than hurt her; it had rocked her world on its axis. She closed her eyes, absorbing the impact. Opened them again. And in that instant her world changed.

Her head was spinning, mind reeling. She looked at the TV, still spitting out news. It didn't seem important now, not as real as what was happening here. She felt like crying. She felt like screaming. So she did both. It woke the baby but it also made her husband appear.

Shut it, woman. What's that fuckin' noise for?

'They've got her.'

Who?

'They, they've got her. They know about the babies. And that means they'll be comin' for us . . .'

Tell me.

She told him. Everything. Where the list came from, who had supplied it. He listened, silent. Not a good sign.

I knew, he said eventually. *Where the list came from. You really think I didn't? You thought you were bein' clever, keepin' it from me, but I knew.*

'But . . . why didn't you say somethin'?'

Why should I? Was what you wanted. What I wanted.

'But it was . . .'

Didn't matter.

She was relieved that he wasn't angry. But that wasn't important now. She could feel panic overwhelming her. 'So . . . we've got to do somethin'.'

He didn't reply.

'I said we have to do somethin'!'

The baby started crying. Hester ignored it. This was more important.

'We could run,' she said. 'Yeah. Go somewhere where they wouldn't find us. Take the baby. Be a family.'

No reply.

'Talk to me! Tell me what to do!'

The TV was still on. He stared at it, tried to concentrate, decided what his next move should be. The news. The smooth detective was still talking. Then the image changed and it was the woman from last night, the one he had seen outside the leisure centre. The pretty one. The pregnant one. He thought she was saying the same things again until he realised it was just a recording of the previous night. He watched her mouth move. Smiled. A plan was forming.

All hunters needed a strategy. Especially an exit strategy.

He put on his overcoat and went outside.

Work to do.

67

Phil parked the Audi in the car park, got out, closed and locked the door. Then leaned against it, sighed. Eyes closed. Clayton Thompson. His DS. Dead.

He shook his head, whether in disbelief or to clear it of the images from Clayton's flat he didn't know. Probably both. His DS, the one who had irritated him no end but who somehow he had still found likeable, lying twisted and broken on the floor of his flat. The walls and floors covered in his blood, thrashed out of his body as he fought against death, struggled to live. All in vain.

There was a moment in every murder investigation in which Phil had taken part that made him contemplate, usually after a couple of drinks on his own, the big issues. Life and death. The human condition. Why we were here, alive in this universe. God and a divine purpose versus blind evolutionary chance. He would look into the faces of the family left behind as they struggled to fill the void that the death of their loved one had created and know they were thinking the same things. If the victim was one of the lost souls he saw all too often, with no one to love them in life or grieve for them after it ended, his questioning was just intensified.

It was a regular process he went through. And he never

found any answers, formulated any convictions or reached any conclusions. But during those alcohol-fuelled dark nights of the soul, he often imagined the dead were calling to him. Asking him to be their champion, to avenge their deaths, bring peace to their families. He would usually sober up the next day; carry on with his life, his job. Rationalise the night before as merely bottle-induced dark fantasies. And then, more often than not, he caught the murderer. Solved the crime. And the ghosts would disappear.

But he was never completely sure they were truly gone. Because when the next murder occurred, they returned, another added to their number. And now, on top of all the pregnant women, Clayton would be joining them. Joining the three a.m. line-up, imploring Phil to help them, avenge them. He knew it.

He shook his head once more, opened his eyes. The station was directly in front of him. He played the events of the inquiry over and over again in his mind. Re-examined Clayton's every word, every look. Tried to find something, some clue or indicator that might have told him what was going on. He found nothing. His heart felt as if it had been attached to a rock by bonds of guilt and regret and thrown into the River Colne. Sinking fast, on a one-way, bottom-bound journey. As that happened, he felt the familiar bands begin to constrict his chest, like an invisible boa constrictor he carried with him always that had to remind him of its presence every so often.

His breathing quickened, pulse speeded up. He couldn't take it any more. He needed rest. He needed escape. He needed . . .

Marina.

The thought hit him like lightning cracking a tree trunk. Marina. It was so simple. It was so complicated. Marina.

Taking strength from that thought, he crossed the car

park, went into the building. All the way to the bar. As he entered, he felt all eyes on him. Unspoken questions, condolences, affirmations of solidarity. He knew they wanted to step forward and speak, all of them, but he also knew that none of them would dare. Eventually they stopped looking, went back to their work. They needed something. They needed him to say it.

'Listen up,' he said, standing still. 'Everyone.' He waited until he had the whole team's attention. Took a deep breath, ignored the tightening in his chest. 'Right. You all know what's happened. And it's a blow. One of the biggest we've ever had. But we've got the person who did this. So that's something. And we're going to make sure that the rest of this case is wrapped up as tightly and securely as possible. Clayton was a good copper. He was a friend to a lot of you. He was my friend too. And I'm going to miss him.' He took a deep breath. Continued. 'But we've got a job to do. So let's get on with it. Thanks.'

He sat down.

Silence.

One person clapped. Then another. And another. Until the whole team were applauding. Phil smiled, blinked wet eyes. 'Get back to work,' he said.

Refocused and re-energised, they did as they were told.

Phil put his head down, looked at the work in front of him, the reports. Knowing they weren't going to write themselves, he got on with it.

Eventually he became aware of someone standing before him. He looked up. There was Marina. Coat on, bag over her shoulder.

'Hey,' she said.

'Hey yourself.'

'Good speech.'

'Thanks,' he replied. 'They needed something.'

She nodded.

'You heard.'

'Whole place has heard. Everyone wants to get her in an interview room, have a crack at her.' She glanced round the office. 'They're taking this one personally.'

'How could they not?'

'What about you?' she said. 'You still on the case? Personal interest and all that.'

He rubbed his eyes with the backs of his hands. Thought of the questioning he had undergone at Clayton's flat. They were his own people, they had been sympathetic. He and Anni had brought in Sophie Gale and there was no question she had killed him. But, like him, they had their jobs to do.

'Well I suppose I shouldn't be. But the Super at Chelmsford wants me to do the interview. So . . .' He shrugged.

She smiled, nodded. But her eyes were downcast. 'Good.'

'I want you working with me again. We've got to get this one right.'

'Well . . .' She glanced about, at anything and anyone but him. 'Sorry. I can't.'

He frowned, looked at her. 'What d'you mean?'

She lowered her voice, as if she was almost embarrassed by what she was about to say. 'I . . . can't stay. I have to go.'

'What? But I need you.' He closed his mouth quickly, wondered how that statement had been received. Wondered how he had really intended it.

'Sorry. I can't.'

'Why not? Is it money? I know we can stretch the budget, get some cash from the Home Office—'

'It's not money. I want to stay. Believe me.' Their eyes locked. Honesty passed between them. He believed her. She sighed.

His voice dropped. 'What then?'

'I need . . . I have to go to the doctor.'

'A doctor's appointment?' Phil almost laughed. 'Well that's okay. You can get it rearranged.'

'No. I can't.'

'Yes you can, just—'

'No.' Her voice louder, sharper than she had intended. She looked round quickly to check no one had heard. They hadn't. 'I'm pregnant.'

Phil stood, unblinking, unbalanced, like he had been hit and was reeling, about to fall backwards.

Marina put her head down, averted her eyes from his. 'I'm sorry. You shouldn't have found out like this.'

Phil said nothing. He looked round, saw the office, felt the unreality of the situation.

'I've got to go.' She made to move away. He put his hand on her arm, stopped her.

'Is it . . . mine? Ours?'

She looked away once more. 'I'll talk to you later.'

'Is it?'

As he spoke, her hand went involuntarily to her stomach, massaged the bump that her baby made. Phil saw the action, looked up. Caught her eye to eye. A sheer, nakedly emotional connection. Neither could look away.

In that moment he knew. And she knew it too.

The baby was his.

'Look, I have to go. There's a . . . something's not right with it.' She reshouldered her bag even though it didn't need it. 'There's a chance I might lose it. Stress, the doctor said. I'm sorry.'

'Marina . . .'

She looked at him then, eye to eye once more. 'I really didn't want you to find out like this. I'm sorry. But we'll talk. Soon. I promise.'

'We need to talk now.'

352

She looked round, like a cornered animal checking for escape routes. 'No, not now. No stress, remember . . .'

'But—'

Anni appeared at the end of the room. 'Boss?'

He looked between Anni and Marina, torn. 'Marina . . .'

'Later,' she said, using the distraction as an excuse to leave. 'We will talk. Later. Promise.'

And she was across the room, out of the door.

Phil watched her go, then caught sight of Anni, still waiting in the doorway. He shook his head once more, went to see what his DC wanted.

68

Phil stood outside the interview room. Flattened himself against the wall. His head was spinning, everything spiralling and pinwheeling, making him feel nauseous and giddy. He closed his eyes, breathed deeply. Tried to clear his mind of everything that was going on around him, jettison the lot, narrow his attention down to just one thing. One person. One objective.

Getting Sophie Gale to talk.

Brotherton's interview had been big, but this was even bigger. The biggest so far.

He took a deep breath, then another. Willing his heart rate to slow as he did so. Calm. Concentrated. Focused. Not an angry man wanting to avenge the death of a colleague. Not a grieving friend. He couldn't allow any of that to spill over in the room. There would be time enough for that later. For now, he was a professional with a job to do.

He checked the file under his arm, flicked through the pages once more. Paid close attention to the paper that Anni had given him. Then he closed the file, opened the door, went inside, closed it behind him.

Sophie Gale sat at the table, staring straight ahead. She was sitting upright, not slumped, as he might have expected, her hands on the table in front of her, crossed at the wrists. Her hair hung down lank at either side of her face. She didn't look up as he entered. The only sign that she acknowledged his presence was a double blink.

He sat down in front of her, put the file on the table, looked at her. And was surprised at what he saw. What glamour she'd had was now gone, her cheap sexual allure dissipated. Her face was blank, white, her eyes inexpressive, like a death mask. She wasn't even looking at him, just staring in his direction.

Phil studied her. His first reaction would have been that she was in shock. But that didn't seem right; he didn't get that feeling from her. He got no sense of the emotional imbalance that shock often engendered. He looked at her once more, deep into her eyes. And found a spark there, a dark, burning spark. He sat back, understanding. She had no more need to pretend. The masks she wore, the ones that had fooled Brotherton and Clayton, were no longer necessary. She had stripped them away, leaving only her death-like face on view, her rage-fuelled inner core still driving her.

Now, thought Phil, he had to find the reason for that rage and work with it. That would be the only way to get answers about what had happened, to work out what was going on, to find the baby and stop a murderer.

He took a second or two to compose himself; then, aware that the custody clock would start ticking with his first question, he started. First he introduced himself to the tape, then he introduced Sophie; he remarked that she had waived the right to legal representation at this stage.

'So what happened, Sophie?'

No response, just those same staring eyes.

'Come on,' he said, 'you killed Clayton. Clayton Thompson. Why?'

Nothing.

'Did you have an argument? A fight? Did he . . . did he try to come on to you?'

A slight reaction, a twitch of her lips, then nothing once more.

Phil sighed. 'Come on, Sophie, help me out here. How can I understand, how can I try to help you if you won't let me?'

He waited, sure that his words would get a response, one way or another. He was right.

'You can't.' Her voice was small and empty. It perfectly matched the expression on her face.

'What d'you mean, I can't? I can't help you or I can't understand you?'

She shrugged. 'Both.'

His voice dropped low, talking like a counsellor or a friend. 'Why? Tell me. Make me understand.'

She sighed. 'It's too late for that.' She shook her head, her lips lifting in an approximation of a smile. 'Too late.'

'For who? For what?'

'It's always been too late.' Her head fell forward, her hair forming a curtain between herself and Phil's questions.

Phil tried a new approach. 'Why Clayton, then? Hmm? Why my DS, why him?' He mentally pulled back. Kept his rage and guilt in check. 'Why not Ryan Brotherton or . . . I don't know. One of your earlier clients. Why Clayton?'

She put her head up once more, her eyes still staring straight ahead. She seemed to be giving the question some thought. 'Because . . . because he stopped helping me.'

'Helping you? Helping you to do what?'

'To . . .' She shook her head, looked away. He had lost her once more.

Another change of approach, Phil thought. He opened the file he had brought with him. This one wasn't for show. This one had facts and details in it. 'Sophie Gale,' he said, reading down the first page. 'Real name Gail Johnson. First came to our attention six years ago, when you were arrested for soliciting. You came to an agreement. Became a paid informant. Then you gave it up and disappeared. Why?'

'Got sick of the life.'

'Fair enough. Then you turn up again with Ryan Brotherton. And he's wanted for questioning in relation to a murder inquiry. At first we think he may be the killer. There's a lot of evidence to suggest that. Hell of a lot. But it's not him, is it?'

No response.

'No. It's not. But it does look like someone has gone to a lot of trouble to get us interested in him. Now why would that be?'

No response.

Phil sat back, looking at her again. 'You like magic, Sophie?'

Her eyes met his. She looked confused.

'It's not a trick question. D'you like magic? Illusions, I mean. Not like Harry Potter and stuff.'

She shrugged. 'S'pose so.'

'Thought you might. You know how magic works? You don't have to answer, I'll tell you. Misdirection. If a magician's very good, he gets you looking where he wants you to look, seeing what he wants you to see. You don't see what he's really up to. You don't see the coins being tucked away and palmed, ready to be pulled out later, the cards placed where he wants them. The things up his sleeve. Just what he wants you to see. Right?'

Another shrug.

Phil leaned forward, his words hard, his voice soft. 'And that's what you did with us, Sophie. You got us looking at Ryan Brotherton. Got us thinking that he was a murderer. Looking for connections with all the other victims, not just

357

Claire Fielding, throwing doubt on his alibi, making yourself out to be a poor little battered wife-in-waiting. Scared of the big bad man. All the while you were playing him. And us. Covering for the real killer, making us miss the real connections. Misdirection.'

She said nothing, but the set of her jaw had changed. Phil wasn't sure, but he sensed that she was taking pride from his words.

He was pleased that what he was saying was having the right effect. 'Regular little Paul Daniels. Except it all went wrong, didn't it? That last one, that wasn't mean to happen, was it? Not so soon. Certainly not while we had Brotherton in custody and could give him a watertight alibi.'

He studied her face once more. She took his words in, processed them. Clearly not happy with what he was saying.

'Now we know it isn't you. Because you were here when the last one happened. But we do know that you know who's doing it. So tell me.'

Nothing.

Phil sighed. 'Look, Sophie. We've got you for murder. No argument. You're going to do time for that. And since it was a policeman you killed, lots of time, I should imagine. So if you want to make it easier for yourself, tell me what I want to know. And I'll do what I can to help.' He couldn't believe he had said that, but he needed her on side.

He sat back, waited. Sophie smiled. That humourless grin she had given earlier, just a skeleton display of teeth. 'It doesn't matter. You wouldn't understand.'

Phil felt himself getting angry and knew that wouldn't help. He had to channel it, make it work for him. He leaned in to her. 'Then make me understand, Sophie. Tell me.'

Nothing.

'Look,' he said, trying not to give in to his anger, 'Clayton Thompson had a family. A mother. Two sisters. I've lost a friend and a colleague. They've lost a son, a brother. How d'you think they feel? Hmm? How d'you think they feel about what you've done to him? To one of their own family?'

Sophie reacted. The word 'family' did it. She sat back, recoiling as if she had been slapped. Phil saw the advantage, pressed on.

'Yeah, Sophie, his family. They've lost him. Because of you. How would that make you feel? Have you got a family?'

And then she laughed. It was a dry, rattling sound, matching her grin. 'Yeah,' she said, the words drawling out of her. 'I've got a family.'

'And how d'you think they'd feel if they knew what you were doing?'

She gave another laugh. 'You really have no idea, do you?' she said.

'What d'you mean?'

'The family. That's what it's all about, isn't it?'

'What d'you mean? Tell me.'

'Family. Family ties. Blood. Thicker than water. Stronger than . . .' Her eyes fixed his. 'That's right. Isn't it?'

'Is it?' Phil didn't know what she meant, though he knew it wasn't good. But there was something in those words that struck him. On impulse he took out the piece of paper Anni had handed him before coming into the room. Turned it round, slid it across the table.

'Would this be a member of your family, then?'

Sophie looked at the paper. It was a photo of the man seen entering and leaving Claire Fielding's apartment on the night of her murder. She glanced up quickly.

Phil caught the expression on her face. Tried to keep the emotion out of his. Because he had her.

69

Tony Scott stared at the page, read the line again. And again. He sighed, stretched. No good. He just wasn't taking this book in.

He put it down on the side table beside the armchair, open at the place he had left it, where it lay, pages curling outwards and upwards, like a cumbersome bird unable to take flight. He gave a small smile of enjoyment as he picked up his glass of wine. The perfect simile for a book he was unable to get into. He should write that down.

He took a mouthful of wine, replaced the glass. Stretched out in his chair, Ray LaMontagne playing in the background. Tony was the first to admit he didn't like much pop music, but this guy had it sussed.

He checked his watch. Almost six. Marina had phoned, said she was finished, on her way home. He had scanned her voice for hints as to her emotional state but found nothing in particular that gave her away. She sounded tired, distracted even. But Tony was sure the work was to blame for that. And the baby. One must be putting a strain on the other. That would be it.

He took another mouthful of wine, thought of picking up the book once more. Looked at it, thought better of it. He had heard so much about it that he'd felt sure he would enjoy it, but that clearly wasn't the case. But then, he thought, taking yet another sip of wine, perhaps it wasn't the book. Perhaps it was him.

Marina had stayed out last night. That thought wouldn't dislodge itself from his mind. He had thought things were getting better between them. They had hit a bit of a rough patch around the time of Martin Fletcher. That was understandable. Then there was the pregnancy, and her desire to leave the university. A decision he was completely behind. But now she was working for the police again.

On the last job she had been fired up, talking about the case all the time when she came home. One name in particular kept cropping up in her conversation: Phil. The CIO on the case, she told him, proud of the new phrase she had picked up. For a couple of weeks it was Phil this, Phil that, so much so that if Tony hadn't known better, he would have assumed she was having an affair. But he knew she wouldn't. Not Marina. Well, maybe he didn't actually know, but he felt pretty certain.

But then came the business with Martin Fletcher, and everything changed. Only to be expected. She'd nearly died. And he had been there for her, comforting, offering words – and gestures – of support. Consoling her. She had responded. And everything had been fine.

Until she'd stayed out again last night.

The track finished and another one came one. It sounded the same to Tony, but then that was why he liked the album. Well-crafted tunes, not much variation, but solid and dependable. You knew what you were getting. Qualities that, if he was honest, he admired.

He checked his watch again. It shouldn't be long now until she was home. He hadn't cooked; he was going to take her out for dinner. To celebrate her finishing the job and just to show how much he loved her. He hoped she would appreciate it.

He picked up the book, took another mouthful of wine. He waited, drinking, unable to concentrate on the book, listening to safe music in his small house. Yeah. He sighed. That was him. His world and everything in it.

A knock on the door stopped any further thoughts. Tony stood up, the book still in his hand, crossed to it.

Must be Marina, he thought.

Another knock. Harder this time, more insistent.

'Coming,' he called. Maybe it wasn't her. Jehovah's Witnesses, probably, he thought irritably. No one else called round. Most of their friends they met in bars or restaurants or at their homes. Shame he had called out, though. If it was Jehovah's Witnesses he could have pretended he wasn't in. Avoided any potential confrontation.

'Marina?' he called. 'Is that you?'

No reply. Just another knock.

Tony sighed, opened the door. Ready for whoever was there. Frowned. Didn't know this person but didn't like the look of them.

Then the hammer appeared.

His book fell to the floor.

And before he could speak – before he could even think – his world, and everything in it, went black.

70

'You know him, don't you, Sophie?' Phil tapped the photo. 'You know who this is.'

Sophie said nothing. Just moved her body slowly back from the table. Eyes on the photo all the time.

'Good likeness? Yeah?'

Again, nothing. Phil could see that she was thinking. Deciding what to say next. What he most wanted to hear. What would help her most.

'So,' he said. He leaned forward, looked at the photo with her. They had done the best they could with it, but it was still blurred, impossible to make out sharp features. But Sophie knew who it was. That was enough. 'What relation is he to you?'

She sat back, unmoving. The overhead lights shadowed the hollows of her eyes, made them appear as empty sockets in a skull.

'Brother? Husband? Father?'

She closed her eyes as he said the words so Phil couldn't read her response. He pressed on. 'One of them, is it? Which one, then? Which member of your family killed Claire Fielding and Julie Simpson? Not to mention Lisa King, Susie Evans and Caroline Eades. Come on, Sophie, tell me.'

Again Sophie said nothing, and again Phil was aware of the calculation behind her eyes. But they held something more than that. He had seen it before. Madness. And something else. Damage. He could guess which one came first.

He kept his voice low, steady. As unemotional as possible, despite the subject matter, despite the adrenalin that was pumping round his system. 'So, this member of your family, he's stealing babies. To keep the family going, is that it? And you've been setting up his victims.'

She gave a slight nod.

'Why?'

'You know why.'

'Tell me.'

'Families have to grow. Or they die.'

'And this was the only way to do it? Ripping unborn babies out of their mothers' wombs?'

'They're not mothers, they're just carriers,' said Sophie, her eyes alight. 'Babies have to bond. You don't want something second-hand.'

Phil sat back, trying to process everything she was saying, tamp down his rage and revulsion, keep going with rational questions that would make her open up.

'So where is he now? Where can we find him?'

She shrugged. Then a smile spread over her features. A sick, twisted smile. 'Out hunting, probably,' she said.

A shiver ran through Phil. 'Out hunting?' He leaned forward. 'Where?'

She shrugged.

'Where is he?'

Sophie said nothing, just closed her eyes.

Phil balled and unballed his hands, tried to hold his emotions in check. If he gave in and railed at her, he knew he would lose her completely. He leaned forward once more, measuring his words carefully.

364

'Sophie, tell me. If you don't, his picture, this photo' – he held it right in front of her face – 'will be on the TV, newspapers, the internet by tonight. I know, it's not a great likeness. But someone will recognise him. And then we'll have him. So you may as well tell me now.'

Nothing.

'Does he know you're here?'

A nod. 'I phoned when I came in.'

'You didn't need a solicitor?'

She shook her head. 'Had to warn . . .' She paused. 'Him. Had to warn him.'

Shit, thought Phil. That was probably the worst thing that could have happened. He had to think quickly, find a way to turn the situation round, make it work for him.

'He'll think you did this to him, Sophie,' he said, hoping his words worked, 'whether you tell me or not. If that picture goes out and we get a tip and go after him, he'll think it's because you gave him up.' He sat back. 'D'you want that?'

No response.

'So tell me.'

Nothing.

He leaned back in to her, his voice low and confiding, like a priest about to take a confession. 'Look, we're going to get him. One way or the other. So you may as well tell me all about it.'

He waited. Eventually she looked up, those mad eyes catching his once more. And that same twisted smile returned. 'I'll tell you. Everything.'

Phil tried not to breathe a sigh of relief. 'Good.'

'But it's a long story. You have to listen to it. You have to *understand*. I can't tell you if you don't understand.'

Phil breathed deeply. And again. He wanted to leap across the table, grab her by the throat, scream at her to give him up, tell him where he was and what he was doing. Slap her,

365

punch her, whatever it took. But he didn't. Instead he just said, 'I'm listening, Sophie. I'll understand.'

He looked at the grainy photo and hoped that, whatever he was doing, wherever he was, they would still be in time to stop him.

Marina opened her front door.

She walked into the cottage, her head down as she removed the key from the lock. She was tired, aching and wanted a bath. She needed to relax, along with a bit of privacy, give herself time to think about what to do next.

She stopped moving.

The cottage was wrecked. Furniture tipped over, books pulled off the walls, ornaments and crockery smashed on the floor. The polite, tasteful, carefully ordered life she had built up with her partner was gone. The breath went out of her as she surveyed the damage, her hand going automatically to her mouth. Then she saw the centrepiece of the display. And her whole body began to shake.

Tony was lying in the middle of the room, on his back, his body twisted. At first she didn't recognise him because his face was covered in blood. She identified him by his clothes. She crossed to him, knelt down beside him. Blood was pooling around his head. There were injuries to his forehead and the side of his head. She touched them. His skull was soft, yielding, like an empty, cracked eggshell, only held together by an inner membrane.

She pulled her hand away quickly, feeling revulsion at the touch, and let out a whimper.

Behind her, the front door slammed.

She turned quickly, jumping as she did so. A figure in an old overcoat was blocking her exit. In one of the intruder's hands was a hammer, blood still dripping from it. In the other, a hypodermic needle.

Marina knew instinctively who it was.

She tried to get to her feet but couldn't do it fast enough; her maternal instinct to protect the baby meant no sudden movements. Then her assailant was on her. She opened her mouth to scream, but they were too quick for her. They dropped the hammer, clamped a meaty hand over her mouth. It was rough and callused, yet slick and wet with Tony's blood. It was held firmly on her mouth. No sound would pass.

She struggled, tried to grab on to her attacker, punch, kick. No good. They were bigger, stronger than her. She was held firm, pulled right into the overcoat. She breathed through her mouth. The overcoat stank.

She was twisted round, but the intruder still held her tight. Marina saw the needle coming towards her, tried to fight even harder. She barely felt it break the skin as it entered her neck.

She didn't feel her eyes close or her body go limp.

She was unaware that her attacker held her until she was completely unconscious, then, careful not to put too much pressure on her stomach, dragged her out of the house.

71

'You know what they used to say about those villages, the ones that are miles away from anywhere?' said Sophie.

'I've heard lots of stories about them,' said Phil. 'Which ones do you mean?'

She gave her twisted smile once more, the overhead light glinting off her mad eyes. 'That you never knew whose baby is whose.' She laughed, then her face became more serious. 'Do you know what I mean?'

'Ah,' said Phil. 'Those ones.' Growing up in the area, he had heard all the stories about the isolated coastal and rural communities. And knew from experience that most of them were true, at least at one time.

'If a baby died in a family, then one would go missing from another family to replace it.'

'That kind of thing, yeah.'

She nodded. 'And nobody would ever say anything.'

'No,' said Phil. 'Because then they would have to admit where the first baby came from.'

Sophie laughed. 'You've heard them as well.'

'But those villages aren't that isolated now, are they?' said Phil.

Sophie stopped laughing. She looked almost regretful.

'Main roads and all that.' But they were still bleak, he thought. Windswept and inhospitable.

Sophie sighed.

'So where are we talking about?' said Phil, probing for her home town. He mentally scanned a map of the Essex coast. 'Was it coastal? Jaywick? Walton? Not Frinton?'

She didn't respond.

'What about on a river? Bradfield? Wrabness?'

A flicker of something behind her eyes. He hoped there was someone watching on a monitor to catch it.

'So come on,' he said, trying to hurry her up. 'You're telling me a story. About your family. I'm here, I'm listening.'

Sophie put her head back, her eyes upwards, as if receiving a signal or instructions from some unseen source. 'There were four of us . . .' she began. 'Me, my brother, my father . . .' She paused, her eyes changing, an unreadable expression on her face. 'And my mother . . .'

She stopped talking again, lost in her reverie.

'What about your mother?' Phil prompted her.

Sophie's head snapped forward, her eyes on Phil once more. 'She died.'

'She died.'

'Or . . . disappeared. I don't know which. Something like that.'

'So then it was just the three of you.'

She screwed up her eyes, her forehead, as though she was thinking hard. 'I remember . . . other kids. Or at least I think I remember other kids. I don't know.' She shook her head as if to dislodge the memory. Like it was an awkward shape that didn't fit in properly. 'Anyway, there were the three of us left. Me, my brother and my dad.'

'And this was when you were Gail?'

She looked confused for a moment, then smiled. 'I was

never Gail. Not till I came here, to Colchester. I was always Sophie. Or Sophia.'

'Sophia.'

'My mother loved film stars.'

'Sophia Loren,' said Phil.

Sophie nodded. 'Right.'

'And your brother?'

'Heston. After—'

'Charlton Heston.'

Another nod. Then her face darkened. 'Yeah . . .'

'Go on then, Sophie,' said Phil, trying to get her back on track. 'You were telling me about your mother. She died? Or disappeared?'

'Yeah . . .'

Phil waited. Nothing. She needed another prompt. 'And then what happened?'

'It was just the three of us. And that's how it always was from then on.'

'And were you . . . happy?'

Another darkening of her eyes as more memories swam through her mind. 'My father . . .' Her forehead creased up. 'My father . . . he had . . . needs . . .'

Oh God, thought Phil, here we go. He had been expecting this. The damage that came first, that led to the madness. He dropped his voice still further, asked a question he knew the answer to. 'What kind of needs?'

'Man's needs.'

'And . . . you took care of them?'

She nodded. 'Yes.' Her voice seemed to have shrunk, regressed. Smaller, more childlike. 'I had to take care of them.'

'And how old were you then? When he started?'

She shrugged. 'When Mother died. Disappeared. From then on.'

'Remember how old you were?'

She shook her head. 'Little,' she said, in a voice matching the word.

Phil swallowed hard, kept going. 'Just you? Not your brother?'

Another furrowing of her eyebrows, another darkening of memory. 'No. Just me.'

She fell silent. Phil waited, wondering whether to interject, hurry her along. Then she began speaking again.

'He did try, though.'

'Who? Your father?'

'No . . . my brother. He tried. Tried to stop my father. From . . . doing stuff to me.'

'And did he succeed?'

She looked at him as if she couldn't believe he had actually asked that question. 'Course not. He was just a kid. Our father smacked him about if he did that, played up. Really smacked him about.'

'He hurt him?'

She nodded.

'Bad?'

She sighed. 'He was always on at him. Heston wasn't good enough. Heston was useless. Worthless, no good. Heston couldn't even do what Sophia did for him, he was that useless. Then he would beat him. Hit him. Whip him. Anything he could.'

'And did he ever hurt you? I mean apart from . . .'

She shook her head. 'No. Never. I could do no wrong. Not like Heston. He could do no right.' She fell silent again. Then gave a small, unexpected laugh. 'You know what? What was funny? Heston got really jealous.'

'Because . . . you were getting the attention?'

Sophie nodded. 'He hated what our father was doing to me. He was always shouting, what's wrong with me? Why won't he do it to me? Because he was jealous that our father

371

was doing it to me instead of him. Because that was love. What my father was doing to me was showing love, he said. And Heston hated not having that.'

Phil was silent. He couldn't think of anything to say in response.

'So,' he said eventually, 'how long did this go on for?'

Sophie shrugged. 'Dunno. Well, yeah. I do.' Her hands on the table began to tremble. 'I . . .' Her head went down, her hair flopping forward, making her features unreadable.

Phil waited. Sophie had reached the stage, he thought, that often happened in interviews like this. No matter what they had done or what had been done to them, they wanted to unburden themselves. Speak it out into the open. Remove the weight from themselves. Not caring about transference, that the person listening would then be carrying that weight.

But not this time. All Phil could think about was what she had done to Clayton.

She continued talking. 'He . . .'

Phil's voice dropped even further, barely above a whisper. 'He made you pregnant.'

She nodded, head still down. Her hair swayed backwards and forwards as she did so.

'And . . .' Phil's voice careful, compassionate. 'And did you . . . have the baby?'

She shook her head. 'I . . . it died. In me. I wasn't . . . wasn't strong enough, he said . . .'

Phil felt rage and confusion rising within him. Sophie had done some awful things, he thought, but they didn't happen in a vacuum. Someone had formed her, made her capable of doing them. And that man was a monster. Phil stamped on his emotions. He couldn't allow himself to feel sympathy for her, no matter what had been done to her. In fact, he couldn't feel anything for her while he was questioning her. So he kept his professional mask in place.

372

'You lost the baby.'

She nodded.

'And then what?'

'I'd had enough. I got some pills. Tried to take them . . .' Her shoulders began to shake; her breathing became erratic as her words were intermingled with sobbing. 'Heston found me. Put his fingers down my throat. Stopped me. Saved me, I suppose. Then we talked.' She looked up, her face streaked with tears, her eyes red-rimmed. 'And I knew I had to get away. 'Cause I mean, what's the worst that could happen to me? Nothing. It had already happened. So I . . . I felt strong after that. Like, like I was reborn. I told Heston, I told him I had to get away. And he said he'd help me.'

'Why didn't he go with you?'

'Because . . . because someone had to stay behind. Look after our father.' She spoke the words with a simple clarity.

'Okay,' said Phil. 'So you ran away. And Heston stayed.' Sophie nodded. 'What happened to him? When your father found out you'd gone?'

A bitter laugh. 'He went mad. Really mad. He wanted to get at me but he couldn't. He tried to find out where I'd gone, but Heston couldn't tell him, 'cause he didn't know. Didn't stop him trying, though. Beat the shit out of him.' She gave a childlike giggle, as if the memory was too horrific to contemplate and the only response was to laugh. 'Nearly killed him, he did.' She sighed. 'But Heston recovered.'

'And he's still there now?'

'Heston?'

Phil nodded. 'Yes.'

'Sort of . . .'

'What d'you mean?'

She looked over his shoulder, not answering. Phil decided to let that one go for now, continue questioning her.

'And you came to Colchester. And you started—'

'You know about me.' The words clipped, snapped. 'You know what happened to me from then on.'

'What about your brother? What happened to him?'

She put her head back, thinking again. 'Things changed. The village changed. Like you said, we weren't so cut off. People from town started to move in. New houses got built. New estates. Luxury executive homes.' The words curled out of her mouth like soil-covered worms.

'I bet your father hated that,' said Phil.

Another bitter laugh. 'Yeah. People talking to him, wanting to be friendly . . . He hated it. He hated attention. And he couldn't find anyone to . . . provide for his man's needs.'

'So what did he do?'

'Made Heston do it.' The words as matter-of-fact as possible. 'But not like he was. 'Cause he wasn't queer, my dad.' Another laugh. 'Oh no. Whatever he was, he wasn't queer.'

Phil felt a sense of dread building with each word he heard. He had a feeling he knew where this confession was going. 'So . . .' He was almost frightened to ask the next question. 'What did he do?'

'Dressed him up.'

Phil nodded. That was what he had been expecting. He looked at Sophie's face, sensed there was something more. 'What else?'

'Did what he wanted, made him . . .'

'Into you?'

Sophie's eyes were downcast. She nodded. Phil felt a small sense of victory amongst the unease about what she was saying. That look, that movement meant there was still something in her, some basic shared humanity underneath all the damage, the madness. He had to work on that, bring it out.

'So Heston took your place.'

Another nod. 'But our father wasn't happy.'

374

'Because he wasn't queer.'

She nodded again. 'He went along with it at the time. But afterwards . . .' She shivered, as if recounting it from personal experience.

'Afterwards, what? What happened afterwards, Sophie?'

'He hated himself,' she said, bitterness dripping from her words. 'He hated himself and he hated Heston. For what they were both doing. He used to beat him. Whip him again.'

Phil suppressed a shudder. 'And Heston took all this?'

Another nod. 'He was scared. He didn't have any option.' She looked round then, as if coming out of a trance, seeing the room for the first time. 'I want a drink. I want to stop. I want a drink.'

'Not long now, Sophie. Let's keep going. Just a little while longer.'

No. I want a drink. I want to stop.'

Phil couldn't stop, he had to go on. He wanted to go on. He was making a breakthrough, just about to reach her. He couldn't stop now. She had to keep going. Had to . . .

He looked at her. All vestiges of her earlier self were now long gone. No sexuality, no allure. Just a damaged woman with a damaged mind. She had clammed up and wouldn't start again until she was ready. He sighed, checked his watch. Leaned over to the tape.

'Interview suspended at . . .'

72

H ester's husband had returned. She had felt his presence but hadn't heard his voice. She had tried talking
to him but got nothing in return. So she had given up. And
then, just as suddenly as he had appeared, he had gone
again, leaving her alone. With the baby.

She felt anxious, uncomfortable. Unable to concentrate
on anything. Her heart was pounding, her mind spooling
through all the possibilities of what might happen. They
could storm into her home, take the baby away from her.
She looked down at it, sleeping again after her husband's
departure. She was still trying to feel something for it, something positive and nurturing, but it wasn't happening.
Maybe they should take the baby. Leave her in peace. In
peace with her husband.

She closed her eyes, tried to call him. Nothing. No
response. She called again, louder this time. Nothing. The
baby stirred as she did so. She ignored it, waited, listening.

Still nothing.

A shudder ran through her. Maybe he had gone, her husband. Maybe he wasn't coming back; maybe he had left her.

Her head was spinning, her mind reeling.

No. He couldn't do that. Couldn't leave her alone once

more. Like it used to be. Like the old days. She tried not to think about those days, it just made her sad. Made her cry, if she thought about them too much. But she couldn't help it.

She tried to block them out, but those times, years ago, when she was alone and afraid, scared and crying all the time, came into her mind. Before her husband turned up to love her, before they became one. There was an unpleasant emotion rising inside her, one that was mixed with loneliness and fear from the old days, one that she had dragged with her all her life. Her most hated feeling: fear of being alone. Of being unloved.

And now her husband was unreachable. And *they* were closing in on her.

Well she couldn't have that. Couldn't be left alone. It would kill her. She needed him. She had to find him.

She called for him, shouted as loud as she could.

Nothing.

And again.

Nothing from her husband. But the baby began to stir. Crying in exploratory little gasps, getting louder and bigger as it got more air into its lungs, felt more confidence in doing so.

And there were those old emotions again, welling up inside Hester, waiting to break.

The baby kept crying.

She dropped to her knees, unable to stop those old, horrible emotions. They had to come out. She put her head back and screamed as loud as she could. Pounding her fists on the floor until her knuckles ached, beating her head against it too. Screaming all the while.

Eventually she stopped, but there was still screaming inside her head. She opened her eyes, expecting the screaming to stop, but it didn't. That was when she remembered that the baby was there with her.

More emotion welled up inside her. Easier to identify this time. Hatred. If it wasn't for the baby, she wouldn't have got into this mess. Her husband would be here and *they* – whoever they were – wouldn't be after her. After *them*. The baby. It was all the baby's fault.

She got up, crossed over to it. Stood before the tiny, wailing figure. Looked hard at it with tear-filled eyes.

It screamed. She screamed back. It screamed louder. Hester screamed louder still. Whatever she did, it wouldn't shut up.

So she bent down, pulled it out of the cot, held it in front of her face, screaming at it, her mouth fully open, like she was about to swallow it. Screaming, screaming . . .

Eventually it stopped. Hester was surprised. She looked round, not wanting to believe her luck. But yes, it had stopped screaming. She smiled to herself. That wasn't in the parenting books. She had invented that one.

She placed the baby back in the cot, still pleased with herself. And then that black feeling began to return. Her husband absent. *Them* after her.

She tried not to give in. She had to hold on, had to think. Do something.

She looked at the baby again, fought down the rising hatred within her, the urge to blame it for everything going wrong. Because it was the baby's fault. She was sure of that. The rage inside told her so.

She could kill it. That was what she could do. Place her hands round its neck and squeeze. Wouldn't even have to squeeze very tightly, it was so small. Bones would snap like firewood kindling. Easy.

She placed her rough, callused hands round its smooth throat.

It looked up at her. Big blue eyes. Vivid and bright, fully rounded in an unformed face.

Her hands dropped away. She couldn't do it. Not when it was staring up at her like that. No matter how much she might hate it.

She watched it, kicking in the cot, stretching its arms and legs, clenching and unclenching its fists. Her expression was blank.

When it's asleep, she thought. Its eyes closed.

That's when I'll get rid of it.

And then run.

73

'We've checked,' said Anni in the observation room. 'I flagged that up. Wrabness she seemed to stumble on, so I went for that. Nothing. Gail Johnson, Sophia Gale, Sophia Johnson, nothing.'

Phil sighed, looked through the glass. Sophie had sat back in the chair, legs spread out, arms on the table, in sharp contrast to the rigid, upright person he had encountered on first entering.

I'm getting through to her, he thought. I'm breaking her down.

The observation room was full of bodies. Just about everyone who was involved with the investigation was there, Anni, the Birdies and as many other officers and uniforms as could fit. They were all waiting, watching, desperate to see the killer of one of their colleagues, their friend, break down and crack. Phil was well aware of the pressure that placed on him.

'Keep trying,' he said. 'I'll try and get a proper surname from her.' He sighed. 'Even if I do, there's no guarantee the baby'll actually be there. But it'll be a start.'

'Just get a name,' Anni said. 'Something I can go on.'

'Okay.'

'And we still don't know who the figure in the photo is. Brother? Father?'

'I'll get there,' Phil said, wishing he felt as confident as he sounded. He looked at Sophie again, picked up a mug of tea to take in to her.

'Wish me luck,' he said.

Anni wished him luck. His DC looked almost beyond tiredness. She seemed to have aged a year for every hour of the day. He gave her what he hoped was a confident smile and left the room.

He stood in the corridor outside the interview room. Leaned against the wall, mug of tea in hand. He took a deep breath, let it go. Another. Let it go.

Right, he said to himself, go in there and do the interview of your life.

Phil switched the tape on.

'Interview resumed at . . .' He checked his watch, gave the time and the other formalities. Slid the tea across the table to Sophie, sat back. She took it, cupping her hands round it. She drank, closing her eyes as she did so.

'Right,' he said, once she had placed the mug on the table, 'where were we? Oh yes. You were telling me about your brother. And your father.'

The ghost of a smile disappeared from her face, replaced by something altogether darker.

'Heston, was it?'

She nodded.

'Johnson?'

She frowned, looked slightly confused.

'Johnson. Your surname. Does he have the same surname as you?'

She shook her head. 'My surname's not Johnson.'

'Gale, then.'

She became thoughtful. Deciding whether to lie or not, thought Phil. 'No.'

'So what's your real name?'

She paused, a look of cunning entering her eyes. 'If I tell you, you'll go straight there. I can't tell you.'

Phil shrugged, tried to make out it wasn't important. 'Doesn't matter. We'll find out one way or another. Anyway, I want to know more about your father. And your brother.' His voice dropped to the lower, compassionate register he had used previously. He leaned forward across the table as if it were just the two of them talking conspiratorially, sharing secrets. 'You were telling me about what your father did to your brother. And how much he hated it.'

He watched her face, the pain and anguish on her features. Asking her to relive the events was like forcing a child into a room that contained their worst nightmare. His heart was breaking for her in that instant. Then he remembered that she had murdered his DS and felt that familiar surge of hatred excise the compassion. He held on to it, worked off it.

'He . . . hated it . . .'

'You said. So what did he do about it? Fight back? Walk out?'

She shook her head. 'No. He couldn't do either. He wasn't strong enough. He just . . . took it.' She sighed. 'Until . . . until he couldn't take it any more.'

'He killed himself?'

She shook her head. 'Would have been easier if he had. No. He . . . he was in a dress. He'd just had . . . just taken care of our father's needs. He wanted to please him. Our father kept hitting him, beating him, hurting him. Saying all sorts of stuff, horrible stuff . . .'

She looked at the tea. Didn't raise it to her mouth. Phil waited.

'He told me this. He crawled into the kitchen. He couldn't

walk. He was bleeding from . . . from what our father had done to him. Crawled. And he took a knife. One of the big ones. For killing the hens.'

Phil flinched, hoped she didn't see it. But Sophie was back in her story.

'He took it and . . . he . . .' Her voice dropped away. 'Cut his own cock off.'

74

Phil said nothing. Her words had hit him almost physically. He felt light-headed, his legs shaking, his breathing difficult. He hadn't been expecting that. Nothing as bad as that.

'Oh my God . . .' He couldn't help it. The words just slipped out.

Sophie nodded, as if agreeing with him. 'Cut his cock off,' she said in a hushed, almost reverent tone. 'Wanted to be a woman. Wanted to be loved . . .'

'Did he . . . survive?'

Sophie nodded. 'Lost a lot of blood. Nearly died. Our father found him, helped him.'

'Took him to the hospital?'

She shook her head, gave a bitter laugh. 'Don't be stupid.'

'What did he do?'

'Cauterised it.'

'With what?'

She shrugged. 'Something hot. Metal. Some tool.' Her voice matter-of-fact.

Phil still felt short of breath. He didn't know what to ask next. Thankfully, Sophie kept talking.

'After he was well again, I helped him. On the quiet. Said

if he wanted to live like a woman I would make him one. Found people to do stuff. You know, procedures.'

'What kind of people?'

'Extreme body modifiers.'

'How did you find them?'

She shrugged again. 'Few contacts from work.'

'And what did they do?'

'Made him a woman. Changed his body. As much as they could.' Sophie frowned, thinking. 'But I think something happened to him. To his mind.'

'What, he lost it?'

'He was never the same again. In any way.' She took another mouthful of tea.

'So did he move out then? Or stay with your father in the house in Wrabness?'

'Stayed with him in Wrabness.' She stopped talking, looked at him. 'How did you know that? I didn't tell you that.'

She sat back from the table, angry. Phil kept looking at her, his gaze level, his voice steady. He knew Anni would be trawling through documents right now.

'You told me yourself.'

'No I didn't.'

'Maybe not in so many words. But you told me.'

She still looked angry. He shrugged.

'There's no point in being mad at me, Sophie. It's all going to come out, so you may as well tell me. What's your surname? Your real surname.'

The anger dissipated, to be replaced by a cunning smile once more. 'Not yet,' she said. 'I'm telling you about my brother.'

'Okay. You keep telling me about him, then. He was living in Wrabness.'

She nodded.

'With your father, still?'

She opened her mouth to answer, stopped herself. Smiled once more. 'No. He's gone.'

'Gone where?'

She shrugged. 'Just gone. And Heston's not Heston any more. He's Hester. My sister.'

'Right. Hester. And he – your sister, she lives alone?'

Again that crooked, sick smile. 'No, she's not alone. She's got a husband now.' She laughed.

Phil was confused. 'Why is that funny?'

Another shrug. 'Just is.'

'And he's there with her?'

Another laugh. 'Always.'

'Right.' Phil had to move on. 'So . . . Hester wanted a baby, is that right? And you went and got one for her . . . for them?'

Sophie looked at her fingernails. They were painted, but broken and chipped. She sighed. 'Yeah.'

He sensed he was losing her. He had listened to her story and he was sure she felt better for putting it on to him. With that done, she could revert to type. But he was not going to let that happen. It was time for him to ramp things up, he thought, get the answers he wanted.

'So tell me if I'm right. Hester and her husband want kids. But they can't have them. So they ask you to find pregnant women so that they can rip the babies out of them and claim them as their own?'

Sophie kept her eyes on her nails. 'Yeah. That's it. Yeah.'

'Ones that were nearly full term. Ones you knew.'

Another nod. 'Yeah.'

'So. You made Ryan Brotherton the scapegoat. Shifted the blame on to him, deflected attention away from yourself.'

Sophie yawned. 'Right.'

Phil was starting to get angry now. He tried to keep it

down, work with it. Channel it. It was a struggle. 'What about Clayton? Why him? Why kill Clayton?'

She shrugged. 'He was useful. Then he wasn't.'

Phil leaned in closer, his voice rising. 'Because he got too close? Because he knew what was going on?'

'Yeah, something like that.' She picked up the mug, put it to her lips, grimaced. 'This tea's cold. Can I have some more?'

Phil slapped the mug from her fingers, snapping off one of her nails in the process. The mug went flying across the room, hitting the wall and breaking, leaving a wet brown explosive patch where it had hit.

'Fuck the tea!' he shouted. 'Talk to me!'

Sophie looked up at him in shock. She flinched, pulled her hands away from him, curled up into herself. Phil kept on at her.

'You fucking listen to me! You fucking murderer! Wrabness. Hester is in Wrabness, yes?'

Sophie nodded hurriedly.

'Where? Which house?'

She kept whimpering.

'Where?'

She jumped at the sound of his voice. 'There's a . . . house off the main road . . .'

'Name? Number?'

She curled herself further into a foetal ball. 'Please don't hit me . . .'

'Name of the house. Number.'

'It's . . . Hillfield.'

'Right. And your real surname?'

She whimpered once more, subsiding into tears. Phil didn't care. 'Now!'

'Croft, it's Croft. Please, don't hit me . . .'

Phil stood up, his head spinning. He didn't know how

387

that display would stand up in court against PACE procedures, but he didn't much care. He could deal with that later. Right now, he had a solid lead to go on.

He looked at Sophie sitting curled in the chair. He should have felt pity and knew that once his anger subsided he might do. But not at the moment. His eyes fell on the photo on the table. And he was hit by a sudden thought.

He pointed to the photo. 'That's him, isn't it?' he said.

Sophie didn't reply.

'In the photo. That's him, your brother. Heston. Hester. Is that right?' He didn't wait for an answer, kept talking. 'The husband doesn't exist, does he? There's just your brother. That's why he wants these babies. Because he can't have children himself. That's it, isn't it?'

Sophie didn't raise her head, just nodded.

Phil was breathing heavily, like he'd just run a marathon. 'Hillfield. Wrabness. Croft . . . yes?'

She nodded again. 'But he won't be there . . .'

He looked down. Sophie was still curled in on herself.

'What d'you mean?'

'I phoned him. When I was brought in. If he's got any sense, he'll have gone by now.'

'Where?'

She shrugged. 'In the wind . . .'

'Shit . . .'

The door opened. Phil turned, ready to shout at whoever was there, throw them out physically if need be. But it was Adrian Wren. And Phil knew he wouldn't interrupt if it wasn't important. The look on his face told him so.

'Boss . . .' Adrian gestured to him.

Phil told the tape the interview had been terminated, stepped outside.

'We've had Wivenhoe on the phone,' Adrian said. 'Marina's place has been trashed. Her . . . partner?'

'Tony,' said Phil, remembering his name this time.

'Right. He was found lying on the floor, head smashed in from the look of it. Ambulance is on its way.'

'Any sign of—'

'No, boss.'

Marina. The baby . . .

Phil felt the familiar bands stretch across his chest. His head was spinning, his breath coming in ragged gasps. He hoped he had heard wrongly, but he was sure he hadn't. Then something struck him. 'Ambulance? He's still alive?'

'Barely. But they'll see what they can do. Attacked with a hammer, it looks like.'

'Just like Caroline Eades . . .'

Phil nodded, eyes on the floor. He remembered his promise to Marina. He would always be there for her. He would never let her be harmed again. Panic rose within him. He fought it down. He looked at the closed door of the interview room.

'And she knows? Sitting in there, she fucking knows . . .'

He lunged for the door, ran inside the room. Sophie looked up from the table, startled, then terrified as Phil came hurtling towards her.

He didn't get far. The door opened and two uniforms rushed in, restraining him.

'Bad news?' said Sophie, once she realised she was in no immediate danger. She laughed.

He was screaming as they pulled him away. Out of the door and into the corridor.

'Oh God,' he said. 'Marina . . .'

75

Marina opened her eyes. It made no difference. It was as dark with them open as it was with them closed.

She tested her arms. They were sore, as was the rest of her, but untied. Was that a good thing or not? Was it an oversight by her captor? Or had she been placed somewhere she had no chance of escaping from?

She stretched out one hand, felt around. Slowly, cautiously, not sure what unpleasant, unexpected surprises she would find in the dark. Nothing. Just a hard-packed earth floor. She lowered her head, smelled it. Musty, damp. Underground, she thought. A cellar or basement?

Panic began to well inside her. Trapped. Underground. Palpitations took hold of her chest, made her breathing difficult.

'No, oh no . . .'

And there was Martin Fletcher in her mind. Standing in her office, blocking the only escape route. And she was once more praying for Phil to come and rescue her but fearing he wouldn't.

'No, not again, not again . . .'

Sobbing now, in terrified desperation, she stood up.

Stretched her hands tentatively towards the ceiling. It was low, crossed by wooden beams. Definitely underground.

She sat back on the floor once more. Curled into herself.

Phil said he would never let her down. Never place her in danger again.

Phil had lied.

She screwed her eyes up tight, opened them again quickly, hoping that light from somewhere would filter in once they became adjusted. Nothing. Just pitch-black darkness as before.

She felt her stomach. No rest now. No relaxation now.

She tamped down the hysteria that was rising once more within her.

Hoped that Phil – or someone – would be coming to get her.

Ignoring that little voice in the back of her mind that said she had been lucky with Martin Fletcher. She had got out alive. She wouldn't be that lucky again. No one would find her. She had been abandoned.

She hugged her arms about herself.

Not daring to move.

And cried.

'I don't know what came over me,' said Phil. 'Very unprofessional. Won't happen again.'

He was in Fenwick's office, facing him over the desk. Sweating and dishevelled and wanting to get moving but knowing he had to go through this before he could do anything else. He had been hauled in as soon as he had been pulled off Sophie Gale. Anni and the rest of the team were following up the leads that had come from the interview.

Fenwick regarded him from the other side of the desk as coolly and levelly as possible. It looked like he was also struggling to remain calm and professional.

'I shouldn't have done the interview, sir. I was too closely involved. And you probably don't want me to go to Wrabness now. I understand.' Phil's voice, his stance said he didn't understand at all.

Fenwick sighed. 'What a mess,' he said. 'All round. And I can't have a go at you for what you've done because you can just come back at me for . . .'

'Your earlier interference.'

'Thank you for reminding me.' Another sigh from Fenwick. 'But at the end of the day . . .'

Here it comes, thought Phil, King Cliché rides again . . .

'At the end of the day, we've got to work together. So you're still CIO on this case and you're going to Wrabness.'

Phil felt relief flood through him. 'Thanks, boss.'

'But no more mistakes. If we screw this up, the CPS will be on us like a ton of bricks.'

'Sir.' Phil turned to leave the office.

'And Phil?'

He stopped.

Fenwick looked pained and tired. As if he'd learned something but that knowledge had been forced on him. 'I don't blame you. I'd have probably done the same. But well done on the interview.'

'Thank you, boss.'

Phil left the office, went to the bar. It was alive with activity. The team were getting suited and tooled up, uniforms putting on protective gear. A firearms unit had been called out. Anni was in the centre of it, co-ordinating. She looked up as he entered. He crossed to her.

'I'm still on the team,' he said to her unanswered question, taking in everyone within earshot as he spoke. 'In fact I'm still your CIO.'

'Glad to hear it, boss.'

'So, what we got?'

She checked the computer in front of her. 'Hillfield is owned by the Croft family. Smallholding.' She looked up. 'Farmer . . .'

'Right,' said Phil. He felt that familiar tingle when a case began to fall into place. 'Fits the profile. Name?'

'Last name on the deeds is Laurence Croft.'

'The father?'

'Looks like it, judging from the date of birth. No date of death, but he's not listed as living there now. Just . . .' She scrolled down the screen. 'Hester Croft. One person. That's all.'

'Sex?'

'Female.' She looked down further. 'The house is on a couple of acres of land. They own some cottages.' She read on. 'No they don't, they were demolished a few years ago, land turned into a caravan park.'

'And I'm assuming it's in a suitably out-of-the way location?'

Anni gave a tight smile. 'Well, it is in Wrabness.'

'Right,' he said. He looked at the rest of the assembled team. They stopped what they were doing, looked back at him. Expectant. Fired up. 'We ready? Then let's go.'

76

The baby was still crying. Hester was on the floor in the corner of the kitchen, as far away from it as possible. Her hands over her ears, her long, thick legs tucked underneath her body, she had tried to curl herself up as small as possible.

'Ssh . . . ssh . . .'

But the baby kept on crying.

She had wanted to get rid of it but couldn't bring herself to do it when it was awake. So she had waited for it to go to sleep. But it wouldn't go to sleep, it just lay there, wailing.

The baby was bad enough, but something worse than that had happened. She had called out for her husband but he hadn't appeared. She had closed her eyes, tried to will him to her. Nothing. No sound in the house, except her sobbing and the baby crying. She had to face it. She couldn't hear his voice any more, couldn't sense his presence. Could feel they were no longer joined. She was all alone.

Her husband had left her. He had gone.

She kept her eyes tight shut, tried to drown out the noise of the baby with her own crying. The baby. It was all the baby's fault. If the baby hadn't come along to disrupt things, then they would still be happy together, like they used to be.

Just Hester and her husband. Alone and together. Their whole world each other. But no. They had to have a baby. It was supposed to make their lives complete. Instead it had forced them apart.

Hester felt impotent rage build up within her. Her body thrashed as she screamed, forcing it out of her.

'No . . . no . . . no . . . no . . .'

She wanted it to be over. She wanted time to be rewound, things to go back to how they used to be. Just the two of them. She stopped screaming, and the sound withered and died in her throat. Hopeless. It was hopeless.

She didn't know what to do. She knew that if her husband had gone, there was no point in her staying in the house with the baby. But she couldn't believe it. She wouldn't believe it. He had to be there, had to be coming back.

Hester stood up. She would make one last attempt to find him, and if that failed then she knew that he was gone for good and she had to decide what to do next. She crossed the floor to the back door, closing her eyes as she passed the baby, not even wanting to see it, acknowledge its presence.

She opened the back door, stepped into the yard. Stood still, listening. The river was making its usual background sound, low static on an untuned TV. She found it comforting, usually, something that reminded her of home. Now it just sounded lonely, like a call for help or attention that would never be answered.

She waited for her eyes to adjust to the darkness, then looked round the yard. She knew all the shapes and the shadows of shapes. It was her home. She knew everything that was there. She scanned, checking. Saw nothing, no one. He wasn't there.

But she wouldn't give up. Not just yet. She would make one last attempt. She opened her mouth and screamed. No words came out, just inarticulate yearning and desire, lone-liness and abandonment. She knew that would be enough to make him come calling if he was there. She *hoped* that would be enough to make him.

She stood still, listening. Nothing. Just the river.

Hester sighed and turned, going back into the house. The baby was still crying, and this time she didn't bother to cover her ears or avert her eyes as she walked past. It was there and he wasn't and that was that.

She went back to her place in the corner, staring at the baby. Making her mind up. She was thinking, trying to sort out in her mind what had happened. She came up with some things. Everything was fine before the baby arrived. Life was good. But now the baby was here and her husband was gone. So, she thought, if she got rid of the baby, her husband might come back . . .

She didn't know if that was true, but it was worth a try. She had thought that earlier, though, and hadn't been able to get rid of it while it was still awake. Now, however, with the constant screaming in her ears, she thought that didn't matter. She could get rid of it. If it made her husband appear again, she could get rid of it.

She stood up.

Walked towards the cot.

77

A light went on. At first Marina thought she was imagining it. It was distant and weak, but it was still a light,
nonetheless.

She sat up, focused her eyes, managed to assess her surroundings. Brick walls, dirt floor, overhead rafters. It
confirmed her earlier impression. She was in a cellar or basement. But not just a square space; it was a room with alcoves
and archways. Crouching, she slowly and silently made her
way towards the light. Before her were other rooms, knocked
through and interconnected with tunnels. Where it needed
it, the ceiling was held in place by heavy wooden struts and
supports. Electric cable was strung along it.

She shivered with the cold, looked at herself. She was
filthy, her clothes black with dirt. There were cuts and
bruises up her arms and legs.

She looked at the walls. There was a workbench set
against one of them, huge and heavy-looking, with a scarred
and pitted surface. There were tools nailed to a board above
the bench, old and rusting but still workable. Marina looked
round, tried to listen. She couldn't hear anything, see
anyone. But she knew someone was there. They must be.
Moving slowly, she crept over to the workbench, looked at

the tools hanging on the board. Hammers of varying sizes, chisels, a hand drill. Her eyes alighted on the screwdrivers. All different sizes, displayed in order from the smallest to the largest. She took the largest from its hook, looked at it. The wooden handle was worn, the paint flaking, but still solid. The metal shaft was rusted but intact. She checked the end. Flat and sharp. Used often. That would do.

She held it in her hand, clutching it hard. She looked round again. There was no way out from where she was; the only way forward was down the tunnel that the light was coming from.

Her heart was hammering in her chest. There were still pains in her stomach but she didn't dare think about the baby, whether there was anything wrong with it. All she knew was that it needed protecting. And as a mother, it was her job to do it.

A mother. That was the first time she had ever thought of herself in those terms.

Clutching the screwdriver as hard as she could, she slowly began to creep down the tunnel towards the light.

The circus was on the move again.

Phil and Anni were in the lead car on the way to Wrabness. Other cars and vans followed, creating a heavy police presence on the road. They had used the sirens and lights to get out of Colchester, moving the remains of the rush hour to one side. But on the smaller roads just their sheer number had been enough to get other vehicles to move out of the way.

Phil sat in the back seat. He ignored the satnav, looked at a map of Wrabness, tried to focus his mind on the task ahead. Trying not to think about Marina. He sighed, unable to concentrate. It was always the same in situations like this. He was supposed to be trained for what was to come, to evaluate matters on the spot and take appropriate action according to what was needed. But every situation was different. He could look at the map, prepare all he wanted, but he knew it would be pointless. He had to wait until he was there, actually in the thick of it, before a course of action would present itself.

He looked across at Anni sitting next to him. She had been silent since they got in the car. No doubt psyching herself up in the same way he was.

'You okay? Up for this?'

She looked at him, startled, as if pulled out of a trance or a power nap. 'Yeah. Fine.'

'Sure?'

She nodded. Phil sensed there was more, so waited, still looking at her.

'I'm just trying to . . .' she said. 'Trying to get my head round it all, I suppose. Clayton; now this.'

'Tired?'

'Utterly shagged. Caffeine, sugar and adrenalin, that's all I am now. But that's not what I meant, boss. It's just . . . everything's fine now. But tomorrow, whenever, when the comedown hits, what happens then?'

Phil shrugged, tried to show nonchalance. He had been asking himself a similar question. 'That's why we have counsellors, I suppose.'

She nodded, seemingly satisfied, and fell silent again.

Phil couldn't think about tomorrow. He couldn't think about the rest of the night or what they were about to do. He tried not to think about Marina.

But failed.

He had once read a story, in a comic when he was a boy, about a supervillain who had all the powers you could think of. When the hero thought of a particular power, the villain ceased to have it. That was how he felt about Marina. He tried to imagine all the fates that she could be undergoing. No matter how horrible or upsetting. He hoped that, like that superhero, if he could imagine it, it wouldn't happen.

He couldn't think of the comedown or the day after. All he could think of, all his world had come down to, was catching a killer, making sure Marina and Caroline Eades' baby were safe. And Marina's baby. But that wasn't due for months. A shudder ran through him. Maybe Hester had already taken her away, absconded to somewhere they couldn't find them. He hoped not. He couldn't . . . He just hoped not.

It was a hope he clung on to as the angry procession approached Wrabness.

78

Hester picked the baby up. Looked at it. Eyes screwed up. Still wailing.

'Time to go to sleep,' she said.

She held the baby girl almost tenderly, rocking her from side to side. Shushing her as she rocked. Talking all the while.

'Yes,' she said to the baby, her voice low, 'sleep. Sleep. That's right . . .'

The baby's wailing began to subside slightly. Hester looked at it, at her, smiled sadly. 'You've got to go to sleep, little one. Yes . . . Because my husband won't come back while you're here. No . . . he won't . . .' Shushing her again. 'So I'm afraid you've got to go . . . got to go . . .'

The baby was quietening down. Listening to Hester's words, or at least the tone of her voice, allowing herself to be calmed by them.

'Ssshh . . . that's it . . .'

Hester smiled as the baby became still, settled.

'Good, good baby.' She remembered its sex. 'Good girl . . .'

She smiled again, pleased she had remembered that.

The baby began to close her eyes.

'That's it, good girl . . . go to sleep . . . everything will be easier once you've gone to sleep . . .'

Hester began to stroke the baby's neck.

The baby's eyes shut.

'So this is Wrabness, then,' said Anni, looking round. 'Drabness, more like.'

Phil gave a tight smile. 'Bet they've never heard that one before.'

They couldn't see much in the dark, but Phil doubted it looked better in the daytime. It was flat, bleak. Fields and trees stretched away behind them, back to the horizon. In another place those features might have seemed bucolic, but here they just made the few houses that sat on the lane look abandoned, cut off.

They had followed directions to Hillfield, the Croft house. It had taken them off the main two-lane road and on to a single-track one. They had parked at the side of the road, blocking access if anyone or anything wanted to get past. Uniforms had already started stringing up tape at either end of the road, erecting barriers.

Phil joined Anni in looking round. The trees were winter bare, the fields desolate in the darkness. He could see the river and, beyond, the lights of Harwich port burning far away on the other shore, looking as distant and unreachable as a mirage. A sign by a five-bar gate gave directions down a dirt track to the beach.

'House is down there,' said Phil. 'That's our route.'

Everyone was piling out of cars and vans. The firearms unit were good to go, guns ready, body armour in place. Everyone had been briefed. Everyone knew what they were supposed to be doing, where and when. The night was cold and sharp, yet hot and alive with adrenalin and testosterone.

'Right,' said Phil to the assembled team, 'we all ready?'

402

Grunts and nods of assent.

'Everyone know what they're doing?'

More grunts and nods.

'Good. Come on, then.'

He went to the gate, opened it. Started to walk down the dirt track. It sloped downwards towards the beach. It was unlit. The further they got from the streetlights, the darker it became. They had been issued with torches and, loath though Phil was to use them for fear of giving themselves away, he had no choice. He switched his on, still leading the way.

Down past an old house with so much junk collected in the back garden that it looked like a contemporary art installation, then past a series of brick walls, overgrown with moss, lichen and ivy. A gate at the end. Phil shone his torch in. A caravan site. Small, the vans old, at least thirty years, he would have said. Most of them were well maintained, but one in particular stood out. Even older, mildewed and rusted. He wondered briefly what kind of person came to Wrabness for their holiday. Kept going.

At the bottom of the track they came to the beach. He stopped.

'When we reach the beach,' said Anni next to him, 'it means we've gone too far. It's before that.'

Phil looked around. He made out the silhouettes of stilted beach houses against the starless sky, looking like marauding misshapen aliens from a fifties sci-fi film. The beach was dotted with old, rusted boats sitting marooned on the dirty wet sand. Chained and abandoned, it looked like they had come there to die. He squinted back up the track. On the opposite side to the caravan site was a field. Beyond the field was what looked like a large shack or barn. Black slatted wood, partially derelict in appearance. He turned to Anni.

'Think that's it?'

'I reckon so,' she said.

He turned to the assembled team. 'There's the target,' he said. 'Come on.'

He stepped into the field.

'Now remember,' he said when he had the attention of the whole team. 'According to the witness, we're dealing with someone who has a separate identity. The name is Hester, she's a transsexual. But there's another identity she calls the husband. And that's the one we have to watch out for. The murderous one. She might be Hester at the moment, she might not. But whatever we do, we don't want to deal with the husband. So let's do this quickly and cleanly, right?'

The team followed him, as carefully and quietly as they could.

79

The baby's eyes closed.

'That's it . . . good girl, that's it . . .'

Hester held the baby with one hand, stroked her neck with the other. So fragile, so small, the difference between life and death. Like a toy, a child's toy. You could play with it for years but then one day you decide to burn it, or hack away at it. Just to see what happens. And you do see what happens. But after that moment's gone, you're left with a melted lump of plastic, or something broken and useless. Only good for throwing away.

And that's what the baby was now. It would only take a moment, just a few seconds, less than a minute, even. And it would all be over. Then things could go back to normal. Her husband could return and they could be together again.

Just one moment.

The baby's breathing changed. She was asleep. Hester smiled again. She had done it. She had talked to the baby, rocked her, got her to sleep. Like a real mother would do.

She sighed.

A real mother.

But it didn't matter. Not now. She had a plan. She had to follow it through. She had to make things happen.

She placed the baby back in her cot, careful not to wake her. Covered her with the blanket. Looked at her. Then knelt beside her, placed her hands gently round the baby's throat.

And something sparked within her. Stopping her.

She. She had called the baby she. Not it. She. Like a mother would do.

Maybe that meant something. That she was a proper mother after all. That she didn't hate the baby; she was capable of looking after it.

She closed her eyes, her head starting to hurt. No. She had to do it. Had to kill it. It was the only way for her husband to return. He wouldn't come back so long as the baby was there, she knew that. Whatever else she felt, she knew that.

So she had to do it. Had to.

She placed her hands round the baby's neck again. Tried to speak. Couldn't get the words out. Noticed for the first time that she was crying. It stopped her.

'Buh-bye bye, buh-baby . . .'

Still sobbing, but as quietly as she could so as not to wake her, she placed her hands tenderly around the baby's neck.

And began to squeeze.

80

The house was surrounded.

Phil couldn't believe anyone actually lived there. His initial impression had been right. It looked almost totally derelict, with black plastic sheeting and hardboard patching up holes and rotting areas in the wooden cladding. Tiles were missing off the roof and the yard outside was so full of junk it looked like a health and safety officer's worst nightmare.

It was the right place. He was sure of it.

The team were in place. Phil was standing beside what he supposed was the front door, next to a team armed with a battering ram, ready to break it down. He spoke into his radio.

Gave the signal.

The battering ram was in place.

The door was smashed off its hinges.

They charged in.

Hester's hands were round the baby's neck when she heard the noise.

It was a huge crash, like an explosion. At first she wondered if it was an earthquake or a bomb. And her immediate thought: she hoped it didn't waken the baby.

But then she heard movement behind her. Shouting, running, lights, bodies.

In her home. In *her* home.

She turned, shocked, tried to take in what was happening. Couldn't. Didn't know what was going on. All she knew was that she was scared.

There were men. And women. Some holding fearsome guns. All shouting at her. Telling her to do things. Step away, lie down, things like that. She looked from one to another in turn, trying to make out what it was they wanted her to do. Lie down, step away. Pointing their guns.

Her heart was beating like it was ready to burst. She didn't know what to do. She turned away from them, heard them shout even louder, move closer to her. She looked at the baby. She was starting to wake up. They had made so much noise they were waking up the baby.

In desperation, she grabbed hold of her and pulled her out of the cot. She had to rock the baby back to sleep. Couldn't have her awake, not now. She clutched the baby to her chest, turned round again.

They had taken a step back. Still shouting at her, but there were more words in the orders now. Put the baby down, step away, lie down, put your hands on your head. It was like a game she didn't know the rules for and that she couldn't keep up with.

So she clutched the baby to her.

The baby started to cry.

She closed her eyes. Tried to will them all away.

Anni focused on the scene before her. She saw Phil at the front of the team, commandingly issuing orders. She quickly took in her surroundings. First she checked for exits and entrances, anywhere they could be attacked from. Task-force members had positioned themselves there. She looked round.

She had seen squalor before, but this place was one of the worst. It looked like someone had been squatting in a dilapidated garage or outhouse. There were attempts at homeliness: armchairs and a settee with antimacassars draped over them. But the furniture was worn and old, like it had been salvaged from some tip. A rusted old tin bath had been set up as a cot; there was an attempt at a kitchen area, but Anni wouldn't have wanted to eat anything prepared there.

The most frightening thing was the person holding the baby. She had expected something, or someone, out of the ordinary. But she hadn't been prepared for the sight of the figure that greeted her. Tall, over six feet, wearing a faded flowered sun dress over what looked like at least two layers of vests and T-shirts, with filthy old denims and boots. A badly fitted wig had slipped back to reveal a shaven head, and make-up had been applied as if without a mirror. There was also facial stubble where this person hadn't shaved for a day or two.

Anni tried to hold her revulsion in and concentrate. She thought instead of Graeme Eades, and the last time she had seen him as he lay sobbing in the cheap chain hotel, thoroughly repentant and guilt-eaten, begging them to return his baby, the only link to his dead wife. That sharpened her concentration.

She looked at Phil, standing in front of her, using the calm and reasonable voice he used in interviews to make suspects open up. The earlier shouting and gun-brandishing hadn't worked, just made Hester cling even tighter to the baby. So he had changed his approach. He was asking her to put the baby down, to move away. But his words, no matter how softly spoken they were, didn't seem to be having any effect either. Anni thought she knew why.

She softly placed her hand on Phil's sleeve. He looked at

her, stopped talking. She gestured with her eyes: let me try. He nodded. She stood alongside him.

'Listen to me,' she said. 'My name's Anni. Is your name Hester?'

Hester's eyes were all over, roving about, trying to take in what was happening. Fluttering round the room like a swallow trapped in a barn. Her hands were back on the baby's neck. Anni knew that the slightest application of pressure could kill the baby.

'You are Hester, aren't you? That's your name?' Anni tried to keep her voice soft, but had to raise it to be heard over the crying of the baby. She kept looking at Hester, willing her to look back.

'Hester . . .'

Hester's eyes stopped fluttering round the room, began to focus on Anni and her softly spoken words.

'Your name is Hester, isn't it?'

Hester held her eyes, blinking rapidly. She nodded.

'Good. Listen, Hester, I'm not here to hurt you. Nobody wants to hurt you, okay? We're just worried about you. You and the baby.'

Anni waited, hoping the words had sunk in. She kept on talking, still using that soft, soothing tone.

'Look, Hester, why don't you put the baby down, yeah? Then we can talk. Talk properly.'

Hester looked down at the baby, began shushing and soothing it. The baby's crying began to gradually subside.

Anni edged a couple of centimetres forward.

'You're good with babies, Hester. Very good. Now why don't you put it down, yeah? Then we can talk . . .'

Hester frowned, still clutching the baby tightly to her. Rocking it from side to side. 'Wh-what about? Why . . .'

'You're out here on your own, you've got a baby to look after, you need help, Hester . . .'

410

'I've got my . . . my husband, he'll . . . he's away, he's . . . got to come back . . .'

'Your husband. Right.' The last thing they wanted was for the husband to return while Hester was holding the baby. 'Listen, Hester, don't worry about your husband now. He's not here. Just think about what's best for you and the baby. I can help you, Hester. Give you the support that you and the baby need.'

Another step forward.

'Come on, Hester, let's talk, yeah? Just two women together.'

She risked another step. Hester, still rocking the baby, had reacted when she had said 'two women'. Clearly that was the right thing to say. Anni kept going.

'Look,' she pointed at the team behind her, 'don't worry about them. They're men. They don't understand. Guns and that, shouting, that's how they respond to things.' She turned back to Hester, looked her directly in the eye. 'Women are different, aren't we? We know how to talk properly, without all that. So come on.' Another step forward. 'Let's talk. Just you and me.'

Hester looked between Anni, the baby and the tooled-up task force. It seemed, from the confusion in her eyes, that she genuinely didn't know what to do. She kept rocking the baby from side to side. It was silent now.

Anni risked another step forward. She was almost level with her now.

'Come on, Hester, you must be tired standing there. Are you tired?'

Hester thought about it, nodded.

'Thought so.' Anni held out her arms. 'Let me put the baby down, then we can talk. Properly. You and me. Yeah?'

Anni smiled. Hoping she looked trustworthy and honest.

Hester looked at the baby and then at Anni, her world

having shrunk down to that choice. She began to release her grip on the baby, to hand it over.

Anni's heart was racing, her hands shaking. She hoped it didn't show too much.

'Come on, Hester. Let me take the baby and we can have a chat . . .'

Hester, with the simplicity of trust that a child would have, hesitantly stretched out her hands, the baby held firmly in them.

Anni stepped up close to her, smiling all the while. She placed her hands beneath the baby, took her gently from Hester.

She held the baby tightly to her. She looked up, saw Hester's face. Expectant, waiting. Trusting. It really was like betraying a child, she thought.

She nodded to Phil, who gave the order. Hester was rushed. Grabbed by the task force, pushed to the ground. She let out a cry of rage that turned into a wail of sorrow.

'I'm sorry,' said Anni, but her words were lost in the noise.

She carried the baby away from Hester, right to the back of the house. Phil followed her.

'Well done,' he said.

'Get the paramedics,' said Anni, without turning round. 'I'm going outside.'

And she left the house, clutching the baby to her chest. Still not turning round.

Not allowing anyone to see the tears on her face.

81

'We've searched the whole house, sir,' said one of the uniforms. 'No sign of Marina Esposito. No sign of anyone. But we found this.' He handed Phil a piece of paper. 'It was nailed to the wall in the kitchen.'

Phil looked at it. Couldn't believe his eyes. They were all there. Lisa King, Susie Evans, Claire Fielding, Caroline Eades. Other names followed them. Beside each name was a date. Due dates, thought Phil. But it was the name at the bottom of the list that concerned him most.

Marina Esposito, it said in handwriting different from but no better than the earlier entries. And next to it, *from the coppers*.

Phil tried to keep panic, desperation from his voice. He addressed the uniform again. 'You've looked everywhere. What about basements? Lofts? Anything like that?'

The uniform shook her head. 'Nothing. We've checked.'

'Outbuildings?'

'Checked them too. Apart from some chickens and pigs, there's no one else here.'

'Keep looking.'

Phil moved swiftly outside. Hester was just about to be escorted away. He ran to the van, confronted Hester. The policemen holding her didn't let her go.

'Where is she?' he said. 'Where've you put her?'

Hester just stared at him, mouth hanging slackly open, fear in her eyes.

Phil brandished the list before her face. 'Here,' he said, stabbing the name with his finger, 'Marina Esposito. Here. Her name. Now where is she? Where've you put her?'

Hester tried to back away from him, terrified. She started whimpering. Phil kept going.

'Where is she? Where is she?'

Hester cowered away from him, turning her face into the arms of one of the officers holding her. 'No . . . no . . . don't, don't hurt me . . . go away, go away . . .'

'Where is she . . .' Phil realised that his words weren't working. Hester didn't know.

It wasn't her. She didn't know.

He turned away. 'Oh God . . .'

They bundled her into the police van.

Phil stood there watching her go, his heart as black, dark and heavy as the Wrabness night.

He was lost.

Marina crept along, bent low, walking slowly. The light was getting brighter as she reached its source, the shadows lengthening, flickering as they came round the corners. It was accompanied by noise. Rhythmic pounding. Hammering.

She pressed herself in tight against the wall, gripped the screwdriver firmly in her hand. Risked a look round the corner.

The walls were lined with shelves containing canned food, cartons of milk, bottles of water. It was like a survivalist's larder. In the centre of the space, a figure was kneeling down, hammering nails into wood. Marina looked closer, tried to work out what was being made.

There were huge squares of wood, metal mesh. The wood

414

was being turned into frames, the mesh covering the frames. Marina was chilled by something more than just cold. She knew what was being made.

A cage. A cage for her.

She gave a gasp. Involuntary, unplanned. Cursing herself for doing it.

The figure stopped hammering, looked up.

He smiled. It wasn't pleasant.

'Hello,' he said. 'Welcome to your new home.'

82

The baby had been taken to hospital in an ambulance. The paramedics had given her a cursory examination and decided she was quite well, considering, but really needed full nursing care. Graeme Eades would be contacted.

Anni was sitting on the step, looking out towards the beach, her coat pulled tight round her, a blanket over that.

Phil sat down next to her.

'Hey,' he said.

She nodded, kept staring straight ahead.

'Well done in there,' he said.

She sighed. 'I lied.'

'You did what you had to do. What was best.'

She shook her head. 'I lied to a vulnerable, damaged human being. I just made someone who's lonely and fucked in the head feel even worse about themselves.'

'You did your job, Anni.'

She didn't reply, just continued to stare.

'You coming back inside?'

She didn't reply at first. 'I think I'll stay here a bit longer. If you don't mind, boss.'

'Okay.' Phil stood up, looked round. Took in the desolation of the place once again. He looked across the field the way they had come, passing his eyes over the caravan site. Who would want to come here for their holidays? he thought, not for the first time.

Something jarred within him.

The caravan site.

'Anni . . .'

She looked up.

'When you checked the details on the Croft family, didn't it say something about owning a caravan site?'

Anni looked up, startled out of her reflective mood. 'Yeah, yes it did . . .' She stood up, joined him in looking. 'D'you think . . .'

'Worth a try,' he said. 'Tell the rest of them where I'm going. If I find anything I'll come back, let you know.'

He picked up his torch, started hurrying across the field.

Marina started to back away from the man. She held the screwdriver out in front of her.

'Don't . . .' Her throat felt dry, parched. Her voice small, croaking. 'Don't come any nearer . . . I'll . . . I'll stab you . . .' The words sounded unconvincing, even to her.

The man smiled again. Shook his head. 'No you won't.' His voice sounded like he looked: rough, callused, feral and powerful. He was tall, his body thick-limbed and bulky. Dressed in old suit trousers, braces and a once-white shirt with the sleeves rolled up, he was sweating and dirty. Work boots on his feet, an old, festering overcoat on the floor beside him. He was bald, but his thick, powerful arms were covered in hair. He had a large stomach protruding over his trousers and straining his shirt buttons, but it looked as solid as granite. He turned, giving Marina his full attention. His eyes looked like dark, stagnant, treacherous pools, his unshaven face red like bad blood. He smiled, his teeth yellow and stained.

417

'It's . . . it's you, isn't it? You're the one who's been taking all the . . . all the babies . . .'

'That idiot bitch of mine. She wanted them. Wouldn't fuckin' shut up about it. On an' on . . . so I had to. Kept her quiet.' He smiled again. It reached those stagnant eyes. 'Can't say I didn't enjoy it, though.'

'So . . .' She kept backing away as she spoke. 'Why . . . why am I here?'

He pointed to her stomach. 'What's that you got growin' inside you? Eh?'

Marina felt her legs weaken.

He laughed. Deep and rough, it sounded like the prelude to an animal roar. 'Can't keep goin' with her any more, can I? Not when your lot are on to me.' His voice dropped, became cold and sharp. 'An' I'm not givin' up. I might have to hide for a bit. Go underground. Keep out of their way.' Another smile. 'An' I'll need some company down here. Then when the kid's born we'll go up again. Find somewhere else. You an' me an' the kid. Bring it up properly.'

Marina shook her head. She could barely comprehend what she was hearing. It seemed so unreal. A nightmare. 'But . . . but why me?'

''Cause I saw you.'

'On TV?'

'Yeah. An' outside the leisure centre. Filed you away. I've had my eye on you. Knew you'd come in handy.'

'They'll . . . they'll be looking for me . . .'

'Look all they want, they'll never find you.'

Marina stopped moving, stared.

'An' you won't escape neither. There's no way out for you. Not down here. So get used to it. You're gonna be here for a long time.' He picked up the hammer. 'I'm gonna get this done. Your new cage. Then you an' me are gonna get to know each other properly.'

And with that he turned his back to her, knelt before the frame, started hammering.

Marina's heart was beating so fast she felt it could grow wings and escape her body. That was it, she thought. That was it. No Hollywood rescue. No escape. And Phil. No Phil. Despite his promises, despite what he'd told her. How he would never let her down again, always be there for her. He wouldn't be. This was it. For the rest of her life.

She crumpled into a heap.

Started sobbing.

83

Phil reached the brick wall, shone his torch past it into the caravan site. He stepped off the dirt track, on to the grass. Looked round.

There weren't many vans. And each of them was in darkness. He stood still, listening. He could hear distant movement from his team in Hillfield, but there was no movement from the site. He shone the torch round again, settling on the caravan tucked in behind the gate nearest the wall. It was the one he had looked at on the way down. Filthy, old, rusted and mildewed. The others didn't look like anything special, but this one was completely uninviting.

Phil stepped nearer to it. And tripped over something.

He dropped the torch, beam shining back at him, bent down to pick it up. As he did so, he tried to see what had caused him to trip. He ran the beam along the ground, found a raised edge that he traced back to the brick wall. He knelt down, examining it. It was the remains of another wall, knocked down but not completely.

He turned in the other direction, followed the raised line with the torch. It led to the middle of the site, turned left. He walked along it, following. There were raised areas all the way up the field. Like the grass had grown over foundations of houses that were once there.

Phil thought. Something about owning houses . . . He remembered. Laurence Croft had owned a row of houses that had been knocked down and the land turned into the caravan site. It figured, he thought. Judging from Croft's DIY legacy in the house, he would have expected a job like this.

He turned back to the mildewed caravan. Something wasn't right about it. The others had their Calor Gas bottles hooked up outside; this one didn't. The others had their curtains open; this one had them closed. And he really couldn't imagine anyone coming to stay in it. So why was it there?

He moved in closer, shone the torch over it. He bent down to look at the step beneath the door. There were tracks in the grass, muddy tracks, like someone had been dragging something. Or someone. The tracks led up the step and into the caravan. Heart thumping, Phil turned the handle. It opened.

He pulled the door open slowly, kept his head back, his body out of the way, not knowing what might jump out at him. He shone the torch in. Held himself ready to fight.

Nothing. He swung the torch round. Dirt everywhere, seating with rotting covers, work surfaces with chipped and peeling Formica, a table with a broken leg, filthy curtains. But nothing else. No one else. The caravan was empty.

Phil stepped inside. It wasn't just the dirt, it was the smell. Like something that had been closed up too long. A tomb. He looked round, swinging the torch, taking it in. It definitely wasn't a holiday home. But it had some purpose, he was sure of that. He just had to find out what it was.

He shone the torch round the cupboards, under the table, on the chairs, on the floor. And found it.

The muddy track marks led to a square in the centre of

the floor. It was of matching carpet to the rest of the van, but had been cut out. Phil knelt down, rolled it back. A square had been cut out of the floor, hinged, then replaced. A trapdoor.

He knew what he should do. Call the others. Get a team over here, get that trapdoor open. See what was in there. But he couldn't leave it to them. He had made a promise to Marina. If she was here, then it didn't matter. He would have found her, one way or the other.

Taking a deep breath, he opened the trapdoor.

It wasn't what he had been expecting. It wasn't a crawl space or a shallow grave. It was a tunnel leading downwards. A wooden ladder was clamped to the side, a thick black cable fastened to the opposite side of the shaft. Electricity, Phil thought. Whatever – whoever – was down there, they had rigged up power.

He shone his torch along the floor, found a ridge in the carpet where the cable snaked in. Must be a hidden generator somewhere, he thought.

He looked down the hole again. It was dark down there, pitch black.

He should call the others over, let them lead the way.

He looked down again.

And swung his legs over, began climbing down.

84

'Shut up! Fuckin' shut up! If there's one thing I can't stand it's a whingein' bitch!'

Marina's kidnapper was standing over her, anger blazing in his eyes. He had walked towards her, exuding an almost primal energy, bent down and smacked her across the face.

It stopped her crying immediately. It also hurt like hell. The blow had been so fierce she had felt like her head was coming off.

She had no doubt that he was more than capable of killing her. And she realised that, even with everything that had happened to her – Martin Fletcher, finding Tony on the floor of their house – until now she had never truly experienced fear.

He bent down again. She tried to get to her feet, but couldn't. Still sitting, she scuttled away from him.

He reached her quickly. She pushed herself back into the wall. He stood over her, bearing down. She began to whimper.

Then remembered the screwdriver, held it out in front of her with both hands, point towards him. Hoped he wouldn't notice how much her hands were shaking.

'Don't . . . don't . . .' Her voice was failing her.

He looked down at her. 'You gonna use that? Eh?'

She kept pointing the screwdriver at him, her hands still shaking.

'You gonna use that on me?' He laughed. It wasn't pleasant. 'You'd better. You do that again, pick up somethin' and point it at me, you'd better be ready to use it. 'Cause baby or no baby, I'll stop you.'

He moved in towards her, his hand outstretched again.

Marina started to cry once more.

Then the lights went out.

'Bastard . . .'

The darkness was all-enveloping. Phil was trying to use the torch as he went down, hoping to see how far he had to go, but he was finding it difficult to hold on to it and the ladder at the same time. He missed his footing and the torch fell from his grasp. The light bounced and swung as it dropped down to the bottom of the shaft.

He put his arm out, tried to grab it, and lost his balance, almost following it. Desperately he cast around for something to grip on to and found the black cable attached to the other side of the shaft. He grabbed at it, hoping it would steady him, but when he pulled, transferring all his body weight to it, it came away in his hand.

He flailed around in the dark, trying not to fall. Luckily, his other hand managed to get a grip on the ladder once more. He clung to it, steadying himself. Took a few deep breaths, continued his descent.

As he neared the bottom, he noticed a dim light shining upwards. His torch. Thank God it was still working, because he was sure he had pulled out the power cable. He stepped off the ladder, picked up the torch. Looked round.

He quickly worked out that he was in the cellar of the house that had once stood above him. A quick examination of the walls bore that out. Bare brick with overhead rafters and a hard-packed dirt floor. He swung the torch's light into every corner. No sign of Marina.

He looked round again, saw a door set into the wall. Heavy and old, made of solid timber. He almost ran to it, trying the handle. Locked. He tried pulling it. Too thick to budge.

'Shit . . .'

Then something caught his eye. Against one wall was an alcove. He assumed it must have been a fireplace at one time, with a chimney leading up to the rest of the building. Someone had customised it. Bricks were piled at one side of the opening and it looked as if a tunnel had been hollowed out through the fireplace.

He examined the hole with his torch, making mental measurements. There was no other opening in the room, no door in or out, so this must be the only way through. Phil hated confined spaces. Tried to avoid lifts, even, whenever possible.

But he got down on his hands and knees, the torch clenched in his teeth. He really should go back, tell the others, get them down here. Send them into the tunnel. He tried to look along it, see if there was any light, hear if there was any sound.

Then came a scream.

'Marina!'

And he was on his knees and into the tunnel, his fear of enclosed spaces on hold.

In the sudden darkness, Marina could feel her assailant in front of her. She didn't think something like this would stop him getting hold of her. Stop him hurting her. Using the wall behind her as a brace, she pulled herself up to a standing position. Adrenalin kicked in. It was either do something or submit. And she wouldn't give in without a fight.

'Bloody generator,' he mumbled. 'Bloody power cuts . . .'

It was now or never. She gripped the screwdriver tightly in both hands and thrust it forward as hard as she could.

It connected. She could feel it hit something solid. She kept pushing, hard. Harder.

He screamed. In anger or pain, she couldn't tell.

She put all her weight behind the screwdriver, drove it in as far as she could, letting it take her body with it. Then, when she could push no further, she let go of the handle.

'Bitch . . .'

She closed her eyes, tried to remember the layout. Turned right, away from where he had been building the cage, and, keeping as low as she could, moved quickly away from him.

'Fuckin' bitch . . .'

She could hear him thrashing about behind her, coming for her.

Her heart felt like it was about to burst as she felt her way along the wall. Her fingers came to a corner. She followed it round. It was some kind of alcove, a recess. An old fireplace, perhaps? Something like that. She didn't care. It was somewhere she could pull herself into, curl up and hope he wouldn't find her.

She squeezed inside, aware that the baby was stopping her from getting any further in. She hoped the baby was still all right. There was nothing she could do if it wasn't. She had to save her own life first.

She made herself as small as she possibly could, held her breath.

Prayed to a God she had long since ceased to believe in, that he wouldn't find her.

Prayed that she would just survive.

85

Phil crawled.

Using his elbows to propel him, he worked his way through the tunnel. The torch was heavy in his mouth, his teeth gripping it as hard as he could, his jaw cramping up. He wanted to let it drop, take a rest, but he knew if he did that he would never get it back between his teeth again. There wasn't room in the tunnel to move his arms, get his hands to place it back there. So he kept moving.

He was committed now. He couldn't go backwards. There was just enough space for him to keep moving forward. The walls and ceiling of the tunnel were right in on him. Brick, stone and dirt all around, with what looked like prop shafts keeping the ceiling up. It didn't look too sturdy. If he disturbed it in any way, pushed too hard, it could all come down on top of him at any second.

He was starting to feel light-headed. Air was in short supply. He tried to keep calm, not panic, concentrate on moving forward. The only alternative he had was to stop. And that was no alternative at all.

And then it started. A panic attack. He felt his chest constrict, his breath come in ragged gasps.

'No . . . not now . . .'

He screwed his eyes up tight. Willed it to pass quickly. It wouldn't. He had to fight against it, keep going. But he had no strength in his arms, no power in his body. He couldn't move.

He had to. He didn't have the luxury of staying still. He had to fight it, work through it. Not give in to it. He pushed, pulling himself along with his arms, taking huge breaths in between. And again. And again. Good. He was doing it, he was fighting it, he was winning . . .

Then the tunnel began to narrow.

'Oh God . . .'

And it was on him even more. He closed his eyes, kept going. Felt tears begin to run down his cheeks. Ignored them. Just kept going.

The air changed. Became slightly less stale. And he knew. He had done it. He had come through to the other side.

He pulled himself out of the tunnel and lay on the ground, on his back, panting like he had just run a marathon. His legs felt weak, his chest ablaze, but he didn't care. He had made it.

Then there was another scream.

'Bitch, sow . . .'

He had found her. Marina screamed as he grabbed her hair, pulled her out of the alcove.

'Come 'ere . . . thought you would escape, eh? From me? I built this place, bitch, I know every corner of it . . .'

He dragged her free. The pain shot through her head and down her neck. She struggled, screamed, fought. No good. He was too strong for her.

'You hurt me, bitch, you pissin' well hurt me . . .'

'Well don't hurt me,' said Marina, 'because if you hurt me you'll hurt the baby. And then I'll be no good to you, will I?'

He paused, seemingly thinking about what she had said. Then resumed pulling her. 'I can still have fun with you, though . . . don't you worry 'bout that . . .'

He was breathing heavily, his grip not as strong as she had expected. She felt a small elation. She *had* hurt him. Good.

But it didn't make things any better.

Without her realising, tears were running down her face as he dragged her back to the cage.

Phil shone the torch around quickly, trying to find where the scream had come from. He took in his surroundings. A workbench against one wall, an ancient collection of tools above it. Some kind of survivalist's store room, he thought. Crossing to the workbench, he picked up a heavy claw hammer and moved in the direction he thought the sound had come from.

Marina was kicking her legs out behind her as he dragged her along the passageway. Her hands were on her head, trying to release his grip, or at least make it less painful for herself. He was walking slower, his wound affecting him now, but still strong. Too strong for her to deal with.

As he dragged her, Marina started to be able to see.

At first she thought it was just her eyes becoming accustomed to the dark, but after blinking a couple of times, she realised that there was a light coming towards her.

Her heart began to beat faster; hope rose inside her. This was it, she thought, this was the rescue. But then just as swiftly as it had arrived, that same hope plummeted within her. What if he had an accomplice? What if there was more than one of them?

She didn't know what to do. But she had to do something.

She took a chance.

'This way,' she shouted. 'I'm here . . .'

Her assailant grunted, turned. Saw what she was looking at.

Then paused for a few seconds, dropped her and ran.

Phil rounded the corner and stopped dead. At first he thought the light and lack of oxygen was playing tricks on him. He blinked. Again. No tricks. There was Marina. Lying on the ground ahead of him.

His face split into a grin as relief flooded his body. He ran to her, dropping down beside her, laying the hammer down, taking her in his arms.

'Oh God, oh Marina . . .' He held her tightly to him. 'I told you I wouldn't leave you . . .'

But he sensed that Marina didn't share his relief.

'He's here, Phil, he's around here somewhere . . .'

Phil sat back, looking at her. About to ask more questions, but they were stopped in his throat. Because Marina's assailant was on him.

'Phil!'

He felt hands round his throat, choking him. A feral roar accompanied the action. Phil felt himself go light-headed. He put his hands to his neck, tried to pull the hands away. No good. The grip was too strong.

He dropped the torch, tried to scrabble around for the hammer, couldn't find it.

The beam of the torch etched the whole thing against the wall in a grotesque shadow play. He saw the man behind him, his shadow making him look seven or eight feet tall. He had to fight back.

He pushed his elbow back as hard and as fast as he could. The man grunted in pain, loosened his grip. Phil pressed the advantage, did it again. The grip round his throat loosened.

He grabbed the man's thumbs, twisted them away from the rest of his fingers as hard as he could.

The man shrieked in pain. Howled like a wild beast. Phil kept pulling until he heard them snap. Then he let go, wriggled away from him. Turned and faced him.

The man was older than Phil had expected, tall, well built and bald. He looked like an older, meaner version of Hester. Phil knew straight away who it was. Laurence Croft. Hester's father. Hester's husband.

Sophie had been wrong. Or she had lied to him.

Croft lunged at him. Phil tried to dodge out of the way, but Croft's right hand came down as a fist, crashing into his face. Phil spun away, lost his footing, the blow was that strong.

He hit the ground on his back and was winded. He spat out blood, felt a tooth amongst it.

Then Croft was on him, aiming another punch at his face. Phil tried to move, but was too slow. He felt his nose break as the knuckles connected. Felt blood spurt out of his battered face.

Croft knelt over him. Phil tried to sit up, fight back, but his head was spinning.

Croft laughed, brought his fist back for a blow that would cause Phil serious, if not fatal, damage.

Then stopped.

His eyes went wide, his head jerked to the side. His arms fell to his sides.

Phil opened his eyes, confused.

Croft's head jerked again, his eyes once more widening.

Then again.

Then his eyes rolled to the back of their sockets and he fell over sideways, hitting the ground with a huge, echoing thump.

Phil looked up. There, standing over the inert body of

Laurence Croft, was Marina. Holding in her hand the hammer he hadn't been able to find, the head coated with blood and other matter.

It dropped to the floor. Phil stood up, went to her.

Had her in his arms before the tears started.

Both hers and his.

86

November gave way to December, and with it Christmas. But there would be no celebrations for Phil.

He sat in his house, the only seasonal decorations a couple of Christmas cards from colleagues, one from Don and Eileen. And one from Marina. He opened it. There was a letter inside.

Phil sighed, decided not to read it, not just yet. He couldn't face it without his props. He got up, went to the kitchen, fetched himself a beer, came back to the sofa. Flicked the remote at the stereo. He knew which album was in there.

He closed his eyes, rubbed his hands over his face. His nose was healing. He hoped the rest of him was too. He took a mouthful of beer. Thought back over what had happened since that night in Wrabness.

He had found the key to the door in the pocket of Croft's overcoat, saving another crawl through the tunnel. But Marina was clearly in pain, clutching her stomach as soon as they made it out. He bundled her straight into an ambulance and off to the hospital.

Then it was a question of mopping up, sorting out.

After having his nose patched up, he had gone back to the

station, Anni alongside him, trying to come to terms with what had just happened.

'So Hester's husband was real after all,' said Anni, sinking exhausted into her office chair.

Phil nodded. 'Sophie played us.'

'Why?'

He shrugged. 'Protecting her father?'

'After all that?'

'Who knows? Maybe she still loved him.'

'Or maybe she just lied.'

'They all lie to us. Haven't you worked that out yet?'

'What?'

'I'm sorry. Something I said to Clayton . . .' He sighed, his eyes moist. 'Christ. What a mess . . .'

The media spotlight was intense. Phil kept out of the way as much as possible, leaving it to Fenwick to deal with. After that, things moved quickly.

Laurence Croft was pulled out of the cellar. Dead. Phil knew there would be an inquiry, but it was strongly intimated that no charges would be brought against either him or Marina. If anything, he would receive a commendation.

Hester was taken to a secure hospital and placed under psychiatric supervision. Phil believed it was only a matter of time before he – he couldn't think of him as she – was declared insane. The baby was doing well and would soon be released to her father. Phil hoped that Graeme Eades would be able to cope.

Brotherton was going to stand trial for attempted murder. And Sophie Gale/Croft had been formally charged with murder.

Which led Phil to recall Clayton's funeral.

That was the toughest part of all. It was held at the Colchester Baptist Church in Eld Lane, right in the middle of town. The Georgian building looked out of place sitting alongside the eighties red-brick shopping arcade that took up most of the town centre.

As Phil stood inside, holding on to the curved wood of the pew in front, he was struck by how small the coffin looked next to the huge organ pipes behind it. How insignificant.

The minister was talking about man having but a short time to live, and Phil knew that everyone in the church was well aware that Clayton's had been shorter than most. Twenty-nine years. He was also aware of the divide between Clayton's family and his work colleagues. He had been asked to say something as part of the service but he couldn't bring himself to do it. Too much pain, too much guilt. Had asked Fenwick to do it instead.

The minister went on to talk of the gift of hope. Phil had looked around the congregation. Clayton's mother and sisters looked shell-shocked. Even Anni was in tears. He didn't think there were many there sharing that gift.

Afterwards, walking out, Fenwick had approached him.

'There's a reception back at the family home. We've been invited.'

Phil nodded. 'You go,' he said.

'I think they'd like it if you were there.'

'You go, Ben.'

Fenwick nodded. Didn't move. There was something else he wanted to say. Phil waited.

'You know, it might all come out. About . . . Clayton. At Sophie Gale's trial.'

'I know.'

'I mean, I'll do what I can, but . . .'

'I know you will.' Phil looked across to the other mourners leaving the church, Clayton's mother having to be helped. 'Do what you can, Ben.'

He walked away.

★

435

He had tried to contact Marina, but couldn't get through to her. She wasn't at work and she certainly wasn't at home. She had been told by her doctor to take some time off. She needed rest if the baby wasn't to suffer. *Their* baby, Phil thought. No one knew where she was.

Tony Scott had survived the attack, but his head injuries had left him in a coma. Phil knew, from questioning the nurses, that Marina had been at his bedside.

He kept his regular Sunday dinner dates with Don and Eileen.

The first time was the worst. Eileen made an excellent roast, and the smell of it, the taste of it, was something Phil had always associated with comfort, safety. But not that time. Sitting round the table and dutifully eating, he found he couldn't smell it, couldn't taste it. Couldn't appreciate or savour it.

Don had been a career policeman. He knew what Phil was going through. Or thought he did. They knew about Clayton, Hester, Croft and the rest of the case. But not about Marina. They didn't ask him about it, but he knew that if he wanted to talk, they were there to listen. And if he didn't want to say anything, they were there for that too.

He put his knife and fork down, pushed his plate away, murmuring apologetically.

Eileen nodded, said nothing.

Phil didn't move. Barely realised he was crying.

Eileen placed her hand on his. Don was there.

They sat like that for a long time.

So now Phil sat alone in his house. Drinking beer, listening to music.

He looked again at the letter, took another mouthful of

beer, draining the bottle. He put the bottle down, picked up the letter. Began to read.

Dear Phil,
I'm sorry I haven't been in touch. I know what you must think of me. But I had no choice. Sorry. I've got things to sort out in my head. Big things. It's not just you. I thought after Martin Fletcher that things would never get that bad again. I was wrong. Though you were there for me this time. Eventually.

You know this baby is ours. I know you do. And maybe we should both be there together for it. For him. Or her. I don't know. And then there's Tony. I feel guilty over what happened to him. I feel in some way responsible. Whatever was happening between him and me or you and me. I've got to honour him too.

I know this is rambling and my thoughts aren't articulated very well, but that's how I feel at the moment. All messed up. I need time to think. Sort things out. I hope you'll give me that.

And I hope you know that I love you. Whatever happens, I love you.

Marina x

Phil put down the letter, picked up his beer bottle. Empty. He got up, went to the fridge for another one. Marina's words going through his head all the time. Guy Garvey was singing about it looking like a beautiful day; Phil was a long way from agreeing. The words of the minister at Clayton's funeral kept coming back to him too. The gift of hope.

He took another beer out, came back to the living room, sat back down. Started drinking.

Thought about how a gift could be a curse.

And then came a ring at the door.

Phil ignored it.

It came again, more insistent this time.

Sighing in irritation, he put his bottle down and went to the door. Opened it.

And there stood Marina.

She looked at him, gave a tentative smile.

'Hey.'

'Hey yourself.'

Phil opened the door fully, stepped out of the way. She walked into the hall, went straight to the living room. He followed her.

He entered the room, saw her standing there. He was unsure what to do, how to talk to her. Then he looked into her eyes. Saw what was there. And there was no uncertainty any more.

He crossed the room, put his arms round her. Held her as tightly as he could.

Guy Garvey was still singing about it being a beautiful day.

This time, Phil had to agree.